"LET'S GET READY!"

Murdock shouted to his SEALS. "When we touch down, one squad out each door—then we spread out, find out where the hell we are and how we can find the Veep. Halverson's with me!"

He looked out the hatch and saw the ground coming up fast. Over the sound of the rotors he could hear the faint popping of enemy fire, searching the sky for an American target. The bird made a sharp turn above a burning tank, and Murdock saw several buildings demolished by the artillery barrage.

Murdock felt the big bird touch down. His men lined up alongside the doors at the ready. Time for the fun to begin.

"Go, go, go!" Murdock bellowed and the SEALS jumped off the chopper into enemy-held territory, their weapons loaded, unlocked, and fingers on the sensitive triggers. . . .

SEAL TEAM SEVEN
War Cry

Don't miss these other explosive
SEAL TEAM SEVEN missions:

Seal Team Seven
Specter
Nucflash
Direct Action
Firestorm
Battleground
Deathrace

SEAL TEAM SEVEN
WAR CRY

KEITH DOUGLASS

BERKLEY BOOKS, NEW YORK

If you purchased this book without a cover, you should be aware that this book is stolen property. It was reported as "unsold and destroyed" to the publisher, and neither the author nor the publisher has received any payment for this "stripped book."

This is a work of fiction. Names, characters, places, and incidents are either the product of the author's imagination or are used fictitiously; and any resemblance to actual persons, living or dead, business establishments, events or locales is entirely coincidental.

Special thanks to Chet Cunningham for his contribution to this book.

SEAL TEAM SEVEN: WAR CRY

A Berkley Book / published by arrangement with the author

PRINTING HISTORY
Berkley edition / October 1999

All rights reserved.
Copyright © 1999 by The Berkley Publishing Group.
SEAL TEAM SEVEN logo illustration by Michael Racz.
This book may not be reproduced in whole or in part,
by mimeograph or any other means, without permission.
For information address: The Berkley Publishing Group,
a division of Penguin Putnam Inc.,
375 Hudson Street, New York, New York 10014.

The Penguin Putnam Inc. World Wide Web site address is
http://www.penguinputnam.com

ISBN: 0-425-17117-5

BERKLEY®
Berkley Books are published by The Berkley Publishing Group,
a division of Penguin Putnam Inc.,
375 Hudson Street, New York, New York 10014.
BERKLEY and the "B" logo are trademarks
belonging to Penguin Putnam Inc.

PRINTED IN THE UNITED STATES OF AMERICA

10 9 8 7 6 5 4 3 2 1

This work of fiction is
gratefully dedicated to
all those real SEALs who
do the covert work we never hear
about, those dirty little bits of patch and
heal in the world of international politics and
day-to-day practical government
that make the world
a safer place to
live in.

FOREWORD

A reader asks me, "Will there ever be a woman SEAL?" Another reader asks, "Why was a woman along in *Deathrace*?" Why? Just seemed like a good idea. The whole principle of fiction is conflict. If you don't have conflict, you don't have a story or a book. That's why Kat was there. What could be more out of phase with a SEAL operation than to have a woman along? Most of the readers I heard from said it worked.

Some asked to see Kat again in other books. Two or three said no more women on missions . . . ever! So it goes.

The gist of it all is I like to hear from you. Hey, like it or knock it or have suggestions, let the cards and letters come. Any more votes on the woman-on-mission question? Get your oar in the water. You can do that by dropping me a line at:

Keith Douglass
SEAL TEAM SEVEN
8431 Beaver Lake Drive
San Diego, CA 92119

Thanks, and I hope to hear from you.

Keith Douglass

SEAL TEAM SEVEN

THIRD PLATOON*
CORONADO, CALIFORNIA

Lieutenant Commander Blake Murdock. Platoon Leader. 32, 6'2", 210 pounds. Annapolis graduate. Six years in SEALs. Father important Congressman from Virginia. Murdock recently promoted. Apartment in Coronado. Has a car and a motorcycle, loves to fish.
WEAPON: H&K MP-5SD submachine gun.

FIRST SQUAD

David "Jaybird" Sterling. Machinist Mate Second Class. Platoon Chief. 24, 5'10", 170 pounds. Quick mind, fine tactician. Good with men in platoon. Single. Drinks too much sometimes. Crack shot with all arms.
WEAPON: H&K MP-5SD submachine gun. Administrator for the platoon.

Ron Holt. Radioman First Class. 22, 6'1", 170 pounds. Plays guitar, had a small band. Likes redheaded girls. Rabid baseball fan. Loves deep-sea fishing; is good at it. Platoon radio operator.
WEAPON: H&K MP-5SD submachine gun.

Bill Bradford. Quartermaster First Class. 24, 6'2", 215 pounds. An artist in spare time. Paints oils. He sells his marine paintings. Single. Quiet. Reads a lot. Has two years of college. Squad sniper.
WEAPON: H&K PSG1 7.62 NATO sniper rifle or McMillan M-87R .50-caliber sniper rifle.

Joe "Ricochet" Lampedusa. Operations Specialist Third Class. 21, 5'11", 175 pounds. Good tracker, quick thinker. Had a year of college. Loves motorcycles. Wants a Hog. Pot smoker on the sly. Picks up plain girls. Platoon scout.
WEAPON: Colt M-4A1 with grenade launcher.

*Third Platoon assigned exclusively to the Central Intelligence Agency to perform any needed tasks on a covert basis anywhere in the world. All are top-secret assignments.

Kenneth Ching. Quartermaster's Mate First Class. Full-blooded Chinese. 25, 6'0", 180 pounds. Platoon translator. Speaks Mandarin Chinese, Japanese, Russian, and Spanish. Bicycling nut. Paid $1,200 for off-road bike. Is trying for Officer Candidate School.
WEAPON: Colt M-4A1 rifle with grenade launcher.

Harry "Horse" Ronson. Electrician's Mate Second Class. 24, 6'4", 240 pounds. Played football two years at college. Wants a ranch where he can raise horses. Good man in a brawl. Has broken his nose twice. Squad machine gunner.
WEAPON: H&K 21-E 7.62 NATO round machine gun.

James "Doc" Ellsworth. Hospital Corpsman First Class. 25, 5'10", 160 pounds. One year pre-med, then he ran out of money. Prefers small dark-eyed girls. Single. Competition shooter with pistol. Platoon corpsman.
WEAPON: H&K MP-5SD/no-stock, 5-round Mossburg pump shotgun.

SECOND SQUAD

Lieutenant (j.g.) Ed DeWitt. Leader Second Squad. Second in Command of the platoon. From Seattle. 30, 6'1", 175 pounds. Wiry. Has serious live-in woman. Annapolis grad. A career man. Plays a good game of chess on traveling board.
WEAPON: The new H&K G-11 submachine gun.

Al Adams. Gunner's Mate Third Class. 20, 5'11", 180 pounds. Surfer and triathlete. Finished twice. A golfing nut. Binge drinker or teetotaler. Loves the ladies if they play golf. Runs local marathons for training.
WEAPON: Colt M-4A1 with grenade launcher.

Miguel Fernandez. Gunner's Mate First Class. 26, 6'1", 180 pounds. Has a child with a woman in Coronado. Spends his off time with them. Married and is highly family-oriented. Wife: Maria. Daughter: Linda, seven. Speaks Spanish, Portuguese. Squad sniper.
WEAPON: H&K PSG1 7.62 NATO sniper rifle.

Colt "Guns" Franklin. Yeoman Second Class. 24, 5'10", 175 pounds. A former gymnast. Powerful arms and shoulders. Expert mountain climber. Has a motorcycle, and does hang gliding. Speaks Farsi and Arabic.
WEAPON: Colt M-4A1 with grenade launcher.

Les Quinley. Torpedoman Third Class. 22, 5'9", 160 pounds. A computer and Internet fan. Has his own Web page. Always reading computer magazines. Explosive specialist with extra training.
WEAPON: H&K G-11 caseless-rounds, 4.7mm submachine gun with 50-round magazine.

Jack Mahanani. Hospital Corpsman First Class. 25, 6'4", 240 pounds. Tahitian/Hawaiian. Expert swimmer. Bench-presses 400 pounds. Once married, divorced. Top surfer. Wants the .50 sniper rifle.
WEAPON: Colt M-4A1 with grenade launcher.
            (Replacement for Gonzalez after he was shot up in Iraq on the first phase of that mission.)

Joe Douglas. Quartermaster First Class. 24, 6'1", 185 pounds. Expert in hand-to-hand and unarmed combat. He's an auto nut. Rebuilds classic cars. Working on a 1931 Model A Ford Roadster. Platoon's top driver, mechanic.
WEAPON: H&K 21E 7.62 NATO round machine gun. Second radio operator.

Fred Washington. Aviation Technician Second Class. A black man. 24, 6'0", 180 pounds. Is driven to succeed. Taking computer college courses. Doesn't carouse much. Is writing a novel about the SEALs.
WEAPON: H&K MP-5SD submachine gun.
            (In sick bay on the carrier from wounds suffered in *Counterstrike* action in the Kuril Islands.)

1

The Yellow Sea
Off the Korean Coast

Lieutenant Commander Blake Murdock felt the salt spray in his face from the light chop in the Yellow Sea as the Pegasus-class eighty-two-foot insertion boat slammed through the dark water just after midnight. He judged the distance to the Korean shore and signaled the coxswain to drop his speed to three knots. The boat slowed to a crawl as it moved almost silently toward the Korean coast a mile away.

Murdock and his Third Platoon of SEAL Team Seven were on a silent mission to the Korean coast. They crouched low in the slender boat awaiting their time to drop into the sea. His platoon worked with a man short, since Fred Washington lay in sick bay on the aircraft carrier USS *Monroe*, CVN 81, ten miles at sea behind them. Washington had taken a serious wound in the last mission on the Kuril Islands. There had been no time to get a replacement.

The SEALs wore their full black neoprene wet suits including gloves, boots, flippers, and floppy hats, but no masks or rebreathers. It was a short surface swim. They had their full combat gear and weapons.

When they were a half mile off the breakers, Murdock gave

1

the coxswain a cut signal across his throat, and the soft purr of the engine died.

Murdock whispered last-second instructions. "You know what we have to do. Let's get in and blow it, then shoot and scoot. DeWitt, take your Bravo Squad in first."

The SEALs slid soundlessly into the water, tied their six-foot buddy cords onto their partners, and began a quiet swim the last half mile to shore. Murdock and his Alpha Squad brought up the rear.

It was a simple mission. They would come out of the surf, take down any sentries or beach watch patrols they ran into, penetrate quietly a quarter of a mile inland, and blow up a small building that had been the center of enemy activity.

Then they would work their way back to the beach, go in the water, and be picked up by the same boat that had brought them. They had done it a hundred times in training and on hot-fire missions.

Murdock stroked silently through the chop of the Yellow Sea. His weapon was tied across his back with a length of black rubber tubing. He was thirty-two years old, stood six-two, and weighed 210 pounds. He had been in the SEALs for six years, the last two commanding the Third Platoon.

His buddy on the swim was Radioman First Class Ron Holt, a twenty-two-year-old in his third year as a SEAL.

Murdock took a long look at the shoreline. Less than a hundred yards away, it looked peaceful. He could spot no guards, or any roving patrols. This was a vital area and should be protected better than this. Their loss, his gain.

Lieutenant (j.g.) Ed DeWitt led his Bravo Squad into the surf, where the black figures lay in the wet sand with waves and foam washing over them. DeWitt watched the beach both ways, then signaled two men to sprint out of the water through the dry sand to the sparse growth twenty yards inland.

Both made it without drawing any notice. Once in the brush, Miguel Fernandez, Gunner's Mate First Class, froze in place. Directly ahead of him a Korean soldier walked along a path heading for the beach. Fernandez waited until he was less than three feet away, then lunged out, slammed into the slight Korean, and rammed him to the ground. Fernandez grabbed the frightened man's mouth so he couldn't scream.

Guns Franklin, Yeoman Second Class, sprinted over from twenty feet away to hold down the struggling Korean while they gagged him and tied his hands behind him with plastic cinch cuffs like those used by cops.

By the time the man was tied, Bravo Squad had crossed the beach undetected. DeWitt gave Fernandez a thumbs-up sign, and they spread out in a defensive line facing inward.

Less than a minute later, Alpha Squad with Commander Murdock joined them. The two officers whispered for a moment, then Murdock took his squad and moved up the faint trail heading inland.

Alpha Squad was in its normal formation, with the scout, Joe "Ricochet" Lampedusa, out in front of the group thirty yards. Murdock followed with his radioman, Holt, next in line. Then came Bill Bradford, Quartermaster's Mate First Class, with his H&K PSG1 7.62 NATO sniper rifle.

Ken Ching, Quartermaster's Mate First Class, was next in line, with Harry Ronson, Electrician's Mate Second Class, following him. James "Doc" Ellsworth, the platoon medic and a Hospital Corpsman First Class, was next to last, with David "Jaybird" Sterling holding down the tail-end Charlie spot.

Lampedusa dropped to the ground. Murdock followed suit, as did the rest of Alpha Squad. Murdock lifted up to a crouch and ran up to his scout.

Lampedusa pointed ahead. "Mounted patrol, Skipper. Truck and four men. Road is about fifty yards to the left."

"Parked," Murdock whispered. "We've got to keep to our time sked."

"Wish we had an EAR," Lampedusa said.

Murdock wished for a pair of them. They were Enhanced Acoustic Rifles, a non-lethal weapon that could put a target down and unconscious for four hours without harming him.

"Diversion," Murdock said. "You have any WP?"

Lampedusa grinned, and brought up his Colt M-4A1 with the grenade launcher under the barrel. He dug a 40mm white-phosphorus grenade out of his combat vest and loaded it. He angled the round to the left, away from their route.

The sound of the grenade firing brought one of the Korean soldiers on the truck up from where he had been napping. He stared in their direction, then reacted quickly when the grenade exploded two hundred yards down the road in a brilliant starburst of hotly burning and smoking phosphorus. The Korean soldiers on the truck yelled, started the rig, and spun the wheels as they raced the truck toward the fire.

Murdock waved the SEALs forward on double time. All fifteen men cleared the road where the truck had been, and plunged into the brush and trees as they moved inland.

Lampedusa worked fifty yards ahead now in the lighter woodland. They had seen no Korean soldiers for the past ten minutes. Lam dropped into the weeds and grass, and the rest of the platoon went down like dominoes behind him. Murdock and Jaybird Sterling slid to the ground beside Lam.

"Fucking lousy way to run a war," Jaybird said.

"Not a war, not yet," Murdock said. "You get the big bucks so you follow orders. What have we here, Lam?"

"Our objective. They have three guards, walking around the place like it's a gold mine."

"It may be," Murdock said. "How close can we get to it without being seen?"

"Twenty yards on this side. Let me do a run around it and see if there's a closer spot."

Lam melted into the woods without stirring a leaf or branch.

Murdock signaled the others behind him to wait, and he and Jaybird watched to the front.

"We got any more of these shit details?" Jaybird asked.

"Two, from what I hear."

"When the hell are they sending us home?" Jaybird asked with a touch of a whine. "We creamed that little Jap general in the Kurils, now we're stuck on the fucking carrier for a month. Nothing is happening over here. Why don't they send us home so I can get in some snowboarding up at Big Bear?"

"You'd break your damn neck, Jaybird. Face it, you love all this shit. Don Stroh says we got to hang tough. If nothing pops in another month, the CIA agent boss man says he'll get our asses back to Coronado."

"Him and his promises. Does that CIA jerk ever treat us right? He's hung us out to dry too many times."

"True, like in Iraq," Murdock agreed.

"Hey, WESTPAC has two SEAL platoons jerking off in Hawaii. Why can't one of them replace us here?"

They both grinned in the dark. Jaybird beat the commander to it. "Because none of them motherfuckers can replace us, nobody in the whole shit-assed Navy can come anywhere near to replacing us."

The SEALs laughed softly. Their platoon had been hand-picked by the CIA to be "on call" for the intelligence agency to do its dirty work around the globe. Whenever the CIA wanted some covert action, they called on Murdock and his Third Platoon out of SEAL Team Seven at Coronado, California. His platoon had even been taken out of the command of NAVSPECWARGRUP-ONE. That was the mother hen of the SEALs on the West Coast. That made the commander of the unit furious. But the Chief of Naval Operations himself had approved the move, so it was done.

Lam appeared as silently as he had left. Murdock swore the kid was half Apache.

"Other side," Lam said. "A place where the woods and brush grow to within ten feet of the buildings and the guards move around there every three minutes. I timed them."

"Go," Murdock said. He gave a moving-out arm swing, and the SEALs caught it back down the line and were on the march silently.

Five minutes later, Murdock settled in just in back of the brush that came close to the target building. Now they could see that the structure had no windows, was two stories high and made of wood.

A Korean guard with rifle slung over his shoulder muzzle-down walked his post around the building. As he came opposite the brush, Kenneth Ching whispered something in Korean. The man stopped and turned, evidently curious.

Harry Ronson charged out of the brush and hit the soldier with a solid body tackle right on the numbers, and they both went down. Ching moved in and clamped his hand over the Korean's mouth. The two SEALs hauled the terrified Korean into the brush, gagged him, and tied his hands behind him with plastic cuffs.

The same pattern held for the other two exterior guards. When all three were stashed a safe distance from the building, Ken Ching and Murdock positioned themselves on either side of the door. Ching jerked the door open and Murdock threw a flashbang grenade into the room. Ching grabbed a surprised Korean soldier who had started out the door and pushed him inside and slammed the door shut.

The six thunderous explosions of the flashbang tore through the enclosed structure, immediately followed by six shatteringly brilliant strobe lights. The sound and light were designed to make the soldiers inside temporarily blind and deaf, but not to injure them.

With the last strobe of light, Murdock, Ching, and Ronson raced through the door into the brightly lighted room. They found four more guards. Two had been sleeping, two others eating. Now all were on the floor holding hands over their ears and with their eyes tightly closed.

It took four minutes to get the Koreans on their feet and propelled outside, where they were bound by their wrists and taken away from the building.

As this took place, Joe Douglas and Bill Bradley had planted four heavy charges of TNAZ explosive in four vital parts of the building. Murdock liked TNAZ because it was fifteen percent more powerful than plastic explosive C-5, and it weighed twenty percent less.

Douglas came around the building and gave Murdock a thumbs-up. Murdock had told him to set the timers for ten minutes. They were ticking away.

"Let's get the hell out of Dodge," Murdock said into his lip mike. The SEALs left their captives in the brush and began to double-time back the way they had come.

About eighty yards away from the structure, Murdock stopped the men and they turned to watch behind them.

The explosives went off within a few seconds of each other, and the two-story building erupted in a roaring, blasting explosion that sent wood soaring into the sky and a huge fireball that surged upward over the treetops. Then all they could hear was the sound of the flames consuming what was left of the building.

To the left and the right they heard truck engines start, and the rigs converged on the fire.

Murdock motioned to three of the men with grenade launchers. They each fired two rounds out as far as they would go back beyond the burning building. The first to hit were HP, the next WP. At once they heard the trucks racing in the new direction.

"Moving," Murdock said into his Motorola. Each SEAL had a personal communication radio with lip mike and earpiece. A transceiver was fastened to each SEAL's belt.

The fifteen men hiked toward the beach. A hundred yards from the sand, Murdock found Lam standing behind a tree. He pointed ahead. A line of ten Korean soldiers, all with rifles at the ready, were positioned across the beach and facing shoreward.

Murdock gave a sigh. He'd hoped that this one was about over. He whispered in his lip mike. "A line of skirmishers up here in the brush. We have ten Koreans out front. Fire between them. Make damn sure you don't hit anybody. Five rounds between them and we'll see what happens."

It took the SEALs three minutes to get into position. Murdock asked for a platoon check. All fourteen men reported ready on the radio.

"On mine," Murdock said, pushing the safety off his H&K MP-5SD submachine gun. He lifted the weapon and aimed between the two nearest Koreans. They stood ten yards apart. He fired three rounds and before the last one was out of the barrel, the other fourteen SEALs opened fire.

Five seconds after the last SEAL weapon fired, the ten Korean soldiers on the beach were screaming in surprise. Some ran to the left, others to the right. In half a minute none of the Korean GIs could be seen.

"Let's take a swim," Murdock said into his Motorola. Then he pulled off the components of his radio and stowed them in the waterproof pouch on his combat vest. He slung the submachine gun over his back and ran toward the dark waters of the Yellow Sea.

After a quarter-of-a-mile swim off the point of land, they made contact with the Pegasas that had been waiting for them.

"About time," the coxswain called. "Figured you guys were gonna hang around for breakfast in there."

The SEALs climbed on board the boat and Murdock fired a green flare. A few minutes later a South Korean patrol craft surged alongside the long, slim boat and stopped. She was the *Sea Dolphin 292,* a craft that Murdock had been on before. Murdock and DeWitt climbed a ladder for a conference on board the South Korean boat.

"That's my report, Colonel. From a security standpoint, there was little or no coverage of the beach. We swam up, ran across the beach, then surprised one sentry who came strolling along. The security inland was worse. The mounted patrol was decoyed off its station and the guards around the 'prize' building were lax, casual, and ineffective."

The South Korean Army colonel scowled in the dim lights of the boat. "Did you use live ammunition, Commander?"

"We fired between the guards they had put on the beach. None was hit, all were frightened out of their skins. They ran away as fast as they could." Murdock paused.

"Colonel, these troops have never been under fire before. They need a firm hand. But if I were grading them on their defense of this sector and their security of the building, it would be a dismal failure."

The colonel nodded. "It is true. Our men need better training. We may ask your captain if you could do some of that training for us."

Murdock smiled. "Colonel, I always follow orders."

The South Korean colonel nodded, turned sharply, and walked to the bow of the ship.

Murdock and DeWitt stood there a moment, then hurried to the ladder to get back in their taxi for a quick ride out to the carrier.

"Glad that's over," DeWitt said as they settled into the

Pegasus. "How many of these test situations have we done now in the past three weeks?"

"That's the seventh or eighth, I can't remember. If I thought it was doing any good, it wouldn't be so bad."

"Hey, could be worse. Better this than the bad guys shooting at us."

Twenty minutes later, Don Stroh met them as they walked into their assembly room on the carrier. The SEALs were not happy.

"Hey, Stroh. When the hell we get off this tub and go home?" Les Quinley, Torpedoman Third Class, yelled.

"Can't tell. Not yet. Hear you kicked ass out there again tonight. The ROKs are gonna be glad to see you go . . . anywhere." He laughed at his own joke as the SEALs stripped out of their wet combat gear and wet suits. He held his fist in the air, and the room went silent in a second. It was a holdover sign from the BUD/S training in Coronado, and still served a good purpose.

"Fact is, I wanted to talk to all of your about that. Things are heating up in Panmunjom. I'm going over there tomorrow morning for a big conflab. The second-highest-ranking North Korean general, Soo Chung Chi, is going to be at the table. On our side will be Vice President Wilson Chambers. We're rolling out our big guns for this talk, and I want to be there. I want to hear what both sides have to say."

"If those two guys kiss and make up, we'll all go home," Jack Mahanani, Hospital Corpsman first Class, roared. Everyone laughed.

Might not be quite that easy," Stroh said. "What happens tomorrow is going to have a huge bearing on whether you go home or not. Thanks for the last training bit. The South Koreans could stand a lot more work, but I don't know who is going to teach them. Now, you guys get some sleep. I've got to get ashore and be ready for the big yahoo tomorrow."

Murdock walked Stroh to the deck, where he would catch his helo.

"Is there really going to be a chance to work things out tomorrow with the North guys?"

Stroh shook his head. "Don't think so. The Vice President

has a lot of packages for the North, if they'll take them. I just can't read the Korean faces, on either side." Stroh shrugged. "Hell, we'll just have to wait and see what goes down tomorrow."

Murdock watched Stroh take off. His men were rested after the hard mission in the Kuril Islands. They were ready. He'd been a SEAL for six years now, commander of this platoon for the past two. He'd wet nursed some of them, come down hard on others. They were SEALs, the best trained special operations fighting men in the world. Quick Response was their middle name. He and his men would be ready, no matter what happened at that conference table tomorrow.

2

Joint Security Area
Panmunjom, Korean Demilitarized Zone

The Joint Security Area at Panmunjom is a green island in a raw brown swatch of land called the Demilitarized Zone that gouges across the width of the Korean peninsula. This neatly landscaped, oval-shaped area is where North and South Korea meet to try to maintain peace through day-to-day discussions. This is where the famous table sits that separates the forces that are often more angry than ready to talk. United States Army soldiers from nearby Camp Bonifas provide protection for the area and the more than 100,000 visitors who come there every year.

The DMZ itself is 151 miles long and two and a half miles wide. It's a buffer zone created by the July 27, 1953, armistice that ended the Korean fighting.

Don Stroh took an observer's position at the back of the South Korean contingent inside the big room where the peace table sat. The South Koreans and their American guests were already in place at the table. The North Korean delegation was not there. It was an old tactic, making one side sit and wait for the other side to arrive.

Ten minutes later, the far doors opened and a short, thickset

man with his North Korean military uniform pressed and
spotless, with all the brass shined and all the combat ribbons
and medals firmly in place, walked quickly down the aisle
and took the center spot in the chairs. Four gleaming stars
perched on his shoulders.

When he was seated, the rest of the delegation, most in
uniform, marched in and sat on both sides of their leader.

Usually the wrangling at this table was reserved for
low-ranking officers of both sides. Perhaps someone had fired
across the line. Some soldier had encroached into the North's
territory. Civilians had been caught rushing across the cleared
and mostly sterile zone.

The sight of high-ranking military men as well as the
second-most-important man in America brought the tension
to a new high.

A minor North Korean civilian spoke first. His words were
at once translated into English.

"The Democratic People's Republic of Korea is pleased to
be at the table today and to welcome the Vice President of the
United States. We hope that this will mean the intransigent
Americans have at last realized that our people can never be
defeated and that we will continue our programs and operations.

"Since the United States has come with its second-ranking
man, the Democratic People's Republic of Korea has also
brought to this table the second ranking official in our
government and our army. It is my great pleasure today to
introduce to you General Soo Chung Chi. General Soo."

One North Korean civilian began to clap, but was quickly
hushed by a soldier sitting beside him. The general rose and
stared across the table at Vice President Wilson Chambers.
The Veep was an imposing figure—six-two, broad shoulders,
forty-eight years old, a head of jet-black hair, and clean-
shaven. He was in better physical shape now than he had been
when he was in college.

Chambers stared back just as hard at the stocky North
Korean general. For a moment the Vice President almost
winced at the anger he saw in the general's face. Then he built

a small frown and his eyes turned icy as he sent his own anger back, until the shorter man looked down at his notes.

An interpreter translated each word into English as the general spoke.

"I am disgusted and angered at this meeting. There is no true purpose here, and no possibility of any agreements. No chance that one of our sides might make concessions to the other. I have watched the United States imperialists function for many years. It is always the same. They attack and subdue an enemy so they can make a profit from that nation and hold power over them. It's an old, old way of life for the Western powers.

"The Democratic People's Republic of Korea has never done any of these things. We have never subjugated another people. We have never made war on anyone for profit or power. We are a small country hounded and threatened by a huge nation with unlimited resources, hundred of warships, thousands of warplanes, and millions of men bearing modern arms.

"We are half of a poor country. A poor nation that could be great if it were unified under one government. We are one people. We should be one country with one government. We must strive for this, to bring eighty million Koreans into the twenty-first century as a new people with tremendous promise and power in the great family of nations around the Pacific Rim."

General Soo looked hard again at the Vice President.

"The United States of America has for almost fifty years shattered the peace and freedom of all Koreans with the presence of her armed forces on our soil. This is nothing but a naked power plot to take over all of Korea and incorporate it into the American union of states, making Korea simply another small part of that union.

"This type of thinking, this type of furious action is nothing short of international criminal aggression, and should be dealt with by the United Nations and other law-abiding security groups.

"The intransient position of the United States leaves the Democratic People's Republic of Korea with only one alter-

native. That course of action is neither pleasing nor easy for
the people of Korea. But at this point it is the only way that
Korea can survive. We are one people. We must have one
government."

The stocky man sat down. There was no cheering by the
North Koreans. Instead they all looked with distaste at the
Vice President.

Don Stroh had watched and listened to the North Korean
with surprise and anger. The man was coming as close as
anyone could to suggesting that an all-out war between North
and South Korea could be the only solution to the current
situation.

Stroh was surprised. War talk from a nation nearing the end
of its economic rope? The North had a 1.2-million-man army,
but much of the equipment it used had come from the Soviets
and the Chinese many years ago and was now rusting and
running out of spare parts and fuel. A MiG pilot who flew his
jet to the South and surrendered had said that many of the
North's fighter pilots had only five hours of flight time a year,
due to a severe shortage of jet fuel. How could they stage an
attack? No, the general was bluffing, and he was good at it.

Vice President Wilson Chambers stood and looked at the
North Koreans. He spoke without notes. A translator on the
North side translated his words.

"This is the start of an interesting exchange. I come
directly from the President of the United States, and he has
made several tremendously generous offers to the North
Korean people.

"The United States does not want to annex Korea. It would
be unheard of. We don't conquer independent countries to
take them into our nation. Rather we help smaller countries
and then free them to be independent, the way we did the
Philippines.

"Today I bring to the North Korean people an offer of more
than a billion tons of foodstuffs, everything from corn and
wheat and rice to powdered milk, baby formula, cornmeal,
oats, barley, soy, and a hundred other nonperishable foods
that can help out a starving people.

"Our only restriction is that these millions of tons of food be used for the civilian population of North Korea. We know that food is in tremendously short supply, and we are not trying to embarrass our guests here today. It is simply a fact that North Korea needs to eat more food than it can produce. We want to help the North Korean people in this matter."

The Vice President paused and took a drink from a glass of water. He looked directly at the Korean general, who had his arms folded in front of him and a look of fury dominating his features. The Vice President hurried on.

"We know that medical supplies and treatment are also lacking in the northern half of the Korean peninsula. To help with this problem, the United States government has made plans to ship twenty fully equipped mobile hospitals to North Korea. They will come with supplies, instruments, machines, drugs, and enough goods to last for a year. A volunteer medical staff can also come along, and will stay and work in the hospitals with Korean medical people for a full year. There is no cost or obligation."

General Soo slammed both hands down on the polished table, creating a loud slap. He stood at the same time. The rest of the North Korean delegation rose as well. The general turned and scowled at the Vice President. He said something in a low voice, then marched stiffly out of the meeting and through the doors he had came in by. The entire North Korean party followed him.

Vice President Chambers stood watching them. Surprise, then a touch of anger, followed by resignation inched across his face.

"What did the general say as he left?" the Vice President asked the interpreter.

For a moment the man frowned, then shook his head. "I must have heard him wrong, Mr. Vice President. To the best of my hearing he said: 'Your fancy giveaway plans will kill you yet.' "

Vice President Chambers asked the interpreter to tell him again, then turned to the rest of his delegation and the South Koreans.

He shook his head sadly. "I just can't understand a man with a mind like that. We offer him a generous solution to two of his country's largest and most serious problems, and he threatens that our good plans will kill us? Does anyone understand what he meant?"

The Vice President looked around, but no one could answer. He lifted his brows. "Well, It seems like my big presentation is over. I didn't get started on it. Now, so we don't have a completely lost day, I want the ten-dollar tour of the DMZ, our troops at Camp Bonifas, the tunnels, the lookout towers, everything I can see, even the tank battalion."

The Vice President looked at his military guide, Major Prokoff.

"Sir, not a good idea. From time to time there are shots across the DMZ. It's always a danger up there."

"Nonsense. I've been in combat before. I have my CIB, and I've even taken a few shots in anger. Arrange it, Major. I want to take the whole delegation along, my staff and the Congressmen. Make them do some work on this pleasure trip."

"Yes, sir. I'll see you back to your quarters, then make the arrangements. You said all of your people?"

"Right, Major. There are twelve of us, my staff and seven Congressmen. Leave the newsmen in the rear this time. Like to get on that today. Might even decide to stay overnight on the line. Bring back some memories for me."

"That would have to be cleared by the commanding general, Mr. Vice President."

"Fine, get it cleared. You tell him that I've already cleared it. I outrank him all to pieces. Now get cracking, Major."

"Yes, sir."

Vice President Chambers smiled as the major hurried off. He enjoyed ordering these officers around. He had barely made buck sergeant during his two years in the Army. Yes, he enjoyed giving the brass orders for a change. He remembered his time in the Army Signal Corps. Lately he'd been fascinated with the military SATCOM radio. He carried one with him everywhere.

He could get in instant satellite communication with the White House or his office anytime he wanted to. He was amazed how well it worked. It transmitted to a satellite and then to the States and into the White House, where the message that had been encrypted was decrypted and came through in voice transmission. The unit was fifteen inches high, about six inches square, and weighed a little over ten pounds. The Vice President remembered the old SCR-300 Army radio he used to carry. It weighed thirty pounds, could transmit no more than five miles, and often didn't work at all.

Two hours later, just inside the gates of Camp Bonifas, the Vice President had the caravan pull to the side. He told his aide, Lukas Young, to bring up the SATCOM radio and get in touch with the White House. Young set up the antenna, turned it to face the satellite, and got the set working.

"I'm sorry, Mr. Vice President, the President isn't here," came over the radio.

"Well, this is Chambers. Tell him it didn't go well today at Panmunjom. Old General Soo went into a tirade about one people and one government. I just got started with our food and medical programs when he snorted, got up, and walked out. Tell the President for me. I'm off on a tour of the DMZ."

Inside the camp, Lieutenant Colonel James F. Lauderdale became the Vice President's official guide.

"Mr. Vice President, it's good to meet you. I command the last American unit stationed inside the DMZ. I advised against this tour for you, but I was overruled. There is a danger here. We've had over seven hundred instances of North Korean commandos penetrating the DMZ and working into South Korea. These units have to be found and eliminated.

"From time to time there is sniper fire across the line. I'll be sure to keep you and your party as safe as possible. I understand you did some Army time."

"Yes, Colonel, I was in the Signal Corps."

"Good. You remember when to keep your head down."

The tour began at the camp, with the colonel's briefing:

"Camp Bonifas is a quarter of a mile from the DMZ. This is the most northern base in Korea that's manned by Americans. This is the focal point of the whole defense system. Our troops here are the sharp blade of the spear aimed at North Korea.

"If anything happens, we'll be the first to know, and then I grab the phone and call General Richard Reynolds, the commanding general of the U.S. Eighth Army. Let's get in the Humvees for a short demo drive into the DMZ. Right here the zone is two and a half miles wide. Down the center are yellow markers. Troops from each side are supposed to stay on their side of those yellow center markers. There have been a lot of incursions by North Korean commandos lately. We'll continue on and see one of our observation points."

It took them five minutes of driving down Military Route 1, through minefields, next to boulder-piled tank traps, and over culverts the colonel said were stuffed with high-explosives that could be set off in case of a tank attack.

Colonel Lauderdale explained that he commanded a light infantry regiment of 250 Americans and three hundred South Korean troops. "This is the last of the one hundred and fourteen posts along the DMZ manned by American troops," he said. "Of course we have our backup tank battalion just to our rear."

Observation Post Oullette stood thirty yards from the yellow and rusting centerline markers in the DMZ. It looked like a training tower or hose-drying building for a neighborhood fire station. The group trudged up wooden stairs to the third floor, which was open on all four sides. On a clear day observers there could see sixteen miles into North Korea. A number of swivel-mounted high-powered binoculars rested on a shelf around the OP.

They went down the stairs and then down some ladders into the underground complex. There were concrete walls and openings. Each opening was a bunker that looked out on North Korea.

"If things get dicey, this is where we'll fire the first shots from if the NKs invade us," Colonel Lauderdale said. "We fight from here and if it's a huge invasion, most of the men here will either die in these bunkers or be captured."

Vice President Chambers looked out one port and noticed a series of switches on the side.

"These for lights?" he asked.

A sergeant shook his head. "Triggers for Claymore mines, sir," he said. The Vice President knew what Claymores were. A chunk of C-4 plastic explosive packed with three hundred ball bearings. The mine could be angled so it fired the balls out one direction and at tremendous speed. One Claymore could kill half a platoon of infantry.

He saw a map on the wall with concentrations of machine gun killing zones. Then the tour was over and they headed back.

"I'd like to see the tanks," The Vice President said. Colonel Lauderdale hesitated only a moment, but it was enough to stir the Vice President's curiosity.

"Are they off-limits, Colonel?"

"No, sir, Mr. Vice President. Theirs is a special unit, highly trained and on a nervous edge most of the time. But for you we can disturb them for a few minutes."

Ten minutes later, they had left the front part of the DMZ and moved to the rear of the American sector. The Humvee drove up to a heavy concentration of barbed-wire fences. There were three parallel ones. The outside fence had steel posts set in concrete, with barbed wire stretched at six-inch intervals up to eight feet. On top of that hung razor wire in circular coils. The next fence was ten feet tall, with concertina on both sides and razor wire stretched on the steel posts.

The last fence was chain link, six feet high and full of caution signs that said in three languages that the fence was highly charged with electricity.

Steel gates stopped them at the guard post. A lieutenant heading the guards insisted on seeing the colonel's ID and that of each of the men in the three vehicles. Then he opened the gate. It slid back on well-oiled rollers operated by electric motor.

"The gate here weighs a little over two tons," the colonel said. "It would take a tank to break through it."

Just inside, Major Donovan Kitts met them. He commanded the 91st Armored Battalion. Kitts was slight, five eight, and looked like a marathon runner. His keen blue eyes missed nothing. He saluted his colonel, said hello, then turned to Chambers.

"Mr. Vice President. It's an honor to have you visit our unit. Is there anything in particular you'd like to see?"

"Just your normal routine. I understand you do some training, maneuvers, preparations for defensive combat, that sort of thing."

"Yes, sir. I could move some tanks around and show you some of your tax dollars at work."

"Thank you, Major Kitts. I'd appreciate that."

They drove a mile away to where six tanks worked back and forth in a barren section of plowed-up dirt just behind the DMZ. The tanks wheeled and charged forward toward the line, then turned, set up a line of defense, pulled out, and each tank drove into a bunker so only the muzzle of the big cannon and the top of the turret showed.

Major Kitts was in the lead tank. When the maneuvering was over, the major climbed out of his tank and came back to where the Vice President and his group stood.

"Major, could I see your outfit's living quarters?" the Vice President asked. "I understand a certain number of you are on alert twenty-four hours a day, and some are sleeping and eating. Where do your men do this?"

Five minutes later they went into a concealed underground complex that looked like a military office, barracks, and kitchen, only it was under the Korean soil. It was a self-contained unit that fed, housed, and supplied the tankers.

Vice President Chambers looked at the facility and smiled. "Major, how would you like to have twelve guests tonight? I want to stay this close to the DMZ and get a notion of what it feels like. We won't be any trouble to you, and we don't eat much. I'm sure the colonel and the general will have no objections."

Colonel Lauderdale built some frown lines on his forehead. "Sir, this is in an extreme danger zone, twice the target that the observation tower is. We usually allow no civilians to be in this area, let alone overnight. Your visit here is most unusual. I don't see how your being here would make that much difference."

The Vice President held up his hand. "Colonel, we appreciate your concern. All but one of this group has been under enemy fire during wartime. You don't need to worry about our safety. We won't need any baggage. We can live in these clothes until we get back to your camp tomorrow morning. It's settled. We'll all stay here tonight." He turned to the other eleven civilians. "Unless any of you want to chicken out on me and run for the camp."

There was some nervous laughter, but nobody held up a hand.

"Good, it's settled. I'd guess that some of this underground facility leads to the bunkers with weapons pointed toward the DMZ. I'd like to see those areas as well."

Major Kitts looked at his commanding officer, who gave the barest of nods, and the tanker led the way to the rest of the underground complex that held the fire-forward areas.

Vice President Chambers settled into position behind a .50-caliber machine gun and grinned. A belt of ammo hung off the gun with one round in the chamber ready to fire. He looked out at the DMZ.

"Damn, but this is tight. Weapons, tanks, and infantry all over the place. I don't see how the NKs could possibly get through the DMZ and even this far into South Korea."

Then the Vice President remembered the angry words of the NK general and the expression on his face as he stood to walk out. For a moment Chambers decided that he would put nothing past this number-two man in the North Korean Army. Absolutely nothing.

3

42nd Tank Battalion
Demilitarized Zone
North Korea

Major Yim Pak Lee frowned as he saw one of his tanks take a slow turn and get bumped by the tank behind.

He used his radio. "No, no, stupid ass in number six. Keep up your speed. You'll get pushed into the gully you keep driving like that. Now. Do it again, all fifteen of you. Back to the starting point, go."

He watched from the turret of his tank on a high piece of ground less than a mile behind the DMZ. It was his maneuver land, where he could put his sixteen tanks through their paces and keep the crews sharp.

He watched the tanks back half a mile, turn, and come into line. Three tanks formed a spearhead in front of five behind them in a line.

Beside that formation was a similar lineup of the other seven tanks. The machines were in top condition. Their crews were hardworking and just reaching the peak of their skills. Each of the sixteen units had a 105mm howitzer and a load of sixty rounds. They could pack a devastating punch.

Major Yim knew his mission. When the orders came down

to attack, it would be at dawn, and his tanks would charge ahead through the DMZ, past the centerline, and smash and blow up all the defenders they could find.

His battalion had won the right to be directly across from the only sector of the DMZ manned by Americans. His men were ready. They would follow orders, and charge into the midst of the sleeping American tankers before they knew it was morning. An attacking force always had the advantage in any kind of battle.

Major Yim smiled. Yes, when the orders came, his sharp battalion would be ready, more than ready, anxious to show its ability to wipe out the sixteen American tanks before they knew there was a war going on.

The major watched the new run-through on the maneuver. Yes, better. The ability to move, take advantage of any cover, and then come out shooting was what his battalion had won honors for.

He saw a military sedan drive into the edge of the tanks' maneuvering range. At once Major Yim ordered his own tank to turn and charge toward the sedan. The rig had stopped just inside the plowed-up ground where the treads punished the land. He brought the big tank to a stop a dozen feet away, lifted out of the turret, and dropped to the ground.

A full colonel stood by the side of the sedan smoking a cigar. Major Yim marched up and saluted smartly.

"Major Yim at your service, Colonel."

The colonel returned the salute, then pointed at the tanks.

"Sixteen still in operation, I see, Major. That's good. You have utilized your spare tank to good advantage. Spare parts is the call I hear from other commanders, but never from you. How do you manage that?"

"Skill and three top-flight mechanics, Colonel."

"Good, good. When your exercise ends here, I need to talk to all of your men. Have your crews and all your battalion support people in your enlisted mess in two hours. I'll see you there."

Major Yim saluted as the colonel stepped back inside the car and it drove away.

Two hours. Plenty of time. The major worked his crews for

another hour, then told them to move the tanks back into their battle stations. Each tank had a carefully built and camouflaged attack position a hundred yards from the centerline of the DMZ. Each position was dug in with ten feet of packed earth in front of the tank, and walls of earth higher than the tank on each side.

It would take a direct hit by a mortar or tank round to hurt any of the tanks. That was the defensive mode. With three minutes of warning, the tankers could be in their rigs, then backed out of the emplacements and sent charging across the centerline fence. It was an order that he prayed for each night.

He used his radio and notified the tankers of the schedule, then warned the support team that even the cooks were to be at the meeting at 1700 in the mess hall. Every man in his command would be there under severe penalty.

Major Yim had worked hard to get into this position. He wanted to be in the very forefront of any attack southward. It was his personal payback.

The major had never known his father. He was born in 1953 after the war was over and the cease-fire had been signed. Now he was one of the oldest tank commanders in North Korea's forces. He had fought to keep his position.

His father had been captured by the Americans late in the war and turned over to the South Korean Army terrorists, who had tortured him for three days. They had used every form of torture that had been devised by man to inflict pain without death. At last, after the third horrific day, his father had died while enduring the torture of a thousand slices. No one knife cut into his flesh would kill him, but the accumulation of blood loss from hundreds of such slices on his body had led to his bleeding to death.

Yim blamed the Americans for turning his father over to the sadistic South. They knew what his fate would be. They didn't care. They wanted the military information about the division across the line from them.

They never got it.

His father had not said a word after he had been captured.

After the war, Yim had grown up without a father. In the highly family oriented society of North Korea, that put him at

a terrific disadvantage. He had no strong male to support him.
He had no older brothers to fight for him.

He remembered that when he was ten, he came home
almost every day with new cuts or bruises after the older boys
had caught him and beat him with their fists.

As he got older, the beatings became worse. He started
carrying a knife that opened its five-inch blade with a quick
flip of the wrist. He used it the first day he carried it. Three
boys two years older than he caught him in an alley a short
way from his home. He warned them. Then he flipped open
the knife and cut two of them so quickly they had no chance
to escape. The third boy ran away screaming. The two he'd
cut had minor wounds on their hands and arms.

The next day the same three boys caught him again. This
time they had knives as well, longer ones than his. His back
was to the wall of a house. The three drove in all at once, and
he couldn't stop all of them. He took a stab wound to his right
leg and a slash on his left arm, but his right hand thrust hard
with his blade and one of the boys took it full in the chest.

He died minutes later in the alley.

After that the boys left him alone, for a time.

The other two remembered that he had killed their friend.

When Yim was sixteen, the two trapped him at the edge of
the schoolyard. By this time he had grown to almost five feet
ten, taller than any of his classmates. He had also studied Tae
Kwon Do, unarmed combat. He was ready.

Chung Sik had come at him from one side and his smaller
friend from the other. Each had a knife. Yim had left his knife
home that day.

He decided the larger Chung Sik was the more dangerous,
and turned and with a side kick stopped him, then turned to
the smaller man, who hesitated.

Yim took advantage of the pause and executed a classic
spinning round kick to the head, slamming the kid to the
ground unconscious.

Then Chung Sik charged in from the side and the battle
was on. Neither had the advantage now, but Yim's kicks and
vicious elbow and hand slashes kept the knife from drawing
any blood. When Chung Sik realized that he couldn't harm

Yim, he waved to two policemen who had been watching the fight from across the street. Chung Sik talked to the policemen, who promptly grabbed Yim and hauled him to the police station.

"Why am I here?" he shouted at them. They beat him with bamboo batons.

"What have I done to be arrested?"

They beat him again.

Three hours later, Chung Sik came to the door and watched the officers beat him again. A policeman behind him watched as well. He wore captain's bars. He looked at Yim.

"You are not greatly injured. You are sentenced to three months in the mountain work camp building roads. Take him away."

It was much later that Yim found out that the police captain was Chung Sik's father.

Yim came back from the labor camp thin, but stronger than he had ever been and angrier. A week later he caught Chung Sik without his friends, and beat him into unconsciousness. Then he broke both the young man's arms over his knee and left him in the gutter.

Yim blamed it all, everything that happened to him, on the devil Americans. They had caused it. They had caught and let the criminal South Koreans torture his father to death.

He would never sleep well until he had repaid the devil Americans in gallons and gallons of their blood spilled on South Korean soil.

The meeting in the mess hall was brief. The colonel was kind in his remarks to the men about their maneuvers in the field that afternoon.

Then he paced in front of them. "You men are here for a glorious purpose. When the attack comes, when we smash across the DMZ into the south, you men will be our spearhead. You will charge through the American tanks like a knife through a ripe melon and you will prevail. Then you will charge south with Seoul in your sights.

"We are counting on you men to be at the very peak of your readiness, to kill the enemy, to slaughter his tanks, and to crash through every South Korean Army unit you find like it was a paper tiger."

The men stood and cheered, chanting: "We are ready! We are ready! We are ready!"

The colonel nodded and headed for the door.

"Attention." The major barked. Every man in the room shot to his feet and stood at a braced attention. Major Yim smiled and followed the colonel out the door.

Yes, his men were ready. They could charge across the border in ten minutes if the order came. He was proud of them.

The colonel stopped at his car. He motioned the major to come closer.

"Major Yim, you're doing a good job. When the order comes, your men look ready." He paused. "That order to charge into the DMZ could come before you expect it. Good hunting, Major."

The colonel stepped into the car with a sly smile, and the sedan pulled away and out of the battalion's rear area.

Major Yim frowned. The order could come before he expected it? What did that mean? This week? This month? Did he mean that they might get into war with the South soon?

American Sector DMZ

"I don't like it, Sarge," Willy Johnson said into the handset. "Too damn much noise out there. Isn't that where the NKs have a tank battalion?"

"Easy, Johnson. Remember last week when the NKs pulled that exercise just at dawn. We had half of our guys out of their sacks and buttoned up in their tanks. We got chewed out for a half hour by the damned colonel himself. I say we sit on it for a few more minutes."

"Yeah, easy for you to say, Sarge, sitting back there at fucking Bonifas. They wouldn't hit you for about three minutes after they squash us like bugs under their tank treads."

"Okay, Johnson, give it a level-one alert. I'll call the

colonel. He ain't gonna be happy getting woke up at four
damn o'clock in the fucking morning."

"Thanks, Sarge. Level-one alert now on the boards. Nobody here gets up, right? Nobody in his tank?"

"Right. Now shut up a minute. Hey, you see anything with
your NVGs?"

"Nope. Too far away. But the sound comes through.
Everything but the tanks starting up."

"Stay on it."

Willy Johnson tried the night-vision goggles again. They
turned the Korean no-man's-land into a dull green, but he
could see the centerline, the bunkers, even some shrubs that
had grown up. But the NK tankers were too far away. He put
down the goggles and listened.

More sounds of metal on metal. Were those closing tank
turrets? Maybe the slap of a wrench on a stubborn nut? How
about a tread getting slammed home with a hammer?

He listened again. Damn, he could just see those damn
NKs swarming over those sixteen tanks over there with their
105 cannon all aimed south. Hell, maybe they were backing
out of their revetments. No, not without starting their engines.

Then the sound came clear and unmistakable: The diesel
engines on sixteen tanks ground over all at once. Johnson
grabbed the phone.

"Sarge, Sarge, the damn tank engines are starting. Sounds
like all of them."

Nobody answered. The line was supposed to be open all
the time. "Sarge, come in, Sarge." He gave up on the phone
and keyed the small radio. "This is Oullette calling Bonifas,
calling anybody, over."

Only a gentle hum came from the radio speaker.

"Bonifas, we've got sixteen NK tanks with engines running. Does anybody copy?"

"Yeah, I copy, Oullette. This is the Ninety-first Tank. That
for real, those NKs fired up?"

"Damn straight. I heard them before. Now I can't raise
Bonifas."

"Let me try."

Willy Johnson waited a long sixty seconds; then the radio came on.

"Yeah, I got Bonifas. The OD said remember last week. He's not excited about it."

"Hell, Nine One, they could be backing those machines out of their holes right now and pointing them at you."

"Right as rain, little buddy, right as—"

The first North Korean artillery round slammed out of the darkness and exploded on the 91st Armored Battalion's communications center. The officer of the day and three enlisted men died from the first shell and all communications were out. Twenty-four rounds rained down so quickly that half the tankers in the center were either killed or wounded.

Deep in their bunkers the tanker crews came awake with a jolt, pulled on boots and helmets, and ran for their tanks. Ten of the sixteen crews made it to their machines and started the motors. Long guns were lifted, trained on the DMZ to the north.

Another barrage of artillery battered three of the manned tanks and four of the empty ones. One tank took a direct hit, and twenty of the 105 shells in its locker went off with a deafening roar.

"Move out, move out," Major Kitts bellowed into his tank-to-tank radio. The big tanks backed out of their assigned bunkers and jolted into the DMZ to escape the killing artillery.

"How many tanks we have left?" Kitts asked his radio. He took reports from seven units. "Okay, we form a line here just in back of the centerline and wait for the bastards. They must be coming. Keep a sharp lookout."

The eight American tanks lined up forty yards apart, twenty yards from the DMZ centerline, and waited.

North Korean 42nd Tank Battalion

Major Yim Pak Lee had his troops up at 3 A.M. and briefed the officers, then the enlisted men. They manned their sixteen tanks at 0415. His orders were to attack as soon as he heard the first artillery shell come overhead.

The shell whispered over at precisely 0420, and the major dropped into his tank and buttoned up the turret.

"All tanks fire one round at predesignated target one on my command. Ready, fire." His own gunner blasted one l05 toward the Americans. Yim reveled in the smell of the burned powder in the tank despite the best fans.

"All tanks move out into attack positions on command. The three-tank spearhead and five. Bravo Team to the right. Move."

The sixteen North Korean tanks swung into position, then angled to their right directly at the enemy tanks they knew had been hit hard by artillery fire. Major Yim lifted the turret of his tank and looked out. He could hear the rumbling of his battalion on both sides of him. There was concentrated artillery fire directly ahead. He would slow enough to miss it. There was the whisper of fighter jets high overhead waiting for dawn. The light would come in three quarters of an hour. By then he hoped he and his men would have punched a hole five miles into the South Korean landscape.

A gentle valley leading southwest was his route. Once he broke through there, there would be little to stop him for twenty miles. He grinned in the morning darkness. They were only a quarter of a mile from the start of the DMV. The machine gunner on his tank cut loose with a ten-round burst, then a second one. Nerves. They all had them, but the MG men could do something about it.

"Target, gunner?" Yim asked.

"Swear I saw some troops out there, Major, maybe an ambush patrol."

Corporal Arley Whitworth had tried for almost three minutes to get a radio contact with Bonifas. Nobody answered. He and his ambush patrol had heard the first artillery. He figured it had targeted the camp's headquarters and then the American tanks.

Five minutes later they all heard the tanks coming from the north. "Tanks, Sarge," Whitworth said.

The older man nodded. Sergeant First Class Benton Crawford had seen it all. Vietnam, Gulf War, and now Korea.

"They're coming, sure as hell. We've got no radio, no phone. We play it by fucking ear. We bring any RPGs?"

The word went around quickly. "We got two pair, Sarge. Holy shit, there they are. Must be twenty fucking tanks."

Sergeant Crawford signaled down the line for all of his nine men to get into a shallow ditch in case the tanks came right at them.

"Get them RPGs up here." Benton sent the word down the line. His men were ten yards apart. The two troopers with the rocket-propelled grenades settled in three yards on each side of their patrol leader.

"Coming our way, Sarge?" one of the GIs asked.

"Looks that way. The only good we can do with those RPGs is to knock his tread off. I want you guys to aim at the tread. So shoot low. Each of you take a different tank. Closer the better. Shit."

He looked up and saw one tank less than thirty yards from them and aimed straight at his men. A machine gun on a tank down the row cut loose. They had another ambush patrol fifty yards down on the right.

"If this bastard keeps coming at us, we crawl through the ditch so half of us are on each side. When he hits the ditch, you two guys blast him with your RPGs. Should be one on the other side. Let's knock this guy out of action."

The infantrymen settled down in the three-foot ditch. It wouldn't be enough to save them if the tank ran directly over them. The dirt would cave in on both sides and smother whoever was under the tank.

The big long gun on the tank fired, the round slamming over the heads of the troops in the ditch.

"Still coming right at us, Sarge," Corporal Whitworth said.

"Spread out," Sergeant Crawford called. "Whitworth, you take half on down to the right. Rest of you, move my way. Remember, hit those fucking treads."

Five of the GIs crawled along the trench to get out of the way of the clanking monster rolling towards them. The tank's machine gun cut loose again, but the fire was well over their heads. The tank rolled forward, aimed at the part of the trench vacated by the men.

Sergeant Crawford grabbed the RPG and sighted in on the tank as it rolled and clanked toward them. When it was thirty feet from the ditch, he aimed at the tank's treads and fired.

At that close range, the RPG barely got started before it hit the tank and exploded with a roar. The big NK tank shuddered, a cloud of smoke drifted upward, then the lumbering metal monster pivoted toward the sergeant. The track on his side had come off and the other track kept turning the rig in a circle. Then it stopped.

The tank was now heading in the wrong direction. The ambush patrol lay quietly in the ditch. The turret of the tank popped open, and a moment later a head and shoulders came out. Four M-16 rifles blasted off three-round bursts and the commander of Tank 22 slumped in the hatch, half his head blown off by the rounds. For a moment, nothing happened, then the body vanished inside the tank.

Before Sergeant Crawford's men could move, they heard another explosion to the right. Then the rest of his patrol came running down the ditch and slid in beside the sergeant.

"We killed a tank, just like you did. Blew his fucking tread halfway back to Scotland."

"Where to now, Sarge," the corporal asked.

"Damned if I know. Most of the tanks are past us. We haven't heard much from the American tanks." Crawford was about ready to move when a machine gun opened up, digging up dirt beside their ditch. They hugged the bottom of the depression, and the tank machine gunner looked elsewhere for targets.

Somebody groaned. The medic crawled over.

"Casualties, Sarge. We've got two dead and one wounded. We should be getting to the rear."

Sergeant Crawford nodded. "Oh, hell, yes, but just where is the rear, and where are the North Koreans? What the hell we going to do when the infantry that's sure to follow these tanks comes running through here?"

"In the dark we have a chance," Whitworth said. "We've got to leave our dead and run like hell to the south. That way we'll have a chance."

The rest of the ambush patrol that had killed two North

Korean tanks turned south and began to jog. The American lines had to be down there somewhere.

91st Armored Battalion

Major Donovan Kitts heard the enemy tanks before he saw them. It was just as he had envisioned it in all the practice alerts and war games they had played. But this was no game.

"I have four tanks breaking through the DMZ," Kitts said on the radio. "Fire at will."

Kitts buttoned up his lid and checked with the gunner. Just as he did, the 105 gun went off with a roar. The gunner had his eyes fast on the scope of the M-21 solid-state analog ballistic computer and the AN/VVG-2 ruby laser range finder to direct the next round. Kitts knew his counterpart across the line had sixteen tanks, but all of his were probably charging across the line right now. Sixteen against eight. Not pretty odds.

Then the battle was on. His gun scored the first direct hit, blasting the tank across the line into a flaming, exploding mass of heavy metal. He lost two of his tanks in the next three minutes and called the rest off, racing to the rear as near to their thirty-mph speed limit as they could go. They twisted and turned and hid behind a small rise and got away, but by then they were five miles into South Korea.

That was when Major Kitts remembered his guests for the night.

"Oh, damn, the Vice President and those Congressmen are still back at the underground headquarters. Holy shit!" He tried to contact somebody with his long-range radio, but all he got in return was static.

Underground Bunker
91st Armored Battalion

Vice President Wilson Chambers jolted awake when the first artillery round exploded fifty feet from him in a tank revetment area. He had heard enough artillery to recognize it even there in the underground. He sat up on the Army cot and shook his head. Another round slammed in and exploded farther away. He pulled on his pants and shoes.

"Everyone up, we're under attack," he bellowed. They had

put the visitors in a room that was farthest away from the access tunnel upward. Some of the other men in the room didn't believe him until the next artillery round landed close enough to make dirt drift down from the ceiling.

"Damn close. Get dressed. See if we can find some weapons. If this is the damn North Koreans' push across the DMZ, we're in deep trouble here, people."

Before the men could get dressed, three others from another room rushed in. They had dressed. All twelve of the delegation were accounted for.

"What's happening?" a Congressman from Oregon asked.

Just then another round hit, caving in the tunnel that led out of the room.

They were trapped.

The men finished dressing, and the Vice President scowled.

"Gentlemen, there's no rush. We aren't going anywhere. That has to be the North Koreans out there attacking the tank battalion, which means they are driving south in an all-out invasion just as the general threatened to do yesterday."

"So where does that leave us?" one of the Secret Service men asked.

"In deep shit," somebody cracked, and they all laughed.

"He's right," Congressman Anderson, Republican from Indiana, said. "If the North has attacked, this is one of the first units that would be overrun, which means right now we're behind the enemy's lines. When they find us, we all say we're Congressmen. We don't even hint that our Vice President is here. We're all Congressmen and we demand to be released at once."

There were some murmurs of approval. The Secret Service men agreed. Then Vice President Chambers took the floor.

"I think the Congressman is right. I was a representative from Ohio. I can play that part. So we're all members of our government and we demand to be released at once."

"Now, we settle in to wait, or do we try to dig out?" one of the younger Secret Service men asked. "Anybody got a shovel?"

The blasted end of the access tunnel wasn't as bad as it

looked. There were some timbers down, but the concrete walls were intact.

After an hour of digging with their hands and some boards, they could see daylight on the other side.

"Hey, out there," one man yelled. "Help us, we're trapped in here."

They heard some shouts, and then a jabbering in Korean. None of them understood a word of it. They all smiled when they heard someone on the other side of the blockage begin to dig it out with a shovel. Now it was just a matter of time.

Eighth Army Headquarters
Seoul, South Korea

Lieutenant General Richard F. Reynolds shook off the hand on his shoulder. It wasn't even light outside yet.

"General. General, sir, the telephone."

"What? What the hell?"

"It's the telephone, sir. Camp Bonifas has been attacked and overrun by the North Koreans."

General Reynolds came awake at once. "No shit?"

"True, sir. The phone." The sergeant handed his commanding general the phone and retreated.

"Yes, General Reynolds here. Who is this?"

"Lieutenant Hardiman, sir. I'm on a cell phone trying to hide from a full-thrust attack by the North Koreans. They've done it, sir. Blasted across the DMV about 0430. They must be eight, ten miles to the south by now. I don't know how much longer I can hide. I'll move south as soon as I can. Bonifas is ruined. Artillery blasted it for half an hour, knocking out communications, flattening most of the buildings. The tank battalion took a lot of hits too. Some of them got away to the south with six or seven of their tanks."

"Thanks, Hardiman. You take care of yourself and stay hidden until dark, then work south. Be careful."

The general hung up. He dressed and rushed to his office. Three of his staff were there taking reports. They established a line on the big wall map. The North Koreans had launched a massive attack along a thirty-mile front with Panmunjom at the center. His troops and those of the South Koreans had taken

large losses. One enemy tank column had penetrated five
miles through the center, but had been blunted and stopped.
North infantry units all along the line were running into
increased resistance from the Southern forces.

Americans were only manning one section of the 114 along
the 151-mile DMZ. The rest of the 37,000 Americans were in
rear-area support and headquarters and supply units.

The first orders General Reynolds gave were for Air Force
support to get off the ground and give close-in firepower.
Then he studied the map. They had to push back that bulge in
the middle. It was aimed directly at Seoul and the enemy
tanks were only about twenty miles away.

"You finally did it, General Soo, you bastard. Okay, we'll
see who has the most firepower. We're going to find out in
one hell of a rush."

4

USS *Monroe*, CVN 81
Off South Korea

Vice Admiral Nathan Kenner came out of his bed at 0437 when his steward knocked on the door.

"Telephone from CIC, Admiral."

"Yes, yes, I'm awake. I have it." He picked up the handset. "What?"

"Word from Seoul, Admiral. The North Koreans just blasted across the DMZ in a thirty-mile-long offensive. They have penetrated five miles in spots. That puts them only twenty miles from Seoul. General Reynolds, CO of the Eight Army, wants to talk to you."

"Put him on."

The phone buzzed for a moment, then came clear. "General Reynolds?"

"Yes, Reynolds here. Admiral Kenner, we've got trouble. Can you send me about fifty ground-attack aircraft? We're in need of more air support."

"Yes, let me talk to my CAG, but I'm sure we can get you F-18's when you want them, and six or eight Cobra chopper gunships. Give me two minutes."

A knock sounded on the door, and CAG Irving Olson walked in.

"I heard. What does the Army want?"

"Ground support. What can we send them on a rotating basis?"

"We've updated our ground-attack capability on the Eighteens. We have fifty-six aircraft that can serve for ground support. We can scrape up about twenty chopper gunships from around the fleet."

"Good, talk to General Reynolds. Work out how he wants to bring them in and the overhead control."

Three minutes later the word went out to the pilots' ready room. The four F-18's on standby would be launched at once. Ten more F-18's would be launched as soon as possible. All with full ground-attack weapons. Aircraft handlers pulled F-18's onto the elevators to bring them to the flight deck. Aircraft crews inspected the planes before the pilots got there.

The first four standby fighters were off the deck in four minutes after the alert; then more began shooting off. As the pilots raced the one hundred miles to the fighting, they were directed to targets by an Air Force AWACS control plane high over the peninsula. The first two Hornets were vectored to the North Korean tank thrust at the center of the line.

The F-18's were loaded for ground attack. Each had its M61 20mm, six-barrel gun and 570 rounds. They carried 17,000 pounds of bombs and rockets, AIM-7 Sparrow missiles for air-to-air defense, and the AGM-65 Maverick for tanks and other major targets.

Captain Olson went to the CIC, the Combat Information Center, where he could talk with his pilots and control the launching of the birds on an as-needed basis. Each flight would have two hours over the target unless they exhausted their armament. Then they would return for another rotation.

A hundred miles to the target was not even a warm-up for the Hornets at Mach 1.8 speed. They would be traveling about twenty-four miles a minute, which put them a little over five minutes away from their combat zone.

In his cabin, well below the flight deck, Murdock heard the flurry of activity of the launches. He came awake at once, dressed, and hurried up to the CIC. Captain Olson saw him come in and nodded, then went back to getting the next flight of Hornets off the deck.

"Damned North Koreans launched a thirty-mile-wide attack across the DMZ this morning. We're giving air support. You guys are bound to get some action pretty soon."

Murdock grinned. "Great, it's about time."

Eighth Army Headquarters
Seoul, South Korea

General Reynolds closed his eyes a moment and shook his head.

"Tell me you're not sure, Major. How in hell could the Vice President of the United States have stayed overnight in a bunker with the Ninety-first Tank Battalion inside the DMV?"

"His request, sir. He said he outranked you. We know he was there last night because one of his Secret Service men has a SATCOM and he talked to us just after midnight. He said all was well, the Vice President was being well taken care of, and they would be back in Seoul today for the ceremony at the war memorial."

"No word from him since last night?"

"No, sir. We have to assume that he was overrun by the NK tanks and captured. Few of the Ninety-first's support people got out. They took over forty artillery rounds when the attack began at 0430."

"We have to get him out of there."

"How, General? He's now five miles behind the front lines. The North Koreans have their Forty-second Tank Battalion out in front, and nothing we have right now is going to push those enemy tanks back across the line."

"So we go inside, through their lines, and lift out the men in choppers. How many are there?"

"Twelve in the Vice President's group, sir."

"Those special Ranger units still with us?"

"No, sir. Both groups rotated a week ago."

"SEALs? The Navy have any SEALs on board that task force off Inchon?"

"Possible, sir. I'll check. Who's in charge out there?"

General Reynolds told him, and said to get back to him as quickly as possible. Then he made another call.

"Commo, get me through to the White House. I have some bad news to tell the President."

USS *Monroe*

Don Stroh boiled into the CIC and spotted Murdock.

"You up already? You know about the damn NKs? Yeah, looks like you do. There's another problem. I just came from the admiral's cabin. He's on his way down."

"What's a bigger problem than a thirty-mile-wide invasion by the North Koreans?"

CAG Olson turned and stared at Murdock. "Bigger? When the NKs overran the DMZ they smashed one of our tank battalions. That was the spot the Vice President picked to use for his hotel last night. He hasn't been heard from since midnight on a SATCOM transmission. We have to assume he's been captured."

"The Vice President a POW?" Murdock blurted out.

"Maybe," Stroh said. "He's a combat veteran. I'd guess his Secret Service men would keep him incognito if they are captured. We'll have to see. The important thing is I'm expecting a call from the President within the next fifteen minutes. Looks like we may have a job for you, Murdock. All we need is a go from the boss CIA man and the President. So when do you want to go in and how will you rescue the Vice President?"

Murdock didn't even blink. "Rescue the Vice President? Fucking carefully. When? Tonight, first dark. We'll take a chopper for a quick jump into Seoul. Then a chopper run into Panmunjom. We'll need a guide who knows the exact location of that tank battalion and who knows the camp and the underground bunkers where the Vice President might be hiding.

"We can use either Cobras or Air Force gunships for protection. Two big choppers to hold fifteen men each for the evac. Who's with the Vice President?"

"Some Congressmen, his staff, and two Secret Service agents. Maybe six or eight lawmakers."

"I wonder if any of them got shot up or hurt in the capture? If so, it'll make it tougher to get them out."

"You won't know until you get there."

Murdock pushed away from the wall. "Captain, can you talk to the Air Force at Seoul about aircraft? Or we could use yours, whichever you want. Might be smoother going from here. Range is right for the Cobras and a pair of Sea Knights. I'll take your advice. Right now I want to get to my men and do some planning. Not much we can do except talk it through."

"We'll get that call soon," Stroh said. "You say you want to go in tonight? What if they move the prisoners before then?"

"Behind the lines about now is one big mass of confusion in a lightning strike like this," Murdock said. "All the troops will be driving forward. First the NKs have to find the Veep. Then they'll have to find someone to interpret for them. These will be low-ranking noncoms, maybe an officer. They won't have the slightest idea what to do with American civilians."

"Right," CAG said. "So they'll have to send word to the rear or to a general or somebody with some field rank to make a decision. By then it should be dark." The CAG stopped. "Yeah, Murdock, let's use our gunships and Sea Knights. They can do the job. It will eliminate one place where things could get fucked up."

Murdock nodded and walked out of the CIC heading for the SEALs' assembly room.

91st Tank Battalion
DMZ bunker

The Vice President pulled the eleven men around him. "We heard someone outside. They'll be in here soon. Jud Ambrose is going to be the headman in here when they come. He knows a little Korean. He's our leader. We're all Congressmen, right? We do what he says. No preference to me or they'll catch on fast. I'm just another lawmaker caught with his pants down."

Four minutes later the North Koreans broke through the litter and fallen dirt and confronted their prisoners. The first man through was a private, and he darted to one side as an officer came in and stared at them.

He chattered at them in Korean, but when he saw no response, he paused. After a quick look around the bunker showed no way out and that they had no weapons, he left the first soldier in the room with his rifle and slipped back the way he had come.

"Just cool it," Ambrose said softly. "The officer must be going to find somebody who speaks English." He checked his watch. It showed ten-thirty. "It took them six hours to discover us and break through. Time is our friend here. In another few hours the U.S. forces could counterattack and recapture this area. We wait them out."

Ten minutes later, three officers came into the room. All carried pistols on their belts. The first one stared hard at them. Ambrose stepped forward. He bowed slightly.

"Konichiwa," he said in Japanese.

The Korean officer frowned. "You speak English?" he asked.

"Yes," Ambrose said. "We are a delegation of lawmakers from Washington, D.C., on an inspection tour. At this time we wish you to provide us with transportation so we can get back to Seoul."

The officer with captain's bars on his shoulders scowled. "Do not make jokes. You are prisoners of war. Civilian not matter. We have captured you. Not matter why you are here. You are prisoners of war."

"That's impossible. We're civilians. We spoke with your people yesterday at Panmunjom. We are lawmakers."

"No matter. I talk to general about you. He say what to do. Easiest just shoot you all now. General will say. You all sit on beds. In two hours we bring you food."

He turned and left. Both the other officers remained in the large room just behind the private.

"Yeah, let's sit down and see how good we can wait," Ambrose said. "This could take several hours. The general won't even look at a message like this until he gets his troops where he wants them."

"Then, we're stuck here?" Vice President Chambers asked.

"For now. It might be the best thing. At least Seoul knows that we must still be here. I made that SATCOM call last night. They'll assume that we are here and captured."

"How will that help?" a Congressman asked.

"If they know where we were, that's the spot where they will start looking for us when they come to pull us out of here."

Another Congressman looked up, his eyes bright. "You think the Army will try to come and rescue us?"

"Absolutely," Ambrose said. "We have the second-most-important man in America in this bunker. There will be a lot of effort made to get him out. When it comes down to a rescue, it might mean that only part of the group gets to go. Can all of you live with that? Some of us might not get on the magic carpet out of here."

"Hell, yes," one man said.

"Hey, if the Vice President can get out, I'll stay," another Congressman said.

Ambrose saw the rest of the heads nod. "Good, that took guts. Our tall friend here appreciates it. Now, we all sit down or lay down and have a nap and relax. We might need to save our strength for later."

Ambrose wasn't sure about the Koreans. He'd been speaking softly so they couldn't hear. Now he went up to the officer with bars on his shoulder. He smiled.

"You fucking bastard sonofabitch," Ambrose said in a softly gentle voice. "You're a low-down dipshit, you know that? Your mother turns tricks at the neighborhood cathouse." He grinned again at the North Korean as the man's face remained calm and unmoving. The Korean didn't understand a word of English.

USS *Monroe*

Most of the ship's crew was up and working by the time Murdock walked into the assembly area the Navy had made available for the SEALs. Murdock sent Lampedusa to roust out the rest of the Third Platoon. It was only 0510.

When the platoon was all there, Murdock held up his fist and the compartment went silent.

"You know we've got ourselves a war out there. The North gents moved south this morning at 0430 and are running wild. Our Navy planes are giving the South some air support."

He filled them in quickly about the Vice President's problem and the job they almost certainly had coming up.

"We move across the front lines at first dark?" Jaybird asked.

"What we want to talk about," Murdock said. "How else can we get in quick and get out with the Veep except with a chopper?"

"No way," Ed DeWitt said. "Got to be a chopper, two of them; the big Sea Knights would do the job. They have enough range?"

Al Adams looked up. "Yeah, a hundred and eighty miles mission radius. She hums along at hundred and fifty-seven miles an hour max."

"But she's unarmed," Bradford said.

"Not with our two machine guns spitting lead out the doors," Adams said.

They went on working on the plan. They could get in and get out in the Sea Knight with four Cobra gunships for protection and four Tomcats to take care of any air-to-air business from the North Korean MiGs.

They went on into details: what weapons they would use, how much ammo, how they would find the bunker, what North Korean troops might be on hand.

By early mess call, they had planned everything they could. Murdock found CAG Olson in the CIC. He had just sent off a flight of six F-14's to handle some MiGs on the western half of the line.

"Murdock, yes. No word from the President, but it'll come through. What do you have for me?"

"If we could move the carrier up another twenty miles toward Inchon, we could use two Sea Knights, four Cobras for protection, and some Tom Cats to watch for MiGs. One Sea Knight would come in to the site to drop us off and scoot to the south side of the new MLR and wait. Then when we have found and recovered the twelve men, both Sea Knights

come back in to pick us up and get us out of there. We can call
them in with the SATCOM on TAC One."

"Sounds good. Two Tom Cats should protect you on top."

"Hey, this is the Vice President we're talking about here,
CAG. Rather be heavy with four up there than be surprised by
four MiGs shooting down our choppers."

"True. You want to go in just after dark?"

"Right. If we could time it so we cross the front line at
dark, that would get us in with the most time left before next
daylight. We have no idea where they took the hostages, or
even if they're still alive. A tank attack on another tank
battalion is a messy affair."

"I've heard." The CAG turned to a crewman. "Get that first
flight of eight Hornets recovered now. We need to get eight
more ready to fly."

The CAG looked back at Murdock. "Yes, near dark the
pressure will be off us for air support. We don't expect much
after-dark action. Your plan sounds good. You know the Sea
Knight is unarmed."

"We'll have a machine gunner at each of the access doors,
sir. We've done it before. A question. Does the Air Force have
an AWACS plane up?"

"Yes, they're controlling the air strikes and air defense.
Doing a good job. Our planes add some punch to their guys.
See me again about 1600 and we'll work out the details." The
CAG turned back to the scopes.

Don Stroh rushed into the CIC, and when he saw Murdock
he grinned. "We've got a go. The boss said to spare no horses.
He's giving the admiral a call right now. This carrier is your
baby. You get exactly what you want where you want it."

"Good. I talked to the CAG. We'll go with two Sea Knight
choppers. Leave so we hit the MLR just after dark. Any
suggestions?"

"How do we know that the party is still in the same bunker
where it spent the night?"

"We don't. Hell, if this were easy, they'd send in some
Marines. We use our noses, grab a prisoner. We'll want to
take two translators with us for Korean speak. They have any
on the ship?"

"I'll find out. If they don't, we'll get two from Eighth Army. They had a call from the Chief too."

"Good. You take care of that. Chopper the translators out here if we get them from Eighth before we leave. I've got to tell the men we've got a go."

The time was just past 0800 when Murdock walked into the SEALs' room. The men were putting together weapons and equipment for a land operation.

"We've got a go," Murdock said as soon as the men looked up. A big cheer greeted him. "Hoo-yah, Commander Murdock," the men bellowed in unison.

"Choppers like we figured?" Jaybird asked.

"Right, the only way to travel. Now, what happens if the Veep isn't where we hope he is?"

"Big deal, we look for him," Ronson bellowed. They all howled.

"How? We don't know the terrain."

"Get some sucker who used to be stationed there," Jaybird said. "Call up that general and get some action."

Murdock nodded. "Jaybird. Hustle your bones and find Don Stroh. Tell him we need a man from Eighth Army who knows the Ninety-first Armored camp. Have that man choppered out to us here with the translators. Go."

Jaybird ran for the door.

"Let's take fifty percent more ammo," Murdock said. "We don't know what or who we'll run into and we won't have a long walk. Bradford, we'll leave the fifty here. We shouldn't need any long-range work. Rest of you the usual weapons. Questions?"

"That'll be a rear area by the time we get there," Ching said. "So how many NKs we gonna have to worry about?"

"Hard telling. Maybe a squad left to pick through the mess hall and the ammo storage. Might be a temporary hospital or a camp for replacements of five hundred men. We don't know. We'll have to play that one by ear when we get there. My guess is that there won't be a lot of men or equipment on-site. The North has advanced so fast, nothing will have caught up with them yet. When the chopper drops us off, it'll attract some interest. Whoever shows up may be packing firearms and be in a bad mood." Two of the men laughed.

Murdock watched them all working on their gear. Yes, they would be ready.

"Remember, it's going to be a bit on the chilly side out there tonight. It's still the end of March, and Korea isn't exactly Hawaii. No wet suits and we won't be using the EAR weapons. If we see any NKs we put them down and dead."

That brought some more hoo-yahs.

"It's now 0812. You have a half hour more to get your gear in shape; then I want a six-hour sleep period. You'll have a special chow at 1400, and we should shove off in our choppers somewhere around 1730. I hear dusk is about a half hour later, so that will put us over our target at about the right time. The carrier is steaming twenty miles closer to the DMZ for us, so we'll have a half-hour chopper ride."

He looked around. "Questions?"

"Am I gonna have any time to do some surfing?" Jack Mahanani asked. "I know one kayabunga of a break off Inchon."

"Oh, hell, yes, Jack," Doc Ellsworth said. "You can just surf right into the tankers' bunker there at Ninety-first and we'll all wait for you." The laughing trailed off, and Murdock went to his gear and began sorting out what he'd take that afternoon.

Jaybird came back ten minutes later.

"Found Stroh and he put in a second request to the general. Don got right through to him. He said we'd have our interpreters and a sergeant who was stationed with the Ninety-first all on the chopper and be here by 1600."

"Good. Now finish your gear. You're on a six-hour sleep period. Do it."

At 1725 the Third Platoon of SEAL Team Seven loaded on board one of the Boeing CH-46D Sea Knight helicopters, the big bananas with large rotors fore and aft. The squads had been checked and triple-checked by the men and officers. Everyone had the right gear and fifty-percent overload on ammo. All wore jungle cammies, and most had on floppy hats and flame-retardant aviator's gloves with the fingers cut out. The camo paint on their faces showed grotesque patterns.

The two ROK soldiers were there talking with the SEALs. They were the translators. Army Sergeant Fred Halverson talked with Murdock when he reported in.

"Yeah, I was on-site there for almost a year. Know the Ninety-first camp inside out. My guess where the civilians were overnighted would be the underground BOQ. It's toward the far side of the complex, away from the tank revetments, so they might not have had any direct hits from the artillery. Shit, what a mess. I hear the tankers lost half their rigs before they got the engines started."

"Advantage of a first attack," Murdock said. "You hang with me, Sergeant, when we land. First I want you to suggest to the pilot where he can put us down nearest to that BOQ."

"Yes, sir, I'll go up front and talk to him."

The access door slammed shut and the crew chief signaled the pilot. The Two Sea Knights lifted off at the same time, followed by four Super Cobra gunships armed with 20mm cannon and 70mm rocket pods.

"Time?" Murdock asked over the growl of the chopper's big blades.

"Seventeen thirty-three," DeWitt said. "Close enough. Heard the pilot say the fighting is now almost ten miles down from the DMZ in some spots. Means we could have ten miles of hostile country to fly over instead of five."

Murdock nodded, and they waited. He watched his men. They had done this before. Two or three showed some prefight tension. Several were taking naps, a good sign. As a whole they were well rested, loose, and ready.

He pulled up Holt. "Fire up that SATCOM on TAC One and see if we can talk to the aviators."

"Our Tom Cat leader will be Tomboy Three. He won't be off the deck yet. I can try for the gunships. They are Shooters."

"Give them a try."

"Shooters, this is SEAL. Do you copy?"

There was a pause, then some static, then the SATCOM's speaker came on.

"SEAL, this is Shooter One. We're with you. As soon as we get dry, we'll spread out and follow you in. Understand no softening up since we don't know the exact location."

Murdock took the handset. "That's a roger, Shooter One. As soon as we're on the location, we'll want you to suppress any sign of opposition. We're on a treasure hunt here with a big prize."

"Understood, SEAL. When you want a concentration of fire, put a red flare on the target."

"That's a roger, Shooter One."

Murdock looked at Holt. "What's the call for the other Sea Knight?"

"This is Knight One, the other one is Knight Two."

"Knight Two, this is SEAL."

"Got you, SEAL. We're in your hip pocket."

"You hear on the ten-mile fighting zone?"

"That's a guess until we get there. We'll stay below that line when you and One head north. We'll be ready for your call for a pickup. Estimate about five to ten away."

"Thanks, Knight Two."

A short time later, the crew chief came back. "You wanted to put MGs at the doors. Now would be a good time. We're about five from the new MLR."

"Let's hope it's a quiet passage," said Murdock.

"We just passed some fighting on the ground," the crew chief said. "New estimate of five minutes to the target."

"Let's get ready," Murdock told the SEALs. "When we touch down, one squad out each door; then we spread out and find out just where the hell we are and how we find the Veep. Sergeant Halverson will be with me."

Murdock looked out and saw the ground coming up fast. The bird made a turn, and he could see a tank below still burning. Several buildings had been smashed by the artillery barrage.

Their forward motion slowed as they settled to the ground. Sergeant Halverson hurried back from the cockpit. The crew chief stood at one access door and Jaybird at the other.

Murdock felt the big bird touch down. His men had lined up at both doors.

"Go, go, go," Murdock bellowed, and the SEALs jumped off the Sea Knight into enemy-held territory, their weapons loaded and unlocked and fingers on the sensitive triggers.

5

91st Armored's Former Position
Near the DMZ
South Korea

Lieutenant Commander Blake Murdock charged out of the Sea Knight helicopter, hit the ground on the run, and rushed fifteen yards straight ahead to the edge of a burned-out building. He dove to the ground.

Gunfire.

Where did it come from? Sergeant Halverson skidded into the dirt beside him.

"We've got some shooters over to the left. That building used to be the HQ. Doesn't look much damaged. Figured we better take them out first."

Murdock touched his lip mike on the Motorola. "Fire from the left, the old HQ building. Ed, take your squad to the right see if you can get behind it. We'll work toward the front and put down some cover fire."

When Murdock looked beside him, he saw his seven Alpha Squad men strung out ten yards apart hugging whatever cover they could find. Horse Ronson had set up his H&K machine gun, and rattled off three five-round bursts at two windows on the building facing them. The glass had already been blown out.

The enemy fire from the building slowed.

"Assault fire," Murdock said into his mike. "Alpha Squad, let's move." He flipped his H&K submachine gun on three-round bursts and ripped off a trio. It was the signal for the rest of the squad to open fire. Then Murdock lunged upward and ran toward the HQ building.

The eight SEALs put down a deadly hail of hot lead as they charged the small HQ structure. No return fire slowed them. Twenty yards later, they leaned against the wall of the building and flipped grenades through the windows.

"I've got a door in the rear," Ed DeWitt said on the radio.

"Go," Murdock said. "Alpha, hold fire."

They heard a door crash in and a half dozen rounds fired, then silence.

"All clear in the HQ building," DeWitt said on the net.

Murdock turned to Sergeant Halverson, who carried an H&K subgun. "Where to?"

The sergeant looked around for a minute and shook his head. "Seems a lot different now with half the buildings flattened. Let's go to the left, down that street about two blocks. This was as close as the chopper could get to the place."

"Ed, we're coming around," Murdock said. "Get your squad out of there. We're moving down the street just in back of your position. About two blocks. Let's all choggie."

They moved ahead like an infantry squad, charging from one bit of cover to the next. First they paused behind an Army sedan that had been tipped upside down and burned out. Next there was a burning building, then a tank that had surrendered with one tread trailing behind it.

Halfway to their goal they met a squad of infantry hidden behind a shattered building and another dead U.S. tank. The surprise fire brought a yelp of pain from one of the SEALs as they all scrambled to find cover. The roadblock was less than fifty yards ahead.

"Ed, we've got some trouble," Murdock said on the mike.

"Yeah, I see them. My squad is to your left slightly ahead. Let me try some forty-mikes on them."

"That's a roger, Ed."

A minute later they heard the Colt M-4A1's firing as they lobbed the 40mm grenades from launchers under their barrels. Murdock lifted from behind a turned-over Humvee and saw two of the rounds hit short, but two more dropped in behind the tank and the building. The rifle fire from the enemy slowed.

"Two hits, Ed. Drop in some more, and some WP."

"On the way," Ed said.

This time eight rounds landed behind the tank and the building. Murdock saw two North Korean soldiers lift up and race to the rear. Bill Bradford with his sniper rifle put two 7.62 NATO rounds into one of the runners. He dropped and lay still.

Murdock motioned to the sergeant, Ken Ching, and Lampedusa, and they ran to the right toward an undamaged building. From there they rushed down its length and just around the far corner. From there they could see behind the dead tank.

Ching and Lampedusa used their Colts, dropped three of the defenders, and sent the other three surging away to the rear. Murdock heard Bradford's sniper rifle speak again, and one of the three runners would run no more.

"Move in," Murdock said, and both squads hit the spot the North Koreans had been defending. One of the Korean translators was with each squad. The one with Murdock ran up as they charged the position.

"I could question any of them still alive," the Korean said.

Murdock nodded. "If any of these are alive, we'll save one for the translators," Murdock said on the horn. Three of the defenders were dead, but a fourth was wounded. Just as the translator began talking with the man, he gave a scream and died.

Sergeant Halverson looked around the tank and stared ahead. "There used to be a small building about twenty yards down there. It was a top house for the entryway into the underground on this end. The officers' quarters were just to the left." He shrugged. "Now there's no fucking building."

"What about that pile of smashed-up lumber?" Murdock asked.

"Maybe, let's go take a look."

Alpha Squad charged the wrecked shack while Bravo Squad was ready with protective fire. There was no gunfire from the direction the NK survivors had run.

At the splintered mass, Murdock found where boards had been thrown aside.

Sergeant Halverson grinned. "Yeah, Commander, this looks like the place. Just a little box to keep out the snow and rain. If we're lucky, your people should be down there."

They moved more of the boards; then Murdock took his penlight off his combat vest and shone it into the hole. Concrete steps led downward. Murdock brought up his subgun and moved down the dark steps slowly.

Without a sound, he made it to the bottom of ten steps. It was pitch black inside. He shone his light on concrete walls. Sergeant Halverson was right behind him.

"Should be a turn to the left, Commander."

There was. Murdock shone his light that way. Another corridor with concrete sides and top. Twenty feet down that way they came to a room. Murdock's flashlight beam didn't reach all the way to the far side. The sergeant snapped on a lighter and moved around.

"Been here and gone, Commander. Looks like they stayed a while, blankets on cots, even a civilian necktie."

"You sure they were here? Any real evidence?" They both searched. Murdock found it in the corner where it had been covered up by a jumble of blankets from a bed.

"A SATCOM," Murdock said. "Looks good as new. The Vice President's party had a SATCOM. They must have been here, and hid the radio. But then they got moved."

"Moved to where is the problem," Sergeant Halverson said. They hurried back topside, and found half of Bravo Squad clustered around Ed DeWitt and one of the translators.

DeWitt looked up. "Cap, we found a live one. He picked up a couple of rounds but he talks real well. This South Korean interpreter isn't the gentlest guy I've ever met. So far the prisoner has earned one broken arm and lost two teeth. Now he's starting to talk."

"Ask him where they put the civilians," Sergeant Halverson said.

The South Korean ROK looked up and nodded. He chattered at the prisoner a moment, got no response, and backhanded the wounded man across the face. The prisoner tumbled to one side, but the other translator lifted him back to a sitting position and the question was asked again.

The prisoner said something.

The ROK shot the prisoner in the thigh with his .45-caliber pistol. The North Korean screamed and spat at the gunman. A moment later the muzzle of the .45 was rammed into the prisoner's mouth and his eyes went wide. The interpreter cocked the hammer and the prisoner nodded.

With the black muzzle of the pistol out of his mouth, the North Korean spoke fast and at length. When the North Korean finished talking, the interpreter looked at Murdock.

"Sir, this unworthy one has guaranteed me that the twelve civilians held in this bunker for several hours have been moved by truck to a building on the other end of the camp. It is guarded by an infantry squad and two lieutenants. The officers don't know what to do with the civilians. One officer wanted to shoot them so they didn't have to bother with them. He was overruled by a major who is now five miles into South Korea."

"Have him show us the building now," Murdock barked.

The North Korean prisoner, with a gunshot wound in his leg, his shoulder, and his arm, ran with the two South Koreans at his side. They kept telling him that if he fell down or stopped, they would blow his head off.

The platoon found no resistance as it moved a quarter of a mile west. They slowed when the prisoner told his captors that the next building was the one with the civilians in it.

Murdock figured the building was a mess hall and kitchen. "Silencers on all weapons," Murdock said into his Motorola. Those who hadn't used them now screwed on the sound suppressors.

They worked up toward the target slowly. Murdock took Alpha Squad around the side of the shielding building, and went to ground behind some sparse grass and weeds.

"Sentries," Lampedusa said into his mike.

"How many?" Murdock asked.

"Two on this side. Fixed posts. No rovers."

"Bradford, take them out," Murdock said.

The first North Korean soldier had just turned to stare at the building near where the SEALs lay when the 7.62 NATO slug took him in the chest just under his heart, splashed two vital arteries, and put him down and dead in a minute without uttering a sound.

The second sentry must have seen the first go down. He blew a whistle and ran toward cover. He was too late. Bradford's second round hit him directly in the heart and slammed him back against the building. In response to the whistle, three more guards rushed around the corner of the building.

"Take your pick," Murdock said, and fired a three-round burst at the men. They were less than fifty yards away and well within the range of the suppressed subgun.

All three guards went down from more than thirty rounds that hit them. One tried to get up, but three more slugs dropped him into the dirt and he didn't move.

"Let's take the back wall," Murdock said. Alpha Squad lunged to its feet and charged the building silently.

Ed DeWitt had his Bravo Squad on the other side of the building to offer covering fire. It wasn't needed. Murdock and his squad pressed against the wooden building, and the men caught their breath. Lam scurried to the far corner and looked around. He waved Murdock up.

"No windows or doors back here, Cap. But there's a door in front. Has a machine gun set up out there with sandbags."

Murdock took a quick look. "Not over twenty yards. You have fraggers?"

Lam grinned, and pulled an M-79 fragmentation grenade from his combat vest. They were on the right-hand side of the building, making a throw by a right-hander easier.

Murdock waved Lam forward. He pulled the safety pin on the grenade, leaned around the corner, and heaved the missile at the target. As soon as he let go of the fragger, he dropped to the ground and Murdock lifted over him and threw his grenade. The first fragger went off with a roar, and three

seconds later the second one shook the sky with sound and
shrapnel.

"Both sides of the building, let's get around to the front
now," Murdock said into his mike. SEALs raced around both
corners and met at the front door. Both North Koreans who
had been on the machine gun lay tattered in bloody rags at
one side. The gun had been slammed to the back and lay
upside down.

Murdock tried the front door. It was not locked. He edged
it open three inches and looked inside. No weapons chal-
lenged him. From the slice of the room he could see through
the opening, Murdock confirmed it was a mess hall.

Lam lay on the floor looking through the same slot. "Cap,
I got some bodies back by the serving line. Looks like some
cots or something back there."

"Any guards?"

"Don't see a shit-assed one, Cap."

"Still should be some inside. They know we're here and
are waiting for us."

"Flashbang?" Lam asked.

"Too many good guys inside."

Murdock made up his mind quickly. "I'm going in at an
angle and get behind that tipped-over table on the right. You
and Doc Ellsworth give me cover, spraying rounds into the
ceiling or the walls up front. Just enough to keep the NKs
heads down. I'll be able to eyeball the place better inside.
Then I'll cover as you and Doc slam inside to the left."

Murdock looked at Lam and Doc. "Ready?"

They nodded. Murdock kicked the door open, took two
steps, and dove in a double roll toward a turned-over table ten
feet from the front door. As soon as he went through the
opening, Lam sprayed three-round bursts of .223 zingers into
the ceiling. Doc hit the front wall with four rounds.

Two weapons returned fire from inside. Murdock heard
one of them fire from high up. He rolled twice, made it to the
table unscathed, and began looking for the high shooter. He
found him on a small balcony near the front on the far side.
Murdock kicked the lever to fully automatic and sprayed the
balcony with ten rounds, then ten more.

A moment later he saw a weapon fall over the rail, then a body pivot forward and hang head-down over the balcony, blood running down and dripping off his head.

In the sudden quiet Murdock heard someone wailing near the front.

"Americans, are you up in front?" Murdock bellowed.

"Yes, yes, all twelve of us. Careful where you shoot."

"Where's the other gunman in here?"

"Don't know, we're all blindfolded and tied."

Murdock scanned the areas he could see. No other balconies or high spots. Had to be someone on the ground floor. He looked at the front again. It had a serving line that separated the mess hall from the kitchen, a typical army setup. Could the other gunman be in the kitchen? Maybe. But now it was going to take a scalpel, not a broadax, to get the Vice President out of this trap and not have any of his party killed.

Murdock motioned to Lam, who jolted through the door and dove for the left side of the big room. Murdock slammed six rounds into the left wall, then six more into the far front wall. There was no answering fire.

Murdock nodded. So it was going to be a cat-and-mouse game. He could do that. He lifted up and stared at the whole area again, trying to figure out where he would hide out in here against a superior force.

Murdock could almost feel the North Korean watching him. He jolted down after the quick scan. There was no gunfire aimed at him. That could mean the other side had a good position and didn't want to give it away as they waited for a telling shot.

He touched his mike. "They must be in the kitchen. We have the hostages tied and blindfolded near the serving line on the right. Let's get all Alpha Squad inside. Come two at a time when you hear covering fire. Shoot into the kitchen, Lam."

Murdock lifted his subgun and chattered off six rounds. Lam did the same. Two by two, the squad bolted through the door and dove to the floor inside the mess hall.

Then they all moved like ghosts along and around the tables and benches in the mess hall working slowly forward.

Lam and Murdock got there first. Thirty feet away a metal shield masked the area below the serving line's metal tables. Murdock figured it was lightweight aluminum and bullets would zing right through it. He could see no one over in the kitchen area. He'd have to sneak a peek. He jolted upright and scanned the kitchen area, then slammed downward.

Three rounds from an automatic rifle sizzled just over his head as he hit the floor.

Lampedusa, twenty feet across, had jolted upward at the same time, then back down. He had in his hand a grenade with the pin pulled and the arming spoon held firmly in place. When he heard the shots at Murdock, he knew the gunman was at the left well away from the American prisoners. He threw the grenade.

The shattering roar of the small bomb in the closed building was magnified ten times. Shrapnel zinged around the kitchen ricocheting off all kinds of metal cabinets, stoves, and utensils.

Murdock squirmed ahead to where the prisoners lay. He saw that none of them was bandaged. He took off the blindfolds from two as he watched and waited.

"Two more grenades far back in the kitchen," he told the lip mike. Lam sent one into another part of the kitchen, and Ron Holt threw the second blaster. When both went off with a resounding roar, Lampedusa was the first man up, vaulting over the serving line and diving behind a large freezer unit. He took no fire.

Ken Chin vaulted over another section of the line and crawled toward the big stove. Slowly the two worked forward, clearing every hiding space on the way.

Murdock found the Vice President, untied him, and took off his blindfold.

"Please stay down, Mr. Vice President. We hope to have this area cleared shortly. Are any of your people wounded or injured?"

Tears brimmed the man's eyes. He tried to speak, but he couldn't. He shook his head—no injuries.

A moment later, Murdock's earpiece came on.

"Kitchen is clear," Lam said. "We have two dead NKs in the back area. The grenades got them."

Ronson and Ellsworth came up quickly and untied the rest of the men and took off the blindfolds. The men sat on the floor for a moment; then some stood, and soon the rest were up.

"Please hold it right here, gentlemen," Murdock said. "We need to make a complete inspection of this place to be sure it's safe. Are any of you wounded or injured?"

He heard some say no, and saw others shake their heads. A man came up with a Marine Corps white-side haircut. He saluted smartly.

"Sir, Ambrose, Secret Service. Ex-Marine, sir. I'd like a weapon. I feel naked right now without one."

"Be glad for the help, Ambrose." Murdock pulled a backup .45 automatic from his combat vest and handed it to the man along with two extra magazines. Ambrose charged a round into the chamber and pushed on the safety.

"Thanks, sir. I feel a lot better now."

Alpha Squad cleared the rest of the kitchen, then two small rooms to one side, and pronounced the mess hall clean. Murdock heard gunfire from the outside. His radio ear talked to him.

"Murdock, we have company," Ed DeWitt said. "Looks like a truck full of bad guys with guns. They see us, we see them."

"Be right out. Ambrose and Ellsworth, stay here and protect the Vice President and his party. The rest of Alpha out the front door, cautiously."

They went out singly, angling for cover. By the time they were out, the North Koreans in the truck had dismounted a hundred yards away.

"MGs set up and go," Murdock said. His own and the rest of the MP-5 subguns were out of range. "Pull the silencers off the MP-5's to reach out. Go." He unscrewed the noise suppressor and put it in his combat vest. The machine guns began to chatter.

"Somebody take out the truck," Ed DeWitt said.

Harry Ronson got his shots in first. He sprayed the truck

until he saw steam jetting from the radiator. By then the rest of them had the range on the fifteen men who had jumped out of the truck and were looking for cover.

One man stood and waved the North troops forward. Miguel Fernandez sighted in with his H&K PSG1 sniper rifle and blew the officer away before he took two steps.

Ed DeWitt hit his mike. "Murdock. I'll take Bravo to the left into that burned-out building. We can get some cross fire."

"Go, find good cover."

Murdock settled down behind a large decorative rock left in front of the mess hall and waited. He had four long guns and four subguns in his squad. All were now firing at the North Koreans, who seemed content to sit behind their cover and take an occasional shot at the intruders. Then two NKs made a dash to closer cover. Both died in the process as Ronson nailed one with a five-round burst from his MG and Bradford picked off the other one with a NATO slug. For a moment all was quiet.

Then DeWitt opened up with his guns from the far side and the survivors of the truckload of men took fire from a new source. Two of the NKs ran for the truck. They fell before they got there. Three more kept firing from behind the truck.

Horse Ronson began searching the rig for its fuel tank. He slammed rounds under both doors, then toward the back. Twice more he punched five-round bursts into the rig, then tried just in front of the rear wheels.

The rounds found the tank and the vapors in the top, and it blew up in a gigantic fireball, instantly cremating the three NK troopers behind it.

All firing stopped.

"Looks like that's all the pages in this book," Ed DeWitt said on the radio.

"Good. We'll use this flat area in front of the mess hall for our LZ. Must have been a sports field." Murdock called up Ron Holt, who turned on the SATCOM to TAC One.

"Call in Knight One and Two," Murdock said. "Tell them we're ready and waiting. We'll put a green flare on the LZ as they get here."

Holt made the call, got contact on his second transmission, and gave the message.

"SEAL, this is Knight Two. Affirmative. We're taking off now. Should be at your LZ in six minutes. We'll have two Cobras with us for shooting fun. Is the LZ secure?"

"Secure for now, Knights. We'll be waiting."

Murdock looked over the playing field. "Let's get some perimeter security around this place," he said to his mike. "DeWitt, take this side. Alpha Squad, on the far side. Ellsworth, hold your guests in the front of the mess hall near the door until you get word to bring them out. Copy, Doc?"

"Copy that, Commander," Doc Ellsworth said. "We stay put, come on your go."

Murdock had pushed the stopwatch button on his timer. "Alpha Squad, let's move out to that cover over there about a hundred yards." He took a green flare from his combat vest and held it as he and the squad ran across the open space and found cover behind two burned-out vehicles and three artillery-shell holes. They settled in and aimed outward to watch for anyone coming toward them. Ron Holt dropped in the same shell hole as Murdock. He kept the SATCOM on the TAC One frequency.

"Commander, I have two Knights and two Cobras on the way. They will have Tomcat flyovers."

Murdock nodded and kept looking past smashed-in buildings and an overturned Humvee. He thought he heard something, then decided he didn't. A jet raced across the sky well away from them. From the sound Murdock couldn't tell if it was a MiG or one of ours.

When the aircraft sound died, he frowned. There it was again, some other sound. Yes, a motor, a vehicle of some kind coming toward them. "Check to the east," he said in his mike. "Anybody see anything, a tank, a truck? I hear a motor."

For a moment the net remained silent. Then Ken Ching broke in. "Yes, Commander. I've got something. Moon is shining off it. Could be an armored personnel carrier of some kind. It's coming hell-for-leather down the road from the east. By the size of the headlights, I'd say it's about a mile away."

Murdock took the handset for the radio. "Tom Boy Cover, can you read? This is SEAL, come in."

He said it twice, then the radio speaker spoke.

"Yes, SEAL, read you. This is Tom Boy Cover One."

"We've got trouble coming a mile east of the former 91st tankers' location. Not sure where you are. We'll put two green flares out to mark our location. Target is coming with headlights on from the east about a mile out. Are you anywhere near us?"

"Not a chance I could find you down there, SEALs. Too many lights, flares and such. I'm a poor risk for that kind of work."

As soon as that transmission cut off another one came on.

"SEALs. This is Cobra One. We're within a minute of you. Put out your two green flares. We can spot headlights easily. Be there in about fifty seconds."

"That's a go, Cobra One. We have no weapons to take on an armored personnel carrier. If you don't get here soon, all bets are off getting our package out of here safely."

"Hang on, SEALs, and pop those flares."

Murdock ran into the open area, lit two green flares, and tossed them into the center of the sports field. Now all they could do was wait and hope.

91st Tank Battalion
Seven miles south of the DMZ
Near Chandan, South Korea

Major Donovan Kitts stood beside his tank and stared hard ahead at the flood tide of the Imjin-gang River. It was too deep right now for a tank to cross. Two bridges capable of holding tanks had been crossed by his six remaining U.S. rigs and then blown up. At the very least that should slow up the North Korean tanks that had smashed his battalion that morning.

Now in the darkness, Major Kitts wondered if he had done the right thing. He'd had no contact with his control headquarters since last night before the invasion.

Ten of his tanks were now piles of junk metal. He'd lost at

least forty tank men and all but a handful of his service and
headquarters troops. He had no idea how many of them had
fled the battalion area just after the bombardment and before
the enemy tanks arrived. As far as he knew there were still
twelve North Korean tanks chasing him. The Navy fighters
with their missiles had destroyed two of the enemy tanks.
They had lost two more somewhere else.

He'd watched the air attack from a slight rise on the other
side of the river. One missile per tank. The Navy needed a
dozen more of those missiles to even things up a bit. He knew
that the NK tanks would be after him come morning. He had
his six armored machines in what meager cover the men
could find. For half the night his men would be chopping
down trees and draping limbs over the rigs for momentary
camouflage.

With the first round fired, each of his six tanks would give
away its position and would be targeted by the twelve tanks
chasing them. How to cut down the odds?

Kitts moved away from his tank and walked the area. He
found one ditch where a tributary ran down to the main river.
He could put one tank in the ditch with room to see and fire
over the bank. Yes. That would give that tank a fourteen-foot
barricade of solid Korean soil ahead of it.

Where else? He went back and brought out his only other
senior officer, First Lieutenant Brady Jolson, and explained
what he was looking for. The officer grinned and went in the
other direction.

By four A.M. they had put five of the tanks in more secure
positions. Three more in gullies formed by tributaries and one
in back of the crest of a ridge where it could fire and retreat
a dozen feet and be safe.

His own tank was the last one. Where in hell could it go?
He had been working up to a half mile behind the river.
Now he moved closer, hiking more than he had done in
months. Less than fifty yards from the river, he found an ideal
spot. Two small streams dumped muddy water into the Imjin-
gang. They formed a small V approaching the main flow.

With only a few yards' movement, he could fire over the

embankment on one side of the V at targets on that flank, then reverse and come up on the other side of the V and fire in that direction.

He pondered it. The main problem was that he could be within a hundred yards of the enemy tanks. Flyswatting distance for their 105 guns, which could fire out over two miles. Also, it was can't miss range for return fire. Could he take out enough North Korean tanks before they found him and blew away enough of the embankment to leave him naked and quickly dead?

Major Kitts never gave it another thought. He ran back to his tank, woke up the crew, and moved it down the tributary to the position. They rolled from one side to the other of the V and where the streams combined, testing out the bi-directional firing that he wanted. Yes, it would work well.

His gunner looked at him for a long moment when they had the tank in its first firing position.

"You sure you want to do this, Major?"

"Yeah, Broadhurst, I'm sure. All we have to do is knock out every tank that finds us, then pick off the rest of them. Remember, we have help."

"Sure, help, six against what, a dozen? We're down here in snot-shooting range, Major."

"True, Broadhurst. You want to transfer to a tank farther back?"

The sergeant shook his head. "No, sir. We almost got one tank early this morning. I'm damn sure not going to pass up a chance to nail about four of the bastards. They killed a lot of my friends today. I'd just as soon blast as many of the sons of bitches straight into Hell as I can."

"Good, Broadhurst, now get some sleep. They'll be coming at us as soon as it's light."

"Major, I had three hours. That's plenty. I think it's your turn. I'll wake you well before dawn. Sack out, sir, and get some rest."

Major Kitts watched his sergeant for a moment, then nodded and flaked out next to a tree. He dropped off to sleep before he knew it.

91st Armored's Former HQ

Murdock kept looking at his watch. The Cobra said less than a minute. He was ahead of the Sea Knights. He looked up the shadowy road to the east and saw the headlights moving toward them. They had slowed and seemed to stop at times. Moving cautiously, not sure what to expect. Good, the longer it took the vehicle to get there, the better for the arriving chopper.

The rig was not gung ho to charge into a fight. It stopped and its machine gun chattered at some foe, real or imagined.

Murdock scanned the dark sky to the south. For a moment he thought he heard an engine; then it faded. The next sensation he had was a hornet's nest right over his head. The Cobra popped up from its ground-hugging flight path and slammed over the green flares at fifty feet, swung to the left, and angled toward the rig with the lights. The radio came on.

"Yes, SEALs, I have him. He just turned out his lights but I know where he is. He can't hide. Thank God for the good moon." The chopper angled toward the vehicle. Murdock heard the cannon firing then, the big 20mm rounds jolting out of the three barrels as fast as a machine gun. He could see the rounds hitting, but didn't know how much damage they did.

"Okay, SEALs, no fireworks yet. I'll make another run with the rockets and see what we can do. Far as I can tell, he's dead in the water there. Not going anywhere."

The Cobra made a tight circle and came in at the rig from a sideways angle. The 70mm rockets thundered out of the pods along the body of the chopper, and a moment later exploded on and around the enemy vehicle. A second more, and the fuel tank exploded, showering the countryside with bits and pieces of metal and flaming gasoline.

"Thanks, Cobra, good shooting," Murdock said on the radio.

Another transmission came in. "Are those fireworks for our enjoyment, SEALs? This is Knight One and Two. We see the green flares. Any enemy fire?"

"A clear pad, Knights. Your Cobra just took care of the bad guys. Welcome to Korea."

Almost at once they heard the sound of the big banana ships coming in. The twin rotors kicked up a storm of dust that blew away quickly in the light wind. Then the bird had landed.

"Ellsworth," Murdock said on the Motorola. "Bring out our guests at a run if they can make it. Their limo is here."

Murdock heard a second chopper circling. The Congressmen and the Vice President and his party came jogging out of the mess hall and into the darkness, then into the splash of light from the chopper's landing lights. Crewmen helped the twelve men on board. Murdock sent the Secret Service man with them, then slammed closed the door and pounded on it twice. The big bird lifted off in another swirling, blinding cloud of Korean dust.

"Clear the area for the next landing," Murdock bellowed when the first chopper had swung away from them. The SEALs in the area scattered.

The second Sea Knight dropped down and landed. In less than a minute the SEALs and their Korean interpreters were all on board. Murdock slammed the hatch closed and locked it, and the helo lifted off.

"Casualty report," Murdock said. There were two.

"You call that a wound?" Doc Ellsworth jazzed at Jack Mahanani.

"Damn right. That's from enemy action. Cut by flying glass in the face. That's Purple Heart stuff."

Doc cleaned up the two slices, which turned out to be minor, and put on closing bandage strips.

Ken Ching had a bullet groove in his right leg. It was no more than a quarter of an inch deep. Doc dosed it with some antiseptic and put on a bandage, and looked around for anymore problems. That was it.

Murdock checked with the South Koreans. Neither of them had been hit. The Army sergeant who'd acted as guide was unmarked. Murdock settled down for the quick trip back to the ship. In a little more than a half hour, barring any lucky ground fire, they should have the Vice President of the United States back safe and sound on the *Monroe*.

The crew chief pushed into the narrow confines of the Sea Knight.

"Commander Murdock?"

"Yeah?"

"Sir, you've got a radio call up front. Some guy called Stroh."

Murdock frowned. Now what the hell could Stroh want to talk about that couldn't wait another half hour until they got back to the carrier?

6

Sea Knight Two
Heading for the *Monroe*

Lieutenant Commander Blake Murdock took the handset from the copilot of the helo.

"Murdock here, Stroh. What can't wait a half hour?"

"Decision time, big buddy. We've got a situation here that the brass wants some help on. There's a vital communications center of ours about five miles behind the North Korean lines. The fighting has settled down now with not much movement.

"Trouble is, that communications center must be kept on the air or totally destroyed. It's a slave unit, no personnel, camouflaged in an old building with antennas hidden in trees. The NKs haven't found it yet. The Army wants to drive a tank force up that way and push the NKs back. But that's going to take a week or more.

"The general wants some security around that unit. Can your platoon go in there tonight at first dark in choppers and hold the place for two days?"

"Can a cat with wings fly, Stroh? How the hell can I tell if we can hold something we've never seen? What's the troop strength in the area? Are there any NK tanks around there? Is it a regular supply route for the troops on line? Is there a command post for the NKs nearby? Get some information for us. Might be good to drop in a company of paratroops while you're at it and some one-oh-fives. You've got us shooting blind here, Stroh."

"Okay, okay. We don't know what the generals will decide to do. What I want to know is can your boys be ready to go at first dark tonight? That's more than half a day away."

"We've had no bad wounds. We can go whenever you need us. First we want some chow and a couple of hours of sleep and time to clean our weapons and resupply. *Dijobe?*"

"Yeah, I kapish. Oh, the Vice President just landed on board. Congratulations on another coup. Just don't let your helmet get too tight."

"We don't wear helmets, Stroh, and our floppy hats stretch to all hell and gone. See you when we get in."

Murdock went back to a spot in the chopper and nodded at DeWitt. The second-in-charge of the platoon slid in beside Murdock.

"Your guys ready to go again?" Murdock asked. "Stroh says they have a situation they may want some help on at first dark."

"The guys look good. Some food and a couple of hours of sack time and they'll be raring to go. What's the mission?"

Murdock began to outline what he knew of it when Miguel Fernandez lifted up and took a swing at Joe Douglas. Douglas took the punch and laughed.

"Fernandez, you're a wimp. Always have been. Shit, don't see how you ever got through BUD/S."

"Eat your own shit, Douglas."

Douglas snorted. "Hell, Fernandez, us guys don't shit tacos like you fucking chili-snappers."

By that time, Ed DeWitt had jumped between the two SEALs and stared them down.

"What the hell is going on here?"

Both SEALs looked away.

"I'm talking to you, Fernandez, and you, Douglas. Just what the fuck is this all about?"

"Nothing," Douglas said. "He kicked me and laughed."

"Not a chance I would mess up my boots kicking him," Fernandez shot back.

DeWitt scowled. He'd never seen the usually easygoing Fernandez so worked up. It had to be more than a small scuffle.

"Douglas?"

"Nothing, L-T. Just some small time teasing. Old Fernandez is on edge about something. Irritable as a virgin in heat."

"You're the only virgin queen in the helo, you queer," Fernandez said softly.

"Fernandez, enough," DeWitt barked. "Fernandez, what's your side of this?"

"Aw, hell. Forget it, L-T. Douglas just ain't my best buddy. Why don't we leave it at that?"

"Cool down, both of you. I don't want to hear any more of this or I'll shack your asses right out of the platoon into Team Seven's supply room. Don't think I can't do it."

Both men shifted lower where they sat in the big chopper.

"Yeah, OK, L-T," Douglas said.

"Right, JG, no supply room for me."

"Then shake hands. I don't want to hear anything more about this, clear?"

Both SEALs nodded, and DeWitt went back to sit next to Murdock.

"Real trouble?" Murdock asked.

"Not sure. I'll talk to some of the other guys. Chance we'll have to transfer one of them, or maybe switch one to Alpha Squad."

"Not in the middle of an operation. Watch them. If it gets too bad, we'll leave one of them on the carrier."

They landed a few minutes later.

Ed DeWitt took Ching and Mahanani to sick bay, where their minor wounds were checked, treated, and bandaged. Both were listed as fit for duty and released.

Murdock found Don Stroh waiting for him at the SEALs' assembly room.

"I want breakfast for my men," Murdock said.

"Breakfast? It's just past midnight."

"Hey, Stroh, this is my carrier. Hustle up some cooks and

get them ready for breakfast for fifteen. Have the works, ham and eggs, flapjacks, bacon, sausage, biscuits and gravy, orange juice, cereal, and buckets of coffee. We'll eat, then we'll talk."

Stroh grinned and found the telephone. Five minutes later he was back laughing.

"Some commander in charge of the whole damn kitchen thought I was kidding. I told him to check with the admiral. He called me back two minutes later. The enlisted mess will be open for your men in fifteen minutes, and you don't need to wear your dress blues. Damn, but you carry a big stick around here."

"Not my stick, it belongs to the President. You really want us out of here by first dark this coming afternoon?"

"Right as rain, Little Beaver."

"Hey, You're not my Red Rider, I can tell you that. We'll be there for chow. Then you and I and somebody over there in the Eighth Army Headquarters gotta have a long talk."

Eighth Army Headquarters
Seoul, South Korea

General Richard Reynolds, commanding general of the U.S. Eighth Army, stood in front of a wall map of the DMZ that had been hastily converted into a battle map. It now showed the progress of the North Korean invasion, and had been updated only ten minutes before.

"The war is only twenty hours old, and already it's bogged down," General Reynolds said. He had been awake since just after 0430 that morning and his eyes were bright with anger and loss.

"This damn bulge in the line right in front of us is the main problem, General," a bird colonel at his elbow said. "So far it's bulged in almost ten miles, which puts it less than sixteen miles from our camp here."

"Our flanks, Colonel?"

"Fairly solid. The line is holding on average about five miles below the DMZ on the twenty-five-mile front. At least it's five miles shorter than we thought early this morning. Our airpower is coming in handy. The carrier offshore has fifty-eight planes that are fitted out for land bombing and close support."

"Reserves?"

"We've pushed half of them up here to the Seoul bulge. The attack up and down the line didn't come at the same precise time, so many of the South Korean troops had time to do some fighting and pull back gradually. That wasn't the case where the tanks hit first. They swamped the Ninety-first with artillery and the T-62's. Cut them in half before the tankers got out of their sacks."

"Air?"

"General, our Air Force bases are far enough away from the attack to be safe. Wish we had twice the number of planes we have, but the fifty-eight from the carrier have helped tremendously. They have more helicopters than we do as well. So that part is going well. They coordinate perfectly with our AWACS combat direction and their turnaround time is amazing."

"So, our biggest problem is the bulge?"

"Yes, that and one other. We have a communications relay station that was built close to the DMZ for maximum coverage. Now it's been overrun by infantry elements. It's about four miles behind the enemy's MLR.

"The center is an unmanned relay point. Most of it's built underground with camouflaged antennas hidden in a grove of trees so they are almost unrecognizable."

"So there are no personnel there?"

"Right. However, there is a lot of sensitive communications gear we don't want to fall into NK hands. We can get along without the relay, doing much of it with the AWACS and other facilities. But the gear on site is the problem. I was thinking about ramming a column of tanks and trucks up there, retaking the area, and getting the equipment out. But now with our shortage of tanks, that doesn't look practical."

"What about an air strike?"

"Possible, but most of the equipment is well underground and it would take a massive hit to do any good. Also, it would attract attention to that site."

"So, send in a team of sappers."

"Sir, we have no Special Forces to do the job. No Delta teams are available. You heard about the SEALs from the carrier who went in and pulled out the Vice President where the Ninety-first tanks had been. Could we request them to do the job? They have the explosive skills and the ability to get in and out quickly. I've contacted Admiral Kenner on the carrier to see about the availability of the SEAL platoon, if we want to use them."

"Are they on tap?"

"They can be ready at first dark about 1730 tonight. Go in at dark. Have all night to do the job and get out."

"Choppers in and out?"

"I'd expect so. Save a ten-mile hike."

"You don't think a column of tanks could fight in, do the job, and get out?"

"Looks like a waste of tanks right now, sir."

"Where are what's left of our battalion?"

The Ninety-first has six tanks left. We brought them up facing the bulge. The other two battalions were not as badly hurt. I think we have fourteen in each group. I'm not sure where they are situated right now."

"Enemy air?"

"Some. The carrier's F-14's are doing a good job overhead. They shot down three MiGs this morning and chased away a dozen more."

The colonel watched his general. "Sir, the communications center?" the colonel asked.

"Yes, go ahead and see if the SEALs want the job and if they can do it. What about the NKs' supply lines to the bulge? Can we hit them hard with air and artillery? If we can keep supplies from coming up, we could blunt their charge, maybe keep them right where they are."

"Yes, sir. We're working on that. Captain Olson, the commander of the air on the carrier, says they are sending out some F-18's to try for some headlight bombing and night strafing. If it works, it will be a big help."

"Good."

"Sir, I'm going to contact the Navy again."

General Reynolds waved him off, and the colonel hurried

away. Communications had been one of his big jobs. Now he didn't want to see all of that highly advanced hardware in the relay station be captured by the North Koreans. It took him almost three minutes to get through to Admiral Kenner on the *Monroe*.

USS *Monroe*

Just after 0100, Murdock, Stroh, Captain Olson, and Admiral Kenner sat in the task force commander's quarters. Stroh had a map that had been faxed to him.

"The Army says that it wants the SEALs to do the job," Stroh said. "It's a straight demolition. That will be the easy part. Getting in won't be so bad; it will be a surprise for any NKs we run into there. Getting out will be tougher when the NKs call in help."

"Where is the center?" Murdock asked.

"It's just north of Kangso-ri, which is about a half mile from the old DMZ and is now in enemy hands," Stroh said. "This is about eighty miles from the carrier's present location."

Could we go in with the Sea Knight again?" Murdock asked. "It's big enough to handle our platoon and equipment and has good speed."

"That's within its range," CAG Olson said. "We can mount two .50-caliber machine guns in the doors for some protection. Night work, so there wouldn't be any enemy air."

"Land the chopper and power it down, or get it back to friendly country and re-enter on call?" Murdock asked.

"A problem," Stroh said. "The general says as far as his people know, this sector has a reinforced battalion of NKs regulars. For them, that's about a thousand men. We're not sure how long their sector is, but there must be some kind of reserves and rear-area units on hand. We don't know if they have found the facility yet. It's camouflaged and mostly below ground."

"Looks like one squad could do the job," the admiral said.

Murdock shook his head. "Not really, Admiral. We work as a team. If one squad goes underground to blow up the equipment, there's no one covering them on top. If we go we need all fifteen men."

"We can't hide a Sea Knight," Olson said. "It would have to come in, drop off the platoon, and come back for the pickup."

"After we blow up the center, we can try to find an LZ where it wouldn't take any ground fire," Murdock said.

"The pilots would appreciate that," CAG said, and grinned at Murdock.

Admiral Kenner turned to Murdock. "Commander, can you do the job quickly and get out?"

"Sir, I don't know. Blowing up a bunker filled with goodies is no problem. Just a matter of identifying the most sensitive and putting enough charges in enough places. As the CAG said, getting out of the area will be the problem."

"Make you a deal, Commander," the air chief said. "You take the job and I'll throw in a Cobra gunship to shepherd you in and out. Then if you run into some firefights getting out, the Cobra can lay on a lot of lead, the way that one did for you a couple hours ago at the tank camp."

"Deal," Murdock said. "Captain, you sure you don't sell cars on the side?" They laughed. "If I could be excused, I have some work to do before tonight. I hope your armament people have lots of C-5 and TNAZ on board."

By the time Murdock found his way back to the SEALs' assembly room, only Jaybird was left there.

"I sent the rest of them to their sacks," Jaybird said. "We almost had another ruckus between Douglas and Fernandez. What's the story there?"

"Not sure, but if it keeps up, we'll leave one of them behind on the next mission."

"I'd say Douglas is the least effective of the two, but that's up to you and the JG. It wasn't anything violent, but there's a strong undercurrent there I don't like to see in the platoon, let alone with two guys in the same squad."

"We're watching it. We've got a go for tonight. We chopper over friendly country for about eighty, then jump in the fucking frying pan for five miles to find our target."

"Sounds like fun. After dark?"

"Right. The CAG is giving us a Cobra gunship for company and putting .50-caliber MGs in the Sea Knight's doors."

"Good. Have the CAG send along the gunners. Then the helo will have protection when we can't man the MGs."

"Good idea. I'm about ready to find my bunk. Catch you in the morning here. When did you tell the squads to be back?"

"Back at 0900, Cap. Figured some work, then some sack time after noon chow."

"See you then. Don't stay up all night."

91st Tank Battalion

A half-hour before dawn, Major Donovan Kitts had his tankers in their shielded firing positions seven miles below the former DMZ. They were ready to rumble. Solid Korean embankments hid everything on the tanks from the top of the treads down. The long guns and turrets were masked by tree limbs and branches.

They waited.

"I hear something coming, Major," the radio crackled in Kitt's ear.

"Make sure," the tank battalion commander said. "I don't see anything. Which direction?"

"Due north."

They all listened. Major Kitts was closest to the enemy, less than fifty yards behind the rushing river. The water was still much too high for the North Korean tanks to swim across. They would have to stand and fight.

Kitts looked across the roiling water. He could die right there today. The idea had never occurred to him before. He was twenty-eight years old, single, had his West Point ring, and the gold leaves of an Army major . . . and he could die there today.

Not by damn if he could help it.

He heard the tanks coming then, not one, but three or four heading directly at him. Three or four!

He slid down in the hatch of his tank until he could just see over the rim.

"Company," he said.

"Got them, Major," Broadhurst, his gunner, said. "I've got two of their Russian-built T-55's at about six hundred yards. Should we take a shot or let them get closer?"

"Closer, Broad. I want them bastards to die hard and fast. Yeah, I see them. Just two." He flipped the radio switch. "All units, all units. I have two NK fifty-five crawlers straight north at about six hundred. Hold your fire as long as you can. If they spot you, shoot. I'm buttoning up. Good hunting."

He clapped the top down on the tank and took his position.

"Yeah, let's rock and roll," he added. "Broad, what's the range?"

"Five hundred. No change in direction. They probably don't know the bridge is out and the river is too high to cross."

"Yeah, when they see that they'll turn to the side, east or west, giving us a good broadside shot. Let's see how it plays out."

The edges of dawn faded away and it was fully light. Kitts watched the smaller of the two Russian-made tanks the North Koreans used roll forward. Their course hadn't varied a degree since they'd come over the slight rise a mile away.

"You've got the left one?" Kitts asked.

"Roger that, Major," Broadhurst said. "Zeroed in and computer laid, ready to shoot. Continual update."

Kitts watched the rolling tanks again. In a moment he saw the gun barrel of the T-55 swing to the left, then back again until it centered on his tank.

"Fire," Kitts barked. The 105mm round went off with the familiar roar. Some smoke and powder fumes tainted the inside of the steel box, but none of the four men noticed it.

Kitts watched through his AN/W2 ruby laser range finder as their round hit the North Korean tank just below the long gun and penetrated the armor. A moment later the T-55 lifted a foot off the ground, then careened to the left and tipped on its side.

"Sighting in on number two," Broadhurst said.

"Go, Broad. Nice shooting. One more round and we get out of sight. Keep the engine running."

The second round only grazed the NK tank as it jolted into a quick left turn. The round exploded behind the T-55.

"Hope they had some infantry back there," Kitts said. "Now, Anderson, get us behind the other bank. We'll hide for a few minutes and see what that other gent out there does."

He wanted to get out of the tank and check the rest of his teams. He used the radio instead. "All units, pick out targets when you can see them. Let's fire and hide. Wait for the last minute before you fire. You know the routine. We're six against eleven. We clobbered one."

"Major, I had one bogie in my sights," Broadhurst said. "It was one of the bigger T-62's, and he suddenly vanished. Something blew him all to hell. Couldn't have been one of our rounds. We have any air support out there?"

Kitts frowned. "Damned if I know." He used the radio again. "Anybody who can, unbutton and take a look upstairs. See if we have any air support. Anybody else see that T-62 get blown up?"

Two of the tanks had seen the T-62 disintegrate.

Kitts opened the turret and looked at the sky. At first he saw nothing, only heard the rumble of tanks from across the river. Then another sound came, a high whining kind of sound.

Jets. Fighter-bombers? He hoped. He edged higher on the tank, then stood up. He could just see over the ledge of dirt they were parked behind.

To his right he saw a North Korean T-62 slanting to the left a hundred yards across the river. He never saw the plane, but he heard it, a roaring, whistling sound as the jet slashed through the air overhead. At the same time something long and dark jolted into the moving tank and exploded. All Kitts could see a moment later were refrigerator-sized parts.

"Yes!" he shouted. Kitts slid back in his tank, closed up, and moved it to where he could see across the river again. A T-55 turned at the water and presented him a side view two hundred yards away.

"Broad, nail him," Kitts said.

"Take a second," the gunner said. "Now, oh, yeah."

The tank lurched as the 105mm rifle fired off, a messenger

of instant death. The computer-guided round jolted into the side of the rushing T-55 and exploded, blowing off the near-side track, tearing off the turret, and causing a dozen secondary explosions as some of the rounds inside detonated.

"Yes, scratch one more NK machine," Kitts yelled. "The fucking odds are getting better. Let's get back in our hidey-hole and look out the other side."

High overhead, two F-18 Hornets from the *Monroe* circled for another run at the rumbling North Korean tanks below.

"Hey, Top Hat One, I nailed that bastard. Did you see that? Secondary all over the place. Good old shaped charge. Does the job."

"Roger that, Top Hat Two. Just keep that three thousand feet of altitude and hang tough. Lots more targets down there."

The Hornets came in for another run with their television-guided 460-pound missiles ready. Each plane carried four of the Maverick missiles especially designed for use against tanks. The 115-pound high-explosive charge was aimed at the top of the tank where the armor that could deflect certain kinds of rounds was weaker.

"Got me another one lined up," Top Hat One called. Then he slanted down with his F-18 Hornet, checked his airspeed to be sure he was above the Mach .09 firing speed, and launched.

"Top Hat One, this is Calico Cat."

"Yeah, tomcatting around again. We're chomping up tanks."

"We have two MiGs approaching your position, Top Hat. Two of us are on the way to meet those visitors and give you some top cover. Stay low."

"That's a roger, Calico. Wham, we just erased another NK tank. Good hunting up there, Calico."

On the ground, Major Kitts watched two more enemy tanks get blasted into piles of junk by the aircraft. He didn't know what kind they were, but the stars on the wings were reassuring. He spotted no more tanks in his immediate area.

"All units, how many NK machines can we count that are not dead?"

"I've got six," one radio voice said.

"I can see only five."

"Everyone still in his nest?" Kitts asked.

"So far as I can see," Lieutenant Olson said. "I'm back about a half mile. None of our guys is moving. Time to leave the nest?"

"Let's play bird dog a little longer. Maybe the planes will drive some more of them into the open for our guns. How many for damned sure kills do we have?"

The men reported in four for sure dead NK tanks from their guns. That, with Kitts', made five. The fly guys must have killed four or five. Maybe the NKs had lost ten tanks today. But five or six of the Russian tanks still made up a potent force.

"Let's go hunting," Major Kitts said.

The six U.S. tanks powered out from their hiding places and aimed north. At once one of the gunners on the east flank saw a T-62 doing a slow turn away from the river. After two rounds from the American tank, the NK machine pivoted on one track and went down the bank upside down into the river.

Two T-55's were caught in a hasty retreat. One was damaged, but ground out of sight over a small hill. The other one took a direct hit, and the 105 round blew off the top of the tank.

Major Kitts came to a stop on the crest of a small hill and scanned the land to the north. There were no more North Korean tanks in sight except the dead and the burning.

He slid back down and tried his long-range tactical frequency.

"Ninety-first calling Second Regiment."

He made the call three times; then the speaker came to life.

"Ninety-first, you still out there? We lost track of you. What's your position and your strength? Good to hear from you. We've got a spot where we need your tanks. I'll want a complete report. How are you on fuel? Tell me. Now is a good time."

Major Donovan Kitts grinned and punched up the send button. He told his colonel exactly what had happened since early morning the day before. It was great to hear a friendly voice from headquarters on the radio.

USS *Monroe*

The second day of the war dawned bright and clear on the carrier. Murdock slept in until 0700, had a quick breakfast, and beat Jaybird to the assembly room. He phoned the munitions man on board, and came up with a commander who knew every ounce of powder, ball, and missile on the carrier.

"Damn right we have TNAZ, all you can carry. You want timer/detonators too, I'd guess. You'll have to sign for it. How much?"

Murdock tried to decide. Smaller charges on individual hardware, or one big blast to bring down the ceiling and bury everything?

"Quarter-pound blocks?"

"Aye."

"Make it twenty-five pounds."

"Twenty-five? You planning on blowing up half the damned countryside?"

"Just about. Nice stuff to have around. Oh, some primer cord too, and we'll need more ammo. My chief will get back to you on that this morning. We'll pick it up all at once."

"Night trip?"

"Seems to be. Thanks."

The men came in on time, and settled down to cleaning and oiling equipment and weapons. They gave Jaybird a list of how much ammo they needed. They would go fifty percent over normal for the chopper run in and out.

"Wish to hell we had some RPGs," Bill Bradford said.

"Oh, hell, yes, you want to carry a dozen?" Lampedusa asked.

Everyone laughed.

They had a quick lunch, then three hours of sack time before they assembled again to get ready for the 1730 flight.

"If we get there early, we'll set down in friendly territory and burn a few minutes until it gets dark," Murdock said.

"Take an interpreter?" DeWitt asked. "We still have those

two on board we used yesterday." They decided to take one along.

Promptly at 1730 they stepped on board the Sea Knight and got ready to rumble.

7

Sea Knight Two
Near Kangso-ri, South Korea

The flight in from the carrier took thirty-six minutes, so it wasn't fully dark. They landed two miles below the MLR, the main line of resistance, where the fighting took place. They were still in friendly territory. They waited for fifteen minutes.

When the black Korean night settled over the peninsula, they lifted off and swept over the small town of Kangso-ri, then flew two miles to the left, where they found the designated target site by the small grove of trees with two antennas in them and a small wooden farmhouse.

Murdock, riding in the small cabin, nodded at the pilot. "Put it down here before we have company."

The door gunners had their .50-caliber machine guns charged with rounds and waiting. No enemy troops appeared. The SEALs hadn't seen any signs of military once they'd passed the MLR. Strange.

As soon as the chopper touched down, the fifteen SEALs boiled out of it, half on each side, and stormed up to the farmhouse. Access to the underground was through the building, which had been gutted, with some security put in.

Ching, Quinley, and Bradford had the bulk of the TNAZ. Murdock waved them forward. By arrangement, Ed DeWitt put the rest of the platoon in a perimeter defense around the building.

The front door of the small house stood open. Murdock went in first right after he threw a flashbang grenade inside. Once through the door, Murdock could see no soldiers through his NVGs. He called in the rest of the sapper squad, and they rushed to the second room, where they found the trapdoor under a small bed. They used flashlights going down the wooden steps. Ten feet underground, they found a concrete-box room. It had dozens of electronic boxes and computers and relays, all tied into cables going out through pipes in the overhead.

"Let's do ten charges with four timer/detonators set for thirty seconds," Murdock said. "Sympathetic explosions will trigger the rest of the juice. Go, go, go."

The three men planted the high-explosives where they would do the most damage. There was a chance the ceiling wouldn't fall in if it were laced with rebar. They'd have to take the chance.

It took them a minute to locate the right spots, place the bombs, and insert the detonators. When they were done, each man held up a hand. When the third hand went up, Murdock nodded, they punched the timers to the on position, and all four men hurried up the steps and out the door.

"Move it," Murdock said to his lip mike on the Motorola. "Get out of there, Ed. At least fifty yards. Go."

By the time Murdock and his three men were out the farmhouse door, the other SEALs had vanished. Murdock took the left-hand side, and had led the way out forty yards when the explosion jolted the ground. It felt more like a small earthquake than an explosion. Smoke billowed from the farmhouse door, and part of the roof collapsed.

Murdock had hit the dirt when the blast came with its small rumble, and before he could get to his feet he heard small-arms fire from the right, where Ed DeWitt must be with the rest of the platoon.

Murdock's ear piece activated.

"We've got company," DeWitt said. "Not sure how many, but they know we're here. Coming from the north, must be fifteen or twenty. So far only small arms fire, no MGs."

"Hunker down, buddy, find some cover," Murdock said. "We'll swing around to the left and see if we can track the visitors."

Murdock and the three men ran bent over to the left, entered the grove of trees, and kept going to the other side of the thirty-yard-wide thicket.

Murdock hit the dirt and the other three followed. Directly ahead not more than fifty yards, they saw the winking of muzzle flashes. The rounds were not coming at Murdock. He reviewed his weapons. Ching had a colt with grenade launcher, Quinley had the caseless-rounds H&K G-11, and Bradford had his sniper rifle. His own subgun was out-ranged.

"Ching, drop in four HE forties on them. As soon as they hit we'll open up. Faster the better."

Ching loaded and fired, and had two rounds in the air before the first one hit. He was slightly short, moved it up, and fired twice more. With the first explosion of the 40mm grenade, firing from the North Koreans slackened off, then built back up. The second two rounds came down right in the middle of them, and the firing nearly stopped.

"Good shooting, buddy, we didn't have the opening here." It was DeWitt. Murdock fired his H&K MKP-5 submachine gun. He'd taken the suppressor off and now had the range. Two minutes of rapid fire from the four men silenced the attacking soldiers.

"Where to?" DeWitt asked.

"South," Murdock said in his Motorola. "Let's link up. We're to the south, you come to us. Just past the trees on your side."

Before Murdock stopped talking he heard it. Then he knew for sure what it was. "Belay that, JG. We've got a fucking tank breathing right down our naked necks over here."

The tank loomed out of the night directly ahead of them and rumbled forward. It was a big sucker.

"What the hell we do about him?" Bradford asked.

"Take him out," Ching said.

"Sure, wiseass, how?"

Murdock wondered the same thing. Then he remembered the TNAZ. "How much of that explosive you guys got left?" Murdock asked.

They had about three pounds.

"Quarter of a pound should boost the tracks off the rollers," Murdock said. "All we have to do is get close enough to him. Each of you take a quarter pound and give me one too. Put in detonator/timers and set the timers for thirty seconds. Whoever gets a chance at a tread, jam in the soup and push the timer, then get the hell out of there."

"This could turn out to be a fun trip," Ching said.

They split, two on each side of the big tank that kept coming straight at them from about forty yards. Murdock wondered if the driver had nightscopes. He bet the man didn't.

Murdock crawled twenty feet to the left of where the tank should come, and waited. He used the mike to tell DeWitt what they were doing. The 2IC was to go south when he got the chance. They would link up later.

The tank rumbled ahead. Without warning, the .50-caliber machine gun on the front of the tank blasted, sending a stream of big slugs out front but nowhere near the SEALs. It kicked off seven rounds, then another seven-round burst.

Murdock grinned. He was shooting at shadows, and drawing attention to himself. Dumbass.

The tank clattered ahead at a walking pace. Murdock crawled forward so he'd have a chance at the tracks, but still room to get away if the brute pulled a locked-track ninety-degree turn on him.

The tank was ten feet away when Murdock lifted up, held the quarter pound of explosive in his right hand, and ran for the churning tracks. His foot hit some brush and he stumbled, but kept his feet. The tracks kept grinding around. Where to put the bomb? He decided on the up side of the track, just before it started its downward trip to grip the ground.

He waited, walking along beside the beast. Now. He pushed in the timer, dropped the TNAZ on the inside of the rollers, and sprinted away. Behind him, he saw Ching running in the same direction.

"Sixteen tanks, seventeen tanks, eighteen tanks," Murdock counted trying to work off the seconds. At twenty-eight tanks, the sky lit up with a small sun and a roaring sound cascaded toward him, jolting him forward a step before a storm of hot air slapped him forward another step.

Ten seconds later the second bomb went off—on the other side of the tank, Murdock figured. The blast effect on Murdock was not so great, but he dove to the dirt anyway. Behind him twenty yards away, he saw the tank through the soft moonlight. It had stopped. The track on Murdock's side was completely off the rollers, and the rig had slewed around in half a turn as the other tread had kept grinding before it blew up.

"We just nailed ourselves a tank," Murdock said on the mike. "Where the hell is everyone?"

"Commander, we're about two hundred yards south of the grove of trees," Jaybird said. "That tank blast was north of us."

"You have eleven bodies?"

"Roger that."

"We're moving that way soon, so hold your fire."

The four SEALs lay where they had dropped when the tank blew. All waited for the turret to pop and a head to show.

"How the fuck long we gonna wait?" Quinley asked in a whisper into his lip mike.

"Long as it takes," Murdock whispered back. "He's still got that fifty up there that can chew us up."

Murdock squirmed in the dirt and weeds. He had his subgun up on three-round-burst setting, and a fragger in the other hand. Another minute. He'd give the tank commander another sixty damn seconds.

Before the time was up, Murdock heard the grating as the tank turret rattled, then lifted up. A moment later an Asian head lifted out. Three weapons slammed rounds into it and the man slid back into the tank, dead in a thrice.

Quinley was closest to the top. He jumped up the tank's tracks and dropped a cooked grenade down the hatch. The almost instantaneous explosion rattled the tank, but set off no rounds inside.

"Move out," Murdock said to the mike, and the four SEALs joined up south of the tank and headed for where they figured DeWitt would be with the rest of the platoon.

They found them five minutes later flaked out in a small patch of brush.

"Time to call in the chopper?" DeWitt asked.

"We have any more company around here? A chopper is gonna kick all kinds of bad guys out of the brush."

Lampedusa, their chief scout and the best set of ears in the platoon, lifted his fist and they all quieted.

"Company, trucks, five, maybe eight on that road over there about two hundred yards. I saw it before on a little recon."

"Maybe they'll just drive by," Murdock said. "Heading north or south?"

"Coming our way, Cap."

"We were close there. Now we have to wait and see what these newcomers are going to want."

"Us probably," Jaybird said.

They moved into a line of skirmishers fifty yards from the road. Each SEAL had an open field of fire to the road. It was more a track through the countryside than a highway. One truck wide, dirt surface, but showing a lot of use, Lam had told the officers.

Two minutes later the first beams of the headlights showed to the north, and swept down the roadway at a hazardous thirty miles an hour.

Murdock called up Holt, who had the SATCOM tuned to TAC One. Murdock took the handset.

"Cobra, this is SEALs North. Do you copy?"

"Roger that, SEALs. This is Cobra Alpha."

"We have some company up here we might need some help on. Convoy of six or eight trucks that look to have troops in them. Figure they came up to give us a good old-fashioned welcome."

"We're five minutes away. Your position?"

"About three hundred yards south of our target. Grove of

trees, just behind us. We'll put a red flare on the trucks if they are still there. You coming?"

"On the way. Count the minutes."

Murdock watched the trucks roll into sight. The first two stopped directly across from them, the others to the north. At once twenty to twenty-five men jumped out of each truck and formed up next to the vehicles.

"Let's get out of Dodge," Murdock whispered into his mike. The men crawled back twenty yards until they vanished into the darkness, then stood and jogged away from the road before turning south.

"If they sweep across from the road along that stretch, it'll cover the communications center," Murdock said to Jaybird right beside him. "Then they'll know somebody is here and come looking for us at top speed."

"They can't track us at night," Jaybird said.

"No, but they can get lucky, leapfrog ahead of us. Where the hell is that Cobra?"

A minute later they heard the *whup-whup* of the chopper blades as an aircraft came from the south. Murdock looked behind them and to the north and could still see the truck headlights burning. One set went off, then another, but that left another six or eight. There was no chance to get a flare on the trucks.

The Cobra made a run on the length of the column, 20mm rounds pounded into the vehicles. Murdock heard one explode as the fuel tank went. Some ground fire lanced up at the chopper, but it didn't seem to be affected.

On the next run from the other way, the Cobra rained on the column with 70mm rockets from the four LAU-68/A pods on its stubby wings. The rockets exploded in deadly fashion along the line of trucks, setting two more on fire and demolishing a third. None of the vehicles would ever run again.

Murdock and his men took advantage of the attack and jogged again to the south. They crossed a side dirt road, went around a group of three houses and outbuildings, and kept moving south.

Lam came up to Murdock and fell in beside him.

"May have some trouble, Cap. I can hear some guys tailing us. Not sure how many, but they must be from those trucks. They could be damn mad now because they have to walk wherever else they're going."

"Drop back and see if you can find out how many. Don't take any chances, but be good to know."

Lam veered off and set up in a patch of brush. He'd wait for the followers and then get back with the main body.

Lam wormed down into the brush and weeds until not even his mother could find him. He checked his stopwatch. It was three minutes before he could see anyone coming. They had a scout out front twenty yards. Not far enough. Behind them came two groups of men, all with weapons and all jogging. Lam scrunched lower and counted. Twenty men in each group. Forty men on their tail, which was not good.

When the last NK trooper went past, Lam faded away to the left side farther from the tail-end Charlie on the NKs and ran. He kept two hundred yards to the side of the North Koreans as he rapidly caught and passed them.

Lam guessed he was about three hundred yards ahead of the trackers. He used his Motorola.

"Third Platoon. Where the hell are you?"

"In your hip pocket, little buddy," Jaybird said. "You're not as quiet as you used to be, I heard you coming. Small hill ahead and to your right. We're going up it. You can't be more than fifty yards behind. How many of them rice-snappers are there?"

"Forty, and they look like regulars. I'm moving."

He caught up with the platoon a few minutes later, and told Murdock about the men behind them.

The hill had a few low bushes on it, no real timber. Murdock passed the word on his lip mike.

"We'll meet our friends at the top of the hill. Just over the slope find firing positions. Who has Claymores?"

Guns Franklin and Al Adams did.

"Set them up in sequence with trip wires about forty yards down the slope. You know the routine. Aim them to spray downhill and then catch up. Adams put one here. Franklin ten yards higher. Go."

Five minutes later, Murdock had his platoon spread out on the reverse slope of the small hill with every man in a good firing position. Adams and Franklin had returned and had the Claymore mines set. All suppressors were taken off to increase the weapons' range.

The Claymore is a chunk of explosive, fronted with two hundred small steel balls. When the trip wire sets off the charge, the explosive blasts the balls out in the direction the mine has been aimed in. They can cut down a dozen to fifteen foot soldiers in single blast.

Lampedusa touched Murdock's shoulder. "They're coming."

Murdock grinned. He couldn't hear them. Lam had ears like an elephant. A minute later Murdock did hear them. He knew they had a lead scout out. Maybe he'd miss the trip wire and they would get a better body count.

Seconds later one of the Claymores exploded with a shattering roar, followed by screams of pain and fury. Nothing happened for almost five minutes. Then Murdock could hear the NKs moving up slope again. The second Claymore burst into the night sky with a roar, and Murdock lifted his subgun and chattered off two three-round bursts.

That was the signal for the rest of the platoon to fire downslope where the sounds had come from. After two minutes of concentrated fire, Murdock gave a cease-fire.

"Let's move," Murdock said. "Not many of them are going to try to follow us, if any are left standing."

They were half a mile down the other side of the hill and looking for a good LZ when Lam came back and shook his head.

"Cap, we've got something ahead. Not sure what it is. Lights up half the fucking sky. Must be some kind of a supply depot or a replacement depot or some damned thing. No secret it's there."

"So, no LZ around here. What about to the left?"

"Some kind of a main highway over there. Lots of truck traffic. You hear that plane few minutes ago? Probably an F-18 just blasted to hell a half-dozen trucks."

"So we move to the right. Find us a black hole where we can call down that bird."

Lam nodded and vanished to the right. "We'll take a break here," Murdock said in his mike. "Ed, put out two security, north and south. We're looking for a good LZ."

Lam came back in ten minutes. "Something you should see up here, Commander." He led Murdock and Ed DeWitt over a quick two hundred yards. They came on a small farmhouse with lights in the windows. A woman's screams billowed out of the place. An NK jeep sat in front of the house and one soldier lolled in the driver's seat, evidently sleeping.

"Let's take a look in that window. Ed, keep the driver covered. If he wakes up, take him out."

Lam and Murdock slipped up on the window and lifted up to look inside. It was a one-room house with a bed against the far wall. There a woman lay spread-eagled on her back and tied to the bed. A North Korean officer had just taken off his shirt. Another one was getting into his pants.

"Through the window?" Lam asked.

Murdock nodded. "I'm right, you left." Both weapons had sound suppressors back on them. They each took a side of the window. Murdock let Lam sight in. "Now," he whispered. Both men fired. Murdock's three-round burst took the man trying to get into his pants full in the chest and blasted him against the wall, where he died instantly.

Lam's Colt M-4A1 slashed out five rounds on fully automatic. Three of the slugs hit the NK officer in the neck and the head, putting him in instant touch with his ancestors.

For a moment all was quiet. Murdock pressed against the broken window, but could see no more men inside. He checked Ed DeWitt, who had moved up beside the jeep driver and now wiped the blood off his knife on the dead Korean's shirt.

"Inside," Murdock said. He and Lam hurried through the front door and saw that the room was clear. Murdock cut the bindings on the woman's hands and feet and pushed a tattered quilt over her naked body.

She hadn't opened her eyes yet. Her sobbing tapered off. Murdock waited a moment. She sat up and motioned to a

smaller room to the back he hadn't seen. He went to the door
with his subgun ready. Inside the room lay two Korean men,
both well over sixty, Murdock guessed. Both had slit throats.
He closed the door.

Back in the main room, the woman dressed. She put on
flip-flops and pointed outside. There she bowed low.

"*Arigato,*" she said in Japanese.

"*Doi tasta maste,*" Murdock said, trying to remember how
to pronounce the Japanese for "you're welcome." He knew he
had clobbered the phrase. The woman smiled briefly. She
understood. She was about twenty-five, Murdock figured.
She bowed again, then hurried off through the night moving
to the south.

They met DeWitt at the jeep. He held a fragger in his hand
and motioned to the rig.

"Why not?" Murdock said.

Murdock and Lam ran to the right, and Ed DeWitt pulled
the safety pin on the grenade, laid it on the fuel tank, and let
the arming handle pop. Then he ran like hell away from the
jeep. He had four seconds to get clear of the blast.

He made it. The grenade exploded, vaporizing the gasoline
in the tank, which led to an instantaneous roaring explosion
that melted down the jeep and set some dry grass on fire.

The three SEALs ran for the rest of their platoon.

A half hour later, Lam came back from the right flank.

"Got an LZ, Cap," he said. "No troops around and a nice
flat spot with no trees. Should be a piece of cake."

"Let's do it."

They came to the place ten minutes later. Murdock used the
land version of the MUGR to give an exact position to within
ten feet with the use of global satellite triangulation. Holt
fired up the SATCOM and made contact with the Sea Knight
on the first try.

"Yes, SEALs, this is Sea Knight Two. Where?"

Murdock gave him the coordinates.

"Any ground fire expected?"

"Negative, looks clean now, Sea Knight. How long?"

"Eight minutes, unless we get into trouble. A red flare on
the LZ? We're lifting off now."

"You got the flare. Blink your landing lights twice, so we'll know it's you."

"Not many NK choppers out there. Will do."

The SEALs automatically formed a perimeter defense around the cleared spot, all prone and facing outward. Murdock pushed the light on his wristwatch. It was only 2030. They had been on land less than two and a half hours. A damned warm-up. Unless something else went wrong.

Nothing went wrong.

They landed on the *Monroe* a little after 2130. Don Stroh knew they were coming in, and nailed Murdock as soon as he stepped out of the chopper.

"Good work, sailor. Now the boss has a really important one that we need to talk about. Oh, you have any casualties?"

"Nice of you to ask. No wounded. Now what's this about a really important mission?"

8

US *Monroe*
Off Inchon Harbor
South Korea

Don Stroh and Murdock talked about the new assignment all the way to the dirty shirt mess, where Murdock had a steak dinner.

"You say this frigate is the largest and most powerful Navy ship that the North has. Why don't you just put an F-18 on it and blow it out of the water with a missile?"

"Because we can't find it when we want to. For instance, the first morning of the war at four-thirty A.M., the frigate showed up three miles off Inchon Harbor and shelled it for fifteen minutes. Then before it was light, it vanished back north into some of the many inlets and harbors up there."

"The whole U.S. Navy can't take care of one little frigate with what, a hundred and eighty men that's about three hundred and forty feet long? I don't believe it."

"True. Second day it did the same thing, and just after dark today it shelled the harbor and the city, then slammed out of there at twenty-four knots and we never laid a hand on her. But we know where she hides out."

"You didn't find her with all the air the Navy has during daylight hours?"

"She vanishes. Now we know why. The Caves of Pon-hyon."

"The what? Caves? You telling me she slips into a cave during the day? That's an awfully big cave."

"Short of blasting down the whole damn mountain, there's no way we can get her in the cave. Except . . ."

"Except by the SEALs. Good choice. How do we get in there and get out?"

"You tell me. The admiral wants this one. He doesn't like to get slapped in the face by a little frigate."

"Yeah, I understand that. Let me sleep on it. We can't do anything until tomorrow night. We could meet her leaving the cave, in the cave, or coming back to the cave."

"Give it your best shot. The admiral's really pissed about this one."

It took Murdock a half hour to get to sleep that night. He kept going over the ways they could get to the ship, how they would blow it or disable her, how to get away. It would be wet, that was the best part. A real SEAL-type job for a change. When he drifted off to sleep, he was imagining the long hull of the ship edging out of the largest cave he'd ever seen.

The next morning in the SEALs' ready room, Jaybird and Ed DeWitt were delighted with the idea. By 0830 they had the details.

"Yeah, this will give us something to get our teeth into," Jaybird said.

"Good," the JG said. "I was wondering if I remembered how to swim. How do we go in?"

They worried it.

"Why not an RIB dropped off a destroyer out about ten miles from the target," Jaybird said. "We can get that middle-sized one that does twenty-five knots. It's got plenty of range."

"They can carry nine," Ed said. "Do we take two of them and both squads, or just one?"

"Both squads," Murdock said. "We might need the fire-power. These NKs get trigger-happy sometimes."

"So we would take two of the RIBs," Ed said. "We have them in Coronado. Are there any in the fleet?"

"Get on the horn and find out, Ed. One of the amphibious ships could have some."

Ed left the small table and moved to a phone.

The rest of the SEALs were cleaning weapons, restocking ammo pouches, and repairing anything that had worn out or been broken. Murdock called them around and told them about the new mission.

"Just one little old frigate?" Douglas asked.

"Hell, Douglas can take care of that himself," Fernandez said. "He can piss it to death easy."

Murdock watched the exchange. He didn't like the tone, or the way Fernandez stared at the other SEAL.

"She hides out during the day, so it'll be a night run," Murdock said. "Maybe early, maybe late, we're not sure." As he spoke, he moved to disrupt the war of stares between the two SEALs. He'd have to ask Ed again about the problem. "How we go in there, all depends on what kind of transport they have in the fleet."

"We could go in on our IBS," Lampedusa said.

"Maybe, let's talk about it," Murdock said. "There are some islands and outposts up there where we might get in trouble. A faster boat might be better if we can wrangle it. Talk to me."

"Hell, we know the IBS," Jaybird said. "We know them inside out. The bigger boat can go faster, but it makes a hell of a racket."

"Have to throttle down when we get in close," Quinley said. "We'd want to swim in the last mile or so anyway."

"Hell we can carry a lot more stuff in the bigger boat," Ron Holt said. "We'll want some limpets or some such to put that sucker in the bottom of that cave, or the channel. I'd vote for the new ten-meter-class RIB. It's got Furno 1730 radar and GPS. Get us in and wait for us and snake us out of there."

They talked it over for another half hour, laying out the tools they'd want to take in, the explosives, the limpet mines, TNAZ as well, and the personal weapons.

Murdock had the whole picture by 1000. Ed came back from a trip to see some supply officer and at last had a report.

"The amphib *Boxer* LHD4 has four of the RIBs. They're the new ten-meter class, which the XO over there said should work fine. He can have one or two of them here for us within two hours of our call."

"Good, let's you and me go see Stroh and then the XO. Looks like we might have a handle on how to do this one."

The XO was Captain Barney Waterton, former CAG and former Wing Leader and F-14 pilot. He grinned at Murdock.

"Damn, we're in the thick of it here, making more combat sorties than anything since the Gulf War. We're geared up to the max on close ground support and rear-area strikes, and still you SEALs can make the admiral jump. Amazing."

Murdock smiled. "Captain, I understand the feeling. But our boss just slightly outranks everyone on board. Of course this one is for Admiral Kenner. His request."

"Roger that, Commander. Well, your outline looks fine to me. I'll order the two RIBs over here now and you can check them out. They come with a crew of three, but you can cut that to two if you want to. You have all the ordnance you need?"

"Check that out this afternoon, Captain. Your powder room should be able to supply us with plenty. We can go with TNAZ if nothing else."

"You want to swim in the last mile?"

"I understand the NKs don't have much coastal radar, and what they have probably won't pick up the RIBs. A mile swim is a walk around the block for us, sir."

"Right. When will you push off?"

"Captain, I figured with the ride on the destroyer for forty miles north, we'd need to allow an hour and a half. We've decided to hit the cave just at dark, before the frigate can get out of its nest. Dark comes about 1800. We'll need fifteen minutes to move the last nine miles in the RIB, and then a half hour for the swim to shore."

Ed had been adding up the times where he sat beside Murdock. He showed Murdock the figure.

"So, about two and a quarter hours for insertion. We'd need

to leave here at 1530 to make our time sked. We don't mind being a few minutes early."

"Sounds reasonable. I've assigned the destroyer *Cole* DDG 67 for your transport. We'll lift your men and the two RIBs over to the *Cole* by helo. No sweat there. Have your men on deck at 1520 and we'll take care of the rest. Anything else?"

"Crews on the RIBs. Keep all three men on board. We'll only have fifteen SEALs."

Murdock and DeWitt stood.

"Thanks, Captain. We'll try to get this NK frigate out of your hair."

After noon chow, Murdock told Jaybird to put the men down for a rest period. They had their personal gear ready, regular loads of ammo, and room for explosives and mines. Murdock and Jaybird went to the ordnance officer and laid out their plans.

Lieutenant Commander Morton smiled when they told him their mission.

"Yeah, more like it," he growled. "What the hell would do the best job the quickest? A frigate, you say. That's about three hundred feet long. Blow her stern off, she'd sink like a bulldozer in heat. We've got some new limpets that really pack a wallop. Only trouble is they weigh about fifty pounds each."

"Flotation collars?" Jaybird asked.

"Yeah, make them neutral buoyancy," the commander said, his eyes sparkling. "Yeah, we've got some of those. Want four of them beauties? If you can get them going off within twenty seconds of each other, they should just about tear that old frigate to pieces. What is she, an old Russian tub?"

"My guess," Murdock said.

They picked out the flotation devices, made sure they would hold the big limpets, then asked the commander to have them on the flight deck in half an hour. Murdock left Jaybird to shepherd the mines upstairs and to make sure where they were when the SEALs arrived later.

By 1430 Murdock had his platoon moving up the ladders toward the flight deck.

Topside, they found the two RIBs and the limpet mines

with their flotation gear. The SEALs brought ten pounds of the TNAZ and timer/detonators.

A destroyer steamed alongside the carrier a quarter of a mile off. A flight deck officer checked with Murdock, and shortly two Sea Knights rolled on scene. One rigged the two RIBs on slings, and lifted away with the cargo. The limpets and their flotation collars and the SEALs loaded into the second chopper, and it took off chasing the first one.

Two hours later, Murdock and his SEALs hunkered down in the sleek ten-meter RIBs as they motored at five miles an hour toward the just-visible North Korean shore through the dusk. They were twenty minutes behind schedule, but it wasn't the SEALs' fault. There had been a small mix-up by the destroyer on its speed to the ten-mile-limit line.

Close enough. Just so the raider didn't slip out of the cave before they got there. All they needed were three or four minutes in the water under the ship. Then five minutes more to get out of the immediate vicinity so the underwater concussion didn't knock them unconscious like a school of flopping fish.

Murdock checked his watch. It was 1750 and they were nearing the mile mark. In a half hour it would be dark. The seals wore full black neoprene wet suits, caps, boots, and gloves. The neoprene traps water inside the suit, which is warmed by the body to help insulate the diver. Each man had a face mask and LAR V Draeger rebreather unit, which allowed the reuse of oxygen and emitted no telltale bubble line to give away the diver.

They had the insulated jungle boots and flippers ready in hand to slip on just before diving. Each SEAL had his individual weapons strapped to his back. This time they didn't bring the heavy .50-caliber sniper rifle.

"We about there?" Ed DeWitt asked Murdock on the Motorola. The rest of the men had already put their personal radios away in waterproof pouches on their combat vests.

"Looks like it," Murdock said. "You ready for a swim?" Both the motors cut off and the sleek RIB boats coasted to a stop. The men were paired and tied together with buddy cords, eight to ten feet of thin nylon line to help them stay together. The line also was a good communication tool underwater.

By pairs, the SEALs went overboard. They swam down fifteen feet, leveled out, and moved toward the coast. Murdock had the attack board, a piece of molded plastic with two hand grips and a bubble compass in the center. It also held a depth gauge and a Cyalume chemical tube to twist to turn on and regulate the amount of light needed to read the instruments. Murdock moved until he had the right compass heading, and stroked out underwater at the normal rate of travel.

Each man in the platoon knew exactly how many strokes it took him to swim underwater a half mile. They had practiced it so much it came as second nature. They were totally at home in the water.

Murdock watched Holt, who shepherded one of the fifty-pound limpet mines on its zero-buoyancy collar. It slowed Holt, just as Murdock figured the big mines would be slowing the other three teams that were responsible for the limpets.

Murdock slowed his stroke to match Holt's.

After a quarter of a mile he tugged on the buddy line and took over the mine, giving the attack board to Holt. The problem was more one of bulk than weight, but still, the blunt collar had to be pushed through the water.

At the half-mile point, they traded off again.

Murdock expected no guards, sentries, or even patrol boats in this area. The South had taken no offensive action against the North's Navy, so they would be snug and feel secure.

Less than a half a mile from the shore, Murdock heard an engine sound coming at them fast. He gave three quick jerks on the buddy cord and he and Ron Holt moved upward to sneak a peak. Murdock's face came out of the water only enough so he could see. To the left he spotted the boat, one of the larger patrol craft that North Korea had. Their Navy was miniscule. The frigate they were going for tonight was the largest boat in the NK fleet.

As Murdock watched, the patrol craft continued on its way toward shore. This could have been the farthest it ventured off the home country. Murdock concentrated on the landfall.

From there they would parallel the shore for about one more klick; then the town and the caves should show.

Murdock didn't worry about losing any of his platoon. Ed DeWitt had an attack board as well. By previous arrangement the swimmers began to surface after every half mile. Murdock counted his four teams, which came up within twenty yards. He saw DeWitt break out of the water and wave. He had his six men. All accounted for.

Murdock swam over to Ed.

"Another klick or so along this point of land and we should have it. Any trouble with the mines?" DeWitt shook his head. "Good, stay alert."

Murdock put the mouthpiece from the rebreather back in his mouth and kicked underwater.

They surfaced the next time at the edge of the small inlet. It was about a hundred feet wide, and ended with a huge cliff and the darkness of what must be the cave. The inlet grew larger as they worked slowly into the tiny port. They surfaced for a moment, took their bearings, and saw the gaping black hole in the side of the mountain that came down to the water's edge.

At this point the swimmers stayed just below the surface, and Lampedusa and Jack Mahanani swam forward on a scouting mission. They couldn't go in blind. Were there surface guards? Were there divers in the water? How about a closing gate across the cave or a net of some kind? All were questions that needed answering.

When the scouts didn't come back after five minutes, Murdock waved his platoon to shore, where they rested sitting on rocks under a half-completed dock.

Lam tracked them down five minutes later. He came out of the water and nodded.

"Oh, yeah, she's there. Big and ugly. No gate in front of the bow. No net. Four guards we could see along the dock on each side. Her mast barely clears the top of the cave, which looks like it was chipped away to make room.

"Doesn't seem to be much activity, not like they were ready to get under way any time soon."

"Bow or stern for the mines?" Murdock asked.

"Oh, the bow. They backed her in, so she can come out quickly. But if we drop the bow into the mud, they won't be able to drag her out of there. It'll be like a big long grave for her."

"Let's do it."

Eight men moved out at once, two to each of the four large limpet mines. The teams swam forward and worked underwater down the bow of the 335-foot-long frigate. They moved fifty feet along the side and stopped. The big mines were edged away from their flotation gear enough so they could be gently attached by their magnetic backings to the steel hull of the ship. Each set of two mines was ten feet under the waterline and three feet apart.

When the mines were in place, one of the sappers swam to the front of the hull. A SEAL from the other side was there waiting. They signaled that they should set the timers. The men swam back to the mines on both sides, set the timers for three minutes, activated them, and swam quickly away toward the mouth of the huge cave. Once free of the cave, they stroked faster toward the half-completed pier, which was two hundred yards from the ship. They came to the pier and surfaced quietly.

Lampedusa nodded at Murdock. The mines were in place and the detonator/timers started.

All the SEALs had their heads out of the water. To be this close to a heavy blast such as was coming could damage or kill a diver with his head underwater.

"About now," Mahanani whispered.

The words were barely spoken when a rumble filled the air around them, then a muted roar, and a wave of water two feet tall rushed toward them. Almost at once, two more blasts went off underwater in the cave, which brought another surge of sound and racing water.

They could see the dark outline of the big ship, and watched as it tilted and then sank heavily forward to the bottom of the inside of the cave.

"How deep is it?" Murdock asked.

"Maybe twenty feet," Mahanani said. "Her deck won't be in water, but she sure as hell ain't going nowhere."

Sirens wailed. Lights flashed inside the tunnel. Murdock took a moment to watch the chaos they had started. More lights flashed; then the entire cave blazed with lights. The bow of the frigate had nosed deep into the water. Her deck slanted twenty degrees forward.

More sirens flashed. Truckloads of troops arrived at the front of the cave and in the lights, Murdock could see the soldiers start to work along the side of the inlet.

"Moving time," Murdock said. The SEALs slid into the water, gripped the rebreather mouthpieces, and swam under the surface to their comfortable fifteen feet. Murdock looked upward, and through the water could see bright flares. He checked again a few minutes later, and saw more flares. But no gunfire sounded or showed below the surface. The SEALs swam forward using their regular strokes to eat up the ocean between them and their pickup boat.

After stroking a half mile, the SEALs surfaced. They were still close to the point of land that extended south from the cave. Murdock counted his men; then Ed DeWitt came to the top of the Yellow Sea and indicated he had all of his men.

Behind them they could still see flashing lights and flares that went off high in the sky and floated down on parachutes. Far off they heard gunfire. None of the rounds came their way.

"Let's go a mile on the same compass heading before we surface this time," Murdock said. The men nodded and dove below the water, where many of them felt more at home than above, or on some enemy land mass.

When they surfaced the third time, Murdock knew they were in the approximate area where they had been dropped off. He couldn't see any boat, but the RIBs were small and painted black, which made them harder than ever to see.

They waited.

Far behind them, Murdock heard a growling sound of an engine.

"Patrol craft," Lampedusa said.

Soon they saw a searchlight sweeping the ocean in front of the craft as it came closer.

"Could be one of their large patrol crafts," Ed DeWitt said

from nearby. "They have a batch of them. Some are a hundred and forty feet long with one three-inch gun and some thirty-seven-millimeter guns and MGs. These guys could give us a bad time. Only good thing is they can't do over eighteen to nineteen knots."

"That's a lot of help," Jaybird said. "Where the hell is our RIB?"

"These patrol craft have radar?" Murdock asked.

"Far as I know they have surface-search only. Something called the Skin Head with an I-band. Whatever the hell that means."

"It means we're gonna have company in about five minutes," Murdock said. "Check your buddy lines. When he comes this way we go down to twenty feet and wait. We don't want anybody getting chewed up by a propeller."

"We don't even have the SATCOM," Holt said. "Why didn't we bring it, Cap?"

"Piece of cake like this, we didn't need it. Up to now, that is."

Ron Holt growled and got ready to dive. After this, wherever he went the fucking SATCOM was on his back.

"Here he comes," Murdock said. "Let's go down deep and hold."

The SEALs dove into the Yellow Sea as the North Korean Chodo-class patrol craft raced toward them.

9

The Yellow Sea
Off North Korea

Murdock felt the patrol craft go past them. It was twenty or thirty yards to one side. He surfaced slowly, then took a peek. The large-looking craft did a slow turn to the left and headed back the way it had come, missing the SEALs this time by two hundred yards.

The SEALs surfaced and moved together within talking range.

"So?" Ed DeWitt asked.

"Fucking long swim out another nine miles to that destroyer, then we probably couldn't find her," Jaybird said.

"We left the SATCOM back on the carrier," Holt said. "Sorry. Never do that again."

"Any ideas?" Murdock asked.

"Sonobuoy-type gadget," Ching said. "One of them little sonar balls we carry sometimes."

"Don't have one," Doc Ellsworth said. "Besides, we don't have a sub listening for us."

"Big fucking ocean out here," Fernandez said.

Murdock unzipped the waterproof compartment on his vest and took out his Motorola. He keyed it and spoke.

"This is SEAL Seven. RIB, do you copy?"

"Sonofabitch!" somebody growled.

"You had it planned all along," Bradford yelped.

The speaker came alive. "SEAL Seven. This is RIB, we copy. You have a light stick? Give us a pink one and we'll come fetch."

There was a small cheer. Murdock broke out a Cyalume light stick, twisted it, and held it up as high as he could. He put the radio back in the zippered wet-proof pouch.

"How the hell did you guys think those RIBs were going to find us, with a Ouija board?"

"A what?" Quinley asked.

"That's a fake game from the fifties that you ask questions and then shove a little pointer around to the answer you want," Mahanani said.

"I knew they'd find us all the time," Fernandez said.

"Like shit you did. You sounded dumb-assed scared," Douglas snapped.

"Can it you two, or you'll both swim back to the destroyer," DeWitt barked. "I want to see both of you as soon as we get to the carrier."

Three hours later, Ed DeWitt had the two SEALs from his squad braced at attention in front of him in the assembly room. The rest of the platoon had finished putting gear away and headed for their compartments.

"Now, we have this place to ourselves. I want to know what the fuck is going on. You two have been at each other's throats for half of this mission. Who wants to tell me what it's all about?"

Neither SEAL said a word or moved.

"Fine. Fernandez, go down to the far corner of the compartment and sit down."

"Sir . . ."

"Move it, sailor."

Fernandez looked back as he walked to the far end of the Ready Room. When he was sitting down, DeWitt stepped up so his face was an inch from Douglas's.

"Talk," he roared.

"Sir. Just a minor disagreement. Nothing more."

"Go on."

"That's it, sir. Stupid little argument. It's nothing."

"It's enough that it could get one of you killed on a mission, that's what it is. You act like you hate his guts, and Fernandez looks like he'd like to make mincemeat out of your heart."

"Yeah, well, maybe."

"No maybe. What happened?"

"Couple of months ago at a party. Little disagreement. I'll forget about it if Fernandez will."

"Just a little disagreement?"

"Right. Bet Fernandez will tell you the same thing."

"Anything else, sailor, before I bust your butt back to the regular Navy and ship you out to Adak, Alaska?"

"No, sir."

"Move it down to the other end of the compartment and sit on it." DeWitt waited until Douglas sat down; then he bellowed at Fernandez. The SEAL ran up to DeWitt the way they did in BUD/S. He braced in front of the JG and stared straight ahead.

The officer took a softer tone with Fernandez. "Miguel, I want you to tell me exactly what the friction is between you and Douglas. I don't care whose fault it is, just lay it out for me."

Fernandez took a deep breath, kept staring straight ahead.

"No big problem, sir. Just a small thing. I can work it out."

"Before or after you get yourself and one or two of the other members of this squad killed on a mission?"

"No worry about that, JG. I'll do my job."

"Douglas said the whole thing was just a little disagreement, is that right?"

"Yes, sir. Just a minor disagreement."

"Happened a couple of months ago?"

Fernandez took a quick look at his lieutenant, then nodded. "Yes, sir, couple of months back."

"What kind of a disagreement, Miguel?"

"Personal kind, sir."

"Kind you can't talk about?"

"Yes, sir."

"Anything more to say about it?"

"No, sir."

DeWitt scowled. If it was personal, he could go no farther. He had to, but he couldn't.

"Douglas, get your ass up here," DeWitt called.

When Douglas stood beside Fernandez, both stared straight ahead. DeWitt paced back and forth in front of them. He stopped and stared hard at each one.

"I've about had it with both of you. Anymore jawing at each other, any physical confrontation of any kind, and you're both out of SEALs, you read me?"

"Yes, sir, Lieutenant, sir," both shouted in unison as if they were back in BUD/S. "Fernandez, you'll walk third in the platoon lineup. On fieldwork, Douglas is next to last in the line. I don't want you to talk to each other, never tie yourselves together with a buddy line, and just the fuck stay away from each other. Maybe I should ship both your asses up to Adak and let you freeze your balls off."

Both SEALs stared straight ahead without saying a word.

DeWitt's scowl was so deep it hurt his cheeks. "Get the hell out of here. You two will be toeing the mark in every fucking jot and tittle or you're booted out of SEALs. You two read me?"

"Yes, sir, JG," the two men roared in unison.

"Good. Dismissed."

Fernandez ran for the door. Douglas let him go ahead, trailing behind, but wanting out of the compartment fast.

Ed DeWitt slammed his palm down on the nearby table. Nothing. He had gotten absolutely nothing out of them. He still had no idea what the problem was. It was the kind of situation that could split a squad in half and cause somebody to get killed. He'd watch them closer than ever the next few days.

Captain Irving Olson, Commander Air Wing on the *Monroe*, sat in the CIC watching the display panels around him. He had ten F-18's out looking for targets of opportunity along the roadways leading to the front lines. So far they hadn't found much.

"Home Base, this is Buzzer Sixteen."

"Go, Sixteen."

"Got me a convoy coming south. Must be twenty-five, thirty miles north of the old DMZ. I'm out of ammo. Even used up my last Maverick on what I figured must be some kind of an Army headquarters just north of the old DMZ. These trucks could use a good hosing down with twenty-mike. Anybody in this area?"

"Come home if you're dry, Sixteen. I'll vector somebody else up that way. The trucks using lights?"

"Home Base, they use them until they hear an aircraft, then go dark."

"Roger that, Sixteen."

"Home Base. This is Buzzer Ten. I'm north of the DMZ about ten. What part of the DMZ has those trucks, middle, east, or west?"

"Buzzer Ten, this is Sixteen. Almost due north of Panmunjom. Follow that road up north and you can't miss them. My guess is about twenty trucks. Good hunting."

CAG Olson rubbed his forehead. The damn headache was back. Too much coffee, no sleep, too many planes in the air. He tried to think when he'd slept last. From 0400 to 0600 way back yesterday. He checked his watch. Just after 0300 now. Hell, he hadn't even been up twenty-four yet.

"Sir," one of the techs said.

CAG Olson thought he heard something.

"Captain, sir, the radio needs you. Buzzer Ten is calling."

The CAG shook his head to clear it, and grabbed the handset. "Yes, Buzzer Ten, Home Base here."

"What a sight, Captain. Like a string of pearl lights. I've got them. Head-on for the first go-round. I've got a full load of twenties. I'll make it a damn sharp angle and get a better concentration of hits. I'm moving and their lights are blinking out. Got them."

"Go, Ten." CAG Olson held the handset so tightly he felt

his fingers go numb. He put it down, eased up, then changed hands, and took it back.

Buzzer Seven landed on the big carrier; then Buzzer Thirteen set down. Olson still had eight out there on a hunting trip.

"Oh, yeah, CAG. This is Buzzer Ten. I buried the first one in line and then some more so they can't get around him. Two of the bastards are on fire. Makes for a better target."

"Scratch them all, Ten. You have any Mavericks left?"

"Yes, sir, two, but I can't find any tanks."

"Use them on the trucks. Hunt some more when you splash those."

"Roger that, CAG. I'm around again, going in for a run. Damn but those burning trucks are a big help down there."

Captain Olson shook his head to fight off drooping eyes and checked the displays. He still had seven birds out there.

"Home Base to Buzzers. Anybody need a drink? Talk to me."

The reports came in with percentages of fuel left. Everyone was in good shape. They were so close to the front that there was little fly time between takeoff and action.

"Home Base, Buzzer Twelve. How wide is the penetration of the NKs on the east side of the line?"

"Five to ten miles on most of it."

"Okay, then those must be friendlies down there. I'll get further north. Thanks."

CAG held on. It would take another two hours to shepherd the last section of the flight to targets and back home. His job. He'd do it. Yeah. Then tomorrow the Tomcats would head out. Sleep? Maybe sometime next week. He reached for the caffeine pills. Two more wouldn't hurt. His eyes went wide as he gulped them down with a shot of cold coffee. He held up the cup, and somebody took it and refilled it. The techs just came on fresh at midnight. Bright and eager and so damn *young*. But they were good at their work.

The speaker broke into his thoughts, and he hit the handset and went back to work.

• • •

Gunner's Mate First Class Miguel Fernandez ran to his sleeping compartment and rushed inside. It was for six men, and the other five bunks were full. At least Douglas was in another compartment. He stripped to his underwear and slid into the bunk.

For a moment his teeth chattered. They did that when he was so angry he couldn't control himself. That damn Douglas. The asshole could get them both kicked out of SEALs.

He hadn't worked all the way through BUD/S and been ground down until he wanted to scream and ring the bell at least fifty times, just to be slammed out of the SEALs because of some stupid shithead like Douglas. Couldn't the JG see what was going on?

No, he couldn't. He didn't know.

Fernandez loved the SEALs. He'd tried four times to get in, and had finally made it. No way he was going to fuck up and get booted. No way.

That first week at BUD/S had been so shocking and traumatic that six men rang the bell and quit. The next week ten more decided the price was too much to pay.

The shock of BUD/S was overwhelming. First there were the extensive physical tests that had to be passed just to get in the front door. He had shuddered when he looked at the list, but he had worked hard and passed. He'd had to swim five hundred yards breaststroke or sidestroke in twelve and a half minutes. Then rest ten minutes and do forty-two push-ups in two minutes.

After a two-minute rest he'd had to do fifty sit-ups in two minutes. Two minutes more of rest, then do eight continuous pull-ups without a time limit. Next came a ten-minute rest before he went on a 1.5-mile run wearing combat boots and trousers. He'd had to make it in eleven and a half minutes.

He had trained for six months before he attempted the physical tests, and just barely passed them. Then he went through six weeks of physical training and orientation to the Naval Special Warfare way of life before the real SEAL training began.

That was the beginning point. The BUD/S six-month course was carefully designed to test the physical and mental capacity of the candidates. They ran everywhere they went in the loose sand around the Coronado, California, base.

The First Phase of BUD/S training was mainly conditioning, with more soft-sand runs, full-out sprints, swimming, a little trick called drownpoofing, calisthenics, and martial arts.

Always there was the mental hazing, taunting the candidates to quit and ring the bell. Forcing them to complete harder and harder physical workouts.

SEAL training concentrated on mental stress and water. If the men couldn't take the hazing, the physical exertion, being in classes and swims and runs for twelve hours a day, then they would never last six months to become SEALs.

Water was the clincher. Early in the training the SEAL candidates were put in a ten-foot-deep pool. It was done to be sure that the men were comfortable in and under the water and didn't panic.

Fernandez remembered this torture especially. He'd never been a strong swimmer. Now he had to be. The men had their hands tied behind their backs and their ankles bound together. Then they had to sink to the bottom of the pool and come back up. This was done repeatedly; then they had to do somersaults in the water and retrieve a diving mask off the bottom with their teeth. This was all done while tied hand and foot. About ten percent of the candidates for SEALs never get past this waterproofing.

Hell Week, all the training including going in and out of the Pacific Ocean's breakers in the small inflatable boats, had been one long and continuous strain for Fernandez. Early on he'd been yelled at by all the instructors, called spic and greaser and wetback. He had learned to let it all roll off his back and grin.

The tough training, and the working closely together, had bred SEALs out of mere sailors. They had learned to support each other, to rely on each other, to trust their lives to the hands of the men working with them. Working as a team became second nature.

Now, after all of his hard work in getting through BUD/S and his two years in SEALs, he wasn't going to be rooted out of the team by some snot-nosed, shit-faced Douglas prick.

Before Fernandez went to sleep he made up his mind about one thing. He would never react to any of Douglas's remarks or looks. He'd ignore the jackass. He'd stay a SEAL no matter what happened to Dirty Dog Douglas. That decided, he slept.

10

USS *Monroe*
Yellow Sea off Korea

Murdock came awake groggy and unrested. He checked his watch. Past 1020. His feet hit the deck and he groaned. When was he going to learn how to wake up bright and alert? He could do it on patrol or a mission where it counted. Without a mission it was groggy time.

Murdock made it to the officers' mess in time to eat, and sat there a target of opportunity when Don Stroh walked in.

"How goes the war?" Murdock asked as Stroh sat down with his usual two cups of coffee.

"Can't tell yet. The Eighth Army is glad the *Monroe*'s fifty-eight planes are set up to make ground attacks. Been a big lift for the Air Force guys." He paused. "Didn't catch you when you got in last night. How did it go?"

"Wet. We got in, did the job, and got out without anyone wounded. That's good news for us."

"Great. I guess by this time you've figured out that you SEALs are firemen on this mission. Bound to be a lot of small fires to put out on a dumb-assed war like this one. Fact is, it isn't even a war. The President and the Congress haven't said it is. What we're doing is responding to an attack on a treaty

ally, and supporting this ally with all of our capability." He
frowned. "Well, not with all of our capability. No nukes are
going on this one."

"Good. Now what is that little twitch under your right eye
all about? Usually it means something is afoot."

"Afoot? You're kidding. I haven't heard that word since I
was in the seventh grade in Connecticut. Mrs. Ambrose
always used it. We got tired of hearing it."

"So, Stroh, what?"

"Hate to tell you. I told Eighth Army it was an Army job
for a team of sappers. Some bird colonel said they had tried
three times. It's a bridge across a river. No way around this
river for ten miles each way."

"The NKs have tanks on the far side and they own the
bridge and want to bring the tanks over when they get their
resupply, right?"

"Yeah, you hear something?"

"Just the wheels grinding around in your head, Stroh. Why
can't the Army blow up a bridge?"

"High ground. The NKs have the high ground on the north
side. It's two hundred feet above the south side of the river.
They just blow away any try our guys make for the bridge.
They control a quarter of a mile with their machine guns and
some fancy quad-fifties they have."

"I thought the Air Force had smart bombs."

"Oh, yeah, they do. The Navy has laser-aimed bombs too,
but somehow they won't do the job right. The Army doesn't
want to blow the bridge into kindling. Just disable it so the
NKs can't get across it."

"Then when the Eight Army decides to go north, they want
to have the bridge repaired for their tanks in quick order."

"Something like that."

"You have pictures?"

"'Deed I do, young man. Plenty. Some marked with where
the Army tried to get their charges anchored before they got
blown away last night."

Murdock took the sheaf of eight-by-ten glossy photos and
worked through them. They showed the bridge, its supports,
the river below, the banks on both sides.

"Can you do it?" Stroh asked.

"Give me a couple of minutes here, sharp stick. Lots of things to consider." He picked out one shot of a side view of the bridge and another from almost overhead.

"We can give it a try. See this section right here?" Murdock pointed to the lead-in to the bridge from the concrete roadway behind it.

"Yeah, it's on the far side of the bridge."

"It's the only place that can be blown out without damaging the structure of the bridge itself. We blow out that twenty-foot approach and the tanks got nowhere to go."

"Yeah, but what about our tanks that want to get across?"

"Easy. Send a tank out there with an engineering team to put up an emergency twenty-foot bridge. Those guys can do that in about three hours. Then shoot over the tanks and you're on your way."

"You sure this will work?"

"Hell, no, Stroh. Nobody gives guarantees these days. It could blow down the whole damn bridge. It's a risk."

Stroh emptied his second cup of coffee. "Easy talk, but how the fuck do you get over to the far side of the bridge to blow it? The NKs have that whole structure zeroed in with machine guns."

"We go in and they never see us."

"How?"

"I have to give away all my secrets?"

"Damn right. If I'm to get a go from General Reynolds."

"We go in upstream a quarter or half mile, come down the flow, and get out under the bridge. We go up underneath the bridge where the NKs can't see us, set the timers, go back to the water, and go underwater downstream another half mile and get out on the south side."

Stroh looked at the pictures. Slowly he nodded. "All right. You have the right explosives?"

"TNAZ."

"Right. Let me talk to the general. I'll get a go from him, but I'll warn him that the bridge should be fit for use, but it might not. It's a better risk than using smart bombs."

Without a good-bye, Stroh stood and hurried out of the

mess. Murdock ordered another plate of hot cakes, and made it into the SEALs' assembly compartment just after 1120.

Jaybird had the platoon working over equipment. Murdock scowled remembering that he still hadn't gotten any higher rate for Jaybird. He was sitting in a senior chief petty officer's slot and still was first class. Murdock was going to twist some tails somewhere. The guy deserved a higher rate and more pay.

"What gives, Cap? Do you have that gleam in your eye again?"

Murdock grinned. It was hard to fool Jaybird. "Not sure. Might have another job to do tonight. If it's a go. Don is talking to General Reynolds now over at Eighth Army. Just never can tell. How are we fixed for line?"

"What kind and how long, sir?"

"Man-weighted for at least a hundred feet. We'd have to have at least six of them."

"Nothing like that in our gear. I'd wager we can pick up some line like that from the big boat here."

"Hope so. Why don't you check it out as a possible."

"Right, Cap. Rope work. Yeah, I like rope work. At least a hundred feet? No sweat, Cap. I'm on the phone."

Murdock still had the envelope of pictures. He pulled Ed DeWitt to one side and showed them to him. Ed looked up.

"So, a bridge?"

"Yeah, look at that first on-ramp-type section before it comes to the first bridge main supports."

"Okay, not all that sturdy. We gonna blow it?"

"Could we blow that section away and not damage the integrity of the main span?"

"Yeah, should work. We'd have to get the juice in the right spots. Yeah, I'd say it would work." He looked up. "Stroh must have caught you. He was here looking."

"In the mess. He's talking with General Reynolds over in Eighth Army now. They want the bridge taken out, but so they can use it later."

"Engineers could throw a tank-proof span over that twenty feet in two hours."

"Yeah, I gave them three hours in the dark."

"How we get in?"

"Wet. Come down the current underwater. Get out right under the span. Then use ropes over the upper areas and go up the lines."

"How far is it from mud to beam up there?" Ed asked.

"Sixty, maybe seventy feet?"

"My guess is about sixty-five. We'd need a hundred and thirty feet of half-inch line."

"We can get by with three-eighths-inch if it's nylon braid."

Murdock called in Lampedusa, Bradford, and Jack Mahanani. They looked at the bridge and listened.

"So they control both sides of the land and we go in wet, right?" Lam said.

Jaybird came back from the phone. "Hey, yes. What's a Navy without some line? We can get whatever we want. They said a hundred feet in nylon would be easiest to use and get through the water. We can pick it up whenever we need it."

The phone rang and Franklin picked it up.

"Commander," he called, and held up the handset.

Murdock took the instrument and listened. "Right. We'll be ready to get out of here just before dark and move in and pick up a friendly local guide. We can get supplies we need here. Right." Murdock hung up. Everyone had stopped talking and looked at him.

"Gentlemen, get your gear ready, we've got a wet job to do. We'll use the rebreathers and the water is going to be muddy. We'll shove off from here in a helo about 1700."

DeWitt kept looking at the photographs. He had one out that showed the top of the bridge and the slope above it.

"Cap, looks like there's about a hundred yards from the crest of the hill back there to the bridge. That area must be under fire from the south side. Be fine if we could have some 105's or some fifty-calibers warm up those areas on call. Give the NKs something to think about besides some body playing with their bridge."

Murdock grunted. "Yeah. Good idea. Get in touch with Stroh and have him put you in contact with the commander in that sector. Set it up so all we need to do is use the SATCOM and ask for the rounds to start. Make it on call. We're not sure when we'll be getting in there. My guess is it would go best after midnight."

"Sounds good. Give the artillery a chance to zero in some firing concentrations to use when we call for them."

Then the platoon gathered around and they began to plan the mission.

"Everybody going, or could eight men do the job?" Jaybird asked.

"Security, we need everyone to give the guys on the ropes some security," Les Quinley said.

"Everyone," Murdock said.

"How many men on ropes?" DeWitt asked.

They kicked it around, looked at the structure of the bridge, and decided that six could do it. They could scramble up the far bank to get their ropes over, then go up the ropes and plant the charges.

Murdock picked out the five men besides himself who were the best at the rope climb on the O course. Franklin, Adams, Lampedusa, Ching, and Sterling.

They decided they'd use smaller charges of TNAZ on the areas next to the main support, and larger charges back where the bridge met the land. That way the whole section should be blown off and drop into the river below.

Ed DeWitt found Stroh, who made the call to the Army people and contacted the commander in the sector where the bridge was. They had concentrations of 105's on the ridgeline behind the bridge. Yes, they would lay in ten rounds on call from the SATCOM to their TAC frequency.

The SEALs left promptly at 1700 in a reliable CH-46 Sea Knight, and set down at dusk near the MLR about ten miles west of Panmunjom. Here the bulge made by the North troops was about seven miles beyond the old DMZ. An ROK captain met them. He would coordinate the artillery. He gave Ron Holt the frequency to use. Holt dialed it up and made immediate contact with the artillery. The ROK soldier there even spoke English.

They were a quarter of a mile from the river. The SEALs wore their jungle cammies, combat vests, rebreathers, and fins. They figured they wouldn't be in the water long enough to need the wet suits.

They found the right spot, then sacked out for three hours. Just at midnight, a guide led them to the water. Murdock and the climbers went in the water first, then DeWitt and the rest of the men. Everyone knew precisely what to do. The timers would be set for ten minutes and coordinated precisely to be activated at the same time.

Each of the climbers carried a 125-foot coil of nylon rope. They figured eight charges would drop the end section of the bridge. They brought twelve bombs all packaged and ready to go.

Murdock eyed the roiling water. It was still in near-flood stage from recent rains. "Buddy lines," he said. "Lam and I will lead. Ed, bring up the rear. No stragglers. Let the current take you, but stay underwater. Don't overshoot. It's only a little more than a quarter mile."

They walked into the water and slipped under the muddy flow. Murdock had no way to count strokes or tell distance. He surfaced twice. The third time he saw the bridge coming up fast. He stroked for the far shore. The river was about forty yards across here. He and Lam came out directly under the bridge. He left Lam at the water's edge to bird-dog in the rest of the men, and went to check on the bank under the bridge. There was a small piece of dry land about twenty feet wide, then the slant up of the bank to the bridge sixty feet overhead. He could climb it with no problem. He went up and tied off his rope to one of the support girders.

No problem for the hot new explosive TNAZ. By the time he got back to the river, all but two men were out of the water. Ed had them in defensive positions. The four other climbers moved to the dry area and looked up at the bridge.

"That section is longer than we figured," Jaybird said. "It's at least thirty feet. No sweat. We use the same eight charges and blow the fucker right out of there without hurting the rest of it."

"Let's get to it," Murdock said. "If it stays this quiet around here, we'll use the 105 rounds for our getaway. Up the hill.

On that rope. We'll hit the girders and take our assigned spots. The faster we work, the quicker we get back to breakfast."

Murdock went up the rope he had just tied off, got to the top, and swung up on the first girder. Under the roadway was a pair of X-shaped box girders on their sides. The charges would go on the ends of the X's on top and bottom on both sides.

Murdock went to the far end of the first girder, and planted the TNAZ bomb where it would cut the steel in half and leave that part of the bridge without support. Above him Lam put a charge on the girder there. The other four men worked their positions. It took them less than three minutes to get the charges in place.

"Ten minutes on the timers," Murdock whispered to Lam. In the dark they couldn't use signs. Murdock contacted two of the other men, and Lam talked to the last two. They all returned to their charges.

"Now," Murdock said loud enough so all could hear. They pushed in the timers on the petards, activating the timers; then all six worked carefully back to the bank and went down the rope to the ground.

Murdock found Holt.

"Crank up that mother and get some artillery in there," he said.

Lam made the call, got confirmation.

"On the way in two minutes, Cap," Holt said.

"Gentlemen, let's get the hell out of Dodge. We've got about five minutes to bang time."

Before they could move, a machine gun chattered on the edge of the bank above them. Rounds slapped into the ground and the edge of the water.

Murdock and the others sent return fire at the MG's position. It stopped for a moment.

"Second Squad, into the water, go, go, go." Murdock barked. "The rest of us, find some cover and burn out that MG up there."

The enemy weapon fired again. By that time the SEALs had spread out and found what cover there was. They sent fifty rounds of return fire.

Murdock saw that the Second Squad was out of sight. He sent a final three-round burst at the MG, then waved. "Let's get wet." First Squad sprinted the twenty feet to the water and slid in quietly. The MG opened up again, this time joined by half-a-dozen rifles as the North Koreans wasted lead shooting where the SEALs had been.

Murdock swam with the current and stayed on top. How far was a quarter of a mile? He saw figures on the far shore and swam across the current. Ed and his squad waved.

Just then Murdock heard the whispers of the 105 rounds going overhead. They landed seconds later somewhere to the rear. The machine gun and rifle fire behind them stopped.

A moment later the sky lit up behind them with brilliant lights, and a roaring wave of sound and wind whipped against their faces. The SEALs looked back, but couldn't see the bridge. Now they could hear a grinding and crashing as something came down hard and hit the ground, sending out a minor shock wave.

"Looks like we blew one bridge," Murdock said. He looked around. "How far downstream are we?"

"Hundred yards at the most," Ed DeWitt said. "Just wanted to get us back together again."

Murdock waved and called softly as his men came by. They all came out of the water. "Somebody count, we got fifteen?"

"Fourteen," Jaybird said. "Who the hell isn't here?"

Before they discovered the identity of the missing SEAL, they heard splashing and Doc Ellsworth came out of the water, one arm pushed into his combat vest.

"He's hit," Murdock said.

They got Doc on solid ground and he shivered. "Damn fucking horseshit fucker got me in the elbow. Fucking elbow. Bleeding like a whore in heat."

Jack Mahanani pushed Ron Holt away, stripped open the medic bag Doc carried, and looked at the elbow in the pale moonlight.

"Keep it tucked in there. I'll wrap it up and stop the bleeding. You need at least one ampoule. They in the usual spot?"

Doc Ellsworth nodded. They could see his white upper teeth biting into his lower lip.

"No more wet for this boy," Mahanani said. "Why can't we walk down this side of the river and then turn inland. The South Ks must know we're out here."

"Yeah, but their MLR is gonna look for us a quarter of a mile on down," Ed DeWitt said. "We don't want to get sliced to pieces by some angry ROK battalion."

"Lam, out front a hundred," Murdock said. "We don't know how close to the river the fucking MLR is along here. We'll have to play it by ear and damn quiet. Quiet, but as quickly as we can. Doc isn't in the best of shape. Usual formation. Let's move."

Ed DeWitt made sure that he put Joe Douglas at the end of the marching order and kept Fernandez right behind himself and Al Adams. He hadn't forgotten their animosity.

Lam worked ahead for a hundred yards, then went to the ground. Murdock slid into the grass and weeds beside him.

Lam pointed to where the moonlight glanced off the river.

"An NK patrol, I'd guess," he said. "I saw them shoot a line across the river. Not over thirty yards wide here. They're moving hand-over-hand across the line."

"How many of them?"

"I can see twelve."

"We sure that they are NKs?"

"No. But a South patrol coming back would already have a line across the river. Right?"

"Yeah. Let's pick off the first two and see what happens." Both men screwed on sound suppressors and leveled in. The silenced rounds made more noise than they wanted them to, but they worked. The first two men on the line collapsed, dropped into the swift water, and washed downstream.

A low wail came from the third man in line. He lifted an automatic rifle and pounded off six rounds into the brush on the south side, but thirty yards from Murdock.

"The rest of them," Murdock said. Murdock and Lam moved back along the rope with their rounds, and soon had company from Jaybird. A minute later, the line was empty and the men still alive on the far side of the river ran up the slope and over the ridgeline.

Lam headed out downstream. Murdock and Jaybird got the men behind them moving as well.

Lam settled in behind a good-sized tree and looked inland. He had led the platoon in a hundred yards from the river, and ahead he could see mounds of fresh dirt he figured were either trenches or gun emplacements.

"Could be the MLR along here," Lam whispered to Murdock, who settled in beside him.

"Yeah. Wonder if any of them speak English?" Murdock sent Lam back to bring up Ching. The Chinese saw the situation.

"Try some Japanese on them," Murdock said. "A lot of the Koreans remember Japanese."

"First we all get some cover. I've heard these bastards are super-trigger-happy."

When the three had pushed behind trees or rocks, Ching gave it a try.

"Hey, you South Koreans. We're Americans out here. United States. Don't shoot." He called it in Japanese. There was no response. He started to repeat it, but a machine gun and about ten rifles opened fire, riddling the small trees and brush where they crouched.

Murdock slithered away from the fire, and went to the rest of the platoon.

"You guys with forty-mikes. We need you to each fire three at max range downstream. Be sure they hit land. Do it now and maybe the distraction will let us slip through the damn South Koreans' MLR here."

The men fired the rounds. Murdock led them back as close to his previous position as he could. Lam crawled back.

"Ching is moving ahead. He says he heard at least half the troops up there bug out downriver for the action down there. Those our forties?"

"True," Murdock said. He whispered to the rest of the men. "We're going to have to go through here like ghosts. Ching and Lam and I will try to quiet anyone left. You hear a morning dove call, you come quickly, quietly."

Murdock crawled away toward the MLR.

Ching was ahead. He moved at a crouch toward the new earthworks. He was almost there when he heard two Koreans talking. He slanted to the left, found a spot without fresh dirt, and eased up the slight rise. He rolled over the dirt and came down in a trench three feet deep.

Ching looked both ways. Nobody. He moved toward where he had heard the two men. He spotted them when he was twenty feet away and the trench made a small turn. They looked over the lip of the berm. One of them sat behind a heavy machine gun.

Ching moved ahead without a sound. He was almost there. He picked up a rock off the new dirt and thew it beyond the two Koreans.

Both yelled.

One swung the machine gun that way. Ching rushed the last twenty feet, clubbed the machine gunner with his Colt carbine, and covered the other Korean, who looked around but didn't reach for his weapon.

"Americans," Ching said.

The Korean grinned. "Melican, OK, GI."

Ching used a pencil flash from his combat vest and blinked it three times toward the river. He got three blinks back.

Five minutes later, all the SEALs were over the berm and moving to the rear. An SK lieutenant had showed up after a few minutes and designated one of his men to lead the SEALs to the rear. Doc Ellsworth was really hurting by that time. Others carried his weapon, his medic bag, and his combat vest. Mahanani walked step for step with him, and caught him twice when he fell.

Holt had the SATCOM up and working on Air TAC One. The Sea Knight had been on the ground waiting for them two miles away. It found them with the aid of a red flare.

Mahanani gave Doc another shot of morphine, and a half hour later they landed on the *Monroe*, where two medics and a doctor met them on the flight deck. Murdock went along with Doc. Ed got the SEALs back to their assembly room.

Murdock didn't like the way the Navy doctors were consulting about Ellsworth's elbow. They had put in half-a-dozen shots to deaden the area. Ellsworth was conscious, but half out of it from the medications.

At last one of the doctors came out to Murdock.

"Commander, it's bad. The elbow is never going to work right again. It's all busted up to hell in there. Maybe a replacement joint down the road a ways."

"It won't be stiff, will it?"

"No, but he won't be doing any fancy gymnastics with it either. Is he a SEAL?"

"Yes."

"Tough. Not a chance of staying with you. You can tell him tomorrow. Now, we have some reconstruction to do and some pins to put in. Understand he was your medic."

"True. Three years."

"Sorry."

Murdock slammed his fist into the wall and stormed out of sick bay.

11

USS *Monroe*

Don Stroh waited for Murdock in the SEALs' assembly room. The men were still in their wet cammies. They spent the time cleaning and oiling weapons, checking out ammo supply, and making a list of what they needed. By this time Jaybird had four boxes of rounds he kept locked so he didn't have to run to ordnance every day.

Murdock came in wet and angry. He didn't see Stroh at first. The CIA man sat in a chair near the back of the big room.

"Listen up," Murdock growled. "We lost Doc Ellsworth. His elbow is shattered. Not a chance he can get back with us. We're down to fourteen men. I need every one of you, so don't go and get yourself shot up or killed.

"If some of you don't know, we nailed that fucking bridge. That thirty-foot span fell into the river. So we should have a breather. What time is it?"

"Just past 0300, Skipper," Ronson said.

"Okay, get out of these wet cammies, grab some shut-eye. That damn Stroh can't have anything for us for at least two days."

Some of the men laughed nervously. Murdock looked up sharply. Don Stroh stood up from the far side of the room.

"Like hell he couldn't," Stroh said. "We've got a war on here, people, in case you hadn't noticed. I haven't been to sleep for thirty-six hours and things are getting a little fuzzy, but General Reynolds called again. He knows it's too late to do anything tonight, so he's calling it for tonight—morning, I guess—at 0500."

"Calling what, Stroh?" Murdock asked.

"This is as bad as the Yalu River retreat. He's had another unit overrun. Not that it's all that important in the scheme of the twenty-five-mile front, but the lost outfit includes a brigadier general and his staff of six officers. They have a SATCOM and they're holed up in a small patch of woods about two miles behind the current MLR."

"Two miles, Stroh? You've got to be kidding. Tell them to get off their fat asses and hike out. They can make two miles in half an hour for shit sakes."

"We're talking about one brigadier, two bird colonels, three lieutenant colonels, and one lowly major. They just ain't used to hiking anywhere."

"Tell them to get used to it. We've got a war on here."

"You can tell them when you see them. General Reynolds wants it to go down this way. We get your platoon to the MLR an hour before daylight. That gives you an hour to get across the MLR and jog in the two miles to the patch of woods. This part of the line is not held in any strength. The NKs are pushing in other sectors, not this one. So there should be almost no opposition for you to get to the general."

"Then what's the Eighth Army have planned for us?" Murdock asked.

"Up to you. They suggest that you might want to wait until dark to make your way out of there. During the daylight you would be a security force for the brass."

"Baby-sitters, you mean?"

"That too. With full dark, you could take your charges, put them in the middle of your platoon, and work your way back to the MLR, where the good guys will create a diversion on one side and you can walk across the main line with not a shot fired."

"Don't count on it. We had to come across an MLR tonight. There were plenty of shots fired."

"That's the assignment. You have time to change into dry cammies, get restocked with ammo, and lift off from the flight deck in twenty-two minutes."

"This general, is he worth it?"

"From what I hear, he is. The two birds are also top-grade."

Murdock nodded. "Don't just sit there, SEALs. Get fresh cammies and some ammo and let's get out of here. This is the new version of Hell Week."

"Yeah," Bradford said. "But here we get to shoot at the bad guys."

Third Platoon made the chopper almost half a minute late, but the bird waited for them. Stroh went along. He sat beside Murdock and shouted so he could be understood.

"You want an ROK interpreter with you?"

"Yeah, one with a good automatic rifle and lots of ammo. I'm two men short now. You want to fill in, Stroh?"

The CIA field man jolted back against the helo and shook his head. It was the first laugh Murdock had had all week.

Nearly an hour later, Third Platoon crawled out of a truck and hurried up a hundred yards to a bunker. An American first lieutenant led them there and pointed.

"The MLR is along here. There's about a hundred yards of no-man's-land out there, then you'll come to the NKs' bunkers. All are freshly made. We'll send one-oh-fives into the sector directly ahead, to soften them up, then send out a raiding party five hundred yards to the left. That should drain a lot of the manpower from this sector so you can get through quickly, and we hope without firing a shot."

He looked at the weapons. "Lots of suppressors. That's good. Use them."

As he finished speaking, they heard the whisper of artillery rounds spiraling over head, then the *karumph* as the heavy rounds exploded along the NKs' main line of resistance.

"Fifteen rounds, then two minutes later the attack to the south," the lieutenant said. "That's your signal to move out. Good luck."

Murdock had changed their usual order of march. They would go single file, Alpha Squad first, Bravo second. All of the silenced weapons would be at the head of each squad. Lam would be out in front by twenty yards.

The last 105 round exploded in front, and Murdock used the NVGs to check the landscape.

"Nothing moving out there," he said. "Let's get a two-minute head start."

Lam moved out as silent as a fresh breeze. Murdock went second, with Ron Holt close behind him. They kept low, moved from one bit of cover to the next. The land between the lines had been shot up considerably. They were halfway across it when they heard the attack on to the south along the line. They waited. Lam nodded. He came back and whispered.

"Hear men moving to the south. Quite a lot of them hiking that way to reinforce. Sounds good."

Murdock used his night-vision goggles again. He spotted a bunker ahead and slightly to the right. Beside that was an earthwork. He had no idea what might be behind it. They moved ahead again, slower this time.

Lam came to within ten feet of the edge of the berm. A figure rose up over the side of the bunker. Lam fired twice with his silenced carbine and the man vanished over the side. Lam ran hard the last few yards to the berm, and lifted up so he could see over it.

Murdock had seen his move and charged up beside him. They looked different ways along the mound of dirt and the shallow trench. The only man they saw was the dead one lying below in the trench.

"Move, move," Murdock said into his mike. The Motorolas would come in handy on this mission. Lam and Murdock, then Holt vaulted over the mound, hit the other side, and ran straight ahead. They passed what had once been a series of bunkers but now were empty.

Behind him, Murdock could hear his men clearing the MLR and running to catch up with the rest of the platoon. Five minutes later they were clear of the MLR trenches and bunkers, and even one kitchen that had been abandoned to send more men to the attack point south.

They jogged forward. The interpreter they had with them carried a new M-16 automatic rifle. Murdock told him to come to the front. The man studied the landscape for a minute. He had been briefed on where the brigadier was holed up. He slanted them to the left and they hurried forward.

There were faint light streaks to the east. Murdock kept them jogging forward. The Korean changed his mind and angled them farther to the left. They saw the tops of the trees and the first real light about the same time.

"Yes, right bunch of trees," the Korean guide and interpreter said. They flat out ran the last one hundred yards, crashed into brush, and through it and into the cover/ concealment of the thick growth and a few towering pine trees.

When all his men were inside, Murdock motioned for them to be quiet. Lam and the interpreter moved ahead slowly, checking any spot where the officers might be hiding.

It was full light when Lam came back grinning.

"Found them, Cap. All eight of them are crammed into the center of a thorn thicket so tough and gnarly nobody would want to try to get through it. The major found it for them, from what he said. Inside it's hollowed out and there's enough room to sit down."

Murdock went up with Lam, and found the brigadier general and his major just outside the thorn thicket.

"General, Lieutenant Commander Murdock at your service."

A big grin spilled over the Army man's face. "Damned glad to see the Navy. SEALs, aren't you. Yes, good. We didn't hear any shoot-outs to the south, so my guess is you got here without much of a problem."

"Right, General. Looks like we're stuck here for the rest of the day. We'll see about getting your group back to friendly lines as soon as it gets dark tonight."

"Yes, we figured that. Did you bring us anything?"

Murdock grinned. "Sure as hell did, General." He touched his lip mike. "Bring up the packages."

Four SEALs came forward, each unstrapping a pack off his back. They handed them to the general, who laughed and thanked them as he and the major hurried back into the thicket and vanished.

"Why do they get all the good food?" Lam asked.

"Because he's a general, that's why. We set up a perimeter defense, then every other man can sack out or eat an MRE for breakfast. You've never had it so good."

Two hours later, Horse Ronson used the Motorola.

"Cap, you best look at this. Some kind of an armored personnel carrier rolling across fields out to the north. Looks like he'll miss our position by a half mile. Must be one of the older Russian-made rigs. My guess is it has a fifty-caliber MG mounted up front."

Murdock and Lam moved to the northern edge of the half acre of woodlands.

Lam checked the vehicle through his binoculars. "Oh, yeah, talk about old. Wonder how they get spare parts for it?"

The Korean slid in beside Murdock.

"Often personnel carrier like that come ahead of column of troops. Could be replacements or just reserves moving up to this sector."

The big rig had stopped a half mile off. Within five minutes, they spotted a column of troops coming over the hill. The men were four abreast and the line at least twenty-five long. A hundred men. All carried weapons, but they couldn't tell just what.

"Will they stay clear of this woodland?" Murdock asked.

"Only come here if they need firewood to cook their meal," the Korean said. "They will have rice roll over shoulder. Full, it good for three, four days. Empty, might steal chickens and roast over fire."

The men watched as the North Korean troops came abreast of their woodland, still four hundred yards away, and continued on past.

Murdock headed back past the hiding spot and heard

raucous laughter. He found the entranceway and crawled forward. Halfway there he met the major.

"Major, no more of that laughing. We're in a precarious spot here. Half of those men in there outrank me, but I'm the commander of this mission. Either you or I will chew tail for ten minutes on those officers insisting that they shut up and be quiet. Clear?"

The major grinned. "You better let me tell them. Generals don't like to be scolded."

"Tell him we just missed being investigated by an armored personnel carrier and a hundred armed troops. They went past us four hundred yards to the east. I don't intend to let him and his colonels endanger the lives of my men."

"Right, Commander. I'll impress him with the gravity of the situation."

Murdock found Holt, and talked on the SATCOM with the American contact officer who had escorted them to the MLR.

"Yes, Lieutenant. We're here, no problems. More North troops moving into the area. We'll be coming out at first dark tonight. Hope you can provide us with a fake attack along the line somewhere. We don't want to have to fight our way through more than fifty to a hundred NKs along here."

"You'll have it. Let us know when you leave the hideout, and about when you'll get to the MLR. It's on the books. Everyone here is anxious to get the package back safely."

Murdock grunted and handed the set back to Holt. "Keep the box turned on and tuned to his frequency. Just in case they want to get in touch with us."

"That's a roger, sir."

Murdock touched the Motorola mike. "Listen up, guys. I want every man to build himself a hide-hole. I don't care if a platoon of NKs come through here, I don't want them to see a one of us. Keep in the perimeter defense, but dig in and cover up. Let's get going on that now. Lam, you stay on the northern side watching for more troops coming."

"Roger, Cap," Lam said.

For the next hour the men of Third Platoon of SEAL Team Seven worked one of their specialties. They called it playing Chiricahua. That tribe of the Apache nation became so adept at hiding themselves in the desert Southwest that they could put a hundred warriors on a flat, desert plain and be invisible. Then when the quarry rode into the trap, they would lift out of the sand and attack. It was said that the only time you saw a Chiricahua was when he wanted you to see him, and that was a fraction of a second before he killed you.

Lam was the best at making a small dug-out hole and camouflaging it with native materials. Here in this woodland it was easy, with lots of native material to work with. Lam had his hole made and himself hidden within ten minutes.

Lam played a little game with himself. He lay on the point of a slight rise in the woods, which gave him slightly longer sight lines to the north. He sectioned the field, going over each part slowly, critically, watching for any movement, any signs of life.

On his second check of the section farthest north he spotted movement. He watched it again, put his 6 x 30 binoculars on it. Yes, had to be. He scowled for a moment. He had to be sure. Another two minutes passed and he was sure. He checked his lip mike.

"Commander, we've got some trouble up here. I'm on point farthest north. You need to look at this."

"Be right up," Murdock said.

A few minutes later he slid in beside Lam's hide-hole and lifted his own binoculars.

"Just past that farthest-out patch of woods, Cap."

Murdock studied the area. "Shit fucker, what are they doing out here?"

"Moving up to the front, I'd say."

"Yeah, three NK tanks, the big ones, T-62's."

"More bad news, Cap. Now I can make out troops behind them. Must be fifteen or twenty men trailing each tank."

"The worst part, all three tanks are headed directly at this patch of woods," Murdock said. Then he scowled. What the hell was he supposed to do now?

Korean Air Space
Over the MLR

"Cat Two-Twelve, this is Home Base."

"This is Cat Two-Twelve. Go, Home Base."

"We have a report of three aircraft heading your direction from the north from our E-2C Hawkeye. Expect some older-class MiGs. They are at fifteen thousand and about forty miles away closing your position at eleven hundred knots. Meet and greet."

"Our pleasure, CAG. Changing course now."

The three F-14 Navy fighters swept into a graceful turn heading due north, their radars reaching out to find the targets.

Cat Two-Twelve was Lieutenant Forest Corey, "Corny" to his buddies. "Got anything yet, Marsh?" Corey asked his RIO in the backseat. The Radar Intercept Officer, Marshal "Marsh" Landower, had his nose buried in his readout radar screen.

"Nothing yet, Corny. Should be coming up fast. We're closing now at twenty-four hundred knots?"

"Near to it."

"That's twenty-seven-sixty miles per hour or over forty-six miles a minute. We should be halfway there by now."

Corey spoke on the plane-to-plane TAC to his two wingmen.

"Gents, they'll probably split when they spot us. We'll take left, right, and middle, as always. Good hunting."

"About time we got some action up here," Pete Platamone said.

"Roger that, Leader man," the other pilot, "Ham" Jones, said. "Free beer for a week for whoever nails the first bastard."

"I've got them," RIO Marsh Landower said. "You're right, they are splitting, still out about twenty miles."

"Stay with them, guys," Corny said. "I've got the middle one."

"No radar-friendly recognition signal from the three," Marsh said. "They are not friendly. I repeat, the targets are not friendly."

"Light them up, Marsh, let's do it."

Marsh had the radar turned on and worked to get a lockup of his signal on the blip on his screen. The MiG was still eighteen miles away and turning hard to the left.

"Stay with him, Corny. Almost had him. Damn. Now, now."

"Weapons free, fire when ready," Corny said.

"I have lock-on and . . . yes, that's a Fox Three," Marsh said. It was the traditional call for a Phoenix missile being fired.

At once the heavy Tomcat aircraft lurched several feet upward as the one-thousand-pound missile dropped from it and the solid-fuel rocket fired, jolting the thirteen-foot-long missile ahead at a speed that would soon reach Mach 5. It left a long cotton white contrail arching into the sky, then turning to the left following the radar input on the target.

The Grumman F-14 is the only aircraft in the U.S. arsenal that can fire the Phoenix. It takes a Hughes AWG-9 or AWG-17 radar/fire-control system, which the F-14 has. The system can be set to track while scanning and lock onto six separate targets while simultaneously guiding six missiles to their targets at the same time.

With its 127-mile range, the Phoenix would have no trouble reaching the MiG less than twenty miles away.

Marsh watched the enemy plane's radar blip do quick and sudden maneuvers to try to outwit the Phoenix, but it never had a chance.

The AWG-9 pulse-Doppler radar in the F-14 never lost contact with the MiG. Seconds later the blip dissolved from the RIO's radar screen as the Phoenix slammed up the tailpipe of the MiG and shattered the complex aircraft into metal confetti that rained down on the Korean land below.

"Splash one MiG," Corny reported on the Home Base and plane-to-plane frequency.

"Damn, lost mine," Platamone said. "Bastard hit the deck and then dodged behind a small hill. The Phoenix liked the mass of the hill better than the MiG. He's to hell and gone down there on the deck. Must be scraping his undercarriage on some of those rice paddies."

"Still playing tag with mine, Corny," Jones said. "Almost had him nailed, then he slipped away. There it is. Yes. We've got a Fox Three on the Phoenix. Shouldn't be long now."

"Home Base, this is CAT Two-One-Two. Anything else for us?"

"The Hawkeye shows that your lost MiG is streaking back north less than fifty feet off the terrain."

"That's a splash on the second MiG," the calm voice of Jones's RIO said.

"Halverson, don't you ever get excited?" Corny asked.

"Hey, it was just one MiG. Want us to chase the other one?"

Home Base cut in. "Two out of three, good hunting. Don't chase the third one, Jones. All three of you stay CAP in that general area. You're now about forty miles north of the MLR. Stack at thirty, twenty, and ten thousand. Good shooting."

12

In North Korean territory

Murdock checked the tanks again through his binoculars. They were over half a mile away heading in his general direction, but he had no thoughts that the tanks would charge through the woods when there was plenty of open ground around.

Unless they knew a general and his staff were hiding in this spot.

If the tanks came close enough, the soldiers might send a detail to the woods to gather firewood to heat up their tea.

The Korean scout and interpreter checked the tanks through Lam's glasses.

"Reserve tanks," the Korean said. "Not first-line outfit. Coming up to replace tanks lost so far in battle. Men behind would be replacement for infantry as well, not fighting unit. Many of these reserves are not well trained."

"Hell, at nine-to-one odds you don't have to be well trained," Lam said. "Cap, we just dig into our hide-holes and wait and hope?"

"Unless you have some outstanding suggestions," Murdock said. "I better go check out my own hole. Come on, ROK friend, you need a hiding place too."

Fifteen minutes later the tanks had rolled even with the SEALs but a good half mile to the right. One squad of soldiers broke off from the main body and double-timed directly for the copse where the SEALs had hunkered down. The weather had turned cold again, but at least there was no snow. Only a few patches of white showed along the back sides of ridges. Inside the woods, the ground had not even frozen.

Murdock had put his hide-hole near the edge of the woods where he could see out north and west. He watched the North Korean soldiers jogging toward them. Eight men. He used the Motorola.

"We have eight visitors coming. Absolute silence. They may penetrate only the edge of the woods for fuel. If you get stepped on, don't yell about it. If we take out one, we'll have to waste all of them, and that would mean a larger force coming to investigate. We hide today and live to fight another way. Jaybird, crawl in and caution the Army to be absolutely quiet. Stay there. Now, no transmissions."

The first NK soldier edged into the woods, his automatic rifle up and his body alert. He looked over the immediate area, and waved the rest of the squad forward.

The soldiers quickly began to pick up sticks and break them into fire lengths, tying them into bundles. Within five minutes they had seven bundles and worked on finishing the last one. One of the North Koreans swore as he stumbled and fell flat in the woods near a large pine tree.

He got up slowly and shouted something to the others. They laughed. The bundles finished, the eight men tramped out of the woods. As they left, two of the eight stepped directly on Murdock's back where he lay near the trail they had chosen. He bit his lip and weathered the last step, then gave a small sigh.

When the NKs were fifty yards away, Murdock used the mike. "Gone for now. Anybody get stepped on?"

Three men reported being tramped over, and Bradford said somebody fell down on him. "I almost shit right there," Bradford yelped.

Major Dan Streib crawled out of the thicket and walked over to Murdock.

"Heard you had some tanks out here," Major Streib said.

"And a squad of NK infantry who gathered some firewood right on top of us and left without seeing us," Murdock said.

A burst of raucous laughter came from the thistle patch.

"Wanted to talk to you, Commander," the major said. He motioned away from the men, and they walked toward the opening to the hideout.

"The general is so relieved that you're here that he's toasting the men with a few drinks."

Murdock glared at Streib. "You mean we brought you food and booze in those packs?"

"General's orders, Commander. I'd wager that you don't outshout your admiral when he gives you an order."

"Not usually, but when that admiral might endanger the lives of my men, I most certainly would. Which is exactly what I'm doing right now. You can come in and be my witness, or sit out here."

"I wouldn't do this, Commander."

"Either I go in there, collect all the damn booze you've got, and chew tail, or my men and I will conveniently lose you and your party tonight before we get to the MLR. Your pick. Which is it going to be?"

"Go talk to my boss. I'm right behind you, Commander. I wouldn't miss this."

Murdock led the way with his MP-5 submachine gun strapped over his back. They crawled on hands and knees into the tunnel of weeds and briars, then twenty feet through the thicket to the opening.

Murdock came to his knees once inside the hollowed-out place. The five men sprawled on the ground. Each one had a whiskey bottle. Murdock swung the MP-5 around so it pointed generally at the men.

"General, I came out here to save your ass and that of these other men. If that outburst of laughter from you drunks had come five minutes earlier, two or three of my men, and probably some of yours, would be dead by now. Do you realize what a delicate situation we're in here?"

"Now just a minute, son," the general began.

"No, General. Major Streib will pick up all of the bottles of whiskey, and then I'll inspect the backpacks of food to be sure there isn't any more. If that doesn't meet with your approval, it's too fucking bad. This is my mission, and I'm in command here. I don't care if you have three or four stars on your shoulders."

"Now look, Navy. You can't come in here blubbering about what we're doing. You have no authority. . . ."

Murdock lifted the MP-5 and put a three-round burst through the overhead of brambles. The silenced rounds caught everyone's attention.

"Hold on, son," the general tried again.

"No, General. You hold your mouth. You have one option. After dark, you and your jolly boys here can have your booze back, only then my men and I will conveniently misplace you somewhere between here and the MLR. You'll stumble around and get caught by the North Koreans and probably get your balls cut off. It's up to you.

"Right now, I'm taking the booze. Anyone with any objections can take it up with Mr. Heckler and Mr. Koch here in my hands. Objections? Anyone have anything to say?"

Murdock looked around. The general had stopped glaring at him. One bird colonel turned away from Murdock's stare. The rest of them shook their heads.

"Major Streib will bring out the SATCOM as well. I don't want a lot of transmissions coming out of this spot. The NKs just might have some triangulation equipment and pay us a deadly visit.

"Gentlemen, my platoon and I kill men for a living. We're good at it. That's why we're here. A little cooperation, and then you can tell all the war stories you want to. But right now, and for the hours until we get back on the other side of the South Korean/American MLR, I'm the man in charge."

Murdock turned his back and knelt down to crawl out. He heard a side arm slide slam a round into a chamber. He rolled on his back and put six rounds through the roof of vines.

Then the black muzzle of the submachine gun lowered and centered on the man who held a .45 in his hand.

"Drop it. Am I going to have to take your weapons away the way I would from a raw recruit? General, control your men."

Before Murdock turned, the general swung his fist and smashed it into the chin of the colonel who had dropped the weapon.

"Better," Murdock said. Then he crawled out holding four of the bottles of whiskey. The major came behind him with two more bottles and the SATCOM.

Outside the tunnel, the major pointed away from the hideout and from Murdock's men. They moved twenty yards, then emptied the booze on the ground and buried the bottles under some leaves and limbs.

"Wow! I've never seen anyone, not even General Reynolds, chew out General Rudolph the way you did. He looked like a buck-ass private. Here's the SATCOM. You mean it about leaving us out here somewhere?"

"If he or any of you causes one of my men to get wounded or killed, I'll dump all of you and have an ironclad alibi by the time I get back to friendly territory. Fucking ass right."

"Okay, okay. I better get back. I'm stuck with these guys. I'd almost stake my life on the fact that there will be no more noise out of the general's compound. Give me a call when you're ready to move out."

"That's a roger, Major Streib. Who was the asshole who pulled the .45? I could have killed him and walked away clean."

"Asshole is right. Colonel Asshole is good enough name for him right now. I'd bet he has dirty shorts and no chance to change them. Serves him right."

Murdock worked up a grin. "Army, you might be OK. Keep your charges under wraps for the rest of the day. We'll pull out of here as soon as it gets dark."

In the meantime, most of the SEALs had drifted off to sleep. Some went to their camouflaged positions; some sprawled under trees. Ed DeWitt had set up a four-man lookout force on two-hour shifts.

Lam and Murdock traded off manning an additional north-looking position.

By 1500 there had been no action. No more Korean tanks showed, no more troops. Even the general and his group had been quiet. Murdock guessed they were sleeping. Some of them had tanked down a lot of whiskey.

Murdock had his men eat their last MREs at four o'clock, and by five-thirty they were saddled up and ready to ramble.

Major Streib came out of the enclosure and said that the general and his men were ready to move.

"Can they walk three miles?" Murdock asked.

The major laughed. "These six officers never take the required PT that the rest of the troops have every morning. I don't know if they can walk even two miles. We'll see. You'll have to impress them with the idea that if they can't walk out, they get captured. As simple as that. I think they'll be able to make it with that kind of psychological help."

Murdock chuckled. He was starting to like this Army major.

They left when it was fully dark. Murdock put Alpha Squad out first, then the Army men in the middle. Ed DeWitt brought up the rear with his Bravo Squad, and they all headed out.

The first half mile went easily. Then Lam came back and they stopped.

"Got something strange up front, Cap. Wasn't here when we came through. Our Korean scout says it's the minimal kind of a battalion rear-aid station that the NKs use. Six or eight twenty-man tents, fires, vehicles. Maybe fifty to a hundred men meandering around like they're waiting for chow."

"Let's hope it's not preparations for a big attack by the NKs in this sector," Murdock said. He called up the major, who went ahead with him.

"You're infantry, right, Major Streib?"

"Had a battalion for a time."

"Take a look out front."

The major eased back from the OP and shook his head. "Yeah, something is coming. Tonight, maybe at dawn, maybe in a day or two. They're laying in supplies and medical people. That sounds like a push right up front here."

Murdock brought up Holt with the SATCOM, and had him try for the American lieutenant who had led them through the South Korean lines. The lieutenant came on the air after the first try.

"We're a least a mile and a half from the MLR with the package, but we find a problem." Murdock described what he saw ahead.

"Damn, must be true. Some of our intel has reported a buildup in this sector. Did you see any tanks?"

Murdock told him.

"Any big concentrations of men, like four or five thousand?

"No, two hundred maybe."

"Is Major Dan Streib there?"

Murdock gave the major the handset.

"Yeah, Streib here. Who is this?"

"Lieutenant Harley Lewiston. I was in your battalion. What's your eval on the situation?"

"Just the start of a buildup, but I'd say not for an attack today or tomorrow. Maybe three days to bring in more troops, more tanks. The aid station is a precaution the NKs don't usually take."

"Our estimates too. Go around these guys, get back on your course, and contact us when you're a half mile off."

Murdock heard the radio and nodded.

"OK, Lam, head to the left a half mile, maybe more, as we go around these NK fuckers down below. Let's move it, we don't have all night."

They swung to the left and hiked through the Korean countryside. Ahead they saw some lights, but they were far to the side. Murdock sent Jaybird back to see how the general and his men were doing.

Jaybird came back chuckling.

"The old general is walking, but he glared at me like he's really pissed. He thinks they should have sent in a helo for him, I'm damn sure of that. He's keeping up. One of the bird colonels is lagging back a little. DeWitt is prodding him."

Murdock thanked him and used his mike. "DeWitt, send Major Streib up here. I think I can use him."

"Roger that, Skipper," DeWitt said.

A few minutes later Major Streib came up. "Thanks for rescuing me from the brass back there. They are mad as hell about this hike."

"Do them good," Murdock said. "You have a side arm?"

"A .45 auto."

"Keep it loaded, you might need it."

The men were single file now, and moving at a quick pace. Murdock saw that they had just topped a small rise when Lam came back and held up his hand.

"Cap, remember those three tanks we saw? They're right ahead about a quarter of a klick. Looks like they're at a picnic. Lights all over the place."

Major Streib listened.

"The troops with them still there?" Murdock asked.

"Not that I could see. Just the tank crews. No security, no other vehicles. Looks like they knocked off from the war early and are having a late chow."

"Gonna take them out?" Major Streib asked Murdock.

"Tempting, but our mission isn't to kill tanks. We've got a package to deliver across the MLR."

"Three naked tanks," Streib said. "Sounds too good to be true, a gift from the war gods dropped right in your lap."

"How far are they from that medical unit?" Murdock asked.

"A klick, maybe a little more," Lam said.

"We better cut to the left again. Put us five hundred yards to the left of them. They just might have out some security we don't know about."

They hiked again. When they were a quarter of a mile away from the tankers, Lam swung them due south. Half of the line of men had passed the tanks when DeWitt saw movement to his right. He used his Motorola.

"Hit the deck. NKs to the right."

Just as he said it an automatic rifle opened up. The general had not gone down when the rest did. Now he flopped quickly and put his arms over his head.

"How many?" Murdock asked on the man-to-man radio.

"Can't tell, Cap," DeWitt said. "We'll go get them. Bravo, let's go. Silenced rounds only for now."

They moved cautiously in a long line toward the shooters. The NKs fired once more, but DeWitt realized they were firing due south, not at the SEALs.

They found the NKs quickly, less than thirty yards through the light growth of brush and grass. The NKs had a hole dug and were aiming their AK-47's to the south. They fired again. DeWitt spotted them first, two men in a foxhole. He lifted his silenced MP-5 and put two three-round bursts from the submachine gun into the hole. One man whimpered and fell forward. The second man turned and started to fire back, but two more SEALs targeted him and put him dead in his hole before he could fire again.

DeWitt and Adams charged into the hole. DeWitt found what he didn't want to. He hit his mike.

"Cap, they've got a wire in here and a phone. They're gonna be missed soon. Should we finish the job?"

Murdock looked at the major. "Four men to a tank?"

The major nodded. "Usually four. No infantry with them?"

"Not that we saw. DeWitt, you have TNAZ?"

"Roger that, Mr. Murdock."

"Go get them."

DeWitt grinned and waved his men forward. "Silenced weapons only unless we get in a jam. Two men for each tank. First we reduce anyone outside the rigs, silently."

They moved up cautiously. DeWitt sent Douglas and Mahanani to the left for the farthest tank. One of them had TNAZ.

Fernandez and Quinley took the center tank. DeWitt and Franklin and Adams aimed for the far right. Each team had TNAZ and grenades and knew what to do. They worked up slowly, crawling the last thirty yards to get a good field of fire. Three men sat around an open fire. DeWitt saw a soldier working on the treads of one tank.

When DeWitt had his men in position, he used the mike.

"Silenced only. Let's do it." He fired a three-round burst at the men around the fire. One went down. The other two tried to crawl away. They died in the dirt. The man at the tank treads took two slugs from one of the Colts and went down clawing at his weapon. Two more rounds stopped him. Nothing moved around the tanks.

"TNAZ on the tank tread, four-minute timer, then two grenades down any open turret," DeWitt said in his radio. "All of you, go."

Adams ran forward, his Colt at the ready. Nobody tried to stop him. He put the TNAZ on the front roller where it left the tracks, pushed in the timer, then vaulted on the tank to where the turret was open. Adams pulled both pins on grenades and dropped them into the tank top, then jumped off the tank and ran flat out for the place he had left near DeWitt.

The two grenades went off 4.2 seconds after Adams dropped them inside the tank. Smoke drifted up from the turret.

Twenty seconds later the grenades in a second tank went off; then the men of the Bravo Squad were all back together and running hard for the rest of the platoon.

The first TNAZ bomb went off before they made it. The heavy tank lifted up, its tread shattered and the roller blown completely off its axle.

The two other explosions shattered the cold Korean night sky a moment later.

"Let's move, double time," Murdock said. DeWitt got back with the unit, prodded the general and his colonels to move it, and jogged away from the site.

"We nailed the three tanks," DeWitt said on his radio. "Four NKs outside the tanks now in touch with their ancestors."

"Let's hope it doesn't attract too much attention," Murdock said.

Lam led them on down the rise, past a farmhouse and three rise paddies now frozen solid. Ahead Lam saw a small stream, which they crossed getting wet only to their knees.

"I'm not getting my feet wet," the general snorted.

DeWitt was right behind him. "Sir, you either get wet, talk your men into carrying you across, or sit out the rest of this little war in a POW camp, because I'm sure as hell not going to pack you over the stream."

The general glared at DeWitt in the gloom, and stepped gingerly into the water.

A half mile from the tanks, Murdock slowed them to a walk. Lam had found a trail heading south that they took now. It wandered between rice paddies and past two small buildings that had been blown apart.

Murdock went up and walked with Lam.

"We should be within half a klick of the damn MLR," Murdock said.

"Yeah, but maybe two klicks to one side from where we came through. That's two to the west of our spot."

"Where's our Korean guy?" Murdock said into his mike. "Whoever knows, send him up front. Gonna have some work for him to do."

Another two hundred yards ahead, they came to a road. Lam lay near it for five minutes. Two trucks with splashy yellow lights rumbled past.

"We get the men lined up along the side of the road, then go across all at once," Lam said. Murdock gave the orders on the mike, and soon the SEALs and their package were spread along the road at five-yard intervals.

Another truck rolled past. In the rear they could see several NK soldiers.

When it was past, Lam looked both ways, "Now, move," he said into his mike. The man ran from their sparse cover near the road, across it, and to the far side and into a small patch of woods and brush. Even the Army brass made it with no problem.

Lam stared ahead from his position a hundred yards ahead of the men. He didn't like it. They had hit a section of the North Korean MLR that also held a rear camp of some kind. He spotted more than a dozen trucks, some emergency lights rigged on poles, and a dozen or so twenty-man tents.

"Hit the deck," Murdock said on the Motorola as he slid into the dirt and weeds beside Lam. "This is another fine kettle of fish you've got me into, Ollie," Murdock said.

Lam shook his head. "The only luck we've had on this mission has been bad luck. What the hell we gonna do now?"

13

Near MLR
North Korean side

Major Streib had crawled up beside them. He scanned the area, borrowed Murdock's binoculars, and took a closer look.

"Oh, yeah, that is more like it. It's set up like a repo depo, full of supplies and replacements of troops for a big push."

"Supplies?" Murdock asked. "Like any concentration of fuel?"

Major Streib grinned in the darkness. "Great minds have a way of doing it," he said.

Murdock called for Holt, who squirmed up beside him. "See if you can get that Lieutenant Lewiston on the air again."

Holt tried, and got him on the second call.

"You talk," Murdock said, giving the handset to the major.

Streib filled in the American on the situation. "Say you lob in a dozen rounds of artillery and we'll be your spotter. Coordinates? We don't even have a map. Can you see on this side the MLR a half mile? We'll lob some forty mikes in and try to set something on fire. We're about a mile and a half west of where we left your MLR. You take your sightings from the fire and tell the artillery guys."

151

"Yes, sounds reasonable," the American on the south side of the MLR said. "I'll have to go through channels. . . ."

"Murdock here." He had grabbed the handset from Streib. "Look, you take time to go through channels and your package won't get delivered. We need a major diversion and we need it right now. We'll start shooting in ten minutes. You have those guns ready in ten minutes or kiss your general and his friends good-bye. No way they can infiltrate through two MLRs. You read me loud and clear, Lewiston?"

There was a moment of silence. "Yes, sir, Commander. We'll get it done. Ten minutes from now, mark."

Murdock pushed the timer on his stopwatch. "Now, all we have to do is find what we can set on fire the easiest."

They had six Colt M-4A1's with the grenade launchers below the barrels. Murdock called the men with the launchers up and explained what they were going to do. "How many WP do we have?"

They counted up. Eighteen WP rounds.

"We're looking for some stored gasoline drums, but not sure we'll find them. We'll need almost maximum range on these forties. Let's try to hit something. As soon as you fire the last rounds, we'll be moving to the left a quick half klick, then due south. Stand by."

Murdock and Major Streib took turns with the binoculars. It was Lam who found it.

"Just to the left of that second tent, the one with the lightbulb hanging outside. Looks to me like about twenty barrels of fuel."

"Oh, yes." Murdock passed the word to each of the forty-mike shooters and set them up fifty yards closer to the target. He sent Jaybird with the Army brass a half klick to the left. When his stopwatch showed ten minutes had elapsed since they'd talked with Lewiston, he told his Colt men to start firing.

He watched the first round hit. Short of the barrels, but it set a tent on fire. Almost at once three more 40mm rounds landed. One hit a truck and the gasoline tank exploded. Six more rounds hit in rapid order, and one blew up right beside one of the drums of gasoline. They had fire, but the WP wouldn't rupture the drums.

Without being told, three of the shooters went to HE, and a minute later two rounds hit close enough to the stored gasoline to rupture one of the barrels. It blew and exploded the rest of the barrels of fuel into one gigantic bonfire.

"Move it," Murdock said in his mike, and the SEALs double-timed to the left, hooking up with the Army men and running south toward the MLR.

They heard the artillery rounds going over. Just a minor whisper before they hit near the furiously burning gasoline.

Lam held up his hand when they had moved what Murdock figured was a half mile to the south.

"Homeboys right ahead," Lam said. "Must be their MLR. Looks like about a dozen of them along a fifty-foot front."

"See anybody leave, like going back to that camp?"

"No one left while I've been watching."

"Bradford and Fernandez, front and center with your tools," Murdock said in the Motorola. "Move up, now."

Murdock found firing positions for the two by the time they got to where he waited. They were eighty yards from the mounds of dirt ahead of them. The trench behind the mound was open to this side.

"We need as many of them down before we move through here and as quietly as possible," Murdock told them.

They nodded. "Open fire at your pleasure," Murdock said.

Bradford eased down behind his H&K PSG1 suppressed sniper rifle, and sighted in on the last man he could see to the left. Fernandez, with an identical rifle, sighted in on the last man he could see on the right. They both fired at about the same time.

They each moved to the next man in line. Six of the NKs were down in the trench before the others noticed. One gave a high screeching yell, and the six went flat in the trench.

Jaybird pushed in beside Murdock. "They done what they can. How about some old-fashioned fraggers?"

Murdock nodded. He and Jaybird began crawling forward. Now and then one of the NKs lifted up from the trench, but then dropped down. Murdock and Jaybird found some cover halfway there. They paused. Murdock told the others to hold fire, and he and Jaybird wormed another fifteen yards, then took out three grenades each and looked at each other in the darkness.

Murdock nodded. They pulled the pins and each threw a bomb. Before the first fraggers hit, the two throwers had the pins pulled on their second grenades and lofted them at the trench.

The first ones hit short; the second ones hit the berm and rolled back into the trench, where it detonated.

After throwing the third fraggers, the two lay still for a moment until the small hand bombs exploded. Then they came to their feet and charged the trench. They made it with no return fire. Murdock ran one way down the trench, Jaybird the other.

Murdock spotted two NKs twenty feet down the trench trying to get to their feet. He slammed two three-round bursts into them and they went down and dead. He moved another thirty feet, and saw no more live defenders. He heard Jaybird's muted weapon fire down the other way.

"Clear right," Murdock said.

"Clear left," Jaybird reported.

"Platoon, move up to the trench and over the berm," Murdock said in the mike. "This is a flat-out run for this opening. It won't be here long."

Murdock heard running feet to his left. He brought his subgun around and cut down three rushing NK infantrymen as they rounded a slight bend in the trench. He heard Jaybird firing as well.

The fastest of the SEALs sprinted to the trench, went up the berm and over it, then hunkered down just on the other side to wait for the rest of the platoon.

The general was the last one to the berm. Major Streib gave him a hand up the berm, then let him drop over the side. The general grunted and swore as he hit the ground.

DeWitt had been counting. "We got all of our people," DeWitt said on the radio. Jaybird and Murdock rolled over the berm and ran up to the rest of the men.

"Easy now, we don't want to get shot up by friendlies over

there. We go silently until our Korean buddy can make contact. Holt, try for a talk with Lewiston again. He might have some clout down here."

They moved forward slightly, alert. The no-man's-land between the lines was wider here, maybe four hundred yards, Murdock figured. That was good. They began taking some rounds from behind them now. Evidently some of the NK soldiers had filtered in and around the bodies in the trench and figured it out. But the NKs had no targets in the dark Korean night.

Murdock took the point with Lam. Four eyes were better than two, they decided. These South Koreans could get trigger-happy sometimes. Then ahead, they could see the concertina wire and a hastily thrust of dirt that must be the MLR. When Murdock looked around, the Korean interpreter crouched behind him.

"This it?" Murdock asked.

The Korean looked and nodded.

"Can you talk to them from here?"

He shook his head and began crawling forward. He was a dozen feet away and to the left when a machine gun fired from the South Korean side. The little Korean man buckled, then rolled over and lay still.

"Damn," Murdock said. "There goes our ride home." He touched the lip mike. "Ching, get your bones up front, fast."

He came a few moments later. "The MLR," Murdock whispered. "They just killed our Korean. Can you try some Japanese on them?"

"Shit, what if they don't know Jap talk?"

"Worth a try. Find some cover first."

Ching crouched behind a boulder and looked over it. He shrilled out a string of Japanese and ducked. There was a stunned silence behind the SK lines. Then a thin voice came back. Ching grinned in the darkness, and shouted again in Japanese. He told them they were the American patrol that went out the night before.

They answered him. He looked at Murdock.

"They want a fucking password."

"Tell them package. Package. We don't know a password. Try it, package."

Ching shouted the word there times. His only answer was a six-round burst of machine-gun fire. He returned fire with a ten-round burst from his Colt M-4.

Holt eased into the shallow where Murdock and Major Streib lay. "Got the lieutenant. He says we're in the wrong sector."

Streib took the handset. "Lewiston, what the fuck is the matter with you? We're opposite where the big fire is, where your artillery rounds came in. Your Southern Fried Friends are shooting at us. Get over here and stop them. We've still got the package, but we could lose half of them if the North Koreans keep shooting."

"To the west more. Okay, I'll get on the horn. My Korean isn't all that good, but we'll try."

"Don't just try, Lewiston, do it. Just trying is going to bag you a dead general and some dead bird colonels."

The machine gun fired again. Somebody behind them swore.

"All weapons. A thirty-second firing. Go at that South Korean MLR. Let's do it now."

The fourteen weapons of the platoon snarled, rattled, and thundered on automatic fire, shredding some of the trees over the MLR ahead of them.

"Cease," Murdock said to the Motorola. "Ching, say it again."

The big man from San Diego bellowed out the Japanese words again. He threw in that they had twice the firepower the men on the line had, and they would kill everyone there if they needed to.

An American voice came back at them in the silence that followed Ching's words.

"You might be who you say, you might not. So tell me, who is Beavis's buddy?"

"Butthead, you butthead," Ching shouted in English. "You believe us now?"

"Hey, I'm coming over the berm with no weapon," the American said. "Just to show you that I believe you."

"You got a name, friend?"

"Yeah, Master Sergeant Wilcox, and you guys and your fancy weapons almost turned my wife into a fucking widow. I'm coming out. Hold your damned fire."

A moment later they saw a flashlight beam moving over the berm and down the bank; then the light reversed and lighted a redheaded American's face.

"Let's move it, ladies," Murdock said into the mike, and the SEALs and their package of Army officers hurried forward, over the berm, and back into friendly territory.

Again the general was the last man over the berm because he moved slower than all the rest. Once on the ground on the South side, he took over at once.

"Who the hell's in charge here?" he bellowed.

A first lieutenant in the Republic of Korea troops hurried up and saluted. He chattered in Korean. The general brushed him aside.

"Get the SATCOM. Where is it? I want a chopper in here within five minutes. Streib, get your ass over here with my SATCOM and roust those bastards back in Regiment. I want some action, now."

Murdock pulled his platoon to one side. He took Master Sergeant Wilcox with him.

"Stay away from the general," Murdock said. "He's furious that he had to walk out. Now, how do we get out of here to where we can get picked up by a Navy chopper?"

"Sir, I'd say about half a mile down the road here and to the left is a field you can use for your LZ. Be glad to show you the way."

"What sector is this? How can you tell our chopper where to find us?"

"Get me on the horn with your pilot and I can guide him in here like biscuits to gravy."

"Good, come with us." Murdock moved the platoon out without another look at the general. Holt hooked up with the carrier on the SATCOM, and ten minutes later he had contact with a Sea Knight on the way to pick them up.

Holt put the sergeant on, and the noncom gave the directions.

"Right, sir. We're sector twelve. I can give you coordinates; then we'll pop a couple of red flares in the LZ. Yes, sir, a secure area and we'll be at least a klick behind the MLR. Right, sir, we'll see you in about thirty."

With the sergeant leading, it took them another ten minutes to get to the field. It was a former rice paddy, larger than most, and still half-frozen from the winter chill.

Holt kept on the SATCOM with the Sea Knight, and when he was close enough, they threw out two red flares. The big bird settled down and Murdock gave the sergeant a handshake, then ran with his men for the loading door on the big helo.

Just inside, Murdock found Don Stroh with a huge grin.

"You did it, you sonofabitch, you did it."

"Never a doubt, except when that asshole general and his men all got drunk and nearly gave our position away."

"Heard about that. General Reynolds heard about your chewing out your general buddy. He's not the most popular man in the command. But he and his staff knew too much to risk getting them caught. If you couldn't extricate them, they were going to call in an air strike and waste all seven of them."

"Major Streib should get part of the credit for the mission. He's a good man. I want you to pass that along to the general. He was a good help."

Murdock saw the last man in the chopper. He looked at DeWitt.

"We have fourteen bodies, Commander, all ready to move," DeWitt said.

"Tell the crew. Let's get out of here."

Murdock looked around at his SEALs in the faint light. "Somebody got hit back there on that final MLR. Who picked up the lead?"

"Must be me, if nobody else is bleeding," Colt Franklin said, his voice soft, shaky.

Mahanani found him sitting against the side of the chopper. "Where?"

"My side. Don't seem all that bad." His voice trailed off. Mahanani got him stretched out on the floor and with a flashlight checked the wounded man. He put a compress on the entry point of the bullet and felt under the man's back. The slug hadn't come out. He gave Franklin a shot of morphine, and covered him up with a pair of Navy blankets from the helo.

"You take it easy, buddy. Have you in sick bay before you know it. You've got a slug inside somewhere that the docs will find. Looks like no more late-night assignments for you for a while."

A half hour later, Murdock and DeWitt talked with the surgeon in the *Monroe*'s sick bay.

"We'll have to go in and take out that slug. We found it and it's not in a critical position, but it has to come out. It missed most of the vitals, but did nick part of the small intestine. He won't be fit for duty for a month at least."

"Thanks, Doc," Murdock said. "We'll check with you tomorrow." He looked at his watch. It was still in the stopwatch mode. He punched the button for the current time: 2320. Time for a good night's sleep. All he had to do was write up the after-action report. A lot of people were going to be reading this one, including the general they'd saved. No wonder the Eighth Army didn't want anyone else to know the man's name. That sounded like the Army.

14

USS _Monroe_
Yellow Sea

Miguel Fernandez dropped on his bunk and closed his eyes. It had been a long day. He'd cleaned his weapon, shaped up his gear, and repacked everything ready to roll. If and when. He gave a big sigh. The head again. He could go for eight hours on a mission without needing to urinate, but back on the ship it hit him every hour or so. He pushed his feet down to the floor from the three-high bunk, and bumped into Joe Douglas. They stared at each other.

"What's the matter, you never saw a white man before?" Douglas said, his face stitched with a sneer.

"Not an asshole one like you, Douglas."

Douglas had eased away from the other man. Now he lunged forward. Mahanani grabbed him by the cammie shirt and jerked him backward like a weightless rag doll.

"Hold it there, fast stuff," Mahanani said easily. "Hey, you're not getting this berthing into trouble. Thought the JG told you guys to stay apart."

"Just coming to get something from Quinley," Douglas said with a touch of a whine. "Then this fucking spic jumps down on me."

160

"Didn't know you were there or I'd have stomped you good," Fernandez said. He'd been called worse names, but the racist jibe from Douglas was ten times as bad. He glared at Douglas.

Mahanani prodded Douglas toward the door. "Little buddy, best you get out of here. Get whatever you need from Quin tomorrow. We're all tired and hurting. Things will look better in the sunlight."

"Hell, no," Fernandez shouted. "This has been going on for too long. Let's get it finished right here with fists and no rules."

Mahanani laughed. "Fernandez, you're not that stupid. Everyone knows what the JG told you two. One more blowup and you're both out of SEALs digging snow in Adak, Alaska. You want that?"

"I'm not gonna let some—"

Mahanani grabbed Fernandez and pushed him against the bunks. "You'd rather give up what you've worked for for three years—to be a SEAL? You're not that stupid, Fernandez."

He stared hard at both men. "Fernandez, get back in your bunk. Douglas, you get out of here and back to your compartment. If any hint of this gets back to the JG, I'll smash a few heads just for the fun of it. You guys hear?"

Douglas snorted and stalked out of the berthing compartment. Fernandez lay back in his bunk, no longer needing to go to the head. When Fernandez looked up, the big Hawaiian/Tahitian stood there grinning at him.

"Hey, little buddy, it goes down hard, but it goes down. I've had some of that too, through the years. I know how bad you want to stay in SEALs, so do it." He leaned in closer so no one else could hear him. "Yeah, I know what happened at that barbecue on the beach. I was there, remember? Nothing you can't live with for a while. I wouldn't give Douglas a hell of a long time in this platoon. He's a natural fuckup. Just hang on, things will get better. If it gets too bad, I'll go to the JG."

"No, Mahan, don't do that. I can fight my own fights."

"Not if the other guy is always hitting below the belt. Now just relax. It's over for tonight."

Then Fernandez knew he had to get to the head. He eased down, and looked at Mahanani. "You want to hold my hand while I take a piss?"

"I think you can handle that," the big Hawaiian said, and slid into his bunk.

Fernandez took a towel with him and left the compartment for the head. He had just passed the other compartment and turned down the companionway when someone jumped out directly in front of him, and before he could more than try to step sideways, a fist slammed into his face, then again and again, until he went down to his knees.

For just a moment the other man started to kick, then put down his foot.

"Fucking greaser asshole," the man said. That was when Fernandez knew the attacker was Douglas. He tried to get up. Douglas pushed him sideways and he fell on the deck, skidding his right hand and producing a floor burn. Douglas snorted and hurried down the hall.

Fernandez got to his feet, his head still woozy and his vision not what it should be. He tried to clear his head. His face felt like he'd been run over by a tank. He made it to the head, tried to wash his face off with cold water, then half walked and staggered back to his own compartment.

The lights were off inside. Even the Hawaiian was sleeping. Fernandez hadn't noticed much difference in the appearance of his face when he looked in the mirror in the head. Tomorrow morning would be different. Damn, what would he say when the JG asked him how he got his face beat up? Fernandez didn't know. All he knew was that he wanted to stay in the SEALs more than anything else in the world. Well, with the exception of his wife and family. They came first, then the SEALs. But it was a damn close call.

Murdock spent half the morning in sick bay. The doctors had decided to let Franklin rest during the night. They said the operation would be on at 0730.

It didn't get started until 0930. They wanted to do more tests. An X ray found the North Korean slug. It had hit some hard tissue and curved around, and was now lodged two inches from the spine, pushing gently against the Lumbar Five vertebra and a bundle of nerves that controlled the lower extremities. If it didn't come out, it could paralyze him.

The surgery took two hours. Murdock and DeWitt paced the compartment like caged tigers. They took turns filling the coffee cups. Just before 1200 the doctor came out smiling.

"Got the damned thing. Looks free and clear. Ordinarily on a wound like that, the bullet would go in the front of the side and out the back causing little trouble. This man will need at least two months before any strenuous activity. Somebody say he's a SEAL?"

"Right, sir," JG said.

"Put him behind a desk or give him a month's liberty. Don't let him anywhere near that O course of yours in Coronado or I'll have both of you up on charges."

"Tomorrow morning would be too soon to send him to a mission then, I imagine," Don Stroh said from behind them. The doctor scowled, turned and left.

"Way too early, Company man," Murdock said. "We're down to thirteen good men, so from here on let's keep it simple. How is your war going?"

"It's evening up out there. The South Ks are getting their defenses together. Might even be some counterattacks soon. What I'm wondering about is what you did to that general. I still don't know his name. I was having breakfast with the admiral when this Army guy called Kenner. He put it on the speaker phone so I could hear.

"This one-star general called you every name in the book. Said you were insubordinate, refused to follow his orders, claimed you outranked him on this mission, and about a dozen other charges.

"Kenner listened to him, then snorted and asked this general if the SEALs had saved his ass. He said yes, but . . . Kenner cut him off, told him he was lucky he didn't get left behind. Told him he better write up a glowing report about the SEALs' rescue or Kenner would forward to General Reynolds a copy of your after-action report.

"That cooled down the one-star in a rush. He said maybe he was a little hasty and he wouldn't press any charges.

" 'Charges!' Kenner thundered. He said the general should at least recommend you for a Silver Star or a Navy Cross."

Murdock led the other two men to the SEALs' assigned assembly room.

"I'm still going to send a copy of my after-action report to General Kenner," Murdock said. "He probably never will see it, but I owe it to my men to protest that asshole general's actions."

Stroh grinned. "Yeah, you're a real team player, Murdock. Trouble is, I don't have a single job for you to do today. You get to sit fat, happy, and warm while those GIs out there are fighting for their lives."

"Good for them. I hope you had a good breakfast. Now, time for us working stiffs to get to it."

Jaybird had the men going over their gear, doing resupply on their ammo packs, and cleaning their weapons, again.

Ed DeWitt checked over his men. He had five now instead of seven. Fred Washington was still in sick bay from his wound suffered in the action in the Kuril Islands. Now Colt Franklin was also in sick bay with that strange side wound. DeWitt stopped in front of Fernandez, who had his H&K PSG1 sniper rifle broken down on a wipe cloth in front of him. Fernandez looked up and DeWitt scowled.

"Fernandez, into my office." DeWitt walked down to the far end of the room and put the SEAL in a chair.

"Just what the hell happened to you?"

"Fell off my bunk, sir. I'm the third one up. Hit some gear on the floor. Hurt like hell. Then this morning I see I got some bruises. Nothing busted, though. Fit for duty."

DeWitt closed his eyes and shook his head. "Fernandez . . ." He gave up and looked away. "Am I going to have to talk to the rest of the squad?"

"They don't know a thing, Lieutenant. Happened in the companionway. It was dark. I never got a good look at who hit me."

"But you have a good idea."

"No hard evidence, sir."

"You know our squad is down to five men. I leave both of

you behind, that gives me three men. What the hell am I supposed to do with three instead of seven?"

"Sir, this is personal, not professional. I would never violate my job as a SEAL to settle a personal problem. I have no doubts that the other man in this problem would also act like a SEAL in every aspect of a combat situation. We can function in the same squad, sir, and we won't let you down."

DeWitt sat down near Fernandez and stared at him. He was a good man, a fine SEAL, a team player. He was so thrilled to be a SEAL that the vibrations shot out of him in all directions. He knew his job, he did it, he was happy in his work.

Douglas was another matter. He had made the grade, passed through BUD/S, earned his Trident, and was in his second year with the teams. But something just didn't jibe right. Something wasn't 4-0 with him. For the life of him, DeWitt couldn't pin it down. It was nothing right now that would get him ramrodded out of the SEALs. Still . . .

"I'll have a talk with Douglas. In the meantime and from now on, you keep away from him. You're in separate berthing compartments, right?"

"Yes, sir."

"Carry on, Fernandez." DeWitt watched Fernandez go back to his fieldstripped sniper rifle and begin putting it back together. He knew Fernandez was married, the only one in the platoon. Marriage was almost impossible for a SEAL. Long hours, days, weeks, sometimes months away in the field. No schedule, no time together with a wife and family that could be counted on. Most SEALs who got married found that it didn't last long. Miguel had held on.

DeWitt walked down the line and motioned for Douglas to follow him. At the other end of the room, he had a standup talk with Douglas.

"You notice the bruises on Fernandez's face?"

"Yes, sir."

"Any idea how he got them?"

"No, sir. He told Mahan that he fell out of his bunk. Said he had a third-level slot."

"You believe that?"

"No, sir."

"Did you beat him up in that dark companionway last night, Douglas?"

"Me? No. No, sir. Not me."

"Who else?"

"I don't know."

"Douglas, if it turns out you're lying to me, I'll have your ass keelhauled. You know how long it would take you to go all the way under the keel of this carrier and come up on the other side?"

"About an hour, sir."

"Hope you can hold your breath a fucking long time. Dismissed."

Douglas gave him a short grin, then dropped it and hurried back to repacking his ammo. DeWitt watched him go. Dammit to hell. What could he do next? He had to keep them apart. He could do that in the field, but if they had a full day and a night here on the carrier, anything could happen. He'd caution Mahanani to keep a close eye on both of them.

Lieutenant General Richard F. Reynolds studied the wall map that still showed the front lines of the North's invasion. The bulge was greatest daggering at Seoul. It was still twelve miles away, eighteen miles from the Eighth Army Headquarters. What he wouldn't give right now for a pair of fully outfitted U.S. Army quick-response battalions. He quit dreaming. All but one sector of the 151-mile-long front line was manned by South Korean units. They were sharp, well trained, with good U.S. weapons, but they were still ROKs. Some had held, some had fought valiantly in spite of overwhelming odds. Now the front line was relatively stable. Four days of war and not a hell of a lot to show for it.

Yes, the South troops were holding. Partly because the North had a massive supply problem. They had overextended in some areas and were paying for it. There had been some counterattacks to retake strategic high ground, but no big move on either side.

He had air superiority. The Navy planes had been a real help. Now he had to figure where to put a thrust. He had a two-division reserve. Not much, but it would have to do. The bulge toward Seoul would be the logical point of attack. But he and some of his top staff had thought about doing a dogleg. Striking quickly through a weak point to the east of Seoul where the current MLR had been pushed back only three miles from the old DMZ.

Ram through there with tanks and troops and plunge in five miles north, then take a sharp right turn and jolt through mostly unprotected countryside for fifteen miles before turning south and trying to cut off the eight to ten thousand troops and armor that the North must have on line against Seoul. If he could cut them off for three days, it might be enough to bottle up the troops and slice them to pieces with artillery and air.

His senior command had been highly in favor of it. They would start with artillery along the line, then a fake attack near the Seoul bulge, and at the same time launch their major thrust north at Changdan. It should work.

Tanks, how many tanks did he have to have that he could commit? It would take two battalions of tanks, twenty-eight of them. That should do it. They could lead the attack, drop off one here and there for protection along the line, and then race across the bulge if they could toward Songu-ri. Yes. He liked it. His staff had liked it. The ultimate decision was up to him.

He turned to his phone and called Switzer, his tank commander.

"Yeah, I can give you twenty-eight tanks. We patch two outfits together and have Major Kitts in charge of the new Ninety-first. When do you want them and where?"

Reynolds made three more calls, then got his staff together and told them it was a go. They would push off at first light the next morning. All tanks and troops and a supply column with food and ammunition and supplies would be ready to follow the troops.

General Reynolds sat back in his chair and tried to relax. In the morning he was committing over ten thousand South Korean troops to a major battle. He made certain Major Hawkins had all the facts when he talked to the Navy.

Hawkins was his Air Liaison officer with the CAG on the carrier. The Navy ground-attack planes would be there to help the troops. Yes, everything done or in motion.

In an hour he'd fly down to the Point of Departure and see how things were shaping up. They had time enough to get the troops down there and the tanks. Most of the movement would take place after dark so they didn't tip off the North. Yes, if this worked they could trip up the whole invasion and then throw the NK remnants back across the DMZ.

Would the United Nations let them chase the NKs all the way back to Pyongyang and end this thing once and for all? From what he'd heard so far, the North Korean equipment was still basically what the Soviets had given them ten years ago. It was old and wearing out and falling to pieces. He was surprised they had surged as far over the DMZ as they had. He had sent a top-priority radio request to the President of the United Nations General Assembly that morning asking if his UN troops had to stop at the DMZ. He'd hoped for a quick reply. So far, no word.

His sergeant major poked his head in the door. "General, better hit the floor. We've got an air raid warning. Not sure if the planes will get through, but they have ordnance. The North Korean jets are less than three minutes away and could launch missiles at any time."

15

Near Changdan, South Korea
The MLR, five miles below old DMZ

Major Donovan Kitts checked with his men again. He was back to full strength with the 91st, but with only six of his tanks and crews from his former unit. The 32nd, which had been battered as badly as his bunch, was blended in with his machines. He had his six vehicles in the point of the attack.

At the last briefing, General Reynolds himself had told them that their line-crossers had reported no armor and not over a company of North Koreans directly opposite them. The 91st would slash through the first line and see what was in the rear areas. Five miles, then a fast turn to the right for a run across the countryside. He had trained in some of this South Korean land.

His only problem would be holding back so the infantry could keep up with their advance. They had to secure the area as they moved. Maybe three miles an hour. It would work.

He went to each tank and talked to the tank commander, meeting some of the men from the 32nd for only the second time. Urging them to do their level best.

"This is one strike that could put a fatal thrust into the whole invasion," he said. "If we can bottle up those forces facing Seoul, and take them out, the whole damn invasion could just evaporate."

"Yeah, but if they riddle us, kill our tanks, and slaughter these ROKs, our asses are really in a sling," one of the tank commanders said.

Kitts grinned. "Yeah, truly. So let's keep our behinds out of any slings."

He could see some of the vehicles and troops behind his tanks. The other tank battalion would lead a thrust a half mile to the left of them. If all went well, the two columns would merge at the five-mile point north and swing due west.

Kitts slid down through the hatch on his tank and waited. He'd trained for three years for this night. In those three years he'd had exactly two days of combat. Now it would be a little more. They had to do well. They would do well.

The artillery opened up at precisely 0445. It was almost an hour to sunrise. The artillery started far to the west and worked one unit at a time eastward, until the whole thirty-mile front rang with exploding artillery rounds.

He heard the whispers as the 105 and 155 rounds whistled overhead and exploded less than half a mile away. The rounds went in for ten minutes in front of them, three or four a minute exploding in a deadly choreography of death.

Then it was quiet. Ten minutes later jet aircraft dove on the MLR of the North Koreans and unleashed cannon fire and air-to-ground missiles.

At 0510, just as dawn crept over the far hills, the order to move out came. Kitts ordered his tanks to button up and advance with him. He was the first tank in the diamond formation, and thrust forward in his assigned direction. They passed through the South Korean MLR in a narrow path, then expanded in their diamond and charged ahead over the uneven ground at fifteen miles an hour.

Over five hundred troops followed closely behind the clanking, roaring vehicles of sudden death.

"Anything?" Kitts asked his gunner on the intercom.

"Nada, Major." He was using his scope and checking every aspect of the land ahead.

"Okay, I have their MLR, there is some firing coming. Machine gun. We'll work the area with a round."

The 105 round fired, and the familiar fumes seeped into the compartment. Kitts watched on the AN/VVG-2 ruby range finder. He saw the muzzle flash of a machine gun; then the whole area of the berm gushed in one large explosion and the flashing stopped.

The tank's 7.62mm machine gun began chattering. He saw more rounds taking out the MLR fortifications the NKs had quickly thrown up two days ago.

Then his tank was at the MLR. His driver edged through the hole their round had made, found no tank trap on the far side, and gunned through the MLR and charged forward.

They were in a series of rise paddies, with their two-foot-high dikes around small plots less than fifty feet square. Ahead he could see no troops and no vehicles.

"Check in when you clear the MLR," he radioed his tanks. Quickly six checked in, and before they were a quarter of a mile ahead, the rest reported they had breached the enemy MLR with no problem.

A Captain Casemore came on the radio. He was Infantry with the ROK company directly behind his tank.

"Slow it down, Major. We've got a few nasties to put down along here. Not many, but too many to leave in our rear. Take a five-minute break where you are and let us catch up."

Kitts pulled his rig to a stop, ordered his tanks to stay in place and to keep watching ahead. He spotted a six-by truck on a road a half mile ahead. His gunner swung around, used the M-21 solid-state analog ballistic computer, and zeroed in. Before the truck could get under way, a 105 round jolted into it and blew the truck into scrap metal spread over a two-acre field.

Kitts checked his watch. After four minutes of waiting he called the captain on the radio.

"Yeah, we're ready to move, Major. One of your tanks rolled right over a hidden machine gun that was giving my guys fits. Move it now."

Major Kitts rolled his tanks again. They found little opposition. There were no tanks opposing them. Two trucks they saw wound up in the ditch and burning. Along one road, they ran into a string of twenty NK troops, who quickly threw down their weapons and gave up.

Kitts unbuttoned the turret and stood up, checking the terrain ahead.

Twenty minutes later he came to the landmark that had been described, and executed a sharp turn to the right, heading due west.

"Now, things should get more interesting," he told his gunner.

High overhead, Tomcat 204 and 206 flew CAP for the six F/A-18 Hornets from the *Monroe*. They scanned north for any NK aircraft, and usually came up empty.

The Hornets buzzed around the attack to the north; then when the tanks and the column turned west, they worked ahead, attacking any targets they found.

"Horny One-Sixteen, I've got two trucks on that road down there. Want to take turns?"

"That's a roger, Horny One-Twenty. We'll use the twenties, no sense wasting anything heavier. I'm right behind you."

The Hornets turned toward the slow-moving trucks, taking a high angle to get more rounds on the rigs from their Mach .9 speed. The first Hornet dumped twenty rounds from his six-barrel gun. That still left him with five hundred rounds.

"Caught him with three of them, One-Sixteen. See if you can find the fuel tank."

The second Hornet made his run, blasting ten rounds into the lead truck, blowing a front tire, slamming it off the dirt road, and setting it on fire.

"Oh, yes, Doctor," One-Sixteen said. "Now where did that second truck vanish to?"

"Saw him heading for some trees back there, just west of the burning truck. Let's take a look."

"Yeah, got him in there," One-Twenty said. "I'm on him." The F-18 pilot in One-Twenty burned up twenty rounds as he blasted the three trees that hid the North Korean truck. Before the rounds hit, the pilots saw two men running from the woods. After the first run by One-Twenty, the North Korean truck exploded when one round hit the gas tank.

"Now, let's see if we can find a tank or two," One-Sixteen said. "I've still got four Mavericks just looking for a place to call home."

Don Stroh brought the SEALs the latest news about how the war had progressed. The big thrust to cut off the Seoul bulge had gone west fine for five miles, then bogged down with stiff opposition. The North Koreans had six tanks in the area, and evidently were planning a buildup for a thrust of their own.

By noon the big maneuver to end the war had resulted in a stalemate, with neither side getting an advantage. The tanks were behind protection waiting for orders.

General Reynolds was disappointed, the tankers were not happy, and the air support had been less than effective.

This time when Stroh came striding into the assembly room, the SEALs hardly looked at him. He found Murdock and lifted his brows.

"Got a good one for you, Lone Ranger."

Murdock looked up from his MP-5. "Good one what?"

"A mission, an assignment. There's an air base up north that's been giving the flyboys a bad time. It's so well defended with the latest missiles and antiair missiles that they can't penetrate it to knock out the planes that come from there. A lot of the MiGs aren't flying; they're keeping them back for some reason."

"For their big push?"

"Maybe. It's what time now? A little after noon—okay, twelve hundred. You're due at a briefing at one o'clock at Eighth Army HQ. I'll tag along. Don't bother dressing up. Your cammies will be fine."

"When is this party taking place?"

"The mission? If you get the job, it will probably be tomorrow at sunup."

"Sunup, the worst time of the day. That's when a man should be sleeping. I dream of sleeping in to noon every day."

"Sure you do. Let's go for a walk and a jump in a helo."

They arrived at Army HQ south of Seoul with ten minutes

to spare. Bird Colonel Chalmers led the session. There was an Air Force colonel, two majors, a master sergeant, and Lieutenant General Reynolds, commander of the Eighth Army in Korea.

Colonel Chalmers briefed them all. "We've tried to neutralize the Sinuju Air Base. It's the major base for the North. They have most of their MiG fighters there. So far we haven't been able to break through their sophisticated air defense. We tried to send in smart missiles, but they get shot down. Our planes can't get near the place without taking fifty-percent casualties. There has to be a better way." He looked at the Air Force man.

"We have a fine little device we call On Sight Radar Targeting, or OSRT. It works well, but must be used by personnel on or near the target. It works with the ground team lighting up exact pinpointed targets with a portable radar unit, which broadcasts that sighting and it's picked up by the attacking planes, which then lock on to the pinpointed target and fire, with devastating results.

"The only trouble is the signal is not as strong as the target's radar in this case, and the plane would have to be well within enemy radar and missile range before we could launch. So that's not an option here. Sorry, Colonel."

"So, what the hell are we going to do about that air base?" General Reynolds asked. When no one spoke, he looked at Don. "Mr. Stroh, you said you might have a suggestion."

Stroh cleared his throat. Generals always had made him nervous. His highest military rank had been corporal. He pointed to Murdock. "Gentlemen, let me introduce Lieutenant Commander Blake Murdock. Murdock and his Third Platoon of fourteen SEALs went in and brought out the Vice President from behind enemy lines four days ago. I'm sure you heard about it. On the way over here from the carrier, we talked about the air base problem. I think I'll let him tell you his suggestion."

Murdock had been checking a map on the wall. He stood and went up to it. He touched the map at Sinuju.

"Gentlemen, this must be where the air base is. Is that correct?"

Some heads nodded and someone said, "Yes."

"How many of you have seen a sniper rifle, only one chambered for fifty-caliber rounds? There aren't a lot of them around. The best is made by a small machine shop down in Georgia by the name of Georgia Gun Works. My men are specialists in using this weapon.

"My suggestion is this. The McMillan M87R is accurate up to a mile away. We like to get within a thousand yards for maximum efficiency. What we suggest is this. The Navy will put my SEALs into the water a short ways off the coast. We'll swim in, infiltrate to within a thousand yards of the targets, and wait.

"Then the Air Force will launch a raid at the air base and get close enough so the North Korean air defenses will come on-line, antennas will display, and facilities vital to the operation will swing into action.

"At that time, the SEALs will be able to identify and locate these devices, then reduce the antennas, hardware, and sighting facilities and anything else we can touch with our fifty-caliber messengers. The M87R's armor-piercing fifty-caliber rounds are highly effective in putting hardware and antennas out of commission. We think we can do the job.

"While we're at it, the Air Force raid on the field will be diverted until we have the facility neutralized. Then, when we give a SATCOM go-ahead, the Air Force can get back on course and complete the mission.

"During that confusion, the SEALs will move back to the sea, swim out to a pickup by a chopper or high-speed boat off a destroyer. That's it."

"How many of the fifties do you have now, Commander?" the Air Force man asked.

"We carry three. We will need at least six more. The armorer on board the carrier says he has three. We need to find three more in your stores."

One of the majors spoke up. "We have half a dozen in our recon platoon. We can furnish them to you before you chopper back to the carrier." He motioned to the sergeant. "If this is the course of action we're going to take."

"Any other ideas?" General Reynolds asked. He looked

around. Nobody said a word. The general sighed. He looked at Murdock again. "You must be the lieutenant commander who rescued one of my Major Generals three miles inside the North Korean lines."

"Yes, sir."

The general laughed softly. "Good work, Commander. If I could, I'd like to have a copy of your after-action report on that incident. Be good to keep it on file if I need it."

"Be happy to send you one, General."

The oldest man in the room shifted in his chair and stifled a groan. He looked at Murdock again. "Son, are you sure that this will work?"

"No, sir. Fifty-caliber armor-piercing rounds simply don't come with a guarantee, but this sort of action has worked well before. Just to be cautious, you might have the Air Force send three planes over the target in a test run before committing the whole flight. If they don't draw a hail of fire, the whole group should be relatively safe."

The Air Force man nodded. "We've been probing it every day for the past four."

Murdock looked at the general. "Sir, do the SEALs have this assignment?"

The general looked around his staff advisors. Most of them nodded. "I agree, Commander. You and your men have the job. Good luck getting it done, and exfiltrating. No unit in the Eighth could do a mission like this one."

"We'll do our damndest, General. Now, if we could be excused, we'll pick up the weapons and get back to the carrier. We have a lot of planning to take care of."

"You're excused, Commander. Good hunting."

It took them a half hour to sign the paperwork for the fifty-caliber weapons and get them to the chopper and loaded on board. The fifties all had the five-round magazine instead of the ten-rounders the SEALs usually used.

"Ammo?" the major asked.

"Thanks, we've got plenty," Murdock said. "We better get moving."

The major drove them in a Humvee to the airport where the Seahawk that brought them in was warming up.

"How far are we from that air base?" Murdock asked Stroh over the scream of the rotor blades as the craft took off.

"That's what we'll have to figure, and how to get you up there and back. A destroyer?"

"Yeah, too far for an RIB. A chopper might attract too much attention. We don't want to have to swim more than a mile or so to shore."

"We'll talk with the carrier guys."

They did a half hour later. They had the CAG, a captain who handled the fleet screen security, and two commanders Murdock didn't know.

"From the *Monroe* to that town up north is about two hundred and seventy-five miles—if we don't overfly any of North Korea, which we can't do," CAG Olson said.

"A destroyer at thirty knots could get up there in about eight hours," one of the commanders said. "That would be a permanent platform for you, a base of operations."

Murdock nodded. "Okay, up there by destroyer, then we take the two RIBs that we used before and motor in to a half mile offshore and swim on in. We'll have two Motorolas with two in the RIBs. The RIBs will wait for us to come out. Since it'll be daylight by then, they might move in closer and give us some support with their machine guns if we need it. We'll go in to hit the beach about 0300. That should give us time to get through any coastal defenses, find the airfield, and get in position where we'll have the best shots at the antiair antennas. Then we wait for dawn to bring in the Air Force. We send them a go message on our SATCOM. That way we avoid any problem with forwarded messages through the RIB coxswains and the destroyer. We can contact the Air Force on TAC One. Then the Air Force can send in the attack. We'll have it timed down to about a half hour either way. It will have to be light when the NKs bring out their defenses. Otherwise we won't know what to shoot at."

"You'll take the whole platoon?" Stroh asked.

"Yes, all thirteen of us. Nine fifties and four subguns on guard duty. The destroyer can stay six or seven miles offshore away from any surface radar."

Stroh looked at his watch. "Eight hours. It's now almost

three . . . fifteen hundred. You better get your men ready while the captain picks out the lucky destroyer and we get our two RIBs on board and get you a chopper to that destroyer."

"Have your men ready to travel and on the flight deck in an hour, Commander," the fleet screen commander said. "We'll send the RIBs to the destroyer before you go. We'll have chow for you on the destroyer. We'll assign the *Cole* to you, that's the DDG 67. Let's move it, people."

Stroh talked to the Air Force by radio, and found they had some aerial recon photos of the North Korean air base and surrounding area. He had them faxed to the *Cole*, where they would be waiting for Murdock.

Murdock had called Jaybird on the way into the meeting with the CAG and the captain, and told him about the mission and to get the men ready to roll. They would have an eight-hour boat ride to get their weapons and equipment checked.

As it turned out, they were dropped on board the *Cole* moments after another chopper put their RIB boats on the fantail. They had arrived on the destroyer more than an hour before the 1800 departure time.

The SEALs were given a modest-sized assembly room amidships, and there rearranged their weapons. Sterling, Holt, Adams, and DeWitt kept their submachine guns. Everyone else was issued a .50-caliber sniper rifle. All had fired it at least fifty times before.

"Listen up," Murdock said. "We'll go over the mission again. We will be taking an eight-hour ride north near the port city of Sinuju, damn near the Chinese border. Our target is the big air base there south of the town.

"We will be shooting up everything that shows that it is, or even looks like it might be, radar equipment, antennas, firing centers, missile-launching centers, radar of any kind or type. That's our job. We need to blind these folks so they can't see the UN planes coming in.

"We shoot hell out of them, get back to the coast, and take a swim out to our RIBs and we're home free."

"How many rounds will we each have?" Bradford asked.

"How many can you carry?" Murdock asked. "I'm thinking forty rounds per man is about right."

Bradford shrugged. "They weigh nine pounds per dozen. Make it forty-eight per man; that's only thirty-six pounds for ammo."

Somebody groaned.

"Can we get ammo vests, those front and back pouches we've used to carry mortar rounds in?" Ronson asked.

"Jaybird, see what you can find out from the ammo guys on board. You subgun guys will take double ammo, and hope we don't need it. You'll be our close support."

Jaybird finished using the phone and came back to the group. "We've got vests for ammo. Somebody is bringing up ten of them for us. All the ammo we need will be here in an hour."

"Chow time in two hours," Murdock said. "Then some sack time and we'll be ready to get on the RIB at 0200. Any questions?" There weren't any. "We've got some daylight pictures of the target. Can't see much, but we know we'll have good fields of fire at the antennas from the south end of the field. Come up and look at them if you want to."

Half the men moved up to check out the photo faxes that had come from the Air Force.

Six sailors showed up at the door with boxes of ammunition.

"You guys starting a war?" one of the sailors asked.

"No, we're ending one," Jaybird told the man as they stacked the crates of .50-caliber rounds inside the room. Murdock was the first one there to try a load of forty-eight rounds. He put twenty-four in the front of the vest and the other half in the back with it in place over his head. He stood up and winced.

"We'll cut the load to forty rounds," he said. "Thirty-five in the vest and five in the magazine. Let's get it done."

"Move it," Jaybird called. "We've got less than an hour and a half to our special chow call."

16

The RIBs, Rigid Inflatable Boats, moved smartly through the water, covering the seven miles from the destroyer *Cole* toward the shore. There was no nighttime fog, no onshore flow, just a bright night with light from a half-crescent moon.

Murdock, in the lead boat, asked the coxswain to pull up at what he figured was a half mile from North Korea. The last mile had been done at four knots so they wouldn't leave a wake or make so much noise that they could be heard over the surf ahead.

DeWitt brought his RIB alongside.

"How's the time?" Murdock asked.

DeWitt checked his waterproof watch. "Oh-three-ten," DeWitt said. "Close enough. Time to get wet?"

"Right. Make sure the two Motorolas and the SATCOM are watertight. No backup on this one."

"Done," DeWitt said.

"Over the side," Murdock said, and the thirteen SEALs eased off the RIBs, entering the water without a splash. The SEALs wore full wet suits to guard against hypothermia, with cammies over them, full cap, and goggles. They went in

180

without their heavy Draeger rebreathers, so they would be on top of the water.

Murdock powered up out of the water for a look. He spotted a building near the shore that showed one light, and aimed for that. The SEALs stroked noiselessly through the Yellow Sea swells, moving quickly toward shore. The heavy .50-caliber rifles were slung over their backs, and they had to work harder than usual to stay on top of the water with the additional load of thirty-five pounds of ammunition most of the men carried.

Murdock hit the breaker line and body-surfed partway in until he could get his feet on the sandy bottom. He paused and surveyed the beach. No obvious defensive fortifications. He saw no lights or troops. The house with the light he had aimed for was now dark. It was the only building he could see.

He motioned to Holt, and the two moved forward with the next wave, stretching out so they could hand-crawl the last surge of the wave, and lay on the beach like pieces of driftwood.

They were swept in another three feet by the next wave. Holt looked over and shook his head. He found no opposition. He lifted his submachine gun and drained the water out of the barrel.

Murdock gave a hand signal, and the rest of the platoon moved into the beach with the aid of the breakers. Murdock and Holt got to their feet and ran forty feet across wet and then dry sand to a scattering of shrubs and small brush just in back of the beach line.

They scouted the area, both gave thumbs-up signs, and Holt waved the rest of the SEALs to come ashore.

All the men drained their weapons' barrels, checked the loads, and were ready to fire.

Murdock put two of the subguns at the head of the platoon, and the other two men with submachine guns at the end. They moved forward cautiously. Thirty yards inland they came to a dirt road, which did not appear to be highly traveled. The men were spread ten yards apart, and went over the path all at once in a rush.

Murdock checked the map he had memorized and the

aerial shots of the airfield. He could see some lights to the left making a blush in the sky. That was the direction to the airfield.

They turned north and moved like ghosts in the night. The subguns all had suppressors on them. There would be no un-silenced shots fired until the big guns began working over the hardware on the air base.

A jet aircraft took off, passing almost directly overhead of them at no more than two hundred feet.

"Must be the right part of town," Jaybird said.

They moved faster then, bypassed a pair of houses, and detoured across some rice paddies to avoid a small collection of buildings that might be a village.

They lay in the grass near a small stream. Nothing moved ahead of them. The locals were all sleeping by that time. At 0330, Murdock motioned the men ahead. They waded ankle-deep through the tiny stream and angled more toward the bright lights. They heard a plane evidently land somewhere ahead of them on the large air base.

The two lead scouts with their MP subguns had just come to their feet and ran toward a small shack directly in their path when two men came out of it, stretched, and walked toward the platoon. Sterling and DeWitt dropped to a crouch and let the men come to them. Both the North Koreans wore uniforms.

Sterling and DeWitt pulled out their KA-BAR knives and waited. The North Koreans were chattering and not watching where they were going. One almost stumbled on Jaybird Sterling, who lifted up and rammed his knife hilt deep upward in the man's belly just under his rib cage. The blade sliced through three vital organs, then lanced into the heart, killing the soldier instantly.

DeWitt clubbed his man with the subgun, then drove his KA-BAR into his chest, killing the North Korean soldier with one stroke.

Murdock moved up quickly.

"Are there any more?" Murdock whispered. DeWitt and Jaybird took off at once, running silently to the shack and checking it out. Jaybird went around to the front, where he found a door. There were no lights on inside. The structure was about eight feet square. A guard shack?

Jaybird unlatched the door and swung it outward. No reaction came from inside. DeWitt edged around the door and from ground level, aimed his penlight into the darkness. He saw only two bunks, a small table, and two packs and rifles. No more guards.

"Clear shack," DeWitt said into his Motorola, and the platoon moved past the shack toward what looked to be the edge of the airfield ahead.

A fighter swept down the runway from their left to right and screamed into the air. Murdock lifted up and took a better look. They had come to the side of the runway about in the middle. They could see muted lights across the runways and what appeared to be a cluster of buildings. He also spotted two dimly lit antennas.

He and DeWitt checked the area with their binoculars.

"Should be the bulk of their antiaircraft system," DeWitt said. "I'd bet those low buildings in the center will open up and antenna and sensing devices will extend upward during an attack."

"Where are the missiles themselves?" Jaybird asked.

"Doesn't matter where they are. If we knock out their eyes and ears, they won't know where to aim them," Murdock said.

The platoon had spread out over a fifty-yard line facing the runway. The heavy guns lay in the middle, with the submachine guns on each end.

They waited. It was a little after 0400. It wouldn't be dawn for another hour. They had to have the light to identify the right targets.

"Stay in place and keep alert," Murdock said. "Shortly before dawn we'll contact the fly boys. Any problems, sing out on the net." There was no response.

Murdock monitored the air traffic. There was little. He saw two choppers moving around, but nothing that looked like a large buildup for a big push.

Murdock called up Holt who had the SATCOM unbuttoned

and ready to use. Dawn was just breaking and streaking the eastern sky.

"Raise the Air Force on TAC One and see if they're airborne and ready to rumble."

Holt used the satellite communications system.

"High Fliers, this is Ground Zero. Do you copy?"

There was no response. He checked the TAC frequency and tried again. This time a voice responded.

"Ground Zero, you're loud and clear. We're wet here and should be near enough your position for some reaction from their antennas in eight minutes."

"That's a roger, High Fliers. Help us find some bull's-eyes."

Murdock heard the conversations. He used the Motorola. "The flyboys will come close enough to get the electronics activated. As soon as anyone spots a change in the physical makeup of those buildings over there, sound off. The flyboys won't be making an actual run, just come close enough to get them excited. Stay hard and mean."

Murdock had punched up his stopwatch on his wrist when the Air Force responded with the eight minutes trip time. He watched the numbers click by on the lighted dial.

"Targets," Murdock said in the lip mike. "Take the best shot in front of you. Guys on the far left, take the far left antennas and anything else that looks operating. Guys on the right do likewise, and the middle group takes that bunch. Anything operating is a target.

"If these jaspers have any security at all around the field, we should be getting some heat before we get rid of all the targets. Subguns, be watchful. Now is a good time for you four to take the suppressors off your weapons. They'll know we're here soon enough.

"We'll hold this ground until we have eliminated all our targets, if possible. Subguys be our lookouts. The rest of us will be fucking busy. Any questions?"

"We hiking out the same way we came in?" a voice asked.

"We'll play that one by ear, Jaybird. It all depends on the situation and the terrain."

"Four minutes since the last transmission," Holt said on the net. "These snoopers must pick up planes out a hundred miles. When do they activate?"

"Maybe at fifty miles," DeWitt said. "At twenty-five miles a minute, those Air Force guys cover a lot of ground in a rush."

Murdock checked the big McMillan M87R .50-caliber rifle. He had the five-round magazine in place and fully loaded, with one round in the chamber and the weapon locked. He sighted in through the 32-power scope and smiled. The scope amplified not only the distance, but the amount of light as well.

He checked one of the low buildings with a flat roof. As he watched, the roof moved. It pivoted upward in the middle and on each side. An antenna of some sort lifted up what must be ten feet and slowly turned.

"One antenna is activating," Murdock said. "Check through your scopes, get on your targets. It won't be long now."

Thirty seconds later half the small buildings five hundred yards across the runways from them had shifted in shape or character. Now more than twenty antennas, tracking devices, and a few small missiles showed where there had only been nondescript buildings before.

"Fire at will," Murdock said. He had sighted in on his target in the center, and refined his sight, and squeezed the trigger. The big gun went off with a blast that sounded too loud in the stillness of the North Korean morning.

At once more of the big rifles fired. Murdock watched his target and saw a small hit. He lifted his sights to the larger part of the antenna and fired again. This time he saw his round strike and nearly break the unit in half. He switched targets, blasted two more antennas and a nearby facilitating building, then slid in a new magazine of five more rounds.

"Make your rounds count," Murdock brayed into the mike so they could hear him over the blasting .50-caliber rounds.

He saw a small utility rig and tracked it a minute, then fired and saw it careen out of control and crash.

Holt tapped Murdock on the shoulder. "The fly-guys have broken off and pulled back so we could have the fun."

Murdock nodded and sighted in again. He fired the big gun

until he could feel it grow hot. For a moment, he surveyed the antennas under their siege. Some of the buildings had closed their roofs. Some had antennas that wouldn't retract, so the roofs couldn't move.

When the antennas were all wounded or broken, the SEALs attacked the adjacent buildings that did not open up. "Sheds are probably where the electronics are positioned," Murdock said in a lull in the firing. "Use up some of your rounds there. I want each man with a fifty to keep two rounds for the return trip. We just might need them."

Murdock worked the bolt, chambering another big .50-caliber round into the weapon, and found a new target.

"We've got company coming from the left," DeWitt said. "Twin lights. Anybody get him in his sights?"

"Yeah, got him," Ronson said. He got off two rounds, and the lights on the small truck went out and DeWitt growled.

"Oh, yes, scratch one vehicle. Could be some foot-sloggers moving our way. I'll go out fifty and watch for them."

"Easy out there, JG," Murdock said. Then he fired five more times into the complex.

"Call out on the net when you're down to two rounds," Murdock said. He checked his watch. It had been three minutes since they fired the first shot. He checked his own weapon—down to three. One more round.

They began chiming in then when the shooters had two rounds left.

"DeWitt, you have anything?"

"Six men working my way. Don't know I'm here yet. Still thirty yards away. Give them another minute." There was a silence then as the last of the fifties fired.

"Pulling back," Murdock said. "Ed?"

Just then, Murdock and the SEALs heard the stuttering of the MP-5 that DeWitt carried. The weapon jolted out six-round bursts twice, then twice more.

"Coming home," DeWitt said. "Four of them are down or dead and the other two running their yellow asses back the way they came."

"Let's move," Murdock said. "Find us, Ed, and take the tail-end Charlie spot. Back the same way we came."

A minute later they heard heavy motors of trucks grinding toward them.

"Company," DeWitt said. "The old eyeballs show me two six-bys that must have troops. What, about twenty per rig. I'd say we will have forty fresh troopers on our tail in about three or four minutes. Suggest we find a good defensive spot and wait for them."

"Roger that, Ed. Close it up. We're coming to a small rise, not much but a minor little hill and some brush and trees. Better than a rice paddy. Everyone over the top and find a firing position just over the crest. Company coming."

It took them almost three minutes to set up on the small hill. They made just enough noise on purpose to attract the North Korean troops into the right area. Murdock had his four MP-5 subguns in the middle of the line. The SEALs spread out five yards apart. All had a full quota of hand grenades.

"Save the fifties for now," Murdock said on the net. "We'll use the subguns when they get close enough. If any make it through that welcome, we'll use grenades. It's downhill so we'll get a roll."

They waited.

"Coming," Lam said. He had the best ears in the platoon. "Little to the left."

Murdock picked them up on his NVGs. They were still 150 yards down the hill. Some small brush and trees confused the matter, but the NKs had shifted to the left. Murdock clanked a .50-caliber round on the long gun, and grinned as the chasers shifted their angle and came head on.

When they were a hundred yards away, Murdock gave the order to fire.

The four submachine guns chattered on three-round bursts. They were the only defensive weapons they had. They took return fire, but the NKs were firing only at the muzzle flashes. They had no targets and did no damage.

"Wish to hell we had a few Claymores," Jaybird said as he lay on the ground watching below. At the first volley from the top of the hill, the NKs went to the ground and fired back, but didn't move on up the hill. Jaybird said there were about thirty men below.

Murdock could hear shouting from below, and watched as an officer went along prodding the men, screeching at them. Murdock couldn't resist. He chambered one .50-caliber round in the big McMillan and found the officer near the NK troops. The man turned full front to the top of the hill, and Murdock fired. The round slammed into the infantry lieutenant and blasted him ten feet down the hill. Where he used to have a chest now was a huge hole and smashed ribs and shards of his spine. The NK troops sagged back to the ground.

It took them ten minutes to launch an attack forward. Murdock figured the top noncom in the company was prodding them. They stormed upward another fifty yards; then the withering automatic fire from the H&K MP-5's stopped them again. Jaybird threw a grenade. It hit about forty yards down the hill, bounced, and went off near enough to the troops to bring some wails of pain.

"Hold the grenades," Murdock said. "Let them get closer."

"Don't think they'll come any closer," DeWitt said. "They're crawling away."

"Let's do the same thing, the opposite direction," Murdock said, and the platoon came to its feet, strung out five yards apart, and followed Lam, who led them down the hill, across a small stream, and toward the coast.

They came to the guard shack, paused to clear it, and went on past that and the bodies of the two NKs they had dispatched earlier.

They were a quarter of a mile from the road they had passed coming in when Lam gave them a down signal on the Motorola.

"Skip, better come take a look," Lam said into the radio.

Murdock moved up quickly to where Lam lay in the grass behind a small bush. Slightly downhill and ahead of them, Murdock saw the road full of trucks. He counted eight all big enough to carry twenty armed troopers.

"Where the hell did they come from?" Murdock asked.

"We do an end run, or maybe a double reverse?" Lam asked.

"We're not going through a hundred and fifty men, that's for fucking sure," Murdock said. He stared at the trucks. "We get on the other side, then we blow the trucks with the fifties. Yeah, let's take a hard left here."

They worked around the trucks in single file and ten yards apart. The North Koreans had no security out. It seemed the men were simply on the way somewhere, and had stopped to relieve themselves or for chow. The time pushed to 0545. Murdock tried to remember how far to the beach from the road. Not far. A mile, a mile and a half?

No more. He watched the troops below. They weren't moving. The truck engines had been turned off. They handed out food. That would take an hour.

The SEALs' silent line melted into the brush two hundred yards to the side of the trucks. Murdock found what he wanted on the far side of them. He could smell the salt air now. Good, not far.

They set up in the edge of a clearing five hundred yards from the trucks. He assigned the rigs to eight men, and told them to use up their two rounds.

"A fuel tank would be good, but the engine will be acceptable." They could see the rigs clearly in the morning light. Everyone fired except Murdock. He was keeping his one last round for insurance.

The rounds screamed into the hapless trucks. Four armor-piercing messengers found engines and blew the vehicles into worthless junk. One round hit a fuel tank and it exploded, showering burning gasoline on two of the other trucks, which soon exploded as well. Twenty seconds after the fifties began firing, the SEALs were done, lined up, and moved out double time for the surf.

They hit the sand five minutes later, strapped their weapons on their backs, buttoned up their Motorolas in watertight flaps, and hit the water.

They were just beyond the breaker line when Murdock heard the growl of a motor. The rest of them caught the sound too.

"Probably a coastal patrol craft," Murdock shouted so most of the SEALs could hear him. "Stay together. We'll duck-dive if we have to. I don't see any boat yet."

They kept swimming on the surface away from the coast.

They had an appointment out a half mile. Murdock heard the patrol craft again. This time it was accented with twelve-round bursts from a machine gun.

The sound faded, then came back stronger. "Coming our way," Murdock said, and the word passed from SEAL to SEAL. They could all hear it then, and some could see a wake as the craft plowed through the Yellow Sea straight at them. It wasn't going to turn away this time. Murdock waited until it was less than fifty yards away. Then he shouted to dive, and the thirteen SEALs turned turtle and dove downward.

Murdock took six strong strokes down and leveled off, watching above him. The water was clear and he could make out the surface. Then it was laced with hundreds of bubbles as the North Korean coastal patrol craft slashed through the water overhead.

Murdock surfaced slowly, took a huge breath, and checked the route of the boat. It kept moving in a straight line. He had no idea what kind of a search pattern the skipper on board was using.

The rest of the SEALs surfaced, and Murdock called for a sound-off to get a head count. Everyone was there. He called Holt over.

"I'll boost you up and you unzip your Motorola and give a call to the RIB. Make two calls, then listen."

Holt waited for the boost all the way out of the water down to his waist, then unzipped the watertight and took out the Motorola.

"SEAL Three calling RIB. Ready to motor."

He waited ten seconds and made the call again. This time a reply came back faintly.

"Yeah, SEAL Three. We've been playing hide-and-seek with an NK patrol boat. Saw your bonfire. Heading back your way. Transmit every minute. Your volume will help lead me to you. Figure we're almost at the range of the boxes."

They made four calls; then Murdock let Holt back into the water. He took out a green light stick and broke the inside, letting the chemicals flow together and produce a steady green glow.

Three minutes later, the RIBs came alongside and picked up the SEALs.

"You crazy, using a light stick this close to North Korean coast?" the coxswain asked.

Murdock snorted, "Hell, I figured you could outrun those guys. Let's go home. We'll fight about it on the destroyer."

17

The Yellow Sea
Off North Korea

The coxswain of the first RIB yelled at Murdock over the whine of the engine that jolted them through the water at nearly forty knots.

"Nice going with that glow stick, Commander. We've got an NK patrol craft on our tail."

"One of the big ones?"

"Probably a hundred and forty feet," the coxswain shouted. "Hope it doesn't have missiles on it or we're in fucking big trouble."

"How fast can we go?"

"This new ten-meter will hit forty knots, but no way we can outrun a missile. We can hope to hear some eighty-five millimeter rounds coming at us. That will mean they have no missiles."

He used the radio for a minute, and then got back to Murdock. "We're splitting off from the other RIB. Give the fuckers back there two targets to worry about. Hold it, here comes a round."

They couldn't hear any incoming sound, but an explosion blasted a crater in the soft green of the sea.

"He's three hundred meters off," the coxswain said. "Damn good. We'll do some maneuvering. Tell your guys to hold on with both hands."

The V-section-bottom fiberglass boat took a hard right turn, then a left, and plunged through the building seas. They took water over the bow, and in a moment the three crewmen were as wet as the SEALs.

Another round came in, landing far to their right this time. Murdock knew the patrol boat was trying for a bracket, but they had no forward observer. He wondered if they had radar. They must to come even this close. With any luck they'd only have surface-search radar. That was all they needed right now. He hoped it was only a Pot-Head I band. But he couldn't know.

The little craft took another drastic turn, this time to the left, and continued for what Murdock figured was a quarter of a mile before the RIB angled back on its course toward the destroyer.

"Can your chopper help out?" Murdock asked the coxswain.

"Not unless I ask him to," the sailor said. "Hell, I want to ditch this turkey myself. Better have your guys stand up for the rest of the run, easier on the kidneys that way."

The RIB heeled over again as it made a high-speed turn to the left again, held that direction for ten seconds, then whipped back to the right, and continued for another quarter of a mile before it angled away from the coast again.

One more round came in, but it was barely heard over the roar do the RIB's engine.

The craft made another sharp turn, then concentrated on moving to sea. They saw flashes of two more rounds, but the low-to-the-water inflatable boats were hard to spot on radar, and this time they had slipped out of the North Koreans' grasp.

The coxswain throttled back to abut thirty knots to make it easier riding. Still, they were the first of the two boats to reach the *Cole*. They tied up to the stern of the ship and went up ladders dropped down from the helicopter landing pad.

They changed into dry clothes in their assigned assembly room, and Murdock asked for a casualty report.

Mahanani grinned at the commander. "Skipper, not a fucking scratch on this one. The JG has some blood on his hands, but he claims it ain't his. Says he had an up-close-and-personal relationship with a North Korean sentry."

"Good. Now let's get some chow and then bunk out. We've got an eight-hour ride back to the Hotel *Monroe*."

Murdock and the JG had just finished their specially prepared steak dinners when a radioman found them.

"Commander, you're wanted in communications right away."

They both went, and the commo officer pointed to a radio and a handset. "The CAG on the *Monroe* wants to talk to you, Commander." Murdock took the microphone.

"Murdock here, sir."

"Good work with those fifties, Commander. We sent a flight of eighteen Hornets up that way. The first two found almost no enemy missile fire at that air base, and we went in with all eighteen and blew the place into hell. Our first count shows we caught fourteen of their fighters on the ground and demolished them. There were jet fuel fires all over the runway. Three of them tried to take off and got plastered into the concrete.

"The front-line troops won't have any trouble with those fighters, and the rest of their Air Force is on the run. Good work. Oh, Don Stroh is here and panting to talk."

"Thanks, Captain. We appreciate your comments."

"Murdock? Yeah, you came through," Stroh said. "The Eighth Army general is pleased as a cocker spaniel with a raw steak. You have a nice nap and we'll see you when you get to this floating hotel. Oh, I think that the general and his staff have a new job for you, so don't cave in on me yet. This one could be important . . . as the others were."

"Don't try to be nice, Stroh. It isn't like you. And I still say that I caught the biggest fish back there in San Diego."

"Biggest, maybe, but I caught the most calico bass and those were the ones we grilled for the fish fry."

"Wait till next fishing trip. See you later." Murdock gave

the handset to the operator and he and DeWitt headed back to the assembly room.

"He's got another job for us?" DeWitt yelped. "How about a couple of days of R&R somewhere?"

"JG, this is Don Stroh we're talking about."

Eighth Army Headquarters
Near Seoul, South Korea

Lieutenant General Richard F. Reynolds stood in front of the huge map in the war room and studied the red line that showed the present MLR. The Main Line of Resistance had been moving little the last two days. The Republic of Korea troops had weathered the attacks well, and had in some cases pushed back the NK troops after their first dramatic drive southward.

The red marks could be wiped off and redrawn whenever news came in of advancements or attacks.

Colonel Vuylsteke waved at the line north of Seoul.

"We've trapped at least a battalion of NKs in this region. They stormed through with tank support. We actually fell back to sucker them in, then crashed in on them from both sides and the front and cut them off.

"The cleanup process is starting. We saturate the area with artillery, then do daylight bombing in the morning followed by our assault on three sides. We should have it mopped up by noon."

The general looked at the west side of the line. There the red marks extended only two to three miles south of the old DMV, which was still printed in permanent ink.

"What about this side? Any movement?"

"Not much, sir. The NKs simply extended their supply lines too far, too fast, and couldn't keep the troops furnished with ammunition, let alone food and gasoline. We're in good shape on the west front, and should have the NKs pushed back to the DMZ within three or four days."

"So, we're making progress. How long do you think it will take us to win back the real estate that we gave up?"

Colonel Vuylsteke shook his head and laid down his pointer. "On that score, we can't say. It depends a lot on how hard the ROKs fight, how well our own supply lines work. We didn't have the chance to stockpile food, ammunition, and gasoline the way the North did. I'd say two months at least to get back to where we were."

"I'm getting lots of flack from Washington and the Pentagon," General Reynolds said. "They say get it over with quickly. I can't convince them that we have a war on out here. They think of it as a small flare-up, a minor support mission for a needful ally. It's goddamned war if I've ever seen one."

"I agree, sir," Colonel Vuylsteke said. He pointed back to the center of the map. "Sir, you asked about the Ninety-first Tank Battalion. They were in that first cutoff push we made. They held their position, and now have joined in the closure of the trap of that battalion of NKs. They are functioning well, and we have lost only one tank in the strike."

"Yes, good." The general threw his riding crop into a chair and sat down across from it. "We need something dramatic, something swift and deadly to convince the North Koreans to pull back to the former lines. We need to talk again. This foiled attack may have reduced the NKs' military's role in the government."

Colonel Vuylsteke drew a circle in red around Pyongyang, the capital of North Korea. "Here is where we need to strike, General Reynolds. If we hit the capital hard with fifty planes, we might be able to convince them the war is too costly."

"Come on, Colonel. It sounds good, but it won't work. Remember Vietnam and then again in the Gulf War? You can't bomb these people into surrendering. It just isn't practical. We need something else. I want you and G-2 to get together and come up with some ideas. We need a good plan, one that will work. Something like that air raid on the Sinuju air defenses. Now, that worked."

"The Navy gets credit for that one, General. The Navy and a handful of SEALs."

"What I heard. I don't care who pulls the trigger. We need a plan, a surprise, something stunning. Not a nuclear bomb on Pyongyang. A practical, workable plan that will set North Korea back on its haunches. Get to work. I want it first thing in the morning."

Colonel Vuylsteke nodded and hurried out. The general got to his feet and studied the map. Where should their next thrust be to push the NKs back into their own country? The DMZ had been least penetrated on the east. Might be just the place to drive them back across the line and let them stew a little.

A month, maybe two it was going to take to convince North Korea that they had to stay on their side of the lines or there would be shooting. The Pentagon, Washington, and the American people wouldn't stand for it that long. The six-day Gulf land war was too much for the public. Two months more of this Korean fighting, and the Administration and the Army brass would be roasted alive.

What in hell would it take to shake the NKs right down to their bootstraps?

General Reynolds paced his reinforced office for half an hour. No course of action came to him. Damn! Maybe G-2 would come up with some kind of a plan. He hoped so. A glance at his watch showed it was 0135. He'd better get some sleep. When did he tell Colonel Vuylsteke to have a plan ready? He couldn't remember. Shit, now he was losing his memory. No. He remembered. He'd said first thing in the morning. That always meant at 0600. Not a lot of time to sleep.

By the time Colonel Vuylsteke reported to his general at 0600, General Reynolds had been working over his maps and reports for a full hour. He waved his top planner aside and finished what he had in front of him, then looked up.

"So?" Reynolds asked.

"We have a plan we think will work. It should shake the whole of North Korea right down to its floppy sandals."

"Good, put it on hold for two days. Tomorrow morning I want an offensive thrust into the old Changdan sector. The penetration there is less than three miles. I want to get the NKs driven back to the DMZ and held there. How long will it take you to get the troops ready, to bring up a battalion in reserve to beef up the attack, and get out tanks over there to lead the thrust?"

Vuylsteke relaxed and grinned. "General, we have a buildup started in that area. We can finish it today and get the tanks shifted over there and blast out at daylight tomorrow. You want to hear about our plan to end the war?"

"No, not now. Let's get this attack rolling and see how it goes. All we have to do is drive them back to the DMV all along the line."

The general looked at Vuylsteke, who had lifted his brows. "What?"

"All along the line, sir? Twenty-five miles? That's going to take us six months."

"We'll see. Get things in motion. I want to be behind the troops when they charge out in the morning."

"Sir, I hope that means way behind, like five miles."

General Reynolds snorted. "Al, you know me a hell of a lot better than that. Get my Humvee ready. Now, don't you have a few orders to give?"

Colonel Vuylsteke waved a partial salute and hurried out of the room.

During the rest of that day, the ROK forces facing the enemy along the Changdon sector sent out four patrols. Two were set up to make contact with the enemy, judge any strength he might have at that point, and return. Both patrols came back bloodied and with two dead. The NKs appeared to have strengthened their lines at this point.

Near sunset, General Reynolds sent an order for a prisoner patrol. They had to bring back if possible an NK officer who knew what the situation was across the line.

Colonel Vuylsteke shook his head as he reported on the last patrol to come in.

"They were met in force, General. A fourteen-man patrol was to make contact and bug out. They made contact and almost got wiped out. Heavy machine guns, mortars, and some kind of recoilless rifles. They were so close our ROKs could see the back blast."

"So?"

"Looks like the NKs can reinforce a sector too. We've thought for a long time we have some security leaks. Somehow they knew we were building up along there and did the same thing at the same time. There's no point in trying for that attack in the morning. We better call it off before we lose a lot of men and get exactly no where."

"Is that what the South Korean officers think as well?" General Reynolds asked.

"Yes, sir, and this time they're right."

General Reynolds sat in his chair and stared at the big map. "All right, call it off. Leave that battalion in reserve up close until we know that the NKs have thinned out that sector." He threw his favorite riding crop across the room and stared at his top aide.

"Now, Vuylsteke, let's hear about that great plan you have for ending the war. Remember that we can't drop a nuke on Pyongyang."

"Agreed, General, but we think you'll like our plan almost that much. Six of us got together and were up all night putting this together. It's simple, really, and the risk factor is practically nil."

Yellow Sea
USS *Monroe*

Lieutenant Commander Blake Murdock took DeWitt and Jaybird along with him this time when he was called to the admiral's cabin just after evening mess. They had been resting up for the past day and a half, and wondered when the next shoe would fall. It was now.

"Admiral's got something big to talk to you about," Don Stroh had said ten minutes ago. "We best get right up there and have a chat."

In the compartment were the Admiral, CAG Olson, the captain of the carrier, and two more officers Murdock didn't know. The three SEALs and Stroh edged into the room.

"Good, we're all here," Admiral Kenner said. "This one is about as top secret as they come. No one outside this room, except perhaps the rest of the SEALs, is to know anything about what we say here. Is that completely understood?"

The men in the room nodded or gave a curt "Aye, aye."

"I've had a request for a strike by the SEALs from General Reynolds, commander of the Eighth Army and the ROK forces now fighting along the DMZ in Korea. It's a bit unusual." The admiral stood and moved to the back of his chair.

"You may have noticed that I said the general has given us a request, not an order. This mission is top secret, but it also is entirely a volunteer one. I won't give an order for you SEALs to undertake this project. If you want to accept it, it would have to be by the decision of the entire SEAL contingent. Is that clear?" The admiral looked directly at Murdock.

"Yes, sir."

"Fine, then let's proceed. General Reynolds is under extreme pressure to end the fighting. The politicos in Washington say end the fighting with the troops in place and redraw the DMZ. That's not acceptable to the Army or to the South Koreans. The pressure is growing by the day. The American public thinks a land war should last only four days like it did in the Gulf.

"With this in mind, General Reynolds asked his staff to come up with a plan to end the war quickly. It has. They have pitched that plan to us.

"I've been on the phone with the general for twenty minutes, going over this plan. We agree how it might work. Here it is.

"Briefly, it's a head-hunting mission. The idea is to execute the top three men in the North Korean government, all of whom are Army generals. You may remember that the former leader Kim Jong Il was overthrown by an Army coup a year ago. The generals now rule with an iron fist. The fourth man in the government is a civilian who had some power in the Jong government. That's it. This type of an attack is unusual for our military. We had headhunters in Vietnam, but usually for much smaller targets. SEALs, it's up to you. Mr. Stroh has checked with his people, who talked to the President. He has approved the mission if the SEALs okay it. I suggest you men return to your unit and consider this request. I'll expect your decision within an hour." The admiral looked at the SEALs.

"Aye, aye, Admiral," Murdock said. Then he, DeWitt, Jaybird, and Stroh turned and walked quickly out of the admiral's cabin.

"Holy shit," Jaybird blurted out once they were in the companionway. "We go in and do a triple snuff on their top three guys."

"Amazing, outrageous, but it might just turn the trick and get that fourth man to call off the war," DeWitt said.

"Skipper?" Jaybird asked.

Murdock shook his head. "Got to think about this one. We'd be going into the heart of North Korea. Probably Pyongyang, their fucking capital. They'll have massive power and guards and elite troops guarding everything and everyone. We don't even speak the language. How in hell . . ."

They hurried back to the assembly room provided by the Navy, where they had their gear and hung out. Murdock held up his hand and indicated Don Stroh should wait outside. He silently agreed.

"A mission, Skipper?" Holt asked as soon as they got in the room.

Murdock called them around and told them what they were being asked to do, and that it was a volunteer operation.

"Since when does the Navy ask us if we want a mission?" Bradford asked.

"Like now," DeWitt said. "This is not our usual covert job. It's above and beyond. Not the type of action that U.S. military usually does, and when we do, it's under extreme secrecy and always on a volunteer basis."

"We've been headhunters before," Harry Ronson said. "No big deal."

"It is a big deal when you're dealing with the head of a foreign government," Murdock said. "We didn't knock off Saddam, you'll remember."

"Yeah, but we should have," Jaybird said.

After a chorus of cheers subsided, Murdock looked around. "So, talk it up. How do you guys feel about this kind of an action?"

"We'll be in the heart of enemy country, right?" Mahanani asked.

"Probably," DeWitt said. "Intelligence will have to tell us where these guys are. I've heard that they never get together.

Paranoid as hell. They do business by phone and radio. They don't want to invite another coup."

"We get them with the big fifties or our KA-BARs or what?" Lampedusa asked.

"Depends," Murdock began.

The rest of the men chimed in. "On the situation and the terrain!" A lot of hooraying followed.

"Everybody will go?" Quinley asked.

"We still work as a team," Murdock said. "We need every body we have. We're down to thirteen. I'd say everyone would go."

"Hell, count me in," Miguel Fernandez said. "You fuckers want to live forever?"

There came a lot of yelling and shouting and hooraying again. When it settled down, Murdock started to grin as he watched them.

"You realize we've never been *asked* to undertake a mission before. We've had assignments and missions and operations. This is a first. We go in if we want to. Since the admiral said it's a volunteer operation, each of you has a vote. I know, I know, unusual for a military operation. This is an unusual request. What do you say? Everyone who wants to go on this expedition, raise a hand."

Murdock looked around the room. Hands began going up. He lifted his. DeWitt's was the first up. He checked every man. It was unanimous.

"Hands down. Everyone who will not go on this outing into North Korea, lift one hand."

He waited a minute, then another long pause. No hands went up. They had left Stroh in the companionway outside the door. Murdock told the closest man to go bring in Stroh. He came in, his face flushed, and Murdock knew that the CIA man had been furiously pacing the companionway.

"Set it up, Stroh. We'll take your vacation tour of North Korea."

Stroh bellowed out in delight and ran for the telephone at the end of the assembly room.

He came back a minute later.

"Yes, okay, we've got a go. The Navy is figuring out how

to get you up there. Probably be by destroyer again and the RIBs. They are checking with Army intelligence to see if they know where any of the three are. We'll need to know that specifically before you go."

Murdock turned to his men. "Let's get with it. Planning time. What weapons and devices do we take? What mix of weapons and rounds? Wet suits or cammies? Let's get moving it, gentlemen. We've got a pisspot full of work to do before we get off this floating hotel."

18

The Yellow Sea
USS *Monroe*

SEAL Team Seven, Third Platoon, decided to take the jaunt into North Korea slightly before noon. There were arrangements to be made. The timetable was set up. The quicker the better. They would deploy off North Korea sometime after dark that same day.

Murdock talked with CAG Olson.

"We need some kind of air contact. The *Cole* has a landing pad for choppers, but they are usually of the LAMPS III class. They won't do us much good since they have no land-attack capability. If we really get in a hole, we need something with some firepower. Can't you put a Cobra on the *Cole*'s pad and we use it only in an emergency? It should be able to land and take off from the destroyer. The rotor diameter is the same as the Seasprite and smaller than the Seahawk."

Captain Irving Olson smiled. "Commander, you've been doing your homework. Yes, we can fly the Cobra off that class destroyer if we need to. In this case it looks like it would work. You'll want it with a complete load of ground-attack weapons. That would be the three-barrel twenty-millimeter cannon in the nose and wing pylons for the quad seven-tube seventy-millimeter rocket pods."

"Good. Always good to have some backup. We'll go in silent, but if we do our job, we can't stay silent for long. We're waiting for word from the Army's G-2 people about where these targets might be. We hear the generals are never in the same place at the same time, so we'll have some travel time."

"Interpreters?"

"Yes, we'll have two flown out here as soon as the Army picks them. We want Koreans who can help us pass if we have to. We are getting Korean civilian clothes to wear from the git-go."

"You have everything else you need, Commander?"

"Yes, sir. We're still selecting our weapon mix. Right now it's set for 1320. We'll have five hours to sunset, but all we want to do tonight is get ashore and get ourselves situated somewhere. We'll go to work the next day."

"Commander, I hope you make it back. You'll make the SATCOM. We can put a dozen Hornets up there without too much trouble if they can help. The air belongs to us now. But the Cobra is a good idea as well. Quicker response time."

Murdock thanked the CAG, and hurried back to the assembly room. There was no word yet from the Army about the location of the targets.

Jaybird had checked with the admiral. The *Cole* had been alerted, and was standing by a quarter of a mile to starboard. The two RIBs were still on board the destroyer, and it was ready with crews for the inflatables.

They had selected weapons. They would take two of the fifties, four of the H&K PSG1 NATO-round sniper rifles. The rest of the SEALs would carry the H&K submachine guns. All but the fifties could be fired with suppressors. A quiet hit would be best. If they could work it.

Murdock went to communications and got through to Eighth Army headquarters. He was routed to Colonel Vuylsteke.

"Yes, Commander. You and your men have done good work. We hope this mission isn't an impossible one for you."

"We hope so, too. Colonel. Do we have any target locations yet?"

"None for sure. We have one tentative one, who intelligence says is the top dog. He's Kim Bok Hee, a four-star general who promoted himself from brigadier. Said to be the most outgoing of the trio. Enjoys a good time, an avid golfer in a land of few golf courses, and a stern disciplinarian. Is currently commander in chief of the armed forces. We think he's in his vacation house near Nampo, which is about forty miles south and west of the capital. It's a port city, if that will help. It's on the north side of a good-sized bay."

"Thanks, Colonel. That should be enough to get us under way. Use the SATCOM to the destroyer *Cole*. We should have a six-hour ride on her before we move to the coast. We must have all three firm locations before we launch. Are we clear on this point?"

The colonel chuckled. "Commander, I see why you're so good at your work. Yes, we'll have firm locations for you. That's our top priority right now. Call me anytime you have a question. We'll give you all the help we can. What about air?"

"It's a timing situation. That would be a hundred-and-fifty-mile jump for your choppers. Your fighters could help faster, but couldn't evac us if we really get jammed. We'll have a Navy Cobra on call about ten minutes away. That will have to do for now. We'll keep our options open."

They said good-bye and hung up. Murdock looked at the phone. He called the admiral and told him they had the first location and where it was.

"About a six-hour ride in the *Cole*," the admiral said. "Let us know when you're ready to board. We'll put the Cobra on board with reloads of ammo after you and your men are choppered on. Anything else?"

"Not right now, Admiral. Thanks for asking. This has a little bit of a weird feeling about it."

"I've had the same feeling, Commander Murdock. Let's hope they are just pre-mission jumpy nerves."

"Yes, we'll hope."

Murdock put down the phone and hurried back to the assembly room. His men were ready. Jaybird had them in their cammies.

"What happened to the Korean clothes?" Murdock asked.

"Foul-up, Skipper. The Army was supposed to supply them, but something went wrong. They sent the two Korean sergeants who will be our interpreters and fill in with machine guns. They arrived on board and are ready to move. We've given them MP-5's and ammo. The colonel I talked to said the clothing would be choppered to the *Monroe* before we got under way."

"Any other problems I need to know about, Jaybird?"

"No, sir. We have double ammo. Each man carries four fifty-caliber rounds in his combat vest. No rebreathers. We go in wet. We each have our waterproofed Motorolas, and we're taking two SATCOMs. Joe Douglas will carry the backup."

"What about the destroyer?"

"She's standing by. The RIBs are on board with the crews. Our Cobra is standing by, and will land on the destroyer as soon as we have been choppered aboard and the clothing arrives from Seoul."

"Sounds like we're ready, LPO."

Jaybird looked up quickly. "Sir?"

"Yes, I know. I just promoted you to LPO, lead petty officer. You have some problem with that?"

Jaybird grinned. "No, sir, Commander, no problem at all. Only . . ."

"Yeah, it isn't official yet until I do the paperwork and twist some major tail. Call the admiral and tell him we're ready to roll."

Two hours later, the thirteen SEALs and their two South Korean interpreters, and the two large boxes of Korean civilian clothes, were safely on board the destroyer *Cole* and steaming west. The Cobra gunship sat tied down on the pad on the stern.

Word came through that the second NK general had been located. Their agents in North Korea reported that General Soo Chung Chi was taking a short vacation in the Chungsan area on the coast. There was a little-known resort there used only by the military high command and government officials.

Murdock looked at a map with the XO of the destroyer.

"That's another thirty miles up the coast from your original drop-off point," the XO said. "Which one first, Commander?"

"Let's wait and see where our third target is. We might get lucky. Then again, he might be three hundred land miles north up by Musan. We'll have to wait for word from the spooks."

The destroyer had just finished the western leg of its trip, and was about to turn north around the west bulge of the southern part of North Korea, when the radio room called.

Murdock got on the radio at once.

"Got your third general," Colonel Vuylsteke said.

"Good. Where?"

"He's about twenty miles inland from Chungsan at Taedong. Our sources say he has a private estate there that most North Koreans don't know anything about. His name is General Sun Kyu Ton."

"Who's running the war for these guys?" Murdock asked.

"They must have some new generals on the front lines. You get everything you need?"

"So far. What we could really use now is a big batch of good luck."

"Wish I could help, Commander. You stay healthy."

Murdock went up to the bridge and talked with the destroyer captain. They checked the maps again and found the two towns.

The destroyer captain was a full commander with a lot of blue-water time. Commander J. Jenkins was from Oregon and wild about rainbow trout fishing. A yellow gnat and a brown bucktail fly were hooked through his hat.

"Where to, Commander?" Jenkins asked.

Murdock eyed the map again. "We'll continue on up the coast past Nampo to Chungsan. Pull this taxi to within five miles of the coast and we'll take the RIBs in as close as possible. We'll work the coast town first, then move inland to Taedong, and with any luck find some nighttime transport south thirty miles to the port city of Nampo."

"And hope that half the NK Army isn't chasing you by that time. I don't envy you this assignment, Commander."

"That's the damn kicker here, Jenkins. No orders. This is a volunteer mission."

Murdock left with the destroyer captain trying to believe what he had just heard.

Below decks in their assembly point, Murdock had the SEALs strip and put on the Korean clothes. They were mostly cotton, with lots of browns and blacks and dark blue. They had loose-fitting pants, some Western-style shirts, and some light jackets that would help hide their combat vests. They would keep on their regular black jungle boots with black socks turned down over the laces to help prevent snags.

The two Korean interpreters chuckled when they saw the SEALs changing into the Korean clothes. They already had on their civilian garb. They went around helping adjust the clothes. The SEALs had a variety of billed caps, mostly black and dark blue. These were the hats the people wore at this time of the year, the interpreters said. In the summer the Koreans switched to straw hats.

Murdock had a long talk with the two Koreans, DeWitt, and Jaybird.

"We're putting our lives in your hands," Murdock said, staring at the two Koreans. "You must know that. A lot of what we do will depend on your advice. If you don't think something we suggest will work, tell us at once. Don't worry about rank out here. We're SEALs, that's our rank on a mission, no officers, no sergeants. You understand?"

They both said they did. Murdock didn't want to know their names. He tagged one as Pete, and the other as Charlie. He asked if they had fired the MP-5 before. One said yes, the other said no. Murdock had Jaybird take them to the fantail and fire fifty rounds each. They came back looking confident about the weapon.

The SEALs had one last meal, then checked their equipment. They would be on their PD in a half hour. Murdock looked at them and chuckled.

"You are the sorriest bunch of SEALs I've ever seen. Absolutely no class, and let's hope that you stay that way whenever we run into any of the locals. Keep those damned round eyes closed as much as possible. We'll use a minimum of cammo colors so the locals might think we could be NKs in civilian disguise. Lead Petty Officer, is it time to get on deck?"

"Ten minutes, sir."

By the time they worked up to the deck, the *Cole* had slowed to four knots in a whitecapped sea. Rain filtered down from a socked-in sky.

"Rain is good," Murdock said. "Makes it harder for anybody to see us coming in."

"Hell, we gonna be wet anyway," Al Adams said.

Murdock looked toward land. He could just make out the shape of a dark mass and some muted lights.

"Five miles offshore," Jaybird said. "Close as the captain wants to take this tub in."

They worked their way down the deck to the fantail, where the Cobra gunship remained tied down. The two RIBs were in the water on short towlines. Now that the destroyer had almost stopped, the RIBs were pulled up and positioned along the stern. One by one the SEALs went down metal ladders to the bouncing RIBs. It took ten minutes to get everyone on board.

Murdock looked at his motley bunch and laughed. "You guys look more like little old ladies than SEALs," he said.

They lined up in the three forward-facing seats with high backrests. The trip would be made standing up more than sitting. The coxswain cleared his craft, threw off the tie-down lines, and they churned away from the destroyer and toward shore. Murdock was in the center next to the console. He yelled at the coxswain.

"Want you to take us in as far as you can, right next to the surf line if you've got the guts. Shorter the swim, the better for my men."

"Sure, and more danger for me and my men," the coxswain shot back. He grinned. "Hell, Commander, if you can go in on a mission like this one, damned if I can't get you in a shitpot full closer than last time."

They plowed ahead through heavy seas at ten knots. It was a safe speed in the waves, and also held down the noise factor. They were still a mile from the beach when Murdock heard the RIB's radio talk.

The coxswain listened closely, then reached over and shut down his engine. The stillness surprised the SEALs.

"What the fuck?" somebody growled.

The coxswain looked at Murdock beside him. "That was Will on the other RIB. He's got an NK patrol craft with a searchlight bearing down on him. Which means he's coming toward us too."

"So we wait?" Murdock asked.

"Yeah, wait and pray and hope to hell he doesn't come straight for us and find us with his searchlight. Those fuckers have a lot of machine guns and some small automatic cannon. Our only chance will be to outrun him if he spots us in his light."

19

The Yellow Sea
Off Chungsan, North Korea

The ten-meter-long RIB rocked in the waves. The sea was about the same, with whitecaps showing around them. Murdock looked toward the coast. Less than a mile, he figured. They could swim from there if they had to, but the cold water would sap their energy for a land fight if they ran into trouble.

They waited to find out where the NK patrol boat was.

Five minutes later, Murdock heard the growl of the heavy motors. It was a large patrol craft. North Korea had several of the boats over 150 feet. They were set up with a lot of medium-sized firepower, but most had no missiles. The sound came closer.

"Hang tough, guys. If we have to, we go over the side and swim for the shore. DeWitt will decide what to do in his boat."

The sound became stronger, then faded. Once they saw the yellow swath of the searchlight, but it swung away from them. Another three or four minutes, and the RIB's radio came on. The coxswain grabbed it. He listened and hung up the handset.

A moment later he kicked over the motor and the RIB began to move slowly toward shore.

"Our NK patrol boat buddy is moving the other way," the coxswain said. "Will on the other boat figures we have time to get in to the surf line, drop you guys, and bug out for our sacks back on the destroyer. But for now, we're on a max of five knots to hold down the noise."

It was almost forty minutes later when Murdock spotted the first wave breaking ahead of them. The light rain kept coming down, as it had since they left the destroyer. He touched the coxswain's shoulder and nodded. The coxswain brought the boat to a stop.

"Tell the other boat driver to have the SEALs meet at that small point of land directly ahead," Murdock said. "I don't know where the other boat is."

The coxswain relayed the message and nodded.

"Let's get wet," Murdock said. The SEALs went over the side, surfaced at once, and did a fast-crawl stroke toward the breakers. Their weapons were tied across their backs. The civilian pants and jackets acted like anchors for them, but they were used to heavy loads in the surf.

Murdock was the third one to body-surf in on a wave. He lay in the wet sand and eyed the beach area. It seemed deserted. He figured the time as a little after midnight. The next wave lifted him and pushed him another five yards inland. He came to his knees, ran bent almost double off the wet sand into the dry, and headed fifty yards down the beach to the point of land he had identified.

He checked behind him, and saw seven of his squad running with him. Everyone had made it through the surf.

When he came to the point of land, he looked across the dry sand and saw three blinks of a small light. DeWitt had made it there first. Murdock waited until he had all of his men, then waved them to the side, and they ran into the patch of woods where the other SEALs crouched.

"Motorolas," Murdock whispered, and the thirteen SEALs and two Koreans unzipped the watertight sections of their combat vests and hooked up the personal radios. Jaybird had taught the Koreans how to hook up and use the sets.

Murdock found Charley, his squad's Korean. "Which way to the town and the resort?"

Charley scowled. "Town due east. Resort, not know. We have to find out. Two Koreans go into town without weapons and talk to people. We pass as North. Have ID cards."

"Let's find the town and someplace that we can hide out until we know what we're doing. Charley, you and Lam lead the way."

They hiked along the side of a dirt road, past half-a-dozen dark houses, on past a field full of rice paddies, and then toward a small hill that had a few pine trees and a lot of smaller hardwoods. At the top of the hill they looked east and spotted the town.

"Chungsan," Charley told Murdock.

The place was larger than he had figured. Every town in the Far East seemed to be large. He guessed there could be twenty thousand people here in the sprawling array of lights he saw in what must be a valley between several good-sized hills.

"How close can we get and stay hidden?" Murdock asked.

"Never been here before," Charley said. "Sorry. Lam and me go out front for look-see."

Murdock put the men down in the thickest part of the woods. There didn't seem to be any activity here. Nothing would happen until daylight. By then they had to have a hide-hole somewhere. He put two men on guard duty and told the others to relax.

Murdock lay in the weeds and brush trying to get warm. He clicked off problems they could run into. Army patrols. Not likely in this sector so far from the front. Civilians cutting wood? Good chance. Their Korean buddies would have to alibi them. Maybe say the SEALs were a special Army force in civilian garb watching for South Korean infiltrators. Should work.

North Korean Army units on training exercises? Could be, but they probably had all possible units at the front.

His eyes drooped shut, and he jerked himself awake. No

damn time for sleeping. Too cold to sleep. The cotton pants and shirts would dry out in three or four hours from body heat, if they could maintain it. He got up and checked the sentries. Both were awake and alert. He went up to the brow of the hill and stared down at the town below. Somewhere down there was his target. All they had to do was find him.

Lam and Charley came back two hours later. They had found another patch of woods close to the town that was unoccupied.

"Looks good, Skip. Near a road with no traffic, but should be busy in the morning. Bicycles, I'd expect."

They moved the platoon forward and put them into temporary cover and concealment. Murdock called the two Koreans up and spelled it out.

"Your job, go into town and be there when it wakes up. Use any ploy you want to, but find out where the resort is without attracting any attention. Probably too late tonight to nail a drunk going home. We'll expect you back here by noon. Understand?"

Both men nodded. "Noon," they said in unison. They left their weapons and combat vests, and put on floppy sandals they had brought with them. Each had brought a small .22-caliber automatic along, and they hid the weapons in pockets. Murdock waved, and they headed downhill toward the city's muted lights.

"Another hide-hole, gents," Murdock said on his Motorola, and the SEALs fashioned more shallow holes with plenty of camouflage they could pull over them if needed. New guards went out and Murdock talked to DeWitt.

"What have I missed?" Murdock asked. "How else could we get our asses in a sling in here?"

"Depends how many Army units are stationed here," DeWitt said. "My guess is most of their troops have been pulled to the MLR to boost their numbers."

"Leaving few if any armed soldiers in this little town." Murdock rubbed his hand over his face. "Damn, I hope that's right."

"What else? Snakebite? Booby traps, home guards, not

finding the fucking resort, maybe it's got a regiment around it protecting the old hard-nuts general?"

DeWitt chuckled in the darkness. "Come on, Skipper. Relax. When we hit a problem, we'll figure out how to handle it. You're getting on the slightly paranoid side here."

Murdock rubbed his face again. "Yeah, you're right, 2IC. I'm getting old-woman-shit-faced. Let's get some shut-eye and dry the fuck out."

Morning brought the first hint of trouble. Jaybird, who had taken the last watch, poked Murdock awake.

"Commander, you better check this out. Some minor problem."

Murdock came awake at once, both his hands on the submachine gun. "Trouble? Where?" Jaybird led him through the sleeping bodies of the men in the first shafts of light that were eating up the darkness. At the crest of the hill they looked down at a small valley with a road beyond.

"So?" Murdock asked.

"Behind those trees. Watch what comes out of them."

They watched a moment. Then a line of women came out hiking along a trail the SEALs hadn't seen before in the darkness. It wound up the hill and would come within fifty feet of the SEALs' hiding spot.

"Women going to work in the fields somewhere," Jaybird said. "They might walk out ten miles to a field."

"We've seen this before . . . in China. Wake up the men and make sure they keep covered up as the women go past."

Ten minutes later the line of women had passed without incident, and Murdock drew a normal breath.

"Tell them to chow down," Murdock said. Each of the men had brought with him two MREs, the sealed-in-plastic ready-to-eat meals. They weren't exactly gourmet, but they would keep a man alive and ready to fight.

By that time everyone was dry. The rain of the night before had stopped early on, and now the sun came out and dried out the brush and trees. Murdock had out three lookouts. Nobody came near the woods after the women passed by.

A jet fighter streaked across the sky at treetop level less

than a half mile from them and brought all the SEALs alert.
The craft vanished off to the left and didn't come back.

"Training mission," Ron Holt said, and the SEALs went
back to checking their weapons and taking naps. No telling
when they might be able to get any sleep again.

At 1100, the two Koreans appeared in the woods. None of
the guards had seen them approach. They grinned and
showed a narrow ravine choked with brush that they had used
to go from and come back to the hillside.

"Find it?" Murdock asked.

Charley nodded. "Other side of town, five kilometers out.
Plenty guards around the place, civilians. Know for sure that
one general is there. Many persons saw his big car with the
bright red star on it drive in two days ago."

The other Korean nodded. "Five, six young women also go
in, three men say. Plenty women there."

"How can we get there?" DeWitt asked.

Charley took them to the brow of the hill and pointed
around the near side of the town. A small range of hills
showed that were used for what the scouts described as a
reforestation project.

"Plenty cover, no people," Charley said.

"Can we get there right now without attracting any attention?" Murdock asked.

"If careful, quiet, and lucky," Charley said.

"Two out of there ain't bad," DeWitt said.

"Let's saddle up, gentlemen," Murdock said. "We're going
for a walk in the park."

They moved from the hilltop into the gully the Koreans had
used. It concealed them perfectly. A half mile below, the gully
ended at a dirt road. A string of six trucks lumbered past, each
loaded with military supplies. Evidently they were heading
south to the front.

Just when Murdock thought all was clear, two bicyclists
came pedaling along. Charley tugged at Murdock's brown
civilian shirt.

"We go across one at a time. Two, three minutes between.
No one worry about it. We civilians."

An ancient truck filled with what looked to Murdock like

rice straw came by. When it vanished, Murdock gave the order for the men to go across the road two at a time, spaced out. Half of the platoon was across when another convoy of military trucks came past. The men waited, then continued when the trucks were gone.

When they were all across, Lam waved them forward again into the light growth of timber on the small hills. They had just started down the third hill, well concealed in the growth, when Lam stopped.

"Skip, you better take a look," Lam said on his Motorola. Murdock hurried to the front and slid into the grass and weeds beside Lam.

Ahead, Murdock saw the problem.

"Woodcutting crew," Lam said. "Military. They stacked their rifles and began taking down pine trees. Almost looks like they're gonna make bunkers, but no reason to out here."

They heard a heavy truck engine some distance away. It stopped and the NK troops cheered.

"How many?" Murdock asked.

"Twelve, plus an officer who wasn't working and carries a pistol. He went to bring up the truck is my guess."

"Can we go around them?"

"No chance, Skip. The area up there is about fifty, maybe sixty feet wide. We go through them or we go back."

Murdock used the Motorola. "Come on up, and spread out into a firing line. Got a small problem."

Five minutes later the SEALs had set up a line of men spread out and facing the woodcutters.

"Silenced rounds only. We're about fifty yards, so use the MPs, and the snipers. On my count. One, two . . . three." Murdock sighted in with his MP-5 submachine gun and put down a chopper nearest the far end. He saw the officer with the pistol come into the clearing, and targeted him next, but the man spun backwards with a round in his chest. Murdock looked for a new target.

Half the woodcutters were down after the first volley. Two scrambled for their rifles and got them, only to be cut to pieces before they could fire a shot.

There were three behind trees. "Let's move out and clean

it up," Murdock said into the mike. The SEALs came to their feet and ran down the slope in a staggered line. The submachine guns chattered off three-round bursts, and then the SEALs were past the last of the dead woodcutters and moving up the other side of the hill.

Fifty yards into the thicker cover of trees and brush, Murdock stopped them.

"The truck," he said.

"Got it," Lam said. He motioned to Jaybird, and they faded back down the hill and to the left where they had heard the truck. Lam went ahead from tree to tree, watching everything forward. He stopped twice and listened, then moved again. Jaybird followed him in the same pattern.

Lam waved Jaybird up, and they looked down an open stretch fifty feet to a military truck. The driver leaned against the front fender, hands in his pockets.

Jaybird held up his hand with two fingers extended. Lam shook his head. He leveled in with his MP-5 and fired a three-round burst. The driver jolted off the fender clawing at his chest. He slammed backwards and hit the ground. They waited. The man on the ground didn't move. No one else came out of the truck.

Four minutes later, Lam and Jaybird found the rest of the SEALs, and they moved out generally north through the wooded hills.

They crossed one more road, a better one-lane blacktop that had much more traffic. It took them ten minutes to drift across this road one or two at a time, and between old trucks, bicycles, and men and women on foot. The SEALs' new civilian clothing blended in nicely with the locals.

It was just after 1500 when they came to the top of another hill. Charley led Murdock to a vantage point, and they looked north and east. They had come past most of the town, and could see pockets of houses and a few industrial buildings to the north of the main settlement.

"We find two-lane road with line down middle," Charley said. "Resort at end of road, maybe five kilometers from town."

"Let's move," Murdock said. "Like to get this one wrapped up before dark. Is there a swimming pool at this resort?"

Charley laughed. "This not California, Commander. No swim place."

"Then probably no chance for a long-range kill."

They hiked out of the hills and into a brushy area where the soil looked too sparse and rocky to cultivate. It provided enough cover for them. They worked three miles north; then Murdock called a halt.

"Lam, take Charley and go find that fucking two-lane road with a line down the middle. Should be to the east somewhere. Get back here as fast as possible."

Lam and Charley left their weapons with the others and struck out in the open across rice paddies, past a house or two, and kept moving quickly through the land.

Murdock watched them move out of sight behind a slight rise, and wished them luck. He sat down and leaned against a tree. The oversized floppy shirts they wore covered their combat harness, but there was no way they could conceal a canteen. Murdock was thirsty. He knew he had to stay that way. Maybe later Charley could find them some good drinking water. Probably all of the water up here was contaminated. Korea was a night-soil heaven.

A half mile to the left across the North Korean countryside, Lam leaned against a small tree and tried to hold in a laugh. Three young girls were chasing a small pig and not able to catch it. The two men skirted the scene, and found some woods where Lam could relax a little.

On the far side of the woods, Lam spotted a military truck speeding along a road. They edged up another two hundred yards and identified the roadway. A blacktop, two-lane road with a stripe up the middle. It was a superhighway in this area.

It took them a half hour to get back to the SEALs.

"Got it, Skip. Looks like we can jog west a quarter of a mile and find some more low hills. I'd bet that they swing to the east up ahead and that should bring us to the resort, or damn close to it."

"Let's move," Murdock said. He picked up the pace then,

not quite jogging, but more than an easy walk. They found the hills and swung east. The number of farmed plots thinned out, in direct proportion to the thinning soil, Murdock decided.

Just after 1620, Lam called Murdock to the front of the line. He was on the crest of a small wooded hill, and pointed to the east.

Murdock took out his binoculars and checked. There were enough buildings for a resort. One was three stories high. They were built in a square and all looked new. The highway led up to the front of the place, and as he watched, a pair of military vehicles rolled through the gates into the square and vanished.

"Found it," Murdock said. "Now all we have to do is locate our favorite general, Soo Chung Chi."

For half an hour they scouted the place from a distance. There were no easy access routes. No concealment of any kind. No houses or buildings had been left standing for a quarter of a mile around the resort. It looked more like a fortified castle than a playing place.

"Have to go in at night," DeWitt said when he put down his binoculars. They had moved up as close as they could get in concealment.

"True," Murdock said. "Oh, oh. Look at this."

DeWitt pulled up his binoculars again and swore. "An old Russian armored personnel carrier. Old, but it still moves and has a nasty sting in that fifty-caliber machine gun."

"Must have a crew of three," Murdock said. "That kind of eliminates our walking in the front door looking for a handout."

He looked at Jaybird, DeWitt, and the two Koreans.

"Now, just how the hell do we get into this place so we can find General Soo?"

20

Chungsan
North Korea

Darkness had just fallen. The scouts were back with their reports. The place was built like a fortress. It was a quad, with the buildings connected. Two entrances, one on the front with a drive-through arch and gate, and a man-sized door on the rear that evidently was locked or had a guard.

"It has to be the rear door," Jaybird said. "The front gate would be too obvious, and that's where they have the firepower. One guard tops at the rear door. We use our Koreans to get the door unlocked or open, take the guard out silently, and slip in that way. Then we find the general, welcome him into Hell, and leave by the same door."

"All silently and without a shot being fired," Murdock said. "I wish it could happen that way."

"Looks like the rear door is the best bet to get inside," DeWitt said. "I agree there, but once we get in, gonna be a hell of a job just to locate the general."

"Bribe," Charley the Korean interpreter said. "Bribery way of life in North. We offer the guard lot of money, twenty thousand won. That over nine thousand dollars U.S. More money than he'll ever see in lifetime. Will work. Bribery always work in North Korea."

"If that doesn't, can you talk your way in?"

"Yes," Charley said. He took out a banded stack of one-hundred-won notes. "Slip money under the door. I prepared."

"We need to get inside quietly," Murdock said. "We can't blow the door open. Then all the soldiers the general brought with him are on us with their AK-47's at full auto."

"Say we're inside the door," Jaybird said. "It's after midnight. What's next?"

"We play it by ear," Murdock said. "As usual. We try to find a hostage who will tell us where the general is. When we find Soo we eliminate him, get out, and take a hike away from here."

"He'd probably be in the three-floor section," DeWitt said. "On the top floor. So we would probably start at the top and work down."

"When?" Charley asked.

The three looked at him. "When?" Murdock asked himself. "I'd say just after midnight. That will mean many of the troops inside will be busy with their women, or asleep. It will also give us five or six hours of darkness to make our getaway."

"Now, should know where we go next. Taedong?" Charley asked.

"Taedong, right," Murdock said. "Then we'll swing back down to the coast, visit the seaside town of Nampo, before we launch ourselves into the Yellow Sea and hope for a pickup."

They considered using two men for a diversion at the front gate, but decided against it. They wanted to keep it a silent hit for as long as possible.

"We should be able to get to the back wall of the building in the dark," Murdock said. "Nobody reported any floodlights along the walls. That will help."

"We going to stay silent the whole time?" Jaybird asked.

"If we can. We'll use our suppressed weapons and KA-BARs. We find the general, snuff him, and get out of there before anyone knows we've been there."

"No chance," Charley said.

Murdock punched him in the shoulder. "Yeah, not much of

a chance, but we keep silent as long as we can. Now, two hours to sleep, then we move out for that back door."

By midnight when they left the woods, the clouds had blown away and a cold half-moon rode high in the sky. They moved silently the mile to the resort building in a combat diamond. They saw no guards, and no lights bathed the outer walls. The platoon leaned against the wall and waited.

At the door, Charley got a thumbs-up from Murdock, and the small Korean pounded on the wooden door. Nothing happened. He pounded again, longer this time. A thin sliver of light showed under the door.

The third time he pounded, a pair of knocks came in response. Charley talked in Korean, waited, then said the words again.

Nothing happened.

Charley talked again, and slid three one-hundred-won notes under the door. The money vanished as someone grabbed it. He pushed three more of the bills under the door. They were pulled away. The door opened an inch and a Korean voice spoke softly. Charley held a stack of the one-hundred-won notes so the person beyond the door could see them.

A moment later a hand reached through the wider opening. Murdock grabbed the hand, rammed the door open, and pulled the Korean outside. Murdock's hand clamped over the frightened man's mouth. They kept the door open a crack. Then Charley pushed the North Korean civilian against the outside wall and began talking to him. His voice was low and threatening.

Slowly the North Korean shook his head. Charley punched him in the face three times so quick the man had no chance to duck. He slumped against the wall, then slid down to a sitting position.

Charley kicked him in the crotch, and the door guard gurgled in pain and terror. This time when Charley talked to him, he replied in a low voice filled with fear.

Charley stood and grinned. "The general is still here. He's on the top floor in the grand suite. There are armed military guards on the third floor, about a dozen of them. Some of them are drunk, others with women. When this misbegotten one can walk again, he'll lead the way."

Murdock nodded and checked the door. He pushed it inward until he could see around the dimly lit courtyard. In the center was a pool with a garden around it. The buildings on both sides were twenty feet away. This outer wall connected them.

Murdock went back to the North Korean civilian and lifted him to his feet. He motioned ahead, and the man struggled to take a step, then a second one. By the time they were through the door, he walked almost normally. He waved them toward the left-hand building. They saw no one in the courtyard, which was about a hundred feet across. Murdock told DeWitt to keep Bravo Squad near the first building and be ready to come to back him up.

Inside the nearest building, Murdock and Alpha Squad went up a stairway to the second floor, then down the hallway. They saw no one. Loud music came from one room. This building was set up like a good hotel. At the end of the hall they came to another door that led to stairs.

The Korean motioned them forward, but hung back. Murdock pushed him to lead them, and they went up the steps. When they came to the door, Murdock pushed it open an inch and looked through. They were on the third floor. Where were the armed guards?

He spotted two down the corridor. It was only twenty feet long here, and opened into a large reception area with four doors leading off it. The two NK Army men leaned against the wall outside the first door. Both had rifles, which they had slung over their shoulders with the muzzles down.

Murdock waved the man behind him, Jaybird, up to the door. Jaybird took a look. He flattened out on the floor and brought up his H&K subgun.

"I've got the one on the right," Jaybird whispered. Murdock knelt behind him and sighted in with his own MP-5.

"Fire," Murdock whispered, and both men triggered their weapons. The single shots stung the two NK guards. One took a heart shot and went down dead without a murmur. The second one caught the round in the chest, but it missed his heart. He staggered against the wall and tried to lift his rifle. Both Murdock and Jaybird got off single shots at about the same time, and the guard went down and didn't move.

Murdock checked the hallway. He saw no more guards. He was about ready to move into the hall when four uniformed soldiers came out of one room, laughing and buttoning their shirts and pants.

They saw the downed men and yelled. None had a weapon. Murdock and Jaybird switched to full auto on the MP-5 submachine guns and fired into the quartet. Two went down; one stormed back into the room he had just left. The fourth tried for the door beside the dead soldiers, but didn't make it.

"Go!" Murdock shrilled, and he led his seven men through the door. They covered each of the four doors and waited. When nothing happened, Murdock tried the door where the two guards had been. Locked. He stepped back and slammed his boot against the wood near the knob and jolted it inward. He had jumped to one side, but no gunfire sounded inside the room. He peered into it from floor level, and saw only a hotel-type room with two beds and four naked bodies.

Two men and two women looked up and drunkenly waved, then went back to their sexual entertainment.

Murdock checked the uniforms thrown on the floor. No stars. The men were too young. He came out of the room just as four North Korean soldiers with AK-47's barged out of the middle door. Six SEAL weapons fired on them before they had targets, and all four went down dead or dying. Jaybird rushed into the room they had just left and returned a moment later.

"Empty, Skip," he said softly.

Two more doors.

Murdock pointed men to doors, and they kicked down the doors at the same time. Gunfire blasted through one of the open doors. Murdock threw in a grenade, and he and three SEALs stormed in when the shrapnel stopped flying. They found two NK officers, naked and both dead from the fragger.

The other room held six women, in various stages of undress, awaiting the pleasure of the Army officers.

"Ask them where the general is," Murdock told Charley.

He did, and the women giggled and rubbed his crotch until he backed away. "They say general old man, he don't fuck. He's down in the kitchen cooking."

Murdock and his men went down the stairs and picked up their talkative captive, and Charley had him lead them to the kitchen on the first floor.

They went in another building toward the back. They saw no soldiers outside. This was a secure area for them. Charley chattered with the North Korean captive.

"In this door, down a long corridor, and then to the right is kitchen."

Lam led out, with Murdock right behind him. Just as they came into the corridor, Lam saw a soldier come into the hall from the other end. Lam's Colt carbine put three silent slugs into the man before he knew they were there. He bounced off the wall, hit the floor, and rolled on his back, dead of lead poisoning.

They ran on rubber-soled boots down the hall. Lam peered around the corner of the hall, and saw two guards outside another door. Ching leaned around the corner at the same time. Both men fired three-round bursts and cut down the guards.

Murdock and his Alpha Squad lined up on both sides of the kitchen door. Murdock and Ronson jolted through the door and scanned the well-equipped kitchen.

General Soo Chung Chi stood at a stove, a large skillet in one hand and a measuring cup in the other. Behind him stood two naked Korean girls about twelve years old. He wore his Army uniform with the stars on his shoulders, a white apron, and a white chef's hat.

He put the skillet down gently on the stove and the measuring cup beside it. He turned toward the intruders, bowed, and looked at Charley. "Do not hurt the girls, they are innocents. No, I did not molest them. I am an artist by choice. I painted them." Charley translated the words quickly for Murdock.

General Soo turned and waved the girls away. They scampered past the stoves and refrigerators and out a door.

"Now, I am ready," he said. Charley translated.

Murdock lifted his right hand and saluted the general. General Soo returned the salute. Then Murdock lowered his hand to his MP-5 and put three rounds into the Korean's heart. General Soo slammed backwards, knocked the frying pan off the stove, and landed on the floor on his back, his unseeing eyes staring at the ceiling.

"Make sure," Murdock said.

Jaybird walked up to the general and put one round of 9mm into his head.

"Let's get out of here," Murdock said. They picked up DeWitt and his men just outside.

"Trouble," DeWitt said. "They have half-a-dozen armed men at the north gate we came in. Saw only two at the main gate."

"They know where we are?" Murdock asked.

"Don't think so."

Murdock put his four men with the NATO-round sniper rifles at the door.

"Take out the men at the north gate," he told them. "Fire when you're ready."

The H&K PSG1's with their bolt action fired into the men at the north gate. Three went down on the first volley. By the time they knew they were under fire and reacted, two more hit the North Korean dirt. The last one jolted through the door outside and ran out of sight.

"Let's double-time for the main gate," Murdock said. The gate was fifty yards away across the courtyard to the south. The fifteen men ran flat out. They took fire from the rear, then saw the guards on the main gate. The four SEALs in front laid down a frontal assault fire, their weapons on three-round bursts or fully auto. They didn't hit much, but made the NKs scurry for cover.

Halfway there they came to a military six-by-six truck, and hid behind it to catch their breath. A dozen rounds from the gate hit the truck.

"Grenades," Murdock shouted. Four SEALs lofted the small hand bombs at the gate. When they went off, the men threw four more.

"When they blast, we hit the gate at a run," Murdock called

out. Somewhere along the line they had lost their hostage. No matter. The grenades exploded with their 4.2-second fuses, and the SEALs charged the gate. They met no opposing fire. As they charged past the gate and two vehicles they found three men dead.

Murdock checked the rigs. One was a civilian car of undetermined make, the other a military six-by truck.

"Douglas," Murdock called. "Can you make that truck run?"

"Damn right." He crawled into the cab, checked around, and a moment later the engine fired.

"Load up, and we're out of here," Murdock said. The SEALs and two Koreans scurried into the truck and it pulled out. Murdock put Charley in the cab with him and Douglas.

"We need to go east," Murdock said. He looked at Charley. "Any idea how to get to Taedong?"

"No way, Jose," Charley said, and laughed. "We go east. Turn left, go east."

Murdock wondered how long they could keep the truck. Word would be out quickly about the death of the general and the stolen truck. They might not even get around Chungsan. He used the Motorola. "Casualty report, Mahanani."

There was a moment of silence.

"Only one we have back here, Skipper, is a round through the left arm of our buddy Al Adams. Sore as hell, but he can still walk and talk. I've got it bound up. Missed the bone, went right on through. He's fit for duty."

"Thanks, Mahanani."

The paved road they were on heading south came to a crossroad. They slowed. Charley shook his head.

"Too narrow, need better road heading east."

They continued driving. They met a small Army rig, but it continued on north without slowing. Murdock eased his grip on his submachine gun.

A mile closer to the town, they came to another crossroad. This one was blacktopped and had a white line in the middle.

"Turn left," Charley said. The road headed due east, then swung a little south, but if it kept going east they would miss the town. On this road, they met no traffic at all. Murdock checked his watch. It was 0328.

"Three hours to daylight," Murdock said. "We need a good place to hide, with or without the truck." Douglas looked at him quickly. "No sweat, Douglas. We keep the wheels as long as possible. It's a hell of a lot better than walking thirty miles."

Two miles up the deserted road, they came to four headlights facing them. The lights didn't move.

"Nobody is passing anybody," Douglas said. "It's a fucking roadblock."

"How fast we driving?" Murdock asked.

"About forty-five," Douglas said. "Fast as I can get it moving."

"When we get within a hundred yards, start slowing down, then when we can see what's there, we'll decide."

He touched his mike. "Roadblock ahead, look alive. Probably run it, so give us some firepower out the back."

They waited. Nothing was visible through the glare of the four headlights. They came closer. Douglas slowed the rig.

A few more feet and their headlights cut through the glare and they saw the vehicles. One was a light sedan, the other a small jeep-type rig.

"Kick it," Murdock shouted. "Ram through the center. Hit the accelerator." After he said it, Murdock pushed his MP-5 out the front-door window and sprayed the roadblock with 9mm slugs. Two of the headlights blew apart. He could see uniformed men diving for cover.

The big truck gained speed slowly, then surged ahead the last fifty feet and rammed into the sedan, shoving it aside like a toy car. They took a few rounds the last few seconds before impact. Then they were past and the SEALs in the open rear of the truck lanced dozens of rounds into the surprised and dazed defenders.

"Radio?" Douglas asked.

"Yeah, they might have one. If so, we can expect more trouble. Which means we can't vanish in a grove of trees and wait out the daylight. We keep blasting east as fast and as far as we can."

He hit the mike. "Any casualties back there?"

"No hits," Ed DeWitt reported. "A few rounds went through the canvas but missed us. OK up there?"

"We have two stars in our windshield. Outside of that, we're rolling. Up ahead they may know we're coming. If we hit another roadblock, put the two fifties through the canvas in front and be ready to fire over the hood. Maybe we can take them out from long distance. Cut some holes in that canvas."

"That's a roger, Skipper," Bill Bradford said.

They rolled along in silence for a while. Murdock could see the dimly lit speedometer, but he didn't understand the reading.

"How fast?"

Charley looked at the dial. "Almost fifty miles an hour. Good."

They could see the town of Chungsan fading away to the right. Another road joined the one they were on, and Murdock hoped this was the main traffic route to Taedong, about twenty-eight to thirty miles east.

Ten minutes later, Murdock started to relax. The city lights were far behind them. They were in the country. Dirt roads came into the main highway every two or three miles. They met no traffic, and saw few buildings near the road or in the fields.

A millisecond later, the roadway directly ahead of them exploded in a brilliant yellow and orange blossom of death. Murdock ducked automatically. Douglas jolted himself out of a near-hypnotic state and tugged at the wheel to keep the truck straight down the road.

"RPG?" Murdock's radio earpiece asked.

"Sounded like it," Murdock said. "Where the hell did it come from? There aren't even any buildings out here."

As if in answer, Murdock heard a machine gun stuttering.

Douglas killed the headlights and eased the big truck to a stop. Six rounds slapped the hood, and two worked up to the windshield. They punched into the weakened glass and blew the shards back on the three men in the front seat.

"Bail out," Murdock shouted into his lip mike. He opened the door and dropped to the ground, did a front shoulder roll toward the ditch, and lay there as the rest of his men jumped, fell, and rolled out of the NK truck.

The machine gun kept chattering at them. He could hear the rounds tearing into the engine compartment. Murdock heard the left front tire blow out as a round caught it in the sidewall. All became quiet for a moment. Murdock lifted up and stared ahead of the truck, but he could see nothing down that way.

He saw a small flame lick its way out of the engine compartment.

"Get away from the truck, she's about to blow," Murdock said. He jumped out of the ditch and ran into a field, stumbled over a foot-high rice-paddy dike, and fell flat on this chest on the hard ground.

The machine gun chattered again.

Murdock hit his mike. "Lam, Jaybird, you two okay?"

"Roger that, Skip. Lam is with me."

"Move out and see about that MG out front. He's got us by the balls."

"We're gone, Skip."

"Anybody get hit? Sound off if you're hit or dead."

He heard a chuckle.

"I'll accept that. When you have a chance, let's get on the right-hand side of the truck. Watch out for that MG. No idea what they have up there, but somebody had an RPG. Let's assemble over here and then we'll move up slowly. The damn truck is no good to us anymore."

He sensed more than heard the men congregating. Somebody touched his boot. He looked back, and Ed DeWitt came up beside where he lay in the paddy.

"Lucky on that RPG. Hard to estimate distance at night. It could have wiped out half of us."

"Damn lucky. Just hope we haven't used up all of our good luck for this trip. No wounds or injuries?" He asked the last question on his mike.

"Hey, I lost a hard-on when that fucking RPG went off," Fernandez said. "Does that count?"

"Your old lady will weep and moan, but no Purple Heart, buddy," Mahanani said.

"Let's move," Murdock said. "Quiet time. Jaybird, can you talk?"

There was no response. They stood and worked over the hard rice paddies without a sound, slowly, expecting the worst.

Two minutes later two fraggers ripped the dark sky apart with bright orange flashes; then a subgun and a Colt spewed rounds into the night. Some heavy sounds of an AK-47 ruptured the sudden silence, followed by more of the 9mm rounds from the submachine gun.

A long silence followed. Two minutes at least, Murdock figured. Earpieces brought an end to the suspense.

"All clear forward, Skip," Lam said. "Only three of them. A motorbike and two bicycles, a machine gun, and one more RPG."

A moment after the transmission, the six-by-six truck's gasoline tank exploded, lighting up the sky for a half mile around. The sound trumpeted away to the hills, and the yellow flash moderated to a dozen licking green and orange flames as they ate through the wood and canvas on the Army truck.

"On the road, double time," Murdock barked.

They found Lam and Jaybird a minute later, and settled back into formation. Next they hiked down the road to the east.

"We hit the ditches if any headlights show in front or back," Murdock radioed. "Now we make some time to the east."

They had hoofed it down the roadway for twenty minutes when Murdock heard something in his earpiece.

"Oh, damn. Damnit to hell. I won't allow it. Shit. Better hold it up. Guess I got hit after all."

By then Murdock recognized Ed DeWitt's voice.

"Mahanani, check out the JG," Murdock said in his mike. They stopped, and the substitute medic found DeWitt on the shoulder of the highway with his left leg stretched out.

The medic used his pencil flash, holding it in his mouth as he peeled back the black civilian pants leg. Just above the jungle boot DeWitt's leg was lathered dark red with blood.

21

Near Taedong
North Korea
Jack Mahanani wiped the blood away and checked the wound. A bullet had gone in the front of DeWitt's leg, probably clipped the leg bone, and slanted upward. There was no exit wound. That meant the bullet was still there up in the calf muscles somewhere.

"So, JG, you picked up one. Not too bad, lots more blood than there should have been. Probably hurts like hell, though. I'll get it fixed up and we'll see how you walk."

The medic put on antiseptic and bandaged the wound tightly, gave him a morphine shot in the arm, then pulled down the pants leg.

"I'm getting to be a fucking magnet for every stray chunk of lead out there. Why the hell me?"

"Hey, JG, lots of that lead missed you. Come on now, let's see how you walk."

With the medic's help, DeWitt got to his feet. He bleated in pain when he took the first step. He set his jaw and took another step and made no sound, but his face worked. Then he let go of the medic and walked back to the road.

"Let's get the hell out of here," he said. Bravo Squad cheered.

The platoon moved up the road again. Mahanani came up to Murdock and shook his head.

"Skipper, we've got to find some transport. The JG won't be good for more than a hundred yards walking. That slug is in his leg somewhere tearing up things every time he takes a step."

"Stay with him. We'll find transport."

Murdock called up Ching and Lam, and sent them along both sides of the road looking for a cart, a truck, a wagon, anything they could use to haul the JG in.

They were now in country that had more farms and more buildings. The men scurried along each side of the road searching and checking in small buildings, hoping to find an old truck they could steal.

Two hundred yards after they started, Ed DeWitt gave a little cry of fury and slumped to the ground. The men helped him limp to the side of the road.

Jaybird stood beside Murdock. "How much farther is it into that town?" he asked.

"From here, maybe fifteen, eighteen miles. Right now too damn far."

They waited. Five minutes later, Ching came running down the roadway pushing a well-used motorcycle.

"Here it is, but I can't get it to run," Ching said.

Joe Douglas was on it in a second. He checked the spark, then the fuel to the cylinder, and laughed. He took off the small fuel-line filter, blew it out, and without the need for tools, put it back in place. He pumped the starter lever twice, then turned on a switch, and the cycle fired up on the first try.

Murdock nodded. "Douglas, can you ride that thing?"

"In my sleep, Skipper."

"Good. DeWitt will be on the seat behind you. Go up the road two miles and get in some concealment. Wait for us. We'll be double-timing up the road. Best bet we have right now."

The SEALs and the two South Koreans began to jog up the road. A moment later the motorcycle growled past them on low power to hold down the noise.

They made two trips of two miles each; then Murdock
checked his watch. It was nearing 0430.

"An hour and a half to sunup," he told Jaybird. "We need
a place to settle down for the day and hide. Keep your eyes
open."

After the third two-mile hike, they watched the east begin
to lighten. Ahead a dirt road led off to the left toward a small
building and a half acre of trees and brush. It could be a
woodlot.

"Let's check it out," Murdock said, and swung the line of
march off the roadway. Murdock stopped the troops well
back from the shack, and sent Charley up to investigate.

Charley found an old Korean man fully dressed and
rocking gently in a rocking chair in front of the small house.
The man gave the traditional greeting. Charley said he was
lost and wondered how far it was to Taedong.

The old man shook his head. He said in Korean that he
didn't know. He never went to the big city anymore. Twice a
week his grandson came and helped him cook his rice and
kimchee. Mostly he sat in the chair, rocked, and watched the
birds.

Charley asked the old man if he could sleep in the woods
until midday, and the old man simply nodded. Charley
walked back to where the SEALs had waited, and told them
about the old man.

Murdock quietly ordered his men to dig out their hide-
holes and get camouflage ready in case they needed it. He sat
looking to the east. Then he called up Ron Holt with the
SATCOM. He had the radioman turn it on, find the right
settings, and aim the antenna in the right direction. Then he
typed in his message on the pad.

"Completed task #1. Now moving toward task #2. Any
changes in our orders? Murdock."

He waited while Holt pushed the switches that automatically encrypted the message and flashed it out in a transmission burst that lasted less than a tenth of a second. Murdock
wasn't sure how the message made the trip, but somehow it
got to the satellite and back to the ship.

They sat waiting. Murdock got up and scooped out a hide-hole he could stretch out in in case they had to go invisible. Before he was done the box chattered with a voice communication.

"Murdock. Your number-two assignment canceled. Subject has moved. Continue with number-three assignment. Your fishing buddy, Stroh." The voice sounded a little strange going through three broadcasts and relay systems and being encrypted and then de-encrypted. Still, it was Stroh.

Jaybird came up when he heard the radio. He missed most of it. He scowled at Murdock.

"Continue to assignment number three? What about Tae-dong?"

"Evidently the general has moved on to some other spa or point of pleasure. We're off Taedong and back to Nampo."

"Great. Just how the hell you figure we're going to get there?"

"By transport. We need transport. See if you can whip up a six-by-six for me, will you?"

Jaybird dropped to the ground. "We must be twelve miles or so from Chungsan. Then it's another twenty-five down to Nampo. Sure as hell hope we don't have to walk the whole way."

"That's what we've got to work on. Right now, it's time to get some sleep. Then what we need is a truck and a map and a whole lot of good luck. How can you help me?"

"A truck. A nice farm truck filled with rice straw would be nice to hide the men in."

"Or a closed one. I've got an idea what to do as soon as we get to the coast. But we're a long way from there yet. A truck. Wish there was more traffic on this road."

Jaybird sat up straight. "So we hijack a truck on the road down there. We don't care which way it's going. We grab a truck and move the troops out to the wet."

"At least anyone looking for us won't think that we've doubled back on our route. They'll be out ahead someplace."

"Let's go truck hunting," Jaybird said. "If we find the right kind, we can use it during the day. If it's not the right kind, we'll hide it here in the woods and use it as soon as it gets dark."

"Jaybird, Lead Petty Officer, you've got yourself a deal."

They found a place where they could watch the roadway in both directions yet not be seen, and settled in. Traffic was almost nonexistent. One small truck came by, but it wouldn't hold all the men. It wheezed, sputtered, and nearly died. Jaybird shook his head.

The next truck was a better size, but just in time they saw the military designation painted on the bumper. They burrowed deeper in the weeds and grass and let it pass. It was headed for Taedong, which pleased them. By then it was fully light. The sun came up.

After nearly two hours of waiting, a promising rig came in sight headed for Chungsan. It was big enough, had a six-foot-high stake body, and was half filled with some kind of produce. Murdock left his weapon with Jaybird and walked along the highway, then heard the rig coming and turned, stepped into the road, and waved both arms.

Murdock still wore his baseball cap and civilian Korean clothes. His size was against him, but from the cab of a truck it wouldn't matter so much. The rig slowed, then stopped.

Murdock ran up on the driver's side, pulled open the door, and stared at a black pistol aimed at his head. The driver scowled and shouted something in Korean. Murdock shook his head. He was too far away to get a swipe at the weapon. Then the Korean hurtled forward, dropped the gun, and fell half out of the truck.

Right behind the man was Jaybird, who had given him a powerful shove. Murdock picked up the revolver, pushed it in his pants belt, and dragged the driver out. Jaybird grinned and slid behind the wheel. He waited for Murdock to push the driver into the rear of the truck and jump in beside him. Murdock found some twine in the truck and tied the farmer hand and foot.

Jaybird stopped at the lane, got out, and ran up to where the SEALs had stretched out. He got them up, had Douglas take DeWitt, and in five minutes had the SEALs all on board the truck and Douglas behind the wheel.

They threw out half of the produce, some kind of long white radishes and some other green vegetables. There was

soon room for all of the SEALs and their weapons. From the
outside the rig looked like any other on the way to market
farm produce. The men were a bit crowded, but all agreed it
beat walking, especially Ed DeWitt. They kept their weapons
handy and locked and loaded.

This truck was newer than the one they had before, and
rolled along at fifty to fifty-five miles an hour. They passed
two slower trucks, and began meeting more traffic the nearer
they came to the city. They came to a fork in the road, and
Charley in the front seat read the signs. He pointed to the
right.

"We go around town and find coast. What you want,
right?"

Murdock nodded. He and Douglas pulled down their bill
caps to help hide their faces. Murdock changed places to put
Charley on the door side so he could ask for directions if they
needed them.

They rolled along another five miles, and found the
north-south road they had used to come from the resort. They
passed it quickly and came to another meeting of two more
roads. Charley read the signs, and angled the truck into the
one heading south and west toward the coast.

"So far, so good," Douglas said.

The moment Douglas said it, Murdock wished he hadn't.
Ahead he saw a pileup of traffic. There were two lanes
heading in their direction, and he could see half-a-dozen cars
and trucks in each lane. At the intersection he saw two
military police waving people forward. The soldier for the
right-hand lane was on the right-hand side of the street. He
pointed at them and shouted at Charley.

Charley yelled back, and the military policeman laughed
and waved them on through.

"What was all that?" Murdock asked.

"He asked me if I had any kimchee. I told him I was taking
half a truckful to his mother's house right now."

"It worked. Thanks. How much farther to the coast?"

"Not sure. Maybe five-six miles."

The town began to thin out. Soon there was only one lane

going each way. Ahead, Murdock could smell salt air. He grinned. They might just make it yet.

"Charley, we need to find a boat big enough for all of us. A fishing boat? Are there any harbors around here?"

"Last sign say Chungsan Bay. We find."

They drove another half hour, working back and forth before they found the small street that led to a quarter-mile-long bay with two small piers. Boats had tied up at both of them.

"We gonna hijack a boat?" Douglas asked.

"Not if we can help it. We'll rent one, if Charley has enough won."

Charley pulled out the stack of bills. "Nineteen thousand won," he said. "Plenty to rent good boat."

"We steal a boat, the coast patrol boats would be all over us before we got ten miles," Murdock said.

They stopped at the end of the pier. Charley and Murdock walked out on the pier, and Charley talked to the boat people. Murdock didn't have to say a word. Charley said something and bumped into Murdock, and they walked back the way they came.

"No boats to rent there, but on other pier," Charley said. They walked to the next pier and went out on it. The boats were not in as good condition. Fishing had been poor, Charley said. The boat that was for rent turned out to be a thirty-foot fishing boat with a diesel engine and a bad paint job. Charley haggled with the owner for half an hour, and at last made a deal. The owner would go along to run the ship and bring it back.

Murdock went out and brought the crew to the dock. Murdock tried to figure how to get Ed DeWitt out to the destroyer. The chopper on board, the Cobra, had no passenger space. It would take a call to the Eighth Army to send up a bird and overfly all that enemy territory. Too risky yet. Maybe later.

The SEALs and Koreans went on board. Two men carried Ed DeWitt, who protested all the way. Murdock talked to Mahanani.

"Can Ed take it for another day?"

"Slug has got to come out within three days. If I do it I might do a lot of damage. No bullet hole to go into. Have to cut and look around. Damn dangerous."

"Watch him closely, your only job."

"Aye, sir."

The boat smelled of fish. The men could all sit on the deck and around the fish hold. If they came up on a patrol boat, they would have to drop into the hold and damn the smell. Once on board, Charley counted out the bills. Two thousand won. Over nine hundred dollars for the thirty-mile trip. The captain said he would sail them right up to the Nampo main port and get them ashore safely. He didn't care who they were, but he told Charley he knew they were not Koreans. Charley gave him another five hundred won, and the captain grinned.

It was slightly after noon when they sailed. The sun was out and there was no wind or waves. They angled away from the small bay and south along the coast, offshore just enough to miss two small points of land. Murdock figured they were making ten knots. About a three-and-a-half-hour trip.

All went well until they were just rounding the point and heading in toward Nampo, which sat on the far end of a five-mile-long bay. An NK patrol boat came up behind them and Murdock barked at the SEALs, who slipped and slid into the hold until only Charley and the captain remained on the small deck.

The patrol boat went past, and the sailors on it laughed at the way their bow wake rocked the empty fishing boat so hard that it came within two feet of capsizing. The captain waved at the sailors. He told Charley it was a little game they played. The larger craft never went fast enough to capsize his fishing boat. The heavier the load of fish it had, the less it reacted to the strong bow wave.

The patrol boat continued on toward Nampo, and the SEALs moved out of the hold onto the small deck area, glad to be back in the sunshine.

"We're gonna smell like fish for days," Jaybird bellowed.

"You smelled like rotten fish years ago," somebody yelled, but Jaybird couldn't be sure who said it. Everyone laughed.

Murdock sat on the deck beside his second in command. He looked at Mahanani, who was grim-faced.

"Getting hard to bend my ankle," Ed DeWitt said. "I hate this. I don't want to slow down the platoon."

"You won't slow us down. Forget that. What we have to do now is find that general. You rest up. We'll be moving again in a half hour."

Mahanani motioned Murdock to the front of the ship.

"He's getting worse. That damn slug has to come out. Another day and he might not make it."

"Any other way?"

"That chopper on board the destroyer. It's a two-place shooter. But it does have a spot for a second man. If the bird could come in without the gunner . . ."

"Yeah, an idea, but then the bird would be defenseless. Don't think the Navy would let it fly that way."

"Afraid of that. So I'll have to cut. Soon as we get ashore and find some kind of a safe spot, I'll cut. The only way."

"Can you find the slug?"

"An X ray would be handy, but the bullet evidently traveled near the skin for a while. It left a purple mark. I'd say I have a good chance of going in within an inch of the slug."

"We better find a spot where we can be out of the way for a while. We get the JG fixed up, then we'll worry about the general."

Murdock took Charley to talk to the captain. He told Charley exactly what they needed, a place where they could land without attracting any attention and a secluded area where they could hide out for the rest of the day.

Murdock watched as the two Koreans talked. The captain looked at Murdock and frowned, jabbered more at Charley, and at last Charley moved over to Murdock.

"He says could get shot for making trip. He want more money. Should I give more?"

"Yes, another thousand won. If he turns us in, we're all dead. Keep him happy. We don't want to go too close to the town."

Charley talked with the captain again, gave him more money, and the captain smiled.

They moved toward the back of the ship.

"Captain says another few minutes he has private dock he can put in at. No questions. Two hundred won for dock man. We get off easy and no fuckup."

"Sounds good." Murdock turned to his men. "Docking in a couple of minutes. Mahanani, you carry the JG off the boat. We'll find some transport somewhere. Charley, you and your buddy need to find out where the general is. Do it as fast as you can. Understand?"

"Yes, find general fast. Charley understand."

The docking and unloading went quickly. Only one old man was on the slender dock. He took the money and grinned. The area had only one road leading to it, and was surrounded by coastal brush and a few trees. Murdock and his men went down the road until the old man couldn't see them. Then they cut into the brush and found a spot secluded enough to hide them all.

Mahanani and Harry Ronson had taken turns carrying DeWitt. It was late afternoon by the time they settled down. Charley and Pete, the two Korean interpreter/scouts, took off to try to find General Kim. All they knew was that he was an avid golfer, so there had to be one golf course in the area.

Murdock went over to where Mahanani had put down JG DeWitt. He looked pale and listless.

The medic took Murdock aside.

"Skipper, this is it. Time we took that slug out. He can't be in any worse shape after I cut. Hey, I'm no fucking surgeon, but I should be able to get that slug out. I'll need some help. This is going to be twelfth-century surgery. Nothing to knock him out with. I'll need two big men to help hold him down. With any luck he'll pass out from the pain after a few seconds. Then I'll work fast. We need to do it now before it gets dark."

Murdock called up Ronson, Bradford, and Fernandez. He told them what was going to happen. "His screams shouldn't last too long. Fernandez, keep your hand loosely over his mouth so we don't wake up the whole southern half of North Korea."

Murdock then talked with DeWitt. "Hey, buddy. That

Russian bullet has to come out of your leg. No way to get you to the carrier. Just another day in the park. It's going to hurt like hell. You do yourself a favor and pass out, okay?"

DeWitt gritted his teeth and nodded. "Just get the hell to it."

They had him laid out on his stomach on a grassy spot where some of the sunshine still came through the trees. Mahanani had his kit spread out, had sterilized a scalpel, and had swabbed down the calf. DeWitt's Korean pants leg had been pulled up to his thigh.

The two big men held Lieutenant Edward DeWitt by the shoulders.

Mahanani wiped a bead of sweat off his forehead, looked at Murdock, who nodded, and moved the sharp knife toward the officer's leg.

22

Medic Jack Mahanani looked at the blue stain coming up the calf of Ed DeWitt's leg. It stopped about halfway up, so the bullet must have turned inward. How far? He felt sweat beading his forehead again. How damn far?

He moved the scalpel up two inches above the blue stain, and made a cut an inch long. He felt DeWitt jolt from the pain; then a long high wail came from him past Fernandez's hand.

Mahanani bit his lip and cut deeper. The wail turned into a scream that promptly cut off, and the officer relaxed.

"He passed out, Mahanani," Murdock said. "Go now, go, go."

The medic cut deeper into the muscle, and then used a long thin probe to explore inside the leg. He felt a scrape. Bone or lead? He didn't know. Had to be lead. Too far from the bone. He worked that side again. Yes, the slug. He felt around with the probe again, trying to get on the other side of the bullet. It didn't move. He took the long thin pliers-like device, which opened on the end, and pushed it into the cut.

DeWitt groaned in his unconsciousness.

Mahanani wiped sweat off his forehead, and probed again with the instrument. He touched the lead, then again. He opened the tool and tried to grasp the slug. It grated, and then slipped off. He felt blood on his lip as he bit harder, then pressed the tool deeper into the officer's muscle tissue. He opened it again, and this time felt a solid hold on the piece of lead. He began to ease the tool out of the wound.

It moved half an inch, then slipped off the slug. Murdock stood by, mopping up the blood that ran out of the wound.

Mahanani worked the probe again, found the slug, grasped it with the pliers-like device, and clamped it as hard as he could. He worked it slowly outward. It moved a quarter of an inch, then again another quarter of an inch.

Three more times he lost the slug and had to grab it again. Five minutes after he had made the first cut, he edged the dark gray slug out of the hole.

At once, Murdock handed him sterile two-inch squares of bandages. He pressed them onto the wound, then put on four more, and wrapped the leg quickly with roller bandages. They all sat there watching, waiting for the blood to stop oozing out.

It didn't. Mahanani gathered more bandages near the leg, then cut off the blood-soaked cloth and pressed in new squares and bandaged it again. This time they could tell that the blood was stopping. They all breathed easier, and Mahanani wiped his hands on his pants. He gave the patient two ampoules of morphine and sat back.

"Now we wait," he said. "We should be able to move him tomorrow, but he won't be doing any walking for some time."

"Base camp," Murdock said. He touched the Motorola. "This is base camp," he said. "We'll be here until we get the general. Dig out your hide-holes and get the best camouflage you've ever found. The slug is out of the JG's leg, but he isn't running any marathons. We'll find the general, leave some security here with DeWitt, and then jump off from here when we're done. Questions?"

There were none, and Murdock went to scrape out a hiding place for himself. It was starting to get dark, so they should be safe at least until morning. Unless the boat captain figured he could get another payday by turning them in.

Murdock put out two security men and relaxed. Why didn't he tell Charley to bring back some food when he returned? Murdock was getting hungry. He was sure the men were half-starved. They also needed some water. He'd talk with Charley and Pete when they got back.

Murdock had situated his hiding place ten feet from where DeWitt lay. DeWitt had regained consciousness and with it, whimpered with the pain even through the morphine. Mahanani would stay with him until he was better. At least they didn't have a fever to worry about.

Darkness swept down on them suddenly, and Murdock changed guards and told them to stay on four hours, then pick a replacement.

Murdock dozed.

Someone pulled on his shirt. He came awake. He automatically jerked the MP-5 up ready to fire.

"Easy, easy," Jaybird said. "The scouts are back. They brought a dozen big loaves of rice bread, a batch of cheese, and two big bottles of water they say should be pure."

Murdock gave a big sigh, and took a half-loaf of bread and a square of cheese.

"The water bottles will be coming around," Jaybird said.

"What did the scouts find?" Murdock asked between bites.

"Charley wants to tell you."

Charley came up in the darkness. He sat beside Murdock and smiled. "Found general. At golf course closed down five years ago. He opened it, had it mowed and three greens repaired. He play three holes six times for his eighteen holes. High score."

"Where's the course?"

"About five miles from here. Easy road."

"Does the general have any guards with him?"

"Plenty, watch all holes, go with him to some hotel."

"Will he be there tomorrow?"

"Man say he play every day for month. Be there tomorrow in morning."

"Good work, Charley. Get some rest."

Jaybird sat nearby. He looked at Murdock. "So?"

"So, we let the men sleep until midnight, then we move out and find the golf course and plan our hit. We'll use the fifties and hope we can discourage the troops on hand."

"Sounds reasonable."

"We leave Mahanani here with another man for security for DeWitt. The rest of us go and hope for a quick hit and a getaway."

"About time we used the fifties. See you at 2400."

Murdock didn't realize that he had gone to sleep. Douglas shook his shoulder, and he came up with the MP-5 at the ready.

"Wake-up time, sir. It's 2400, time we get moving."

Murdock went to check on DeWitt. Mahanani had been dozing, but came awake when Murdock walked up. He checked DeWitt and looked up.

"Doing better, Skipper. He's been sleeping, the morphine is helping. Hear we're moving out about now."

"You and Adams are on guard duty for security on DeWitt. You probably won't have any trouble. With daylight, work up some kind of camouflage for the JG. We'll see you when we get back. By then we'll need some kind of transport for DeWitt, unless we can grab a boat at that dock."

When Jaybird got back to his spot, Jaybird was there and said the men were ready to move out. Murdock sent Adams over to stay with the medic, and the rest of them followed the two Korean scouts toward the golf course.

At that time of night, there was little activity around the few houses and buildings they went by. The golf course had been built on former farmland, and had gotten in trouble with a stringent North Korean land-use law. But a general in charge of everything can change anything.

They found the golf course after an hour's hike. Murdock scanned the three holes the general had reactivated. There were trees and shrubs growing on the rest of the course, plus lots of weeds. The course had been closed down, but the officials at that time must have forgotten to put it back into farm use.

Murdock and Jaybird chose a natural growth of trees that

must have at one time been between two fairways. They did a little clearing, and had good fields of fire at the third green from just over 150 yards. Fish in a barrel.

Murdock put the two fifty-caliber weapons ten yards apart, and made sure their fields of fire were wide open. Then he put the rest of the platoon on security and backup around them. He placed the four PSGl sniper rifles one on each side of the fifties and two in the middle. They would have six shots at the general before the Koreans knew anyone was there.

Murdock and the men settled down to wait. Charley said that often the general was on the course at daylight. He evidently was an early riser. This might be his last day to get up, Murdock mused. There was no reason that the SEAL marksmen could miss at this range.

Murdock began thinking about his retrograde movement. He'd pull back through the course, make for the small hill they had come over, and then find the dock and his other three men.

Depending on who was chasing him, he'd steal a boat or simply dive into the bay and swim out to sea. But what about DeWitt? He was a SEAL. He would be able to swim better than walk. He would be stronger tomorrow. Other possibilities cluttered Murdock's brain. They could carry DeWitt to the dock, put him on a boat. They might find a truck, drive down the coast, and find a boat or a better place to get into the sea and swim out to contact the RIBs. No, they had to contact the destroyer first with SATCOM before they went into the water. Give a location.

His mind whirled. Everything was so tentative. Play it by ear. What if there were too many alternatives?

Murdock mentally slapped himself. First things first. The general. First the general.

Time crept past, and at last the east streaked with light, then dawn, and finally the sunrise.

He used the Motorola. "Let's look sharp, SEALs. He should be coming soon, if he does today. He wouldn't dare double-cross us and sleep in."

Murdock checked everyone he could see. All were in place. The snipers had their orders. The general first, then his military guard if he brought one. When the guards were down, the SEALs would move back to the dock.

Some distance away they heard motors, heavy ones on trucks and lighter ones, perhaps cars.

"Jaybird?" Murdock asked on the radio. The platoon chief had been spotted halfway to the first tee, in a clump of brush. He came on the personal radio, his voice a whisper.

"Yes, they are here. One truck, ten men all with rifles. Two cars, strange make. The general, two other officers. And the drivers. The three officers have their golf bags on pushcarts."

"Good. Jaybird, can you get back up here without being seen?"

"Affirmative."

"Move it."

Five minutes later Jaybird slid into the thicket beside Murdock.

"From the kowtowing, my guess is that the largest of the three golfers is the general. We better put all of them down just to be sure."

"Will the soldiers come with the golfers?"

"Don't know."

They waited. From their slightly raised vantage point they could see about fifty yards of rough fairway on the other side of the second-hole green.

Another five minutes and they saw the three golfers walking up the second fairway. They all lined up shots and swung. The largest man had a good swing, the other two bad swings. Always play with someone you can beat if you're a general, Murdock decided.

The men followed the first shots. They all had three and four putts on the green, then the tee shots for the third hole.

"We go when I give the order," Murdock said in his mike. "We'll wait until all three are on the third green. Confirm. Alpha Squad?"

He received agreement from the men. "Bravo Squad?" Again the men came on in rotation to say that they understood.

Another wait. The general reached the third green in three shots. He lay about thirty feet from the pin. The green looked like an unkempt suburban lawn, closely clipped but still a lawn.

The other two chipped on. One rolled to within two feet of the pin, and he screeched in joy. The general put his hands on his hips and must have been scowling.

Two more men came behind them. One had a basket, another what looked like folding chairs. Both were soldiers, but neither had a weapon.

Murdock used the radio. "Bradford, take the general. Fernandez, do the golfer next to him. Share the third one and the two picnic guys. Lam and Jaybird. When they're down, you two get down there and make sure. Soon now. They're all on the green."

He waited while the general lined up his shot. When he got ready to putt, Murdock gave the word. "Ready . . . fire."

The six weapons went off almost at the same time. The general had stood up from his crouch to check the line again. The big .50-caliber round caught him in the right side of the chest, blowing out half of his lung and three major arteries. He jolted backward and didn't move.

The other two golfers took rounds in their chests and heart and went down. The two men with the picnic lunch goods didn't have time to run. They got nailed at the same time. Nobody moved after the first volley. Lam and Jaybird took off at a sprint to cover the 150 yards to the green. Their weapons went off six times with rounds to the head; then they rushed back to the cover and concealment of the woods.

They waited a minute longer. Nobody appeared from the direction of the first tee.

"Take the brass and let's get out of here," Murdock said. They pulled back through woods and brush and trees off the golf course and over a small hill.

Jaybird hit his radio. "Commander. I just saw a soldier running back from the second green toward the first. I think we've been spotted."

"Move it," Murdock said. "Ching, take the rear guard. Let's get some distance here, people."

They had started down a slight hill when Lam came on the Motorola.

"Motors, I can hear motors. Are the soldiers in the truck and moving toward us?"

"Or they'll try to get ahead of us," Murdock said. "I don't remember any roads up in here. Let's keep moving."

They were strung out in five-yard intervals in a single line when the North Koreans fired on them. The men evidently had driven ahead and set up a blocking position. They were two hundred yards away down a slight incline. The land was open with only a little brush.

The SEALs went to ground, found what cover they could behind old downed trees and some rocks.

"Hold your fire until they advance," Murdock said. "Jaybird, you saw ten of them at the first tee?"

"Roger, Skipper, but another truck could have come. I see more than ten down there."

"Jaybird, you're leading Bravo Squad. Stay in position. Be sure every man covers the man on his right. We need to get out of this and on our horse. Holt, warm up that box and get in touch with the destroyer on TAC Two. Tell them assignment number three is completed. On our way out but small delay. Tell them we're at Nampo and to get the damn RIBs on their way."

"Aye, Commander. Doing it."

"Confirm when they confirm."

Murdock had been watching the NK soldiers below moving slowly up the hill. They didn't look like seasoned troops. Probably some unit assigned to the general that hadn't fired a shot in months.

Murdock went back on the horn. "Bradford, see if you can pick out an officer down there in your scope. If you can, blow him away. Fire and then move, right?"

"That's a roger, Skip."

Murdock saw three men below lift up and charge up the hill ten yards to some boulders. The NK soldiers below opened fire again, and the SEALs hugged their cover. Murdock looked up and saw fifteen men come out of some brush on the left flank only fifty yards away.

"Left, fire to the left," Murdock bellowed into the lip mike. The SEALs cut loose, and five of the advancing troops slammed into the ground, the other ten dashing back over the small rise of land.

The big fifty exploded as Bradford fired. They heard a long let-out breath; then Bradford came on the radio.

"Yeah, scratch one officer. He won't send no more men into battle, leastwise on *this* planet."

The men below edged closer. Some were now within a hundred yards.

"Let them come," Murdock said on the air. "We can wait." He watched the left flank, but no more men appeared there.

"We've got five of them on the right flank," Jaybird called. "Douglas, Fernandez, cover that sector. Rest of Bravo front."

When four more men below stood and charged upward, Murdock gave the order to fire. The SEALs cut down three of the four. They lay sprawled on the ground in the open, either dead or badly wounded.

"They are coming on the right," Fernandez screeched. He fired his sniper rife as fast as he could pull the bolt and slam it home. Jaybird looked at Douglas. He wasn't firing.

"Douglas, get with it, don't hang Fernandez out to dry," Jaybird screeched in the Motorola. Still, they heard only one weapon firing. Jaybird swore, and turned so he could support Fernandez. He was almost too late. Three of the NK troopers had broken out of the taller timber and were almost on Fernandez when Jaybird cut down the last two. Fernandez got one of them.

"Clear here," Jaybird said. "Fernandez, you okay?"

There was no answer. "Fernandez, come back." When there was still no answer, Jaybird crawled forward and to the right, keeping behind as much cover as he could find. The rest of the platoon kept up the fire to the front.

"Don't let them get away," Murdock said. "Some are pulling back. You sniper rifles, nail them."

Jaybird crawled up to the log Fernandez had used for cover. It was perfect from the front, but he had been fully exposed from the right flank. He saw blood on Fernandez's shoulder and chest.

"Fernandez is hit," Jaybird said. "Looks bad, Skip."

"Don't move him yet. This is about over. Chase the last of

them down the hill. Lam, check that left flank to be sure nobody is left over there."

Three minutes later the firing had stopped. Murdock ran to the right to find Jaybird and Fernandez.

Jaybird looked up, blinking back tears. "He's alive, but he's hit in the shoulder and the chest." Murdock checked Fernandez. Together they helped Fernandez to stand.

"I can walk," Fernandez said. "I can walk."

"Yeah, and pigs fly all the fucking time," Jaybird jawed. "Lean on me, we've got some moving to do."

They walked slowly back toward the home base and the small dock. Lam and Ching acted as rear guards, but there was nobody following them.

"Somebody will be looking for us damn soon," Murdock said. "Holt, crank up that box on TAC Two and get the destroyer. I'll talk." A moment later Holt came beside Murdock and held out the handset.

"They're on."

"Chopper guys, we could use some help."

"This is the Floating Friend. What kind of help?"

"Can that bird of yours fly without the gunner?"

"It'll fly, but the weapons aren't much good."

"Could you pick up a casualty and put him in that seat?"

"Against regulations."

"Yeah, but can it be done? Will you do it?"

"Let me get back to you in two minutes."

"Not a chance, Skip," Holt said. "Those are thirty-year career men out there."

When the set came back on, Murdock answered.

"Land guys, that's a negative. The RIBs went out about twenty minutes ago. We'll put them on fast throttle. Be off Nampo in another twenty minutes."

"We won't be out there by that time. We may still have half the NK marines to fight up here. Let you know. Hey, send in that Cobra now, we might need his guns after all."

"That's a roger. The bird is on a three-minute alert. He's almost gone."

"We're about halfway to Nampo Bay. Have him lay off and we'll bring him in with a smoke flare if we need him."

"That's a roger, SEALs."

A mile back toward the sea, they had to carry Fernandez. He was loosing blood. Jaybird had done some quick bandaging, but it came loose and he bled again. They stopped, and Jaybird put on another bandage made from the sleeve of his shirt.

They heard truck motors, but had no idea how close to a road they were. They hadn't seen any roads coming in. Murdock wondered how quickly the live ones left below could get any kind of military help. It just depended how many real troops the NK had left in this seaport town. Maybe a defense force?

An hour later they came up the last rise to the woods where they had left JG DeWitt. Murdock had briefed Jaybird, and he, Lam, and Charley kept going to the pier and checked it out. The same boat they had come down the coast in was still tied up at the pier. Jaybird boarded her, but the captain wasn't there. A man came out of a small building, and Charley talked to him. He laughed and they nodded and Charley gave him some bills.

Charley ran back to Jaybird. "We rent boat again. Fast before captain sober up."

Jaybird got on the Motorola and told Murdock. Jaybird, Lam, and Charley boarded the fishing boat. Charley checked the fuel supply. Less than a quarter of a tank.

"Plenty," Jaybird said.

The SEALs walked over the hill and down the pier in staggered groups. First came two men carrying Fernandez. They put him on board. The man Jaybird had seen talking with Charley came out, got on board, and started the fishing boat's engine to warm it up.

Ten minutes later all the SEALs and the two Korean scouts were on board and Jaybird cast off the two lines. The fishing boat chugged away from the pier and headed out into the bay. They were well away from the pier when two uniformed soldiers ran on it and waved their hands. They fired some rounds, but missed.

"Straight out the bay," Jaybird told Charley to tell the man at the wheel.

They were just out of the bay and had cleared two small islands when Murdock remembered the SATCOM. He had Holt turn it on to the TAC Two channel.

"Cobra, are you around and do you have your fangs?"

"Must be SEAL power down below. We're about three miles off Nampo."

"Good. We're just clearing the islands off the bay heading due west in a thirty-foot fishing ship." Jaybird touched Murdock's shoulder and pointed to the north.

"Oh, yes, Cobra, we could use some help. We have a North Korean patrol boat heading our way about a mile off. Can you beat him here?"

"Watch us, SEALs."

Murdock got his troops along the rail on the north side of the ship. "If he gets close enough, we hit him with all the firepower we have. That patrol boat has more firepower than we do, but we can make him think about it, especially the fifties, if you tear up his bridge."

They waited. Murdock didn't even try to figure it. At thirty knots, how long would it take the boat to cover a mile? At 218 miles an hour, how long would it take the Cobra to cover three miles? A tie?

They waited.

Murdock checked on the approaching patrol craft. The NKs could fire their guns three or four miles. What were they waiting for? Confirmation?

Murdock told all of his guys to get down so they couldn't be seen from the patrol boat. That could buy them a few minutes.

When he looked again, Murdock figured the boat was no more than a half mile away. He heard a machine gun chatter across the water.

"Down," Murdock bellowed, and his men hit the fishy deck. The rounds landed short.

That was when the Cobra slanted down toward them. Murdock was on his feet waving. Then the rest of the men were up. The Cobra continued past them, and a moment later they heard rockets launch from the Cobra and snake their way across the light blue sky at the fast-moving patrol craft.

Murdock heard the rockets hit. Three missed, but four struck the patrol craft, and it slowed and then went dead in the water. Murdock checked it with his binoculars. Its bridge was blown apart. The chopper made another run and fired another salvo of the 70mm rockets at the ship, which resulted in more explosions and then an oily fire.

The SEALs cheered.

Murdock got on the radio.

"Cobra, I like your fangs. You see a pair of RIBs out there anywhere?"

"Saw them coming over. Check your southwest. They are about a half mile from you. We'll stand by until you board."

"Thanks again, Cobra. When you come to Coronado, I owe you a drink and a steak dinner."

"You're on, SEALs. Standing by."

The fishing boat angled southwest, and five minutes later they saw the RIBs rocketing along to meet them.

Jaybird sat down beside Murdock. "Problem, Skipper. I'm bringing Douglas up on charges, dereliction of duty and failure to follow a direct order, resulting in the life-threatening wounding of a fellow SEAL."

He told Murdock what had happened. "Douglas deliberately held up firing to support Fernandez. If he had helped cover Fernandez, Fernandez would not have been wounded. There has been bad blood between those two for the past three months. You must have heard about it. I'm bringing Douglas up on charges and I want you to back me up."

23

The transfer to the RIBs and the trip back to the destroyer went smoothly. The RIB coxswains throttled back to fifteen knots to reduce the jolting on the two wounded men. DeWitt was feeling better, but Fernandez had taken a turn for the worse. Mahanani didn't know what was the matter. He guessed that the slug must have damaged more in the chest than he'd figured.

Murdock stayed with his wounded men as they were taken to sick bay on the destroyer. Two Navy doctors took over. The medics did some cleanup work on DeWitt's leg, then put him in a hospital bed.

"We want to watch the lieutenant's wound until we get him back to the carrier," one of the doctors said. "With field surgery, there's always a chance some infection could run wild. Tell your medic he did a damn fine job locating that slug without any X ray or a CAT scan. I'll give you a letter for his file."

Al Adams's bullet wound through his left arm got a quick working over. A nurse cleaned the wound on both sides, then gave him a shot of antibiotics and a fresh bandage. He was released back to duty with orders to check in every two days at sick bay on the carrier.

Fernandez was another matter. Murdock looked up from a magazine as the doctor came into the waiting area.

"Fernandez's condition is critical. One of his lungs has started to collapse, but we've taken care of that. The slug shattered when it hit a rib and caused a lot of trouble inside. The wounds to his shoulder are not a problem. We're doing more tests, but it's going to be a watch-and-wait situation. I'll keep you informed about his condition. He's a SEAL, right?"

"Yes sir. One of my best men. I don't want to lose him."

"Right now we can't tell just how bad it is. We should know in eight to ten hours."

Murdock thanked him, and went with Al Adams back to their assembly room. When they got in the door at the room, Jaybird had the men working on their weapons. They all had changed from the Korean civilian clothes back to cammies.

"Feels a hell of a lot better than them damn pajamas," Ronson said. That drew a chorus of cheers.

"The JG is in good shape, but they kidnapped him until we get to the carrier," Murdock said. "Fernandez is still under the knife. They don't know exactly how much damage there was. One of the bullets in his chest shattered and caused all sorts of hell. We're waiting to see what the medics say."

The telephone rang and Murdock took it. Don Stroh was on the radio hookup from the carrier.

"You shit-kickers really get the job done. Damn but I love you guys. Two out of three. The odds around Eighth Army HQ was that you'd only get one of those North Korean generals."

"Any fallout yet from the two men down?" Murdock asked.

"None. Not even an announcement that the two generals had been killed in an accident or due to some serious illness. Nobody is sure what to expect from these crafty Orientals."

Murdock moved away from his men and talked quietly.

"Look, we're down to eleven men, ten really. We can't function this way. Don't cook up any new missions for us. If you haven't heard, DeWitt has a bad leg wound and is out of action. The platoon is dead in the water here."

"Don't worry about it. You might have lots of time. Word at Eighth Army HQ is that the attacks all along the line have stopped. The North seems to be having second thoughts. Our side has halted all offensive thrusts and curtailed the air war. It's like a cease-fire without any talking about it."

"Think they're serious?"

"I'd say so. General Reynolds thinks so. The Vice President is still in Seoul. I hear that he's been authorized to put on the table the same offer he made at Panmunjom the day before the war started. The food supplies and medical teams and goods, if it gets to the civilian population. The offer may already have been made."

"So maybe those two snuffs did some good?"

"I'd say they made all the difference. You took out the top two men. Now the third general has to decide what to do. Besides, he'll be scared to death to put his head out of a concrete bunker somewhere. The civilian guy they brought in might also have some say. Who knows."

"Not me, Stroh. I leave politics to the professionals. Now, I'm heading for a shower. We'll see you in about six hours or so. In the meantime, I'm getting hungry enough to eat your old shoes. See you soon."

Murdock went for a shower and some clean clothes. The men were heading for a special chow. Murdock had no idea what time it was. They had been up since midnight. He looked at his watch: It was 1330. It had been a long day. He had a meal in the wardroom, then hit his bunk hard and slept.

The huge beast with war clubs in each hand kept banging on the castle wall. Murdock told it to get lost. But it banged and banged. Murdock stirred on his bunk, shook his head, and sat up. "Yeah, yeah, hold your skivvies up." He stumbled to the door and opened it. The sailor grinned.

"Sorry, sir, to wake you. You have a special radio call from the carrier. The guy was insistent. A Mr. Stroh."

"Yeah. I'll get my pants on and you point me to the closest hookup."

A few minutes later, Murdock took the phone and whispered into the mouthpiece. "Stroh, you unrepentant chicken-plucker. You better have a good reason for waking me up or I'll pluck you clean when I get back on the carrier."

"I love you too, Murdock. We've got good news. The civilian man I spoke about, who was number four in the government, has been handed the reins of power by the last general, and he's called for a cease-fire. I'd say you boys could be heading home in a day or two as soon as I can make some arrangements."

"You're off the hook, Stroh fish-catcher. Damn you, Stroh, I just got to sleep. While I'm up, find out if there's an NCIS man on board the *Monroe*. I've got some serious charges to bring and I want it done right."

"Yeah, what's the NCIS?"

"You've got to know that, Stroh. It's the Naval Criminal Investigative Service, a civilian operation that works directly with the CNO and isn't subject to any regular Naval authority. Entirely impartial and can investigate anything from a five-star admiral down to the lowliest deck swabber."

"I'll find out. You should be on board in another two hours. Take another nap. You're no fun when you're so cranky."

"Yeah, Stroh, go fish."

Murdock smiled as he hung up. So the Little War was over. He didn't quite know how many days it had lasted, but the SEALs sure as hell had had a lot to do with ending it. Yeah, another nap sounded just about right.

The next day on board the *Monroe*, Murdock listened to the carrier's legal officer explaining it again. He still wasn't sure that he understood it yet.

"While the offense did not take place on the carrier, it was done by an enlisted man assigned here on temporary duty, and as such he comes under the legal control of this command.

"Charges of dereliction of duty and failure to follow a direct order have been placed in proper form and order with this command. We have taken the man into custody and he will be transported to San Diego, where he will be subjected to a hearing to determine if a court-martial should be held. Any such hearing and court-martial would be held at the Naval Special Warfare Command in Coronado. Is everyone clear on this?"

Murdock, Jaybird, and Joe Douglas nodded.

"Then this meeting is over. Return the prisoner to the brig."

Two Master-at-Arms men stood beside Douglas. They indicated he should go with them.

Douglas turned to Murdock. "Commander, you know I didn't do nothing like this. Jaybird hates my guts, always has since I first signed on. He told me he'd get me sooner or later."

Murdock waved him off. "You'll have your day at the court-martial, Douglas. You better just keep quiet now."

Jaybird shook his head. "Damnit, Skipper, I never should have let the two be side by side back there on that hill. Things were coming down damn fast right then. They were the closest ones to cover that right flank. I reacted without thinking about the trouble between the two. Yeah, I knew about it. JG and I even talked about leaving Douglas behind on the last mission. We decided we needed his gun. Fucking bad decision, it turns out."

Four days later, Fernandez had stabilized enough that he could be airlifted on an ambulance plane out of Seoul with other war casualties and flown to San Francisco. The Army wounded would go to Letterman General Hospital there, and three Navy men would continue on to Balboa Naval Hospital in San Diego.

Stroh had made the arrangements for Air Force transport, and the rest of the platoon lifted off a day after Fernandez. Al Adams was well on his way to healing. DeWitt was still using a pair of crutches, and would go into Balboa as well when the platoon checked into Coronado.

Joe Douglas made the trip in handcuffs and leg irons, and was isolated in the farthest back seat of the big transport.

News of the charges against Douglas preceded the SEALs into their base, and Master Chief Gordon MacKenzie stood with folded arms as the platoon jumped down from the six-by that had transported them and their gear from North Island Naval Air Station.

The master chief came to attention in front of Murdock and saluted. Murdock returned the salute.

"It seems we have a bit of a problem, Commander, with one of your boys. The old man is furious. Evidently it got out of hand. We'll deal with it." The master chief frowned and looked away. "One more thing. Commander Masciarelli said he wants to see you the second you hit base. We better humor him on this one."

"We? You coming?"

"Not a chance. I only have twelve more years to retirement. Why would I want to commit suicide?"

Murdock gave his gear to Jaybird and headed for the Old Man's lair. He never liked meeting with Commander Masciarelli. The man was a political animal—sure, a SEAL once, but he was a fucking hell of a long way from there now. Murdock marched his way past the buildings to the headquarters of Team Seven and went in. He was gritty from the long flight, grimy, and probably smelled. Good.

A bright young second-class female with a flat chest grinned at Murdock.

"Boss wants to see you right away." She led him to a door ten paces away and knocked, then pushed it open. She wasn't about to go inside. Murdock went in, put his floppy hat under his arm, and stepped up to the desk with its totally bare and polished top. He snapped to attention. "Sir, Lieutenant Commander Murdock reporting."

Commander Dean Masciarelli put down a report he had been reading and glared at Murdock.

"You intend to go through with these charges against Douglas?"

"Absolutely, sir. It's a definite case of disobeying an order while under fire that resulted in the critical wounding of another SEAL. It's a plain dereliction of duty."

"You're a lawyer now, Murdock?"

"No, sir."

"Good, my advice is to stop the charges now, ship Douglas out to Adak, and forget the whole mess."

"Sir, in my opinion that action would not be in the best interest of the SEALs, nor of the U.S. Navy."

Masciarelli groaned. "Murdock, when are you going to stop fighting the program and learn how to work with the Navy?"

"Sir, I never really . . ." He stopped.

The commander looked up. "Almost blurted it out, didn't you, Murdock. You have no real desire to go up the promotion ladder. You don't want those admiral's stripes on your sleeve. We've been over this before. I hear you turned down an offer to work with the CNO."

"Not my kind of job, sir."

"Yeah, you're probably right there. This Douglas matter. You know I'll be on the hearing board, and if it gets a go, probably also on the court."

"Yes, sir."

"You have no objections?"

"Not a one, sir."

"Good. One other matter. I've let you slide along without a proper platoon organization for too long. I hear you're promoting one man to lead petty officer. I'll approve. I want you to pick out a senior chief petty officer to help you run the platoon. You have the pick of any man in SEAL Team Seven."

"Sir, that will take some time."

"You'll have lots of time before the court-martial. Get a man in there and integrated into your team. No telling when another call will come from the CIA. You know I still despise this arrangement. No chain of command. No Navy control. I hate it." The commander of SEAL Team Seven looked out his window for a moment, then back at Murdock.

"Soon you'll need to have a chief petty officer to fill out your roster. You've got room now. Think on it. Now, I'd bet you're looking forward to a shower. You sure as hell need one. You're dismissed, sailor."

Murdock came to attention, did a smart about-face, and marched out of the room.

Things moved quickly after that. The next day the official papers were filed with the signatures of Jaybird, Murdock, and Commander Masciarelli. The hearing on Douglas was set for a week later. Murdock and Jaybird spent two days at the Balboa Naval Hospital in San Diego, talking with Fernandez and with Ed DeWitt. DeWitt was scheduled to come out of the hospital in three more days.

They dug out every case of conflict between the two SEALs, and after a lot of persuading, Fernandez told Murdock what had started it all at that beach picnic nearly a year ago.

"You remember it, Commander. A beach party with lots of barbecue and good food and plenty of beer. The volley ball was coed and my wife, Maria, was there playing. Douglas was on our team, and he got rude and kept touching her, making whispered remarks. I told him to lay off, to keep away from her. He wouldn't. I pulled him out of the game and told him to stop.

"He called Maria a greaser, a *puta*, a rotten wetback who should have stayed in Mexico. That's when I hit him. The other guys pulled us apart before any real damage was done. Jaybird made us shake hands, but that didn't change a thing. He's been badmouthing me ever since."

Murdock smiled. "Okay, Fernandez, now we've got something. This is enough to get a conviction." He watched Fernandez. "Are you sure you want to go through with this? If you really object, we can withdraw the charges, I'll transfer Douglas out of the SEALs, and we'll never see him again."

Fernandez stared at the ceiling. Then he shifted in the bed. He had just found out today that he would be in the hospital for another two months, but should be patched up well enough to return to duty as a SEAL.

"Yes, let's continue the process. I owe it to Maria. If he gets away with it with me, he'll just terrorize somebody else who isn't a white man."

The day before the hearing, Murdock took a phone call from Douglas's hometown. Murdock had called the local sheriff just to check on Douglas's background, and the answer was surprising.

"Commander, how the hell did Joe Douglas ever get in the Navy? He served a year and a day in county jail for battery, and then had two more arrests for beating up Jews and homosexuals. He got a great lawyer and beat both charges of assault. Damn, I didn't know that the Navy let in felons."

Murdock told him it didn't, if the Navy knew about the convictions. Douglas had covered it up somehow. Murdock had the sheriff FAX him the arrest reports, the jail records, fingerprints, and everything else from Douglas's file.

The hearing lasted only an hour and twenty minutes. Fernandez had given a deposition about how the trouble began, and it was read in the hearing. Then Murdock tried to introduce the records of Douglas's civilian skinhead activity and arrests, but the Hearing Officer ruled it could not be entered there, but should be filed with the appropriate office.

Joe Douglas contended that the trouble at the beach party was petty and not serious and soon forgotten. He denied that he deliberately did not fire to protect Fernandez in Korea, that the charges were trumped up because the lead petty officer did not like him.

The ruling came after ten minutes of deliberations. Sufficient evidence was presented that Joe Douglas would have a court-martial. The date was set two months away to give counsel on both sides time to prepare their cases. Both would be Navy lawyers.

Murdock copied the civilian records on Douglas, and turned the originals over to Commander Masciarelli. He said he knew exactly where to take them.

"If for any reason Douglas is not convicted on these charges, he'll get booted out of the Navy so fast he won't find his ass-end for a month. He never should have been in the Navy in the first place. A goddamned skinhead!"

Murdock went back to his office and got down to the task of building his platoon back to fighting strength. He had wondered when Masciarelli would demand that he install an SCPO and a CPO the way the other platoons had. At least he could pick his senior chief petty officer. He would have to be a top SEAL and a good administrator. Tough to find. He'd work with the master chief. He'd have some ideas.

Men, how many did he have left? Fred Washington, who got wounded on the Kuril Islands, was back at Balboa

Hospital and recovering, but the doctors said he probably would not be able to take the physical punishment the SEALs experienced.

How many? Washington out, Doc Ellsworth with the shattered elbow still in Balboa. He wouldn't be coming back. Fernandez was a possibility of making it back. Colt Franklin with his side wound was recovering nicely at Balboa. He'd be back. Ed DeWitt's leg was healing well. He'd been put on a month's medical leave and told to rest and recover at home, or go fishing. Douglas would never wear the SEAL trident again.

So he needed three new men. Take away one for an SCPO, and he still needed two new SEALs. At least they didn't get anyone killed on the last two excursions. That was a plus.

Murdock reached for his coffee cup and took a gulp. When he looked up again, a familiar figure stood in the doorway.

"Hi there, hero."

"Dad. What are you doing down here?"

Congressman Charles Fitzhugh Murdock smiled at his only son, and came into the room and sat down.

"Coffee?" Blake asked.

His father shook his head. "Just had a cup with your Master Chief MacKenzie. Quite a lad. I just happened to be in San Francisco, so I had them fly down here to see if you were home."

Blake Murdock laughed. "Dad, you knew I was here. I'd bet you knew when we left Seoul and on what flight and when we landed. Good to see you again. How's Mom?"

"She's better all the time. Has a hundred charities she works on. She gets in more hours of work than I do, I think. Saw Ardith last week. She asked about you. She knew where you were and was worried."

"She probably knows I'm home as well. Our nation's security is in total disarray."

"But we're the people who should know where you are. I hear you might just have won the peace over there with your small little band of SEALs."

"We did our part, Dad. I also got two men shot up badly.

But when boys play with guns, somebody is bound to be hurt. You have time for dinner, Dad?"

"Wish I did. Duty calls. We landed at North Island. We can talk on the way back over there. I didn't know it was so close to you."

In the Navy staff car usually reserved for admirals, Blake and his father rode back to Coronado, through the small town, and to the closely connected North Island Naval Air Station.

"Had a chat with the Vice President the other day," the Congressman said. "He had many nice things to say about you. You saved his life, you know, and probably prevented a full-scale U.S. involvement. He told me he wants to adopt you."

Murdock laughed. "Sounds like him. He seems like a down-to-earth kind of guy. He cooperated with us well on our brief trip back to the South Korean side."

The big car drove onto the taxi strip and to the far end of the field, where an Air Force business-type jet waited.

"Your mother is looking forward to another leave for you. When will you be coming to Washington?"

"We have a court-martial coming up. Maybe in three months. Maybe next month. I'll have to work it out. First I have to get my platoon pasted back together and into training. Then I'll figure it out."

The Congressman left Blake at the door of the car, told the driver to take the commander back to the Special Warfare base, and hurried out to the jet. As soon as he went up the steps, they were pulled in after him and the sleek jet revved its engines and rolled down the runway.

Murdock grinned as he leaned back in the leather seat and enjoyed feeling like an admiral for three and a half miles. Then he went back to work, laying out his platoon, deciding what specialists he needed to complete his team. Wondering about an SCPO.

His phone rang.

"Third Platoon, Murdock."

"Hi, will you be home on time? I want to know when to start the baby-back ribs I have ready to broil. I know how you like them and I found this new barbecue sauce you'll love and . . ."

"Ardith?"

"You expected maybe your first wife in your apartment?"

"I've never had a first wife. How in the world?"

"I know just about everything you do, Commander. Has your father left yet?"

"You are a magician, a Merlin, a wonder. No, I won't be home on time. I'm leaving in about a minute. Start the ribs anytime you want to—no, maybe you better wait to start the ribs."

"I like the sound of that. Hey, hurry home. I'm sorry about Fernandez and Doc Ellsworth. At least you didn't get anybody killed these two times. We can talk when you get here."

"Yeah, we will. How did you know about . . ." He shook his head. "Never mind, I'm on my way."

He stopped at the Quarter Deck for just a minute to talk to Master Chief MacKenzie.

"Commander, I have a list of three men you might want to look over one of these days for your SCPO. All good men, all with the rate. I like one of them better than the other two, but I won't tell you which one that is. We'll see you tomorrow, Commander?"

"Not sure. I may take a day of sick leave."

"Thought you might, lad. And be saying hello to Ardith for me."

Murdock took a step back. "How did you know . . ." He shook his head. "I have too many mysterious people of magical powers around me. I think I better leave before I really get myself into trouble. I'll see you when I come over the Quarter Deck, Master Chief. Good night."

It was less than a mile to his apartment. He drove with a nervous excitement he hadn't felt in weeks. Twice he made himself go slower. When he turned into his parking spot in the condo lot, he saw a flash of white at his window on the second floor. He parked and ran up the steps.

"Hi, sailor," Ardith Manchester said as he pushed open the door. He sucked in a breath just looking at her. Tall, long blonde hair halfway to her waist, maybe 120 pounds soaking wet. So svelte and beautiful it made him ache.

"Hi there, pretty lady."

They walked toward each other, and he reached out and kissed her lips without touching the rest of her. She whimpered and caught him with her arms and held him tightly. Her chin went on his shoulder, and she let out a long-held in breath.

"I pray for this day never to end," she whispered, not really knowing if she had said it out loud or only thought it. He picked her up, carried her to the living room couch, and let her down gently and sat beside her.

"Hey," she said.

"Hey."

"I'm so glad that you're back, so . . . so glad." She brushed her hand over her eyes. "I'm not saying things right. Not doing . . ." She clung to him then, her face hard against his chest. "Just want to sit here and hold you, and hold you . . . Oh, God, you're home. I . . . I died a hundred times. Every time I heard about you going in to the Islands or going into North Korea. Five or six times. I yelled at them, I screamed, and my secretary came rushing in twice. I told her what I was doing and we cried together. Girl stuff. Oh, damn."

They sat there, neither saying a word.

"I know, I know, I know. I shouldn't have found out where you were and what you were doing, but I couldn't stop myself. My dad knew and got reports, sometimes daily. What he knew, I soon knew. I'm not sure if I got much work done for him those days."

She pushed back from him and stared hard at his face. "Sometimes I wonder why I'm doing this. Is it worth all the agony, the worry, the pressure? Then I look at your picture, and remember all the marvelous days and nights we've spent together, and I'm sure that it's worth it."

She snuggled down close to him again and felt his arms come around her.

"Oh, yes," she said, and purred. "I may never leave this couch. Just stay here forever."

Murdock caught his breath and tried to say something, but he couldn't. His mouth wouldn't work and his throat felt funny and all at once he wanted to be quiet and simply hold her.

It was ten minutes before the silent mutual admiration broke and Ardith eased back from him.

"Well, now that I've spilled my guts all over your couch and made an utter ass of myself, and puked up all of my worries and agonies and dreams and private-place emotions, I think it's time that you say something."

He reached over and kissed her lips gently, then harder, until he had pushed her down on the couch and lay on top of her. The kiss lasted and lasted.

She eased away from him and smiled. "I guess that's exactly what I hoped that you were going to say. I hope you can get the next three days off. I want to drive up to Moro Bay, above Santa Barbara a ways, and watch the ocean and eat clam strips, and walk along the water, and go in every one of the tourist-trap shell shops on the bay drive."

"Yes, we'll do it," he said, his voice husky. "I've got months of leave time coming. We'll head out first thing in the morning. Now, you want your ribs before or afterwards?"

She grinned. "Afterwards."

The ribs were amazingly good too.

Moro Bay was a delight. Murdock couldn't remember being there before.

"There used to be lots of sea otters in the bay," she said, looking out a restaurant window as they munched their way through heaping baskets of clam strips. "There were so many they decided they were hurting the fishing, so they trapped them and moved them all down the coast. Turned out almost all of them died that they moved. Now it's a rarity to see a sea otter up here."

That afternoon they found an art colony up the road toward the Hearst Castle. A little town called Cambria. She bought an oil painting of the sea and two tall trees framing a foaming wave.

The third day they slept in at the motel and the phone rang. Nobody was supposed to know where they were.

"Don't answer it," she said.

"I better." He picked it up. "Yes." He listened a minute and grinned. "How the hell did you find us, Stroh?"

He listened again. "So you've got a bug on my car? Yeah, probably. You want to talk to Ardith? Sure." He handed her the phone.

"Don?"

She listened. "Dad asked you to find me? I don't believe it. Why?" She listened again, then laughed. "Yes, I can understand that. Tell him I'll be back tomorrow night. Yes, Don, and how did you find us?" She listened again, laughed, and said good-bye.

"How did he find us?" Murdock asked.

"He just said he was CIA. Dad has lost some files and he says I'm the only one who knows where they are. It's a bill he's been working on for months. I have to fly back in the morning."

"Ah-hah! Duty calls, only it's your duty."

"Yeah, some even-up time maybe. We still have tonight."

Murdock grinned. "Oh, yes, tonight's the night."

All the way on the drive home the next morning, he kept wondering who he could get to fill out the platoon. Then what would the next hot spot be? Where would they go? Maybe the Near East was heating up. Old Saddam Hussein might get frisky again, or somebody in Iran, or Libya. Oil would blow up the world again one of these days. When it did, he wanted to have Third Platoon of SEAL Team Seven ready to answer the call.

Yeah, they would be ready. They were SEALs!

SEAL TALK:

MILITARY GLOSSARY

Aalvin: Small U.S. two-man submarine.

Admin: Short for administration.

Aegis: Advanced Naval air defense radar system.

AH-1W Super Cobra: Has M179 under-nose turret with 20mm Gatling gun.

AK-47: 7.62mm Russian Kalashnikov automatic rifle. Most widely used assault rifle in the world.

AN/PRC-117D: Radio, also called SATCOM. Works with Milstar satellite in 22,300-mile equatorial orbit for instant worldwide radio, voice, or video communications. Size: 15 inches high, 3 inches wide, 3 inches deep. Weighs 15 pounds. Microphone and voice output. Has encrypter, capable of burst transmissions of less than a second.

AN/PUS-7: Night Vision Goggles. Weigh 1.5 pounds.

ANVIS-6: Night-vision goggles on air crewmen's helmets.

APC: Armored Personnel Carrier.

ASROC: Nuclear-tipped antisubmarine rocket torpedoes launched by Navy ships.

Assault Vest: Combat vest with full loadouts of ammo, gear.

ASW: Anti-Submarine Warfare.

Attack Board: Molded plastic with two hand grips with bubble compass on it. Also depth gauge and Cyalume chemical lights with twist knob to regulate amount of light. Use for underwater guidance on long swim.

Aurora: Air Force recon plane. Can circle at 90,000 feet. Can't be seen or heard from ground. Used for thermal imaging.

AWACS: Airborne Warning And Control System. Radar units in high-flying aircraft to scan for planes at any altitude out to 200 miles. Controls air-to-air engagements with enemy forces. Planes have a mass of communication and electronic equipment.

Balaclavas: Headgear worn by some SEALs.

Bent Spear: Less serious nuclear violation of safety.

BKA: Bundeskriminalamt: German's federal investigation unit.

Black Talon: Lethal hollow-point ammunition made by Winchester. Outlawed some places.

Blivet: A collapsible fuel container. SEALs sometimes use it.

BLU-43B: Antipersonnel mine used by SEALs.

BLU-96: A fuel-air explosive bomb. It disperses a fuel oil into the air, then explodes the cloud. Many times more powerful than conventional bombs because it doesn't carry its own chemical oxidizers.

BMP-1: Soviet armored fighting vehicle (AFV), low, boxy, crew of 3 and 8 combat troops. Has tracks and a 73mm cannon. Also an AT-3 Sagger antitank missile and coaxial machine gun.

Body Armor: Far too heavy for SEAL use in the water.

Bogey: Pilots' word for an unidentified aircraft.

Boghammer Boat: Long, narrow, low dagger boat, high-speed patrol craft. Swedish make. Iran had 40 of them in 1993.

Boomer: A nuclear-powered missile submarine.

Bought It: A man has been killed. Also "bought the farm."

Bow Cat: The bow catapult on a carrier to launch jets.

Broken Arrow: Any accident with nuclear weapons or nuclear material lost, shot down, crashed, stolen, hijacked.

Browning 9mm High Power: A Belgium 9mm pistol, 13 rounds in magazine. First made 1935.

Buddy Line: 6 feet long, ties 2 SEALs together in the water for control and help if needed.

BUDS/S: Nickname for SEAL training facility and six-month course in Coronado, California.

BUPERS: BUreau of PERSonnel.

C-2A Greyhound: 2-engine turboprop cargo plane that lands on carriers. Also called COD, Carrier Onboard Delivery. Takes people, supplies, mail to and from carriers at sea.

C-4: Plastic explosive. A claylike explosive that can be molded and shaped. It will burn. Fairly stable.

C-6 Plastique: Plastic explosive. Developed from C-4 and C-5. Is often used in bombs with radio detonator or digital timer.

C-9 Nightingale: Douglas DC-9 fitted as a medical evacuation transport plane.

C-130 Hercules: Air Force transporter for long haul. 4 engines.

C-141 Starlifter: Airlift transport for cargo, paratroops, evac for long distances. Top speed 566 mph. Range with payload 2935 miles. Ceiling 41,600 feet.

Caltrops: Small four-pointed spikes used to flatten tires. Used in the Crusades to disable horses.

CamelBack: Used with drinking tube for 70 ounces of water attached to vest.

Cammies: Working camouflaged wear for SEALs. Two different patterns and colors. Jungle and desert.

Cannon Fodder: Old term for soldiers in line of fire destined to die in the grand scheme of warfare.

Capped: Killed, shot, or otherwise snuffed.

CAR-15: The Colt M-4A1. Sliding-stock carbine with grenade launcher under barrel. Knight sound suppresser. Can have AN/PAQ-4 laser aiming light under the carrying handle. .223 round. 20- or 30-round magazine. Rate of fire: 700 to 1,000 rds/min.

Cascade Radiation: U-235 triggers secondary radiation in other dense materials.

Cast Off: Leave a dock, port, land. Get lost. Navy: long, then short signal of horn, whistle, or light.

Castle Keep: The main tower in any castle.

Caving Ladder: Roll-up ladder that can be let down to climb.

CH-46E: Sea Knight chopper. Twin rotors, transport. Can carry 22 combat troops. Has a crew of 4.

CH-53D Sea Stallion: Big chopper. Not used much anymore.

Chaff: A small cloud of thin pieces of metal, such as tinsel, that can be picked up by enemy radar and that can attract a radar-guided missile away from the plane to hit the chaff.

Charlie-Mike: Code words for continue the mission.

Chief to Chief: Bad conduct by EM handled by chiefs so no record shows or is passed up the chain of command.

Chocolate Mountains: Land training center for SEALs near these mountains in the California desert.

Christians In Action: SEAL talk for not-always-friendly CIA.

CIA: Central Intelligence Agency.

CIC: Combat Information Center. The place on a ship where communications and control areas are situated that open and control combat fire.

CINC: Commander IN Chief.

CINCLANT: Navy Commander IN Chief, atLANTtic.

CINCPAC: Commander-IN-Chief, PACific.

Class of 1978: Not a single man finished BUD/S training in this class. All-time record.

Claymore: An antipersonnel mine carried by SEALs on many of their missions.

Cluster Bombs: A canister bomb that explodes and spreads small bomblets over a great area. Used against parked aircraft, massed troops, and un-armored vehicles.

CNO: Chief of Naval Operations.

CO_2 Poisoning: During deep dives. Abort dive at once and surface.

COD: Carrier On Board Delivery plane.

Cold Pack Rations: Food carried by SEALs to use if needed.

Combat Harness: American Body Armor nylon mesh special operations vest. Six 2-magazine pouches for drum-fed belts, other pouches for other weapons, waterproof pouch for Motorola.

CONUS: The Continental United States.

Corfams: Dress shoes for SEALs.

Covert Action Staff: A CIA group that handles all covert action by the SEALs.

CQB: Close quarters battle house. Training facility near Nyland in the desert training area. Also called the Kill House.

CQB: Close Quarters Battle. A fight that's up-close, hand-to-hand, whites of his eyes, blood all over you.

CRRC Bundle: Rolled off plane, sub, boat. The assault boat for 8 SEALs.

CRRC: Combat Rubber Raiding Craft. See above. Also the IBS or Inflatable Boat Small.

Cutting Charge: Lead-sheathed explosive. Triangular strip of high-velocity explosive sheathed in metal. Point of the triangle focuses a shaped-charge effect. Cuts a pencil-line-wide hole to slice a steel girder in half.

CYA: Cover Your Ass, protect yourself from friendlies or officers above you and JAG people.

Damfino: Damned if I know. SEAL talk.

DDS: Dry Dock Shelter. A clamshell unit on subs to deliver SEALs and SDVs to a mission.

DEFCON: DEFense CONdition. How serious is the threat?

Delta Forces: Army special forces, much like SEALs.

Desert Cammies: 3 colors, desert-tan and pale-green with streaks of pink. For use on land.

DIA: Defense Intelligence Agency.

Dilos Class Patrol Boat: Greek, 29 feet long, 75 tons displacement.

Dirty Shirt Mess: Officers can eat there in flying suits on board a carrier.

DNS: Doppler Navigation System.

Draeger LAR V: Rebreather that SEALs use. No bubbles.

DREC: Digitally Reconnoiterable Electronic Component. Top-secret computer chip from NSA that can decipher any U.S. military electronic code.

E&E: SEAL talk for escape and evasion.

E-2C Hawkeye: Navy, carrier-based, Airborne Early Warning aircraft for long-range early warning, threat assessment, and fighter direction. Has a 24-foot saucerlike rotodome over the wing. Crew 5, max speed 326 knots, ceiling 30,800 feet, radius 175 nm with 4 hours on station.

E-3A Skywarrior: Old electronic intelligence craft. Replaced by the newer ES-3A.

E-4B NEACP: Called Kneecap. National Emergency Airborne Command Post. A greatly modified Boeing 747 used as a communications base for the President of the United States and other high-ranking officials in an emergency and in wartime.

EA-6B Prowler: Navy plane with electronic countermeasures. Crew of 4, max speed 566 knots, ceiling 41,200 feet, range with max load 955 nautical miles.

Easy: The only easy day was yesterday. SEAL talk.

ELINT: ELectronic INTelligence. Often from satellite in orbit, picture-taker, or other electronic communications.

EOD: Navy experts in nuclear material and radioactivity.

EOD: Explosive Ordnance Disposal.

Equatorial Satellite Pointing Guide: Used to aim antenna for radio to pick up satellite signals.

ES-3A: Electronic Intelligence (ELINT) intercept aircraft. The platform for the battle group Passive Horizon Extension System. Stays up for long patrol periods, has comprehensive set of sensors, lands and takes off from a carrier. Has 63 antennas.

ETA: Estimated Time of Arrival.

Executive Order 12333: By President Reagan, authorizing Special Warfare units such as the SEALs.

Exfil: Exfiltrate, to get out of an area.

F/A-18 Hornet: Carrier-based interceptor that can change from air-to-air to air-to-ground attack mode while in flight.

Fitrep: Fitness Report.

Flashbang Grenade: Non-lethal grenade that give off a series of piercing explosive sounds and a series of brilliant strobe-type lights to disable an enemy.

Flotation Bag: To hold equipment, ammo, gear on a wet operation.

Fort Fumble: SEALs' name for the Pentagon.

Forty-mm Rifle Grenade: The M576 multipurpose round contains 20 large lead balls. SEALs use on Colt M-4A1.

Four Striper: A Navy captain.

Fox Three: In air warfare, a code phrase showing that a Navy F-14 has launched a Phoenix air-to-air missile.

FUBAR: SEAL talk. Fucked Up Beyond All Repair.

Full Helmet Masks: For high-altitude jumps. Oxygen in mask.

G-3: German-made assault rifle.

Gloves: SEALs wear sage-green fire-resistant Nomex flight gloves.

GMT: Greenwich Mean Time. Where it's all measured from.

GPS: Global Positioning System. A program with satellites around Earth to pinpoint precisely aircraft, ships, vehicles, and ground troops. Position information is to a plus or minus ten feet. Also can give speed of a plane or ship to one quarter of a mile per hour.

GPSL: A radio antenna with floating wire that pops to the surface. Antenna picks up positioning from the closest 4 global positioning satellites and gives an exact position within 10 feet.

Green Tape: Green sticky ordnance tape that has a hundred uses for a SEAL.

GSG-9: Flashbang grenade developed by Germans: a cardboard tube filled with 5 separate charges timed to burst in rapid succession. Blinding and giving concussion to enemy, leaving targets stunned, easy to kill or capture. Usually non-lethal.

GSG9: Grenzschutzgruppe Nine. Germany's best special warfare unit, counterterrorist group.

H&K 21A1: Machine gun with 7.62 NATO round. Fires 900 rounds per minute. Range 1,100 meters. All types of NATO rounds, ball, incendiary, tracer.

H&K G11: Automatic rifle, new. 4.7mm caseless ammunition. 50-round magazine. The bullet is in a sleeve of solid propellant with a special thin plastic coating around it. Fires 600 rounds per minute. Single-shot, 3-round burst, or fully automatic.

H&K MP-5SD: 9mm submachine gun with integral silenced barrel. Single-shot, 3-shot, or fully automatic. Rate 800 rds/min.

H&K P9S: Heckler & Koch's 9mm parabellum double-action semiauto pistol with 9-round magazine.

H&K PSG1: High-precision, bolt-action, sniping rifle. 7.62 NATO round. 5- to 20-round magazine. Roller-lock delayed-blowback breech system. Fully adjustable stock. 6 x 42 telescopic sights. Sound suppressor.

HAHO: High Altitude jump, High Opening. From 30,000 feet, open chute for glide up to 15 miles to ground. Up to 75 minutes in glide. To enter enemy territory or enemy position unheard.

Half-Track: Military vehicle with tracked rear drive and wheels in front, usually armed and armored.

HALO: High Altitude jump, Low Opening. From 30,000 feet. Free fall in 2 minutes to 2,000 feet and open chute. Little forward movement. Get to ground quickly, silently.

Hamburgers: Often called sliders on a Navy carrier.

Handie-Talkie: Small, handheld personal radio. Short range.

HELO: SEAL talk for helicopter.

Herky Bird: C-130 Hercules transport. Most flown military transport in the world. For cargo or passengers, paratroops, aerial refueling, search and rescue, communications, and as a gunship. Has flown from a Navy carrier deck without use of catapult. 4 turboprop engines, max speed 325 knots, range at max payload 2,356 miles.

Hezbollah: Lebanese Shiite Moslem militia. Party of God.

HMMWU: The Humvee, U.S. light utility truck, replaced the honored Jeep. Multipurpose wheeled vehicle, 4 x 4, automatic transmission, power steering. Engine: Detroit Diesel 150 hp diesel V-8 air-cooled. Top speed, 65 mph. Range, 300 miles.

Hotels: SEAL talk for hostages.

Humint: Human Intelligence. Acquired on the ground by human beings as vs. satellite or photo recon.

Hydra-Shock: Lethal hollow-point ammunition made by Federal Cartridge Company. Outlawed in some areas.

Hypothermia: Danger to SEALs. A drop in body temperature that can be fatal.

IBS: Inflatable Boat Small. 12 x 6 feet. Carries 8 men and 1,000 pounds of weapons and gear. Hard to sink. Quiet motor. Used for silent beach, bay, lake landings.

IR Beacon: Infrared Beacon. For silent nighttime signaling.

IR Goggles: "Sees" heat instead of light.

Islamic Jihad: Arab holy war.

IV Pack: Intravenous fluid that you can drink if out of water.

JNA: Yugoslav National Army.

JP-4: Normal military jet fuel.

JSOC: Joint Special Operations Command.

JSOCCOMCENT: Joint Special Operations Command Center in the Pentagon.

KA-BAR: SEALs' combat fighting knife.

KATN: Kick Ass and Take Names. SEAL talk, get the mission in gear.

KH-11: Spy satellite, takes pictures of ground, IR photos, etc.

KIA: Killed In Action.

KISS: Keep It Simple, Stupid. SEAL talk for streamlined operations.

Klick: A kilometer of distance. Often used as a mile. From Vietnam era, but still widely used in military.

Krytrons: Complicated, intricate timers used in making nuclear-explosive detonators.

KV-57: Encoder for messages, scrambles.

L-T: Short for lieutenant in SEAL talk.

Liaison: Close connection, cooperating person from one unit or service working with another military unit.

Laser Pistol: The SIW pinpoint of ruby light emitted for aiming. Usually silenced weapon.

Left Behind: In 30 years SEALs have seldom left behind a dead comrade, never a wounded one. Never been taken prisoner.

Let's Get the Hell out of Dodge: SEAL talk for leaving a place, bugging out, hauling ass.

Light Sticks: Chemical units that make light after twisting to release chemicals that phosphoresce.

Loot & Shoot: SEAL talk for getting into action on a mission.

LZ: Landing Zone.

M1-8: Russian Chopper.

M1A1 M-14: Match rifle upgraded for SEAL snipers.

M-3 Submachine gun: WWII grease gun, .45-caliber. Cheap. Introduced in 1942.

M-16: Automatic U.S. rifle. 5.56 round. Magazine 20 or 30, rate of fire 700 to 950 rds/min. Can attach M203 40mm grenade launcher under barrel.

M-18 Claymore: Antipersonnel mine. A slab of C-4 with 200 small ball bearings. Set off electrically or by trip wire. Can be positioned and aimed. Sprays out a cloud of balls. Kill zone 50 meters.

M60 Machine Gun: Can use 100-round ammo box snapped onto the gun's receiver. Not used much now by SEALs.

M-60E3: Lightweight handheld machine gun. Not used now by the SEALs.

M61A1: The usual 20mm cannon used on many American fighter planes.

M61(j): Machine pistol, Yugoslav make.

M-86: Pursuit Deterrent Munitions. Various types of mines, grenades, trip-wire explosives, and other devices in anti-personnel use.

M-203: A 40mm grenade launcher fitted under an M-16 or the M-15. Can fire a variety of grenade types up to 1,200 feet.

M662: A red flare for signaling.

MagSafe: Lethal ammunition that fragments in human body and does not exit. Favored by some police units to cut down on second kill from regular ammunition exiting a body.

Make a Peek: A quick look, usually out of the water, to check your position or tactical situation.

Mark 23 Mod O: Special operations offensive handgun system. Double action, 12-round magazine. Ambidextrous safety and mag-release catches. Knight screw-on suppresser. Snap-on laser for sighting. .45 caliber. Weights 4 pounds loaded. 9.5 inches long, with silencer 16.5 inches long

Mark II Knife: Navy-issue combat knife.

Mark VIII SDV: Swimmer Delivery Vehicle. A bus, SEAL talk. 21 feet long, beam and draft 4 feet, 6 knots for 6 hours.

Master-at-Arms: Military police on board a ship.

MAVRIC Lance: A nuclear alert for stolen nukes or radio-active goods.

MC-130 Combat Talon: A specially equipped Hercules for covert missions in enemy or unfriendly territory.

McMillan M87R: Bolt-action sniper rifle, .50 caliber. 53 inches long. Bipod, fixed 5- or 10-round magazine. Bulbous muzzle brake on end of barrel. Deadly up to a mile. All types .50-caliber ammo.

MGS: Modified grooming standards. So SEALs don't all look like military to enable them to do undercover work in mufti.

MH-53J: Chopper, updated CH053 from Nam days. 200 mph, called the Pave Low III.

MH-60K BlackHawk: Navy chopper. Forward infrared system for low-level night flight. Radar for terra-follow avoidance. Crew of 3, takes 12 troops. Top speed 225 mph. Ceiling 4,000 feet. Range radius 230 miles. Arms: two 12.7mm machine guns.

MI5: British domestic intelligence agency.

MIDEASTFOR: Middle East Force.

MiG: Russian-built fighter, many versions, used in many nations around the world.

Mike Boat: Liberty boat off a large ship.

Mike-Mike: Short for mm, millimeter, as 9 mike-mike.

Milstar: Communications satellite for pickup and bouncing from SATCOM and other radio transmitters. Used by SEALs.

Miniguns: In choppers. Can fire 2,000 rounds per minute. Gatling-gun type.

Mitrajez M80: Machine gun from Yugoslavia.

Mocha: Food energy bar SEALs carry in vest pockets.

Mossburg: Pump action shotgun, pistol grip, 5-round magazine. SEALs use it for close-in work.

Motorola Radio: Personal radio, short range, lip mike, earpiece, belt pack.

MRE: Meals, Ready to Eat. Field rations used by most of U.S. armed forces and the SEALs as well. Long lasting.

MSPF: Maritime Special Purpose Force.

Mugger: MUGR, miniature underwater locator device. Sends up antenna for pickup on positioning satellites. Works underwater or above. Gives location within 10 feet.

Mujahideen: A soldier of Allah in Muslim nations.

NAVAIR: NAVy AIR command.

NAVSPECWAR: Naval Special Warfare Section. SEALs are in this command.

NAVSPECWARGRUP-Two: Naval Special Warfare Section Group Two based at Norfolk.

NCIS: Naval Criminal Investigative Service. A civilian operation not reporting to any Navy authority to make it more responsible and responsive. Replaces the old NIS, Naval Investigation Service, which did report to the closest admiral.

NEST: Nuclear Energy Search Team. Non-military unit that reports at once to any spill, problem, or Broken Arrow to determine the extent of the radiation problem.

Newbie: A new man, officer, or commander of an established military unit.

NKSF: North Korean Special Forces.

NLA: Iranian National Liberation Army. About 4,500 men in south Iraq, supported by Iraq for possible use against Iran.

Nomex: The type of material used for flight suits and hoods.

NPIC: National Photographic Interpretation Center in D.C.

NRO: National Reconnaissance Office, runs and coordinates satellite development and operations for the intelligence community.

NSA: National Security Agency.

NSC: National Security Council. Meets in Situation Room, support facility in the Executive Office Building in D.C. Main security group in the nation.

Nsvhurawn: Iranian Marines.

Nucflash: An alert for any nuclear problem.

NVG One Eye: Litton single-eyepiece Night Vision Goggles. Prevents NVG blindness in both eyes if a flare goes off. Scope shows green-tinted field at night.

NVGs: Night Vision Goggles. One eye or two. Gives good night vision in the dark with a greenish view.

OAS: Obstacle Avoidance Sonar. Used on many low-flying attack aircraft.

OIC: Officer In Charge.

Oil Tanker: One is: 885 feet long, 140 feet beam, 121,000 tons, 13 cargo tanks that hold 35.8 million gallons of fuel, oil, or gas. 24 in the crew. This is a regular-sized tanker. Not a supertanker.

OOD: Officer Of the Deck.

Orion P-3: Navy's long-range patrol and antisub aircraft. Some adapted to ELINT roles. Crew of 10. Max speed loaded 473 mph. Ceiling 28,300 feet. Arms: internal weapons bay and 10 external weapons stations for a mix of torpedoes, mines, rockets, and bombs.

Passive Sonar: Listening for engine noise of a ship or sub. It doesn't give away the hunter's presence as an active sonar would.

Pave Low III: A Navy chopper.

PC-170: Patrol Coastal-class 170-foot SEAL delivery vehicle. Powered by four 3,350-hp diesel engines, beam of 25 feet and draft of 7.8 feet. Top speed 35 knots, range 2,000 nautical miles. Fixed swimmer platform on stern. Crew of 4 officers and 24 EM, with 8 SEALs.

Plank Owners: Original men in the start-up of a new military unit.

Polycarbonate Material: Bullet-proof glass.

PRF: People's Revolutionary Front. Fictional group in *Nucflash*, **SEAL Team Seven book.**

Prowl & Growl: SEAL talk for moving into a combat mission.

Quitting Bell: In BUD/S training. Ring it and you quit the SEAL unit. Helmets of men who quit the class are lined up below the bell in Coronado. (Recently they have stopped ringing the bell. Dropouts simply place their helmet below the bell and go.)

RAF: Red Army Faction. A once-powerful German terrorist group not so active now.

Remington 200: Sniper rifle. Not used by SEALs now.

Remington 700: Sniper rifle with Starlight Scope. Can extend night vision to 400 meters.

RIB: Rigid Inflatable Boat. 3 sizes. One is 10 meters with speed of 40 knots.

Ring Knocker: An Annapolis graduate with the ring.

RIO: Radar Intercept Officer. The officer who sits in the backseat of an F-14 Tomcat off a carrier. The job: find enemy targets in the air and on the sea.

Roger That: A yes, an affirmative, a go answer to a command or statement.

RPG: Rocket Propelled Grenade. Quick and easy, shoulder-fired. Favorite weapon of terrorists, insurgents.

S&W Mark 1 MOD: Hush Puppy. SEAL name for this pistol.

SAS: British Special Air Service. Commandos. Special warfare men. Best that Britain has. Works with SEALs.

SATCOM: Satellite-based communications system for instant contact with anyone anywhere in the world. SEALs rely on it.

SAW: Squad's Automatic Weapon. Usually a machine gun or automatic rifle.

SBS: Special Boat Squadron. On site Navy unit that transports SEALs to many of their missions. Located across the street from the SEALs' Coronado, California, headquarters.

SD3: Sound suppression system on the H&K MP5 weapon.

SDV: Swimmer Delivery Vehicle. SEALs use a variety of them.

Seahawk SH-60: Navy chopper for ASW and SAR. Top speed 180 knots, ceiling 13,800 feet, range 503 miles. Arms: 2 Mark 46 torpedoes.

SEAL Headgear: Boonie hat, wool balaclava, green scarf, watch cap, bandanna roll.

Second in Command: Also 2IC for short in SEAL talk.

SERE: Survival, Evasion, Resistance, and Escape training.

Shipped for Six: Enlisted for six more years in the Navy.

Shit City: Coronado SEALs' name for Norfolk.

Show Colors: In combat put U.S. flag or other identification on back for easy identification by friendly air or ground units.

Sierra Charlie: SEAL talk for everything on schedule.

Simunition: Canadian product for training that uses paint balls instead of lead for bullets.

Sixteen-Man Platoon: Basic SEAL combat force. Up from 14 men a few years ago.

Sonobouy: Small underwater device that detects sounds and transmits them by radio to plane or ship.

Space Blanket: Green foil blanket to keep troops warm. Vacuum-packed and folded to a cigarette-sized package.

Sprayers and Prayers: Not the SEAL way. These men spray bullets all over the place hoping for hits. SEALs do more aimed firing for sure kills.

SS-19: Russian ICBM missile.

STABO: Using harness and lines under a chopper for men to get down to the ground.

STAR: Surface To Air Recovery operation.

Starflash Round: Shotgun round that shoots out sparkling fireballs that ricochet wildly around a room, confusing and terrifying the occupants. Non-lethal.

Stasi: Old-time East German secret police.

STICK: British terminology: Two 4-man SAS teams. 8 men.

Stokes: A kind of Navy stretcher. Open coffin shaped of wire mesh and white canvas for emergency patient transport.

STOL: Short Takeoff and Landing. Aircraft with high-lift wings and vectored-thrust engines to produced extremely short takeoffs and landings.

Subgun: Submachine gun, often the suppressed H&K MP5.

Suits: Civilians, usually government officials wearing suits.

Sweat: The more SEALs sweat in peacetime, the less they bleed in war.

Sykes-Fairbairn: A commando fighting knife.

Syrette: Small syringe for field administration often filled with morphine. Can be self-administered.

Tango: SEAL talk for a terrorist.

TDY: Temporary duty assigned outside of normal job designation.

Terr: Another term for terrorist. Shorthand SEAL talk.

Tetrahedral Reflectors: Show up on multi-mode radar like tiny suns.

Thermal Imager: Device to detect warmth, as a human body, at night or through light cover.

Thermal Tape: ID tape for night-vision-goggle user to see. Use on friendlies.

TNAZ: Trinittroaze Tidine. Explosive to replace C-4. 15% stronger than C-4 and 20% lighter.

TO&E: Table showing organization and equipment of a military unit.

Top SEAL Tribute: "You sweet motherfucker, don't you never die!"

Train: Formation used for contact in smoke, no light, fog, etc. Men directly behind each other. Right hand on weapon, left hand on shoulder of man ahead. Squeeze shoulder to signal.

Trident: SEALs' emblem. An eagle with talons clutching a Revolutionary War pistol, and Neptune's trident superimposed on the Navy's traditional anchor.

TRW: A camera's digital record that is sent by SATCOM.

TT33: Tokarev, a Russian pistol.

UAZ: A Soviet one-ton truck.

UBA Mark XV: Underwater life support with computer to regulate the rebreather's gas mixture.

UGS: Unmanned Ground Sensors. Can be used to explode booby traps and Claymore mines.

UNODIR: Unless otherwise directed. The unit will start the operation unless they are told not to.

VBSS: Orders to "visit, board, search, and seize."

Wadi: A gully or ravine, usually in a desert.

White Shirt: Man responsible for safety on carrier deck as he leads around civilians and personnel unfamiliar with the flight deck.

WIA: Wounded In Action.

Zodiac: Also called an IBS, Inflatable Boat Small. 15 by 6 feet, weighs 265 pounds. The "rubber duck" can carry 8 fully equipped SEALs. Can do 18 knots with a range or 65 nautical miles.

ZULU: Means Greenwich Mean Time, GMT. Used in all formal military communications.

SEAL TEAM SEVEN

Keith Douglass

❏ **SEAL TEAM SEVEN**   0-425-14340-6/$5.99

In a daring mission of high-seas heroism, Lt. Blake Murdock leads his seven-man unit from Team Seven's Red Squad into bulkhead-to-bulkhead battle—with high-tech buccaneers who've got nothing left to lose...

❏ **SEAL TEAM SEVEN: SPECTER**   0-425-14569-7/$5.99

Lt. Blake Murdock and his SEALs must spearhead a daring rescue mission and get the delegates out of the former Yugoslavia—where the wars still rage—in one piece—and give those responsible a taste of extreme SEAL prejudice.

❏ **SEAL TEAM SEVEN: NUCFLASH**

0-425-14881-5/$5.99

In the New World Order there is only one fear: A renegade state will gain control of a nuclear weapon and incinerate a city of innocent people. It's up to Lt. Blake Murdock and his SEALs to bring the bad guys down.

❏ **SEAL TEAM SEVEN: DIRECT ACTION**

0-425-15605-2/$5.99

During an attack on a terrorist group in Port Sudan, Lt. Blake Murdock and his SEAL team uncover three million dollars of counterfeit currency.

Prices slightly higher in Canada

Payable in U.S. funds only. No cash/COD accepted. Postage & handling: U.S./CAN. $2.75 for one book, $1.00 for each additional, not to exceed $6.75; Int'l $5.00 for one book, $1.00 each additional. We accept Visa, Amex, MC ($10.00 min.), checks ($15.00 fee for returned checks) and money orders. Call 800-788-6262 or 201-933-9292, fax 201-896-8569; refer to ad # 695 (7/99)

Penguin Putnam Inc.
P.O. Box 12289, Dept. B
Newark, NJ 07101-5289
Please allow 4-6 weeks for delivery.
Foreign and Canadian delivery 6-8 weeks.

Bill my: ❏ Visa ❏ MasterCard ❏ Amex _____(expires)

Card# _____

Signature _____

Bill to:

Name _____

Address _____ City _____

State/ZIP _____ Daytime Phone # _____

Ship to:

Name _____ Book Total $ _____

Address _____ Applicable Sales Tax $ _____

City _____ Postage & Handling $ _____

State/ZIP _____ Total Amount Due $ _____

This offer subject to change without notice.

"**Fasten your seatbelt!** *Carrier* **is a stimulating, fast-paced novel brimming with action and high drama.**"
—Joe Weber

CARRIER

Keith Douglass

U.S. MARINES. PILOTS. NAVY SEALS.
THE ULTIMATE MILITARY POWER PLAY.

In the bestselling tradition of Tom Clancy, Larry Bond, and Charles D. Taylor, this electrifying novel captures the vivid reality of international combat. The Carrier Battle Group Fourteen—a force including a supercarrier, amphibious unit, guided missile cruiser, and destroyer—is brought to life with stunning authenticity and action in a high-tech thriller as explosive as today's headlines.

__CARRIER	0-515-10593-7/$6.50
__CARRIER 6: COUNTDOWN	0-515-11309-3/$5.99
__CARRIER 7: AFTERBURN	0-515-11914-8/$6.99
__CARRIER 8: ALPHA STRIKE	0-515-12018-9/$6.99
__CARRIER 9: ARCTIC FIRE	0-515-12084-7/$5.99

Prices slightly higher in Canada

Payable in U.S. funds only. No cash/COD accepted. Postage & handling: U.S./CAN. $2.75 for one book, $1.00 for each additional, not to exceed $6.75; Int'l $5.00 for one book, $1.00 each additional. We accept Visa, Amex, MC ($10.00 min.), checks ($15.00 fee for returned checks) and money orders. Call 800-788-6262 or 201-933-9292, fax 201-896-8569; refer to ad # 384 (7/99)

Penguin Putnam Inc.
P.O. Box 12289, Dept. B
Newark, NJ 07101-5289
Please allow 4-6 weeks for delivery.
Foreign and Canadian delivery 6-8 weeks.

Bill my: ❑ Visa ❑ MasterCard ❑ Amex _____ (expires)
Card# _____
Signature _____

Bill to:
Name _____
Address _____ City _____
State/ZIP _____ Daytime Phone # _____

Ship to:
Name _____ Book Total $ _____
Address _____ Applicable Sales Tax $ _____
City _____ Postage & Handling $ _____
State/ZIP _____ Total Amount Due $ _____

This offer subject to change without notice.

SOMETHING EXPLODED IN THE SKY...

...something metallic, something swirling, something from hell. Four dark beasts filled the southeastern horizon like the lions of the apocalypse. The reflection of morning light off the sand splayed like blood across their wings...

Startled from the half-daze of the monotonous watch, the sentry grabbed his rifle and flung himself against the sand-filled bags at the front of the trench. It took a moment for his brain to register the fact that the planes were coming from the south and not the north—they were friends, not foes. The thick canisters of death slung beneath their wings were not meant for him.

"What the hell are those," he asked his companion as the planes roared over their positions.

The other soldier laughed. "You never saw A-10 Warthogs before?"

"They're on our side?"
"You better pray to God they are."

by James Ferro

HOGS: GOING DEEP

0-425-16856-5/$5.99

Prices slightly higher in Canada

Payable in U.S. funds only. No cash/COD accepted. Postage & handling: U.S./CAN. $2.75 for one book, $1.00 for each additional, not to exceed $6.75; Int'l $5.00 for one book, $1.00 each additional. We accept Visa, Amex, MC ($10.00 min.), checks ($15.00 fee for returned checks) and money orders. Call 800-788-6262 or 201-933-9292, fax 201-896-8569; refer to ad # 839 (7/99)

Penguin Putnam Inc.
P.O. Box 12289, Dept. B
Newark, NJ 07101-5289
Please allow 4-6 weeks for delivery.
Foreign and Canadian delivery 6-8 weeks.

Bill my: ☐ Visa ☐ MasterCard ☐ Amex _____ (expires)

Card# _____

Signature _____

Bill to:

Name _____

Address _____ City _____

State/ZIP _____ Daytime Phone # _____

Ship to:

Name _____ Book Total $ _____

Address _____ Applicable Sales Tax $ _____

City _____ Postage & Handling $ _____

State/ZIP _____ Total Amount Due $ _____

This offer subject to change without notice.